The
Wartime
Mother

BOOKS BY LIZZIE PAGE

THE WARTIME EVACUEES SERIES

A Child Far from Home

The Wartime Nursery

SHILLING GRANGE CHILDREN'S HOME SERIES

The Orphanage

A Place to Call Home

An Orphan's Song

The Children Left Behind

An Orphan's Wish

The War Nurses

Daughters of War

When I Was Yours

The Forgotten Girls

The Wartime Nanny

Lizzie Page

The Wartime Mother

bookouture

Published by Bookouture in 2025

An imprint of Storyfire Ltd.
Carmelite House
50 Victoria Embankment
London EC4Y 0DZ

www.bookouture.com

The authorised representative in the EEA is Hachette Ireland
8 Castlecourt Centre
Dublin 15 D15 XTP3
Ireland
(email: info@hbgi.ie)

ISBN: 978-1-83618-153-8
eBook ISBN: 978-1-83618-152-1

and what seemed corporal melted
As breath into the wind.
Would they had stayed!

— MACBETH, WILLIAM
SHAKESPEARE

1

NEW YEAR, 1941

Francine

Francine Salt had chicken pox spots all over her body and it felt like her face was on fire. Sometimes her friend's mother, Mrs Hardman, patted her with calamine lotion. It was meant to soothe her, but it didn't work, so now not only was she aflame but she was also blotchy and smelled of the sickroom at school. No one would want to come anywhere near her – at least that was one good thing. After all, she just wanted to be alone now.

Francine had lost count of the days since the bomb hit the air-raid shelter where her mother, her sister Maisie and her baby brothers Jacob and Joe were sheltering. Ever since that morning, she'd spent most of the time in her old friend Valerie Hardman's bed in the Hardmans' basement flat in Romberg Road, or on a cushion in the tiny cellar.

There was nobody left. Francine's father was at war and the rest of her family were dead. Mrs Hardman checked on her when she could, but she punched tickets on the buses, so really most of the time it was just Francine.

She gripped the dice her father had given her before he left tightly so that it felt unnatural when she unfurled her fingers. Other times, she traced the tiny frost patterns on the window – they were so beautiful she didn't think they could be of this world. Sometimes it rained, which Mrs Hardman explained was good because 'it puts out fires quicker...' Every day, the sirens pierced the air and the fire engines shrieked their shrieks and the *boosh* of the explosions made the flat shake.

On the fifth day after she lost her mother – or perhaps it was the sixth or the seventh – a teacher arrived. Miss Beedle had come on the train to Somerset when the three friends, Francine, Lydia and Valerie, were evacuated from London. Francine remembered that trip last year almost more clearly than she recalled more recent events.

Some children had been frightened, some full of gleeful excitement, others serious, weighed down by responsibility. As for the mothers... Francine could remember her own mother clutching her. She remembered Miss Beedle had tried to disentangle Francine from her, gently but firmly, holding up her mother, 'Shh, it's for the best.'

This time, Miss Beedle didn't lean in for a hug and she didn't say much, and Francine appreciated that.

'Sadly, you can't stay here,' Miss Beedle said. Her face was paler and thinner than it was a year ago. 'Mrs Hardman has work and London is too dangerous for a ten-year-old to be left by herself.'

'I'm eleven soon,' Francine pointed out.

'Exactly,' Miss Beedle said.

Francine stared at the dice.

'They will put you somewhere nice again.' Miss Beedle

seemed out of breath. 'And I know you'll be a good girl wherever you go.'

She had brought with her a valise and she asked if Francine wanted to grab her things from her flat upstairs – but Francine shook her head, so Miss Beedle went up by herself. When she came back, she showed the contents to Francine. The case was small, but even when everything was in it, there was plenty of space.

'I put in a picture book...' she said hesitantly, before clicking the case shut. 'I always liked *The Princess and the Pea*.'

Then it was time to go. Francine didn't ask where to, she just followed Miss Beedle obediently, like a little lamb. What was the point in knowing? She had nothing left to tie her to anywhere.

At the ticket office at the railway station, Miss Beedle handed her over to someone else. Francine felt like the parcel in pass the parcel. When the music stopped, they'd unwrap more of her, then pass her on.

'Take care of yourself,' Miss Beedle said, and she had tears glistening in her pretty eyes; it was strange, she had been one of the more upbeat grown-ups last year.

The woman she was handed over to had straight yellow hair turned up at the ends and tortoiseshell glasses and she smiled without showing her teeth. She took the handles of Francine's suitcase, carried it onto the waiting train and placed it up on the luggage rack.

'I thought it would be heavier,' she said, then, crossing her arms, she gazed at Francine like she was trying to see right inside her. 'Francine is a funny name,' she observed before correcting herself, 'I mean unusual-funny, not funny ha-ha.'

The woman told Francine her own name, but she didn't

catch it. Francine wondered if she had something wrong with her ears now, along with everything else. Leaning her head against the train window, Francine worried over the woman's name. Was it Myrtle? Or Beryl? She was one of those people who seem to think they're good with children but aren't. Francine preferred the type who aren't but will freely admit it.

Only once the train set off, all smoke and whistles, did Francine realise she was facing the wrong way. The sensation of moving backwards unsettled her. She would have asked to swap seats – to take the one opposite – but she didn't want to ask this woman anything.

Hand in pocket, Francine rotated her dice over and over. The woman asked if she was sleepy and Francine nodded but in this new nightmare world, she felt half-asleep most of the time, stumbling through her days neither awake nor asleep.

The woman kept forgetting where she had put her tickets. Francine rolled one of the dice onto the palm of her left hand: if it were a six, five or four, she would tell her where they were (in the pocket of her shiny handbag). A one, two or three, she would not.

It was a three.

When the conductor came, the woman made him wait, his shaking hands fumbling for the edge of the seat to steady himself while she searched the depths of her coat and each corner of her embroidered purse. Francine felt sorry for the conductor and told the woman where she had put them but the woman ignored her. The conductor rolled his eyes.

Francine wondered what her best friend Lydia would say about all this: She might laugh at 'possibly Myrtle'. She would probably squeal about Francine smelling of disgusting medicine. Lydia had a keen sense of smell and was equally keen on letting the world know about it.

Thinking of Lydia was about the only thing that wasn't dark and heavy right now. People used to say Francine and Lydia were like twins, only opposites: night and day, meat and veg, little and large. And Valerie was like their big sister. But now, both Lydia and Valerie were a billion miles away in Somerset and Francine hadn't heard from either of them since she lost her mother and siblings. Surely she would soon?

'Such sad news!' they would write. Or, 'You are still my best friend.' A letter from them would be better than calamine lotion, better than any lotion in the world.

Once they left London, the view was trees, back gardens and fields and sometimes small hills and rivers. Francine wasn't interested in pretty views. And she would rather it was plain, since her sister Maisie had never got to see pretty things like this and now never would. Sometimes another train would shoot past the other way, towards London, and Francine would try to make out the people at the windows, but she could catch nothing but shadows.

Undeterred by her silence, the blonde woman talked about the Christmas holidays just gone and a husband who was training up north and a daughter whose name was Jane, and Francine did not say, 'funny ha-ha' or 'unusual'.

'Jane's been evacuated too,' the woman said. Did she never take a breath? 'You'll like it, you see.'

Francine glared until eventually the woman met her eyes.

She stuttered. 'I... I do appreciate your situation is complicated, but the important thing is to make the best of it.'

She folded her arms as though she had imparted the wisdom of Solomon.

Francine was not a girl who often scowled at grown-ups. For one, her mummy would have smacked her legs for impertinence, and for two, she was both forgiving and friendly by nature, but this lady was pushing her. Instead, Francine lay down on the facing-the-wrong-way bench seat, keeping her feet on the floor. The woman told her to sit nicely, yet Francine pretended to be asleep. The woman tsked in response, but didn't do anything else.

When the train stopped and people got on, wanting the seat Francine had taken over, she did have to sit up. They mumbled about young people these days having 'no respect'.

'I told her!' blonde woman insisted.

They were two elderly women on a trip to see one of their married daughters. Francine kept her eyes closed, her body going with the train's motion and everything going backwards.

The blonde lady talked about Francine as if she wasn't there.

'The bombings,' she explained self-importantly. 'All her people are dead. The shelter flattened.'

The elderly women looked over at Francine, irritation replaced with sympathy.

'Poor mite.'

Francine had been called this before and she didn't know why. She knew a mite was a bitey insect.

'So sad.'

Blonde woman agreed. 'She looks all right now, but it's bound to hit her later.'

One of the elderly women gestured to Francine's face. 'And why is she...?'

'That's chicken pox.'

'It never rains,' the old woman said incomprehensibly. If

Francine hadn't been pretending to be asleep, she would have told her that it does, in fact – it was raining right now.

'In a way, that saved her,' blonde woman added, excitement in her voice.

Did she think Francine couldn't hear?

'That's why she wasn't in the air-raid shelter. Mother didn't want the babies to catch it.'

When the two elderly women got off at their station, the blonde woman looked around, hopeful about finding someone else to talk at. Mrs Howard liked to say Lydia 'could talk the hind legs off a donkey'. Francine and Lydia used to laugh every time.

'What donkey?' Lydia would giggle. 'Where do the legs go then?'

This woman could talk the hind legs off a rhinoceros.

Now, she called Francine's name. If Francine were cheeky like Lydia, she would have said, 'That's my name, don't wear it out,' but instead, she just whispered, 'Yes?'

'We had to get you out of London. Mr Hitler doesn't care if you're nine or ninety. Or if you're an orphan. Everyone's fair game to him.'

Why was the woman talking about orphans? Francine disliked her even more. The only thing that was keeping her going was Daddy. Daddy had lost four members of his family. He could not lose five. Francine owed him that. He was originally from Holland and he hadn't been able to join the British Army, but he had been welcomed by the Dutch. As soon as he could, he would come home, and he would be overjoyed to see her.

'You understand, don't you?' she pleaded.

'I understand,' Francine mumbled, tracing her spots with a finger. She had become like her dice. Three spots, four. Twenty-four.

The blonde woman strode off, looking for new audiences. She returned not long after, with two black teas, animated with tales of dealing with queue-jumpers.

'You need to stop scratching or you'll get infected.' She caught Francine's wrist, nearly upsetting her cup.

Francine didn't care about getting infected. She didn't care about anything. The rain continued to pour and the windows steamed up.

'Have you heard of Kettering?' the woman asked.

The dice said one.

'No.'

'Neither had I before today,' said the woman. 'But that's where we're going, and you'll be safe there, which is the important thing.'

2

Winnie

Winnie's late husband Trevor used to love all the occasions in the pub: Christmas Day, Boxing Day, New Year's Eve, New Year's Day – but this year Winnie had to drag herself through them, watching the clock until the moment she could call out, 'Time, gentlemen, please.'

It was quiet after the festive period, and Winnie was glad of it. Everyone was all tired out this January – more than ever. The war had been going on for over a year and a half now and Winnie was wondering how much more they could take – how much more *she* could take.

If, twenty years ago, you had told Winnie this would be her life, she'd never have believed it. Certainly not the part about the war, and definitely not the part where she ran a pub. This was never her dream.

It was a nasty day. The sky was mottled grey and the rain lashed at the windows. The weather would put people off coming to the Castle, but those who were already out wouldn't want to go home.

Winnie checked the windows were tightly shut, then moved to the front door and pulled back the bolt, officially opening up for the day. The Castle's sign, with its cartoony picture of a castle with turrets and a great oak door, was swinging and drops of water made their cold way onto the top of her head, making her shiver. Although Winnie had usually been up for hours before unbolting the heavy doors of the Castle at twelve o'clock, the pub opening always felt like the official start of her day.

Outside, the pavements had turned dark grey and slippery. Children were racing home for lunch, gleeful at the downpour and the rain on their cheeks. The drains were overfull. Across the road, the greengrocer was lugging in his damp cardboard boxes and the butcher watched, knee-high in sawdust. She gave them both a wave. Hopefully they'd come in later.

Mac, her twenty-year-old barman, was bored. He kept saying it was going to be 'dead', which she hated. The word 'dead' should be reserved for people, not pubs. But people didn't even say it about people any more – people nowadays 'passed away' or 'were asleep' or 'fell in battle'. Winnie hated those even more.

'It's never busy in January,' she said to Mac. 'Find something to do. It'll make time go quicker.'

Before Winnie had employed Mac she'd been on her own for a while and, although she had managed all right, she'd often had dark imaginings that the cellar door would slam, trap her inside and no one would discover her, so she'd put word out for staff and Mac's mother said she needed him out of the house. He had the blues, she explained, although it occurred to Winnie that Mac's mother might have them too.

He'd tried to join up but 'the recruitment office said he'd do more harm than good.'

Over the months since, Winnie had thought the recruitment office might have had a point. Somehow Mac had broken the till. He had nearly knocked himself out with a tray. Lost one customer's Zippo lighter – 'It's engraved, it is!' – and lost another customer's bracelet – how? He frequently slipped on his own sloppy drink spillages. But Mac was big and strong. A gentle giant, though not always so gentle. If necessary, he could send a grown man flying. He was no Trevor, but he made her feel more secure.

That Thursday, her regular locals Jim, his father Old Jim, Toby and Nathan were the first to arrive, followed by Scott Cuthbert.

'What's he doing here?' Winnie muttered under her breath.

Scott Cuthbert usually worked through his lunchtime. He was a social worker for Kettering Council and a diligent one at that. He was also Winnie's oldest friend. If he was coming in this early in the day, something was amiss.

Pints lined up on the bar like bowling pins. There was a commentary on the weather, on the latest theories about the war; Winnie had heard them all before. She got out the mop and swished around where their shoes had made the floor wet – figures of eight worked best. Old Jim made his usual joke about Winnie being light on her feet: 'Have you never thought about ballet?'

Ordering 'feet up!' as she approached the bar stools, Scott Cuthbert obliged, even though he only had one foot now and even that one had a mind of its own. She swirled around him, already dreaming of a bath and an early night.

'How are you, Winnie?' Scott Cuthbert enquired in the special voice people used with her nowadays. Some people asked: 'How are you bearing up?' Some said, 'How are you getting through?' Susan, Winnie's nineteen-year-old daughter, once said, 'I don't know how you get up in the morning,' and she got short shrift for that.

'Fine,' Winnie said.

Trevor had been dead eight months now. If she pretended everything was fine for long enough, surely she would wake up one day and it would be?

'You?'

'Fine,' he said.

'I'm getting some of that gin your Ada likes next week.'

'Fine,' he said again.

All these *fines*? – something was definitely amiss.

'So?' she said. 'A lunchtime tipple? That's not like you!'

He smiled, folding his beermat.

'You know me well.'

'Yet still, you've always been able to surprise me.'

They shared a smile and then he said, 'I've got a problem.'

There were a thousand ways to respond to that, but Winnie wasn't in the mood for teasing.

'Spit it out.'

'It's awkward,' he said, looking around.

Jim was doing the *Telegraph* crossword, Old Jim was 'helping' him. Nathan was reading D.H. Lawrence and Toby was writing his memoir, which he sometimes read aloud. None of them would give two hoots about anything Scott Cuthbert had to say.

'Whatever it is, you can say it here,' she told him.

Winnie did leave the pub sometimes. The Castle was the kind of pub you could step out of and know all would be well. Trevor had promised her that. He'd made a lot of promises – but that one held. Not like some pubs, where you stepped away from the till at your peril. There was Mac, of course, not exactly eagle-eyed, but another pair of eyes none-theless. Nathan would step in, if necessary, and sometimes had. Jim, too, would probably leap at the chance.

'Fine,' Scott said.

Winnie poured herself a soft drink. She was often tempted, especially at miserable lunchtimes such as these, to have something stronger, to soften the sharp edges of her grief. But no, she wasn't going to succumb. What would Trevor have thought?

'There's this youngster coming up to Kettering about now.' He turned his wrist to check his watch.

'Right...'

Already, she could see where this was going.

'Who needs a place to live. I was thinking, now that Susan's moved out...'

'Sorry, no,' Winnie said firmly – you had to be like that with Scott. He didn't do hints or vague allusions. 'You shouldn't have thought.'

Another one of Winnie's regulars, Sid, arrived and, grateful for the interruption, Winnie slipped away to serve him. Sid used to play the piano beautifully but had stopped after his son was killed at Dunkirk. No matter how often people asked, he refused. Piano was for life, he said, and he was no longer living – he was waiting to die.

Sid took his drink to a corner table as far from the piano as possible. The regulars greeted him cordially, but he preferred to sit alone. No one else played the piano well enough or wanted to tread on Sid's toes, so it was just another thing to dust.

'You've got space,' Scott persisted as she reluctantly made her way back over.

'So?'

'The child has no one else.'

'I'm not doing it.'

How much clearer did she need to be?

'You had an evacuee before, didn't you?'

Brothers. They came on the train the day before the war broke out and she'd picked them up at the village hall. Trevor joked that it was shooting fish in a barrel. They had room and a yearning to help. People did back then, before the deaths, the shortages and the fatigue set in. The hall was packed with good intentions.

Peter and Paul – yes, really – were nice kids. Her only complaint was their appetites. They were constantly on the prowl for food. Susan hadn't been like that, so it took Winnie by surprise. Trevor was no help.

'What did you expect? They're growing lads!'

The brothers were enrolled at the local school, where they seemed happy until, one month later, Peter, the younger, who not only ate more but talked more, announced, 'Dad's getting us this afternoon.'

Sure enough, later that day a man on a motorbike with a sidecar shaped like a rocket appeared. Winnie never found out how the brothers knew he was on his way. Homing pigeon or mind reading or, perhaps more plausibly, a note from a teacher. Whatever it was, she must have missed it. She had wondered if she had done something wrong, but their dad didn't seem displeased. He had a drooping moustache like a Confederate soldier. He thanked her in an accent she couldn't place, offered her a spin in the sidecar ('not today, thank you!') and gave her a package of sixty cigarettes. 'As a gesture of appreciation.'

Paul climbed on the back of the bike, Peter wriggled into the sidecar, the man fixed his goggles and revved the engine.

'Wait...' Winnie had to know. 'Were the boys unhappy here?'

Had she not fed them enough? Had they written home with tales of starvation?

'This country is finished,' their dad explained, honking the horn as though it were an exclamation mark. 'I'm sending the boys to Australia.'

So you couldn't say Winnie hadn't done her bit. Or that it hadn't hurt her heart when they left.

Scott Cuthbert was looking at her eagerly. 'And you used to take lodgers?'

'*Adult* lodgers!' Some of her regulars glanced over at her raised voice. 'Not children,' she added in a lower tone.

And anyway, that was before, when Trevor was alive. Easier to feel comfortable about strangers in the next bedroom if your husband is next to you under the blanket.

'Then what's the difference?'

Good grief, Scott. Couldn't he see? She was pulverised. Bereft. Distraught. Every day, fighting the temptation to drink until she blacked out.

'*Everything* is different now.'

She was suddenly tearful, so she busied herself. She got Jim a glass of water since he was coughing. Fetched an ashtray for Nathan, who was getting ash everywhere. Helped Old Jim with the crossword – 'is it ANTARCTIC? Does that fit – how about if you add an A – ANTARCTIC*A*?' She wiped down the counter even though it was spotless. She unpacked a new stack of card beermats to replace the wet ones. If they weren't pulled apart, they'd have addresses scribbled on, or sometimes, blotchy love notes.

More regulars came in, shaking their umbrellas, making the freshly mopped floor dirty again, and Mac served them.

When she went back over to Scott, pulled by a stupid urge to finish this, he said, 'Whole family wiped out.'

'If she's not got anyone else, then she's not just an evacuee, is she? She's an orphan and I'm not the right person to help.'

Did Scott think Trevor 'falling in battle' was going to send her into a frenzy of compassion? The truth was losing her husband had had the opposite effect. She had nothing left to give – not to anyone. When she heard of death nowadays, she struggled to find an appropriate response. Mrs Warner's husband had been downed in a plane over Holland and Mrs Warner had taken to her bed for a month. Winnie had envied her. Envied the widow who couldn't get out of bed! What a monster she had turned into!

She couldn't understand why Trevor – of all people – had to die. Men who weren't half the man that he was survived! Mean, nasty men lived on while Trevor didn't. It wasn't fair.

Scott probably thought she should have 'got over it by now'. He'd never say it, no one would dare say it directly, but indirectly... Winnie could read minds now, and that was what they were all thinking.

'It's a desperate situation,' Scott continued.

'It's still a no.'

'It would do you good too, Winnie.'

That was the trouble with people who knew the earlier incarnation of you. They wielded it over you like a sword. She tried to take his glass, but he held on, his fingers wrapped round its stem.

'I'm not finished.'

'You are now.'

They were six when they met, twelve when he came to

live with her family, fifteen when he lied to go to fight in the war – the Great War, that was, though they called it the First War now. She wept when he left, wept even more when he came back. He was the same age as her – forty – and he used a stick when his leg was bad, two when it was very painful. They'd told him he would never walk again, he'd proved them wrong. Ada was a nurse in one of his hospitals. He always said that she saved his life.

Scott Cuthbert went back to Ypres every year, although he couldn't now because it was under German occupation, again. He hated missing the memorial services at Menin Gate – hadn't missed one since 1919. If it hadn't been for this war, she and Trevor might have gone to pay their respects too. And if it hadn't been for the pub too, of course. It was always hard to get away, impossible now that it was Winnie's responsibility alone.

Scott would have loved to have joined up again and fought in this war. No, 'loved' was the wrong word – he felt he ought to. She knew he had shed tears about not being able to fight for his country a second time round.

'Haven't you done enough?' she'd demanded one time, when he was venting his frustration at the wireless.

'Never.'

'Looking after children is important work too,' she had said.

Famous last words.

He placed his coat under one arm and made his way to the door. He had two sticks today. The way he walked always elicited sympathy, which he hated, and she didn't want to feel it either. It was just a big contrast to the man he used to be a long, long time ago.

Winnie had to come round the counter and grab the

handle of the door for him because he couldn't manage it himself, but he was in such a mood, he didn't even muster a thank-you.

3

Francine

There were shiny puddles everywhere. The blonde woman pretended that walking round them was 'such fun!', but her expression said she didn't think so. Some of the puddles were so wide you couldn't avoid them, and Francine leapt and landed with a splash, her dice jumping in her pocket. One moment her socks were dry and starchy, the next soaked. It was cold too, blue-lips temperature. Lydia used to say that weather like this made you look as if you'd had too many boiled sweets.

Now the woman was going on about Francine's lack of a gas mask.

'I don't know where it is,' Francine muttered, although she did know. It had been in the shelter that had been hit. The woman was also annoyed Francine didn't have gloves or a hat (also in the shelter).

'Why didn't they pack properly?'

'It's fine,' Francine said, defensive on Miss Beedle's behalf. Her teeth were chattering, her fingers barely mobile. Actually, the puddles and the sting on her cheeks made her feel more awake.

After about twenty minutes they arrived at a recruitment office, where men in civilian dress stood outside, smoking. There were signs on the window: FOR YOUR COUNTRY Another: WHAT WILL YOU TELL YOUR CHILDREN YOU DID IN THE WAR?

'We're upstairs,' she explained, to Francine's relief.

They went up narrow stairways without light all the way to the third floor, where they sat on a bench and waited. It was small and confined, low-ceilinged, just like in the air-raid shelter

After a brief wait a man came in, and introduced himself as Mr Cuthbert. Francine went over this name in her head so she didn't forget it. One of Mr Cuthbert's legs stopped at the knee and the other had a twisted foot, but she told herself not to look. They went into his office, which was more like a cubicle, dominated by steel cabinets with sticky paper attached and dates written on them and folders peeping out of the drawers. It reminded her a little of Mrs Howard's topsy-turvy library, only that library made this place look organised.

'Welcome to Kettering! It's a lovely part of the world, despite the weather.'

The dice said to stay quiet.

'I need to do paperwork. Do you mind if I ask you some questions?'

The dice said four – fine.

He asked her birthday, and Mum and Dad's names and address, and filled out the gaps in the papers. At first the questions were too easy, and then they were too hard. Most of her answers were, 'I don't know'.

At one point he looked up and, in an incredulous tone, said, 'You must remember something!'

Francine nodded, yet everything felt vague and misty, as though she was peering through a smeary train window. The names and addresses of relatives, possible family members, were just out of reach. If only she could give her brain a good clean.

'You lived in Somerset a while?'

Francine had stayed with Mrs Howard at Bumble Cottage for three months the previous year, before returning to be with her family back in London. Francine's mother had struggled without her oldest daughter and Francine had been homesick too. Lydia Froud, Francine's best friend, her opposite twin, had stayed on in Somerset.

Francine thought about Lydia now, all eyes, teeth and golden curls, chasing around the garden or throwing cushions. For a moment, she would have given anything to be back there. But that wasn't going to happen.

Mrs Howard had an elderly dog called Cassie. Within a few days of Lydia and Francine's arrival, poor Cassie became ill and died. A half-demolished fruit cake seemed to have been the explanation – its raisins had poisoned her. Somehow – and Francine was never quite sure how – it turned into Francine's fault for being careless with the cake and for leaving it where an inquisitive dog might get it.

Mrs Howard didn't punish Francine, she was just grimly sad, but since that day she and Francine had never been close. And if there was one thing Francine was certain of it was that Mrs Howard wouldn't want to see her ever again.

Mr Cuthbert was waiting for her to speak.

'Pardon?' she said.

'Do you know where your father is?'

'He is in the army.'

'You sure it was the army, not the air force or navy?'

Francine nodded. Of this she was sure.

Mr Cuthbert seemed animated by this. *Now they were getting somewhere!* 'We'll find him, Francine—'

'Will you just stop!' interrupted the woman.

'What?' he asked.

'Pardon,' corrected Francine. '*What* is less polite—'

'I meant her,' she snapped. 'Stop scratching!'

This was also less polite. Francine folded her arms away. Mr Cuthbert grimaced sympathetically.

'May I have a word in private?' the woman asked, and so Francine was sent out of the room. They may have thought it was private with her out there, but she could still hear every word.

'I thought you had a plan, Mr Cuthbert. Bringing her all—'

'I do have a plan,' Mr Cuthbert interrupted. 'It's just the finer details.'

'We could have put her in a children's home in London.'

'I don't think she'll adjust,' he said. 'They're not for—'

'...rather than bringing her cross-country on a wild goose chase.'

Francine thought of the geese in Somerset and the honking countryside noises that once used to frighten her more than the sound of planes bringing bombs.

'Give me a few days.'

'Mr Cuthbert, I need to get back. There are other children waiting to leave the city.'

'Just a couple of—'

'One night.'

She was far fiercer than Francine would have expected.

'Two?' he suggested.

'I said one.'

Which was funny, because Francine had just rolled a one.

4

_____

Winnie

Winnie polished the pint glasses, the wine glasses and the sherry glasses. You had to be extra careful not to break glasses because it was harder to get replacements these days. Winnie was always getting a rap on the knuckles from the brewery. People thought she was free or self-employed, but running a pub was like being a puppet on a string, and how it went was largely down to the puppeteer in charge and even what mood he was in.

The rain held off and more people came in that evening, so Winnie lit the fire. Scott Cuthbert's earlier visit had disturbed her. They had been in tune with each other for a long time, but it was clear they weren't any longer. She wasn't the Winnie she used to be. She wasn't as strong as she once was. He had to understand that. He had to accept that – as she had.

Scott had always had this vision of Winnie as someone powerful. When they were younger and used to play in the woods together, he once fell out of a tree and crumpled on the ground, howling. She had carried him all the way home to his mum. His mum had pinched Winnie's cheeks and told her she was a hero.

In her memory, it was not long after that his family had died in a dreadful tram accident, and Scott came to stay with them, but actually it was over three years later. The incidents had simply meshed into one over time.

Winnie had always planned to travel the world. That was always her dream, her big goal, but then she met Trevor Eldridge: a no-nonsense, ambitious young man from Birmingham. Trevor chatted her up on the train but, because she thought that sounded uncouth, she told everyone that they met through 'family friends'. She told him he must say that too. It was the only time she ever asked him to lie.

Trevor said, 'When you told me you wanted to travel the world, I thought I should let you go.'

'But?'

'I'm too selfish. I don't want you to leave.'

It was easy to fall for Trevor. It wasn't just his easy way with words, he was free of the anguish or self-doubt that dogged other men. He was so sure of himself, his personality so big, he made her feel like there were no other options, but in a good way – like she didn't *need* other options – and he claimed he was head over heels for her.

Even though Trevor had talked about running a pub, it had taken her by surprise that he actually went and did it, because she hadn't realised yet that Trevor always did what he said he would do. He was old-fashioned in that way, a man of his word.

The Great War had been over for a year and the country was officially in recovery. Or were they still suffering? Or perhaps the country was suffering and recovering at the same time. People were optimistic mostly, until you walked around and saw the decimation. Too many women, not enough men. That was another reason she was happy with Trevor, not that she'd ever admit that. The odds of her meeting anyone had been against her. The girls at school had told her exactly where she stood: At nineteen, Winnie had a curvy figure but a homely face. She shouldn't expect too much, especially when half her generation were dead.

But not only was Trevor alive – he'd spent most of the Great War training recruits in Hull – but he had a nice face, friendly manners and surprisingly large feet (he had to get his shoes from a specialist shop in Birmingham). He had a lot going for him, which made it all the more remarkable that he was interested in her.

It was autumn when he first took her to the Castle. There was a nip in the air and she didn't want to catch a cold, especially with the particularly nasty one going around. The leaves were red or gold, and crunched underfoot. She loved that crunch – 'like crispy bacon,' Trevor said. The trees were proud in their simply unadorned beauty. The birds were rehearsing formations in the sky, 'like soldiers,' Trevor said. He had a weird way of looking at things, yet he always made her think.

'Where are we going?'

'Wait and see...'

A homeless man in the street outside Boots the Chemist asked for money and Trevor dug deep in his pockets to give him something. He could never walk past anyone in need.

'Poor old boy,' he said even though they were about the same age. 'All the things he's seen and this is how he's treated!'

And then there it was. The pub stood alone, double-fronted, orange brick, white columns. At the top, more ornate, it had TE CASTLE in a semicircle. It had porthole windows like a ship. Winnie had walked past this pub for most of her life and never thought much about it. It was just part of the landscape. Her parents weren't drinkers – her father didn't like the loss of control, her mother didn't like the smell. Maybe she'd gone in at Christmas time, or that might have been the King's Head. Weren't they all the same? She remembered her father saying, 'Children and pubs don't mix'. Some people said that women and pubs didn't mix either.

'What happened to the H?' she asked, laughing.

'What?'

She pointed at the sign. Who would take the letter H, she wondered, what would they do with it?

Usually, Trevor liked a laugh. He said they had a similar sense of humour and this was important to him, more than beautiful features but he appeared to see nothing funny in this.

'I guess it dropped off. Be easy enough to replace though. What do you think?'

'In what way?'

He ignored that. He had a bunch of keys – she didn't know where he had got them from – he was opening the door.

'There used to be a Roman castle down the road. It's long gone, but this Castle – the more important one – remains.'

He grinned, sense of humour restored.

'An Englishman's home is his castle, don't they say?'

What about an Englishwoman? she thought, but he held out his hand and she let him guide her inside.

The frosted glass, the mahogany smell, the dark wood – it felt fusty and old-fashioned.

He leaned against the bar. 'It's ours.'

'*What?*'

'If we want,' he added quickly, but she sensed it was a done deal.

'We can run it together. The landlord is retiring. I've chatted with the brewery, so...'

He swept his hand through his hair.

'You did say you wanted to change your job.'

She was always complaining about the old people's home – but it was just habit, it didn't mean anything. She was saving up for her travels. Every night, she leafed through her *Baedeker Guide* from the library and dreamed. She'd renewed the book four times already. She also spent a silly amount of time wishing she had wealthy relatives to send her to Rome or Sicily on a Grand Tour.

'We'll marry. Of course.'

The proposal felt like an appendage or an afterthought. He was so excited about the Castle, he hadn't considered her.

'Marry?'

Trevor had swivelled from businesslike to romantic. Winnie was reminded of those cuckoo clocks where a different character comes out for rain or shine.

'We'll be landlord and landlady.'

Right then, being a landlady felt as unlikely as being a ladybird.

'I'm not sure,' she said. This was too much. 'Are you... proposing?'

He dropped onto one knee – Trevor had lightning-quick reflexes, and, if this was what he had to do, this was what he'd do.

It wasn't the most romantic proposal – in the middle of a silent, dusty public house – but Winnie was a realist. You didn't get through 1914–1918 with silly notions about life. And marriage was the thing, not the proposal, and that was enough for her. So they were getting married. It was decided. That was out of the way.

With renewed interest, she examined the Castle. There was a small swing door behind the bar, and she could see an old till, shelves and carpets full of holes. Trevor hardly looked. He'd already made up his mind.

'How much is it then?' Winnie asked timidly. These carpets needed to be pulled up... yesterday.

'Whatever it is, it's worth it.' Trevor hugged her. 'I'm glad you love it, too.'

'Shall we discuss the details over tea?' she suggested. She felt giddy and she couldn't help wondering what her old friend Scott Cuthbert would say. She didn't think he'd like it. After he had told her he was marrying Ava, he had exhorted her to 'Explore the rolling hills of Tuscany, the sandy dunes of the Arabian deserts, or even the Taj Mahal!' He wouldn't expect her to move less than half a mile from home.

Trevor had no money for tea. He had given his last change to the homeless man. Winnie thought that might be a bad sign, but she didn't say anything.

For Trevor, marriage and pub were inexorably linked – if she wanted one, she'd have to swallow the other. It was his dream, and Winnie knew that if she loved him, she would have to take his dreams on as her own.

The day after Scott's request it wasn't wet, but it was cold, and her regulars arrived wrapped up in layers, like onions, that took a while to unravel. Like onions, the sight of them also made Winnie want to cry. Some of them stood in the doorway, letting in cold air as they stomped their feet. She'd try to keep track of whose scarf and whose hat was whose, but it was often a losing battle.

As she opened up, Winnie suddenly realised she hadn't changed out of her slippers.

'Standards, Winnie,' Trevor would have said.

Everyone was wondering if it would snow. Jim was staring out the window, a childlike grin on his face.

'It's going to tip down!'

'That's the last thing we need,' Winnie exclaimed. The deliveries would struggle to get through. Who'd clear the snow off the pavements? She would, she supposed. Most men between the ages of eighteen and forty-five had left: the town was almost entirely maintained by elderly men and middle-aged women like her.

Jim looked at her reproachfully. He was probably thinking the old Winnie, Winnie-and-Trevor Winnie, would have loved it.

Winnie put her landlady's smile on her face.

'I'm joking! Nothing I love more than snow,' she lied.

They'd done a snowman competition in the Castle garden once. Trevor had fired snowballs at brothers Bobby and Nigel Stone all the way to the high street. Both of the Stone boys were in the air force now, and their mother didn't go out any more.

There was a nice atmosphere that afternoon though, even Winnie had to admit: the Castle was a refuge from the bad weather. The fire gave the air a smoky scent. Old Jim had brought in his dog; Jess was often excitable, but today she nestled under his table like a good girl. You could forget the war for five minutes.

'Canadians are coming to town!' Mac said as he arrived for his evening shift.

But you couldn't forget it for very long.

Winnie wasn't surprised. The Canadians had come the last war round too; it had only been a matter of time before they returned. She expected they would take over the disused airbase less than half a mile away like last time.

Mac's face was flushed with displeasure. 'Their trucks are blocking up the main road right now. It's like an invasion!'

Poor chap, Winnie thought. Her burly barman would love a beau, and she guessed what he was thinking: more competition.

He'd been sweet on her daughter, Susan. He'd been sweet on Mrs Turner after her husband ran off with a schoolgirl. He'd been sweet on Annabelle Stone, but her brothers had warned him off. Mac gave off an air of desperation – Winnie had subtly tried to tell him that, but that was part of the problem; he couldn't read between the lines.

'How long until they are swarming over the town?'

Mac looked like he was going to cry.

'They have their work to do,' Winnie said. 'That's what they're here for – to help win the war. They hardly affected us last time.'

But Mac was obsessing. 'All over our women...'

'They won't bother you.'

'They'll still want to get to know the area,' interjected Toby unhelpfully. 'And in my experience, they strut around like peacocks.'

'You see!' said Mac, slamming a bottle onto the counter so everything on it wobbled.

5

_____

Francine

By the time Francine and the lady arrived at the Good Bed
and Breakfast it had gone six, and they hadn't had a bite to
eat since breakfast. The first thing the landlord, Mr Good,
told them was that they were too late for food. The blonde
woman's cheeks went pink.

'Could we have our breakfast now perhaps?'

You'd think she asked him to assassinate the king! What a
suggestion! Breakfast was for mornings. They didn't do
supper!

'This girl is an orphan,' she told him, and Francine
sensed that once again she was pulling out her trump card.
'Family bombed out in the Blitz. Died all at once. Only last
week.'

'My papa didn't,' interrupted Francine. 'He is in the
army!'

'We have no idea where your father is,' the woman

continued. 'The others were killed. Finito. Four of them. The child is starving.'

Whether this was what convinced him to make two cress sandwiches and two cups of tea so weak that it was more like hot water, Francine would never know, but the woman clearly thought it had.

'She's going to be fostered here in Kettering,' she continued triumphantly once he'd set down the plates. 'Two birds, one stone. Get her a new family and get her out of Hitler's way. Because being unlucky once won't stop him again.'

'Who's going to foster her?' asked the landlord, which struck Francine as the salient issue.

'That's still being arranged,' the woman said, picking at the crusts. 'But whoever it is, has to be an angel to take her on.'

She looked up at Francine as though she had just realised she was there. 'No offence.'

In the bedroom, the blonde lady busied herself pulling the curtains, tugging on the tiny lamp cord to see if it worked (it didn't), opening and shutting the cupboards and drawers and her bag. All the while, she was still talking. Francine didn't listen. It was just a low background noise, like the hum of aeroplanes.

Twin beds took up most of the room, leaving only small gaps in which to walk. But Francine slept better with company – and, much as she had few warm feelings towards the woman, she was glad they were sharing.

Since the Blitz had begun, she had spent most nights in the air-raid shelter, curled up like a comma round her sister Maisie. Her elbow in her stomach, Maisie's hair in her mouth. She still found Maisie's hair – which was curlier and lighter than hers – on her clothes. Did Maisie know what was happening when the bomb hit?

The bathroom was at the end of a corridor. Francine didn't know which tap was hot, nor how to switch it off, and then which was the flush. Then, excruciatingly, she didn't know which door she'd come out of.

She knocked at one and there was no answer. She waited before knocking at a second. A young woman in only a towel flung the door open and a man's voice shouted out, 'The more the merrier!'

She backed off, knocked on a third and, blessedly, the blonde woman answered, her face a panicky mirror of Francine's own. She had changed into a long nightie like the ones Mummy had worn, although hers had a frill round the neckline.

'There you are!' she said, her hand over her heart. 'I would be in so much trouble if I lost you!'

The woman then asked if she wanted to say her prayers. When Francine said she didn't, thank you, she snapped, 'You ought to,' but she didn't say hers either. They lay side by side. Before she leaned over to switch off the light, the woman, now in a softer tone, said, 'If you were my daughter, I'd give you a kiss. Do you want me to give you a goodnight kiss?'

'No,' Francine said.

'Goodnight,' the woman said tightly.

The sheets were cool and the eiderdown crumpled, and Francine thought about the air-raid shelter and the game of dominos they'd been playing before she got the chicken pox. The shelter had felt like home. It was full of toy cars and marbles for the little ones, books and games for her and Maisie. But Mummy hated it. In the day, she was sweetness and light, but in the shelter, she'd grow fearful and morose.

And then, as Francine lay there, struggling to sleep in the unfamiliar bed, her family came to find her – Mummy, Maisie, the tiny boys – and sat at the end of her bed, pawing her. She felt like they were waiting for her to say something but she didn't know what. Maisie kept tugging at the quilt and screeching that it wasn't fair. The babies cried. Mummy looked desolate. They were there when she closed her eyes; the only way they'd go was when she opened her eyes, but she didn't want to do that.

Francine must have fallen asleep at some point though, because the next thing she knew, the blonde woman was shaking her awake.

'You're screaming, child!'

Francine pushed her fist to her mouth. The pillow was covered in spots of blood.

The next morning, the blonde woman ate her boiled egg and soldiers in silence. The only thing she said was, 'I had a terrible night, you kept waking me,' and although Francine felt bad, she also felt relieved that the woman had stopped her incessant chatter.

She looked up for assistance with the eggshell – Mummy used to help – but the woman was scowling into her toast and Francine didn't want to start her off again. She poured salt until the landlord grabbed the salt cellar away from her. The Good Bed and Breakfast did not live up to its name.

Back outside, in the cold air, Francine trotted after the lady to the council office – it wasn't as far as it had seemed the evening before. Some puddles had iced over, and crackled underfoot.

At the recruitment office a man in khaki uniform was

smoking in the doorframe, surveying the miserable landscape.

'Come to join up, ladies?' he said.

The woman tittered, 'Hilarious!'

Back upstairs to the airtight chamber: this time, Mr Cuthbert was on the floor at the cabinet drawers.

'You couldn't stay just one more night?' he asked as they walked in.

Francine wondered if this was another joke.

'I've hardly slept as it is!' The woman snapped. 'And she needs a gas mask, gloves and a hat – as a matter of urgency!'

'Understood,' he said without looking up.

The woman spat on a handkerchief to wipe Francine's cheeks. She pushed and rubbed as Francine winced. Francine guessed this was what she did with her own daughter, her Jane and, although she hated it, it gave her an ache of jealousy. Why did it have to be her family who was dead? Why did everyone else get to keep theirs?

'And remember' – the woman finally stopped her rubbing, but it was like she wasn't clear what Francine ought to remember. 'Stop scratching,' she decided finally. 'Otherwise, you'll be scarred for life.'

And then she left, the door swinging shut after her.

'Not to worry,' Mr Cuthbert said, seemingly more to convince himself than her. 'Let's find you a lovely foster carer.'

6

Winnie

The man who came from the brewery wasn't one of her usual contacts: Mr Bedford and Mr Paley were lovely men. Trevor always said they'd got lucky with them because many brewery folk were uncooperative. They'd have tea from the best china, putting the world to rights. Mr Marshall was different. Straight away, he put her back up by assuming Mac was the boss.

Winnie asked after Mr Bedford and he flicked something off the bar.

'He's in the army now.'

'And Mr Paley?'

'Missing in action.'

'Sorry to hear.'

'Indeed.'

She wondered why he hadn't been conscripted. There were lots of exemptions, but nothing about him – or his work – stood out.

He had brought something for her, he said. 'From the brewery.' A portrait of Winston Churchill, about a metre square with an ornate frame.

'Gosh,' said Winnie, lost for words.

'A gift to all our pubs,' he said.

'Golly...'

'Where do you want him?' asked Mac.

'Over the bar,' Mr Marshall said. 'Where everyone can see him.'

'I'm not sure,' Winnie mustered.

The day they'd opened – or reopened – the Castle in June 1919, everyone was talking about the Treaty of Versailles. Winnie was telling everyone what she thought: it was storing up trouble for later down the line. She had been expanding on this when Trevor grabbed her arm.

'They don't come here to listen to us spouting off!'

'Trevor!' She was stung.

'We need to be neutral, Win!'

She thought of her father, who was always wanting her opinion. A rare man, whose mantra was: 'Don't let anyone tell you that men are better than women.'

'Just in the pub,' Trevor had added quickly. 'Save the rants for elsewhere.'

'They're not ra—'

'Whatever. Customers come here for escape, not to have bad news shoved in their faces.'

It wasn't that she disliked Churchill. Like most people, Winnie was cautiously optimistic that he'd help win the war. And it wasn't that she disliked the portrait. On the contrary, it was nicely done. It was just this was not her and Trevor's way. As Winnie was prevaricating, Mr Marshall was turning puce.

'No one else has a problem with him!' he spluttered and

Winnie realised she was in danger of losing twenty-two years of brewery goodwill.

'I don't have a problem. I just try to keep the Castle non-partisan.'

But all he could hear was that she hated Churchill.

'All right!' She gave in. There were, she supposed, bigger battles.

Once Churchill was up, his jowly scowl dominating, Mr Marshall pulled out a notebook and put on his spectacles.

'Half the pubs in London have closed,' he said. 'And of those that haven't, many of them have evacuated into their own cellars now.'

'The powers-that-be won't like that,' Winnie said.

'They don't mind. I heard one pub got blown apart except for the piano. It was untouched, they say.'

What the people in the cities were going through was horrendous.

'At another, people ran in and nicked sherry just moments after the ceiling collapsed. Get to see the worst in everyone these days.'

'And sometimes the best?' Winnie suggested.

Mr Marshall looked at her like he thought she too could keep her opinions to herself.

'Did you know the government banned all pubs in the Great War?'

So? thought Winnie resentfully. Was she supposed to be grateful? But Mac joined in, exclaiming, wow, he didn't know that.

'They thought pubs would lead to licentious behaviour.'

'Wonder why they haven't now?' Mac pondered.

'They wouldn't dare!' Winnie said, laughing, unable to resist. Mr Marshall scowled.

'Thing is,' he said slowly, 'we might have to shut down some pubs...'

'The government are saying that?' Winnie was so alarmed that she squeaked.

'Not quite,' he said. 'The brewery are saying that. It's financial. We're looking at reducing the numbers of pubs we have open. Just while the war is on.'

Jim, Old Jim and Nathan, who had been pretending not to listen, gasped. Jess, the mood-reading dog, let out an anxious bark.

'Don't let them, Mrs Eldridge,' called Sid.

'Not the Castle!' Toby called in his sonorous tone. 'Never!'

Winnie took a deep breath. Mostly she was annoyed with herself for not seeing this coming. Trevor would have anticipated it. She just reacted to things after they'd happened. Trevor would have defended his castle at all costs. She looked over at the shocked faces of her regulars: Sid nursing a beer, Toby quivering furiously and Jess circling the tables. This is my community, she thought. And not only that, this is my livelihood. My income. My home. My connection to my dead husband. I have nowhere else to go.

'How will you decide which pubs stay open?'

Mr Marshall gulped back his drink and then, like a child, held out his glass for another. 'Double.'

She did as she was told. She knew what the brewery were thinking. She was alone here, she was a target, a widow with a customer base of old men. They weren't important.

Mr Marshall downed this drink in one, a man satisfied with the world.

'Footfall.'

'What's that mean?'

'All depends on your numbers!' He winked. 'If you're doing well, you get to stay open. If not...' He did a throat-slitting sign, which Winnie thought was inappropriate.

'Most men from Kettering have been mobilised,' she said. 'The young people have moved away.'

'You'll have to find other customers.'

'Like who?'

'You'll think of something, Mrs Eldridge.' He paused. 'Or will you just give up? Your choice.'

Winnie looked at Churchill looming over her: She thought of the pubs forced underground, with protective socks over their bottles and boards at their windows. Right. The people in the cities were managing. She could manage. As Churchill might have said, 'We will fight them in the public houses.'

She was going to keep the Castle open if it was the last thing she did.

7

Francine

Even though it was cold, Mr Cuthbert was sweating as they walked. Francine felt for him. He wasn't as much of a talker as the lady either. They staggered past a butcher's shop, a greengrocer, and a pub called the Castle without the H, which had pretty hanging baskets covered in frost and rose bushes without flowers.

He noticed her looking. 'In summer, there will be yellow roses there.'

'They're unusual,' she told him. She remembered her father bringing a yellow rose home. He'd found it in the street, he said. Francine had thought that might put her mother off, but she had put it in a milk bottle and then kissed him on the lips.

'It's an unusual place.' He smiled.

They had gone on another five minutes or so before he had to rest.

'I was about your age when I lost my parents and my sister in an accident,' he said suddenly.

Francine looked at the paving stones. If she didn't step on the cracks, all would be well.

'What happened?'

His expression looked like he was back there.

'Nothing for a while. Eventually a kind family took me in and I was happy.'

'You said you didn't think I would adjust to a children's home.'

He was avoiding looking at her now.

'That's right...'

'What *is* a children's home?'

Usually children's somethings – children's playgrounds, children's books, children's songs – were lovely, but Francine understood that this wasn't.

'It's a place where children without families live – I don't think it would be right for you.'

'Why?'

He made a face. 'I don't think a girl like you should be institutionalised.'

Francine didn't know this word either.

'Children can get lost in those places,' he explained. 'I've found someone to care for you.' He swallowed. 'It won't be like being with family in London, but you will be looked after.'

'Until Daddy gets me.'

'Until then,' he said, staring straight ahead.

On the doorframe of the house they stopped at, about a head higher than her, there was attached a mezuzah, a case about a finger long with a tiny prayer inside. They had one at home, and Mummy and Daddy used to touch it whenever they came home. She remembered Mummy saying she'd put one up on the shelter but she hadn't done it. Maybe that was why it had all gone bad for them.

Mr Cuthbert knocked and a muffled voice called out, 'Wait! I have to put my teeth in.'

Mr Cuthbert grimaced, but said to Francine, 'Give him a chance.'

Francine blinked.

'Sometimes, we can't have our first choice, or our second, but...' He patted his chest. 'Remember, it's what's in here that's important.'

Francine didn't know what he was trying to say.

Finally, the door swung open. The man there wore a kippah, like Francine's father did on a Friday evening, but there the similarities ended. He was so old, he was bent double like he was readying to re-enter the ground, and he had wizened hands that fiddled with his mouth. He was older even than Francine's grandad, who lived in a home for people who can't remember who they are. His back was curved and he had grey stubble and the biggest ears she'd ever seen, each covered by a sort of grey fuzz.

'Come in.'

They crowded in the narrow hallway. He smelled and the house smelled. Dust and sweat and spicy oils and rooms that were cold and hot at the same time. Pictures on the wall: a windmill, the king, a ship. A mishmash.

'I like the landscapes,' he said, gesturing towards a picture. His voice was thick, like his mouth was full of something. 'And the seascapes. And the still lives.'

Still lives, Francine thought. That was her. Still alive.

His mouth made a clicking noise even when he wasn't talking.

'So, my little guest,' he said, looking at Mr Cuthbert for confirmation.

Mr Cuthbert said, 'Francine, this is Mr Cohen, your foster carer—'

'Don't be frightened!' Mr Cohen interrupted. 'I don't bite – I can't!'

They followed him into the living room. It was full of boxes, cups, plates of crumbs and ornaments. It was a mess; you had to pick your way around to avoid banging into anything. Lydia would have fainted at the state of it.

'I've let it go since my Bertha went.'

Francine looked up at Mr Cuthbert. She thought he would be appalled too, but if he was, he didn't show it. He was kind to the old man.

'How long has it been?' he asked, picking his way across the room, his stick inadvertently spearing a newspaper.

'Twenty years,' the old man said. 'Feels like yesterday.'

Francine sneezed and they both turned to her.

'You're not allergic to cats?' Mr Cohen asked.

Francine bit her lip. 'I don't think so.'

He said the cat was for company, but she wasn't good company at all. 'She has terrible manners,' he said. 'I'll introduce you.'

'Will I be institutionalised here, Mr Cuthbert?' Francine whispered as the old man went to seek out his pet.

Mr Cuthbert snorted. 'I shouldn't think that will be the problem.'

She had been passed from Mrs Hardman to her old teacher, to the blonde woman, now to this man. Each wrapper taken off – now the music had stopped and this was what she was left with.

'You'll start school next Monday,' he said. Before Francine could ask anything else, the old man had returned to the room holding, not a cat, but a cup of tea. He said the cat had run off again but not to worry. She'd be home for her supper. Francine had not been worried about the cat. She took the drink and sniffed it. Mr Cohen had called it tea but it was a pale-grey terrible liquid that you would have second thoughts about giving to plants.

She set it down on a wobbly pile of newspapers – there was no other free surface anywhere, not even the floor.

'I'll make the next one, shall I?'

He beamed at her, his teeth slip-sliding. 'We're going to get along famously.'

8

Winnie

On Sunday, Susan dropped by on a flying visit. A friend was driving north and would pick her up on his return. Winnie had her daughter for about four hours – do not say 'only' four hours, she told herself. Be grateful!

'How did he get fuel?' Winnie asked. The petrol cuts ran deep now.

Susan tapped her nose, and then she pointed at Churchill. 'What's he doing there?'

'The brewery brought him in.'

'I thought you and Dad avoided political statements.'

'We did,' said Winnie. Sometimes she felt like everything was slipping out of her control. 'I didn't have much say.'

'I like it.' Susan shrugged.

Winnie was careful not to make demands on Susan or to expect too much of her. Expectations were not fair on a child. Susan didn't exist to fill the gaps in Winnie's life. Winnie knew mothers who lived through their children but, even if she tried that, Susan wouldn't let her.

Susan was a female Trevor through and through. Like Trevor, she hated to feel pressured. And Susan was brilliant. Trevor might have been brilliant too, but he'd had no education. He could add up. He knew when the brewery deals were as good as the brewery said they were and when they were telling porkies, but he had no qualifications to show for it. (Winnie wasn't bad with numbers either, but she still used her fingers to count sometimes.)

Susan was tall. When she didn't stop growing, Trevor used to worry about her height – the tall girls he knew stooped, his mum stooped – but Susan never stooped. And her stride was enormous. Winnie had to do two steps to her one. You didn't mess around with Susan.

That day, she looked especially magnificent, wearing a cape that flapped behind her. Susan never followed fashion, but always looked stylish. At school, a posse of younger girls had swarmed after her, hoping to emulate her. Winnie couldn't blame them.

Mother and daughter smiled at each other. Susan had Trevor's crooked grin, his proud nose, but people said she had Winnie's eyes. Green with black spokes. Trevor used to say he fell for Winnie's eyes, but Winnie suspected he said that because he felt he ought and what he actually fell for was her ample chest and small waist, but he knew that didn't sound so good.

Mac was behind the bar that day and as soon as he saw Susan, he tried it on. He couldn't help himself.

'You walking out with anyone, Susie?' he asked. Winnie knew Susan hated being called Susie, yet she felt for Mac. He always got it wrong.

'I am,' replied Susan deftly and Winnie's stomach

twisted. She hadn't known there was a beau on the scene. 'How about you, Mac? Any luck with the ladies?'

He stuck out his lower lip.

'Someone will come along soon!' Susan said brightly. 'Let's go, Mum.'

It was quiet enough for Mac to manage. Obediently, Winnie followed Susan upstairs to the kitchen. There, she took off her cape and spread herself out. All she wanted was a sandwich.

'What shall I put in it?'

'Don't fuss, Mum.'

Susan never cared less about food. Winnie opened a tin of sardines. It would be Winnie's ration, but Susan needed feeding up and Winnie didn't. She wanted Susan to love it, to love being here, to love her. Winnie felt so powerless lately, she needed a boost.

'You're courting then?' Winnie asked when Susan had finished eating, wondering if the mysterious driver was Susan's boyfriend. He would have to be pretty special.

'Shhh,' said Susan. She got up and shut the kitchen door to prying ears. 'I just said that to put him off, you know.'

Winnie did.

'And no, I hardly have time to brush my own hair!'

Winnie used to dream about Susan's wedding, but she didn't dream about it these days. Susan was driven by work, by the workings of her brain – and now by the war. She was, by her own account, extremely undomesticated.

They had been talking for a while and Winnie was convinced she was doing a good job covering up how low she felt when Susan said, 'Why don't you shut the pub? You always say nothing happens in January – why not go to see your friends?'

Winnie kept up with her friends from school, but they were all doing the same precarious juggling act as her.

'I should be here.'

She didn't want to tell Susan what the man from the brewery had said. She didn't want her to know she was at risk of losing the Castle. Susan mightn't live here any more but this place was her childhood.

'If you're sure...' Susan said. She tried to visit every six weeks or so; she wasn't far away, but sometimes important things came up. When she cancelled, Winnie always said fine, fine.

'I'm glad you've got the pub to keep you busy, Mum.' She took Winnie's hand. 'I miss Dad, too.'

In the old days, whenever there was bad news or big news, the day the stock market collapsed, or when King Edward abdicated, Winnie and Trevor had given drinks on the house. They couldn't do that any more – there was so much bad news, they'd be bankrupt in a week.

The day war broke out, though, there were drinks for everyone. You had to put on a brave face – it was your obliga-tion. People came to the Castle to escape, not to feel worse. They managed to keep spirits up all evening but then, when it was just the two of them in bed, in the dark, they could be themselves again.

'I'm joining up,' Trevor said. He was forty-four years old, forty-five next July. Before she had time to reply, he said, 'I have to do it now.'

'What about the pub?'

When she meant was *what about me?*

'You'll manage.'

She'd had a lifetime's worth of 'you'll manage'. That was

what you got when you appeared responsible. She couldn't argue because Trevor would do what he wanted anyway, and she didn't want her antagonism to be his overarching memory of her. She pictured him squatting in some trench – showing off a photograph of her and Susan. Did he even have a photograph of her and Susan to show off?

'It's the right thing to do,' he whispered. 'We have to stand up to the Nazis.'

They held hands across the mattress and she pretended she didn't feel strongly, pretended it was only his decision to make. Even if she didn't think it was. Maybe it was just the drink talking. Maybe it was just the chatter in the pub. She didn't think he'd go through with it.

But the next day he found a recruitment office. She prayed for them to laugh and tell him he was too old, but, just as the last time they never told Scott Cuthbert he was too young, they didn't send Trevor Eldridge away. Of course they didn't. They were like the three monkeys he'd got her from the market in Leicester, the ornaments that were in the pub toilet: See no evil, hear no evil, speak no evil.

Trevor's last night at home was a normal Monday evening, as normal as nights in the Castle ever were. Winnie was feeling anything but normal, and she was done with pretending otherwise.

'You going to tell everyone?'

'If it comes up.' He was coy for once. It didn't suit him.

'It's hardly likely to, is it? No one's going to ask if you've joined up.' A final jab. 'No one would imagine it!'

He rolled his eyes. When she was like this, he called her a grumpy old bat.

She had Peter and Paul, the evacuee boys, to worry about by then too. And she was worrying about them. When she'd gone through the pockets of their shorts to wash them, she found Peter had a penknife and Paul had a slingshot, and were these appropriate? Susan only ever had pens or notes of equations in hers.

'I don't want the Castle to run to ruin while I'm away.'

'I can look after it.'

'I know you can. I just... I love this pub.'

He loved the pub more than he loved her. She bounded upstairs two at a time, propelled by anger. He'd be thinking she was overdramatic, a quality they both disliked, but so what?

In bed, that last night before he left, Trevor had sneaked his hand across to her – his signature move – and she had rolled on her side, her back to him. It was how she slept best, but it was also a way to let him know she disapproved.

He whispered 'Winifred,' which meant business, and she pretended she was asleep.

She thought they'd have more time.

His last morning, she had done a special breakfast, eggs and bacon, toast, and he said it was a treat, but he left most of it. He looked sick too; he had a green pallor and he kept popping off to the lav. He always got a dicky belly after an argument, it upset his equilibrium. She got a bad head – she had one now.

What a pair they were. Even if he changed his mind, he had set in motion a stream of events that it would be impossible to hold back. Like the tide, it had to come in, and all she could do was see how much devastation it was going to cause.

She walked Peter and Paul to school, chanting their times tables. She kept muddling six times eight and eight times seven, which the boys found hilarious. On the way, she hoped her bloody husband would be gone before she got back – those anguished goodbyes belonged in films, not in the real world – but as she waved off the boys at the school gate, she realised, *My God, I mightn't see him ever again*, and she had alternately fast-walked and galloped all the way home, her bag slapping into her calves, her skirt tangling round her knees. What was she thinking?

He was still there, coming out of the lav, most un-film-like, tucking his shirt into his trousers, when she threw herself at him.

'What's all this about?'

Even his surprise couldn't put her off.

'I thought you had already left.'

'The train is not until ten.'

They hugged. He buttoned up his flies and they hugged some more. Now that she had come to her senses, she wanted to take him to bed. Show him how much she loved him with her body. But there was no time for that.

Why couldn't their lives continue just as they were? Why did the world have to be filled with such maniacs?

'Don't hate me,' she pleaded. To think that this – grumpy old bat – could be his last impression of her!

'I could never hate you!' Trevor was surprised. 'Where's that come from? Keep the Castle going for me, darling, and I'll be home before you know it.'

He flicked her chin up to his, gave her one last kiss, and then he heaved his bag onto his back and was gone.

She touched her lips now. She could still feel the kiss there.

Winnie opened the tinned peaches she was saving for a special occasion. There was no more special occasion than Susan being home. Then she told Susan about Scott Cuthbert's request. About the girl.

'You're a caring person, that's why he asked.'

'Maybe it's time I didn't care so much. For all the good it's done me.'

She wanted Susan to agree with her or to say something like, 'It's too soon, you don't want to be worrying about anyone else,' but what she actually said was, 'It might be helpful for you too, Mum.'

'Su-san!'

'I'd be glad knowing that you weren't alone – that you had company.'

'I've got company coming out my ears.' Winnie sighed.

Susan sniggered. 'They're all over seventy though.'

'Young Jim's only sixty-eight!'

Susan told Winnie how she was struggling to get hold of the cosmetics she liked now, and Winnie said she could have hers, but Susan screwed up her nose. Winnie's stuff was old-fashioned. Winnie smiled as she remembered feeling the same about her mum's eau de cologne. Susan did let Winnie give her one small bottle of perfume – said it had been a while since she'd smelled of anything but sweat and corned beef. Then she put her coat on – she didn't want her driver to have to wait.

'Work all right?'

Susan wouldn't tell Winnie about what she did in Buck-inghamshire, but Winnie guessed she hadn't been recruited for her cleaning skills. Susan was a numbers whizz. She had triumphed at a maths contest and the next thing, serious men in mackintoshes had taken her off for talks so private even Winnie wasn't allowed.

'Don't ask,' she always said, usually before Winnie had – as if Winnie would pry. Winnie prided herself on giving her daughter space.

'You be careful, that's all.'

'I'm probably in one of the safest places in the country.'

Nowhere was safe. Now Trevor was gone, Winnie had woken up to how precarious everything was, and she couldn't go back to how carefree she used to be. Now, everything was a risk – danger was everywhere.

She would like to put Susan in a purse, carry her around with her, never set her down, like a kangaroo with its joey. But she would not say that. This was why she could not afford to feel for anyone else ever again. One precious person – Susan – to fret over was more than enough.

Then Susan's lift turned up and, with a wave of her gloved hand, her brilliant daughter was gone again.

9

_____

Francine

Mr Cohen's uncompanionable cat was called Tiger. She wasn't tiger-coloured, although she did have fetching grey and white stripes. She had a long tail and a loud meow, and she pressed against your calves.

Mr Cohen talked as though he didn't like Tiger, but quickly, Francine realised that he adored her. He let her on his lap, stroked her back and tickled her ears. He called her a whiner and moaner and he said, 'Don't feed her, I already have,' but the cat played starvation so convincingly that Francine was often compelled to give her something off her own plate.

Mr Cohen said she didn't used to meow, but a couple of years ago her brothers had died, so he supposed she was lonely. And now she had probably forgotten why she meowed, it was just a habit! Francine bet she hadn't forgotten, but the story made her like Tiger even more.

Yes, the house was messy and smelled weird. And Mr

Cohen's false teeth didn't fit as they should and he left them around the house in cups of water. Coming upon them unexpectedly, all floaty and pink, made her shudder.

Mr Cohen was almost as small as she was. His first name was Alfie – Abraham. She didn't know how he got to from Abraham to Alfie, but sometimes names took a meandering route. Her mother's name had been Miriam Golda Salt but Daddy had called her Mimi.

At night, Francine pushed open the window of her bedroom and let the ghosts come in. Sometimes only one of them came: Mummy usually; and Mummy would watch her, shaking her head, so miserable. Francine got the idea she hated being dead.

One time, Francine whispered, 'When will Daddy come back?' and her mummy pressed her fingers to her lips – 'Shhh.' Perhaps her mummy not knowing was a good thing, because if Daddy wasn't alive, surely she'd know better than anyone?

Francine helped around the house. She cleared the surfaces in the living room, which were so thick with dust that she could write 'Lydia', 'Valerie' and 'Francine' in it with her finger. Francine also took over in the kitchen – they both agreed her culinary skills were superior – and sometimes after she completed a chore, Mr Cohen would drop her a coin from his shaking hands.

'My daughter, Ruth, is in Paris,' he told her. 'Ruthie Toothie.' Fumbling in his wallet, he pulled out a faded photograph. 'Her husband is a Frenchman. They met at Cambridge, studying biology.'

Francine looked at a pretty woman with a serious expression and bobbed hair. Because her name was Francine – meaning 'from France', where her mother's parents were from – she felt an affinity for this young woman in Paris, though she had never been there herself. The man in the photo had his arm right round Ruth's shoulders, the other hand resting on her waist.

'They are in hiding,' he said gloomily. 'From Nazis, yes?'

'Yes,' she agreed.

'My Daniel is fighting.'

'Do you have a photograph of him too?'

Apologising that it was old, he showed her a laughing boy at the seaside, in shorts, without a top, flexing his non-existent muscles.

His wedding photo came out of the wallet now too. It had been folded and the white cross of a crease divided it into four sections. Mr Cohen's wife looked taller than him and they were both looking to the side: she had a birthmark, a vertical line down her cheek, and she was beautiful. He wasn't bent over then like he was now, his ears and nose were normal-sized, and he had no grey fuzz.

He said, 'I was a young man once,' in a nostalgic tone, which made Francine want to cry.

Francine tidied the living room and decided she would do the kitchen and maybe Mr Cohen's bedroom later. After she'd washed the bedsheets, she hung the sheets out to dry, and then washed the towels and the tea towels.

'Sweet Punim,' he said

'Pardon?'

'You don't speak Yiddish?'

No one spoke Yiddish at home; it had been English with a sprinkling of her father's Dutch swear words. Papa's plan when he came to England shortly after the Great War was to forget the past and integrate as much as possible. That meant dropping anything that made him stand out.

'I can make chicken soup for you,' she said apologetically. 'Mummy taught me.'

His face lit up.

'My Bertha used to. I will get the ingredients.'

'Deal!' She held out a hand and he held out his. His palm was rough and scratchy but not much bigger than hers.

The uniform for Francine's new school was a grey skirt and a white top – and when she first put them on, her heart raced. She had never tried on clothes without her mother before. And she didn't like what she saw in the mirror. Most of the spots had faded but the ones she had scratched had left a mark. And it wasn't just that; she felt she had a look of horror that came from the inside out.

There were four evacuees at the new school; all boys, and, at playtime on her first day, they were brought to meet her. Francine hoped she might know them from her school in London, but they were strangers. They'd been in Kettering for over a year and she couldn't tell them apart from the local children.

Miss Lane, her new teacher, said, 'Boys, I want you to help Francine Salt to settle in.'

'The other evacuees have mostly gone back now,' explained a large boy with a black eye – Barry.

'Their parents didn't want them to stay away any more,' David added.

'Mine want me here until the war is finished – what about yours?' Jack asked.

Many children's lives were complicated, but Francine realised then that her life was more complicated than most, even those of the other evacuees. Perhaps the biggest difference was that they had homes and families in London to go back to.

The smallest boy among them was the same height as her. He had a pinched face full of freckles – he was more freckle than not – and Francine warmed to him immediately.

She showed him her dice and he said, 'I've got marbles, swap you?'

When she refused, he ran off, but over the next few days they did deals. Never for the dice though – they were her most precious possessions. He loved a game of cards, and they played together at break and lunch. Even when people mocked him for playing with a girl, he didn't care. His name was Albert Parsons and he hated to be called Bertie, so every time Francine wanted to wind him up she called him just that.

At first the local schoolchildren ignored Francine, not in an unpleasant way, but more in a 'we're used to people coming and going so we don't get attached' way. Over the next few weeks, Francine proved herself unremarkable in sports, which confirmed to her new classmates that she was a person of little interest.

Nevertheless, she made friends with a red-headed girl, Pauline, who enjoyed skipping, and when she wasn't skipping, Francine had Albert. She was with him the first time they met the foreign soldiers in the street. Albert dared her to ask them for chewing gum. She wouldn't have normally, but she didn't want to be a cowardy custard. The soldiers handed over chewing gum, a small bar of Hershey's chocolate, and said to find them again for more. Albert was impressed and Francine couldn't believe her luck.

The teachers were nearly all women, which was the

same as at St Boniface school in Somerset and her school in London. There was one male teacher, though. Mr Williams was probably too old to enlist. He had comb-over hair that whipped the other way when the wind caught it and some of his back teeth were gold, winking in the sun. Francine usually found a flash of dental gold fascinating, but she didn't like it in him.

If he saw something in the playground he didn't like, say, bulldog, chase or rugby, he blew a whistle. The sound went right through her. It was so bad, she'd stand stock-still, hands over her ears. She couldn't work out why she hated the noise so much until she remembered: they'd used whistles to search for her family underground.

Barry with the black eye was met after school every day by his older sister Marjorie, who was thirteen and fantastically grown-up. Marjorie was what Mummy would have called 'well developed'. She had a chest and wide hips like a woman, and everyone said she was walking out with an older boy called Fred, although Francine had never seen them together.

'Watch out for Mr Williams,' Marjorie warned Francine. 'He's a maniac with the slipper. I heard he nearly killed someone with it once. We call him Willy-bums.'

Francine giggled.

Barry added, 'He's especially not nice to the London children.'

'To *some* of the London children,' Marjorie corrected.

'Which ones?'

Marjorie shrugged, which made her bosom rise and fall. Then she folded her arms. Francine had a feeling that she had an answer but wasn't going to say.

'You'll see...'

· · ·

'Francine is a peculiar name,' Mr Williams said one time as she queued for the canteen, and Francine thought, *Et tu, Willy-bums*. In Somerset, Mrs Howard had often quoted Shakespeare and it occasionally came back to Francine, although she was never quite sure of the occasion to use it.

'Where is it from?'

'My mummy,' Francine said.

'And Salt?'

'My daddy.'

'I meant, what part of the world?'

How would Lydia respond, Francine wondered. Despite the lack of communication, her London friends were still guiding lights for her and she often thought what they would do. Lydia was fearless. Valerie was also courageous, but in a different way – quiet and stoic. Valerie would gather information, then come up with a solution.

'Salt mines?' Francine guessed.

Mr Williams seemed unsure whether she was laughing at him or not. A shiver ran through her as she waited for a response. *He's a maniac with the slipper*.

'Don't be clever,' he said. Francine was scared, but then he smiled and a bolt of light came from his mouth. 'Run along.'

Was she the type of London child he would like to pick on? She had a feeling she might be.

10

Winnie

Winnie was fairly sure that, when Trevor was alive, they had not spent half their time reassuring customers – but it certainly felt like she did now. Her regulars needed comforting. They felt terrible about the war, even though it was hardly their fault and even if they sometimes pretended they didn't. They spent their mornings on allotments and their nights with the ARP. Some of them had sons fighting in France or Holland or daughters nursing in Malta or Egypt. They were the generation who couldn't fight, the ones left behind, watching on in dismay. The aerial bombardment of the cities continued brutally. When the casualty figures were high, a morose shroud settled over the pub.

'Again,' sighed Old Jim. 'I can't believe it. How much can a nation endure...?'

'I wanted more for my grandchildren,' grumbled Toby, who fretted over his little Sandra and her brother Tony whenever he wasn't writing his memoir.

'What can you do?' Winnie would ask as she served up their pints. But she was preoccupied too, by the idea that the brewery was going to close them. The Castle might not be hugely popular, but shutting it would be a disaster for her regulars.

'If it weren't for this place, I would go crazy,' admitted Nathan.

'If it weren't for this place,' joked Jim, 'my wife would go crazy.'

Even Sid raised his glass at that.

Their wives – if they had them – were volunteering at the hospital or running emergency tea vans. It was a collective effort – and the Castle was there to keep their spirits up.

When Winnie was not reassuring the customers, she was reassuring Mac. As he swapped around bottles to disguise the fact that they had so few, he said, 'I don't know what I would do without this job. My mother says the same.'

'I know,' she told him. 'I'm doing my best.'

Three weeks after his previous visit, Scott Cuthbert came into the pub one day on his way home from work. Mac dried his hands ready to serve him, but Winnie got to him first.

'Usual, please,' he said with a smile. 'All's well that ends well,' he continued before she asked. 'With the London girl. You remember I told you about her?'

'Of course,' said Winnie. 'You found her a place?'

'She's settled in a treat.'

He took a sip of his pint and smacked his lips together. He always did enjoy his first taste of a drink the most.

'Do you know a Mr Cohen of King's Road?' he asked.

'I don't.'

'I thought you knew everyone in Kettering.'

'Clearly not.'

'Ah,' Scott said. 'He keeps himself to himself. He's been on the foster register since 1905.'

1905?

'How old is he then?'

'Eighty, maybe?'

Winnie didn't like the sound of that. An elderly man, on his own? How would he know how to look after a young girl?

'Is that appropriate?'

'There weren't many options!' Scott snapped. 'Everyone's stretched to their limits.'

'That's... very old.'

'I checked!' he said, still defensive. 'She's doing better than I expected. Resilient little thing.'

'Good,' said Winnie, though she didn't believe it. 'Excellent news,' she added, since Scott was still looking peeved.

'The only alternative was a children's home. I had to make a decision.'

'Course you did,' she said. Scott was under pressure too, she reminded herself with a deep breath. She knew he wouldn't see any child go to a children's home if he could avoid it. Winnie's parents had been churchgoers and kind people. Outside of home, Winnie had heard phrases like, 'Children should be seen and not heard,' or 'Spare the rod, spoil the child,' but this was not her parents' vocabulary.

The day everything changed, there was a knock at the door late at night, then her father left the house. When she woke up the next morning, Scott was on the living room floor. He was just lying, staring at the ceiling, his hands crossed over his chest. She got a fright: he looked like he was in a coffin.

At the time, she was reading *Wuthering Heights*. She remembered Cathy's father had turned up with Heathcliff, a

strange gypsy boy. It wasn't like that for them. She'd known
Scott Cuthbert and his family for ever. He wasn't a wildling
who dashed around moors. He wasn't half-gypsy or half-mad.
Scott was a popular child from a nice family who'd had, as
everyone put it, 'a spot of bad luck'.

That evening, her father had taken her into the kitchen
and said, 'He's got nowhere else – he's been having a terrible
time. It's not going to make a difference to us.'

Of course it was going to make a difference to them!
They grew even closer and her parents were pleased. 'They
are your parents as much as mine,' Winnie once told him.

Winnie's parents died four months apart, her father first
and then her mother, in the early days of the Great War, and
sometimes Winnie was glad they hadn't lived to see how
terrible the war ended up being or how long it went on for.
People said that her mother died from a broken heart, but
Winnie was sceptical – her parents had rubbed along nicely,
but they weren't Romeo and Juliet.

Scott was stuck in the hellhole of the Western Front
when she wrote the news. She missed him so much. She
couldn't imagine how it must have felt to be orphaned for a
second time. And then he nearly died and everything
changed again.

Scott believed secrets were bad. 'It's no good being silent
about pain,' he said. 'The deeper you bury it, the more scary
it is when it jumps up in the middle of the night.' Everyone
knew how bad his experience was in the trenches: 'Like hell.'
But on the subject of his time in children's homes, Scott
spoke only one time that Winnie could remember. He'd told
her that being badly beaten at the home wasn't the worst
part. It was seeing the others badly beaten. The noises they
made. He would close his eyes and wait his turn, but the
terrible noise he couldn't escape, even now.

'Especially the younger ones,' he'd said. 'The older ones tried not to show it, but the younger ones hadn't got wise to it.'

Winnie shivered at the thought of something like that happening to this little girl. Perhaps the old man really was an angel.

Scott asked, 'How are things here?' and Winnie was also glad to change the subject. She explained that the brewery might be closing them down and that she was waiting for their decision and it depended on 'footfall'.

'What does that mean?'

'I have to get more people into the pub, but I don't know how.'

Scott sucked his teeth. 'You'll think of something. You always do.'

That wasn't true – but it was certainly true that was how Scott saw her.

The day after Scott's visit, Winnie saw the girl in town. Scott hadn't physically described her – he hadn't said her hair was all the way down her back or that her face looked drained and skinny, her legs even skinnier, or that she looked... she looked how Winnie felt – she looked vulnerable.

Winnie wasn't sure it was her, but she didn't look like a Kettering child.

She wouldn't say hello; she didn't want to spook her. Dusk was falling; it was too late for the girl to be out by herself, and she hoped Mr Cohen had all his faculties. The child should be in a family home, not running errands for an elderly man – but she wouldn't say anything to Scott.

The girl stopped often: to pick buttercups. To run her

hand along lavender bushes. She picked the petals from daisies. And she blew a dandelion.

She was trying to get near a bird; she held out something, open-palmed – a biscuit or a crust maybe? – and she kept more still than you'd imagine a child that age could keep, but still the bird hopped away, and the girl's shoulders went down.

As she plodded down the road, Winnie's heart clenched. Please God she'd be all right.

11

Francine

Francine liked tidying Mr Cohen's house – she liked keeping busy. The busier she was, the less the absence of her family pressed down on her. She could pretend they were still alive, squidged together in the shelter, squabbling or snoring.

Mr Cohen didn't have calamine lotion. His solution to most issues, whether it be itchy skin, a headache or a sore throat, was an 'airing'. He had this in common with Francine's mummy. She was open-window crazy. Perhaps that was why she had loathed the air-raid shelter so much – no windows.

These days, it wasn't just at night that Francine's dead family came to her. Sometimes, on the way to school, she saw her little sister, Maisie, hopscotching in the street, jumping on chalk numbers. throwing stones within the confines of the squares, accusing Francine of cheating. Her mummy was telling her off – 'If you can't get on, stop playing together.'

'We are getting on!' Maisie yelled back before bellowing, 'Cheat! Cheat!'

Francine wondered if anyone else noticed.

In the evenings, Francine and Mr Cohen often ate jam sandwiches, but sometimes she made cheese on toast. Mr Cohen had a tiny appetite and it alarmed her that he might be shrinking. One day, he might be smaller than her. One day, he might entirely disappear...

On Fridays after school, she made chicken soup and boiled potatoes, and he would light the candles and slurp it up. She was never hungry after cooking, but she would have soup in a tin mug to keep him company.

He didn't seem to mind what she did. In that way, he was like Mrs Howard in Somerset. It was like he expected the best of her so he didn't need to tell her what to do. Francine hoped she wouldn't disappoint him but, even if she did something bad, she guessed he wouldn't be too disappointed. He'd just say, 'There, there, bubula.'

He wasn't always happy, though. He was desperate for news of his Ruthie Toothie, but all he had was letters from embassies and universities saying, 'We are sorry to inform you that we have no further information.'

Francine knew Lydia's address – Valerie had moved in there too – off by heart and, even if she didn't, writing 'Bumble Cottage, near Chard, Somerset' would probably have got a letter to them. They were once the three bears (Lydia sometimes insisted she was Goldilocks). Or the Three Musketeers. (Although Lydia sometimes wanted instead to be the woman they were fighting over.) Once, the three witches in *Macbeth*: 'When shall we three meet again?' (Right now, it looked like never.)

She waited for their letters. She wanted envelopes fat with the adventures of Lydia's dog, Rex. Tales of how Rex got his ears wet when he drank. Or stories from Valerie: how such-and-such wireless show was hilarious while this other show was the pits. Days became weeks, yet still they did not write. Did they not remember her, she wondered? Did they think she was dead too? If Lydia's beloved parents, the Frouds, or Valerie's put-upon mother, Mrs Hardman, had died, Francine would have written to them, of that she was certain. Francine couldn't bring herself to write first, even though there were things she wanted to ask. She wanted to know if they had ever had chicken pox or why Mrs Howard thought it was Francine's fault about Cassie. She wanted to tell Valerie her mummy, Mrs Hardman, had looked after Francine and if it weren't for her, she would have been in the shelter when it was hit, and maybe that would have been for the best?

It was awfully lonely being out of the shelter now.

Francine had been living with Mr Cohen for about two months when, teeth out, he asked, 'What happened to your family?'

Francine had known this was coming. Nice Pauline at school had asked, and so had Well-Developed Marjorie. Her teacher Miss Lane had asked. Mr Williams had asked. (No way would she tell him!) Albert had not asked, but he had told her: 'My host family said I am not allowed to, because it's upsetting.'

After she told Mr Cohen, he looked tenderly at her. 'Did you go to the burial?'

They had rushed her away. Mrs Hardman and Miss Beedle and then the blonde lady and then Mr Cuthbert. Sometimes, it felt like she had been bundled off like a criminal in a cartoon. It was well intentioned, she appreciated, but a bundling nevertheless. Almost like being kidnapped, only the kidnappers left no ransom note and there was nowhere to go back to.

'No,' she said.

'Did you sit shiva?'

She didn't even know what this meant but that evening, when she came downstairs, Mr Cohen was waiting for her.

'We sit shiva for your mother, your sister and your brothers.'

He scissored the collar of her shirt. He covered the mirrors. Then he prayed the mourning prayer. Francine, tiny on a low stool, her knees pushed to her cheeks, wept.

12

Winnie

Spring came and the days grew longer. The yellow roses would be in bloom any time now. The Nazis were still pounding the cities, but even they must have cottoned on that it was futile. The British were enduring, and they would endure for as long as needed. You couldn't break the spirit of Londoners and you couldn't break the spirit of the rest of the country, either.

The stoicism of her fellow countrymen and women was inspirational to Winnie – if they could withstand it in the cities, so would she have the courage to keep her little county pub going. Do it for Nathan. Do it for Toby, for Sid, for Jim and Old Jim, Leonard and Stanley, for Mac, for Mac's mother, for Mrs Partridge, do it for the community, do it for Jess the dog.

Do it for Trevor. Do it for me.

When Mr Marshall from the brewery came back, he was more officious than ever, reciting *footfall this* and *footfall that*.

Leaning over the counter, stale breath, he said: 'It's between you, the King's Head and the White Horse. My money's on the King's Head staying open. It's popular...'

Good grief. The King's Head was looking favourable? Better than the Castle? In what universe?

Trevor and the landlord of the King's Head had nearly come to blows more than once. There had been a scandal – something to do with overcharging. 'A reputation of a pub is everything!' Trevor roared. And then the landlord may have had a relationship with the barmaid and then sacked her. Trevor was outraged. In recent years, they had an entente not entirely cordiale. After Trevor died, the landlord had sent his barman over with condolences, but it was clear he was also on a fact-finding mission: 'You'll be giving up the pub then, Mrs Eldridge?'

'No.'

You can tell your boss to stick it where the sun don't shine.

'The thing is – we sent someone in here, undercover,' Mr Marshall was saying.

We are in the middle of a war and you are sending people to spy on pubs? Winnie thought, but didn't say. She wondered if everyone was being sent mad by the endless gloom in the wireless stories, the newsreels and the newspapers. Was puffing themselves up and making themselves look important some bizarre coping mechanism?

'Do you want me to read the report?'

Not particularly, thought Winnie, but she said, 'Go ahead.'

Mr Marshall straightened his tie and cleared his throat: 'Observations on the Castle Public House, March 1941.'

He lowered his voice. 'The barman is simple in the head.'

Winnie was appalled. 'Mac is helpful, kind, and everyone loves him!'

Mr Marshall held up his hand.

'Nevertheless, it is evident that he is hard-working and loyal.' He deliberated before going on. 'The landlady is pleasant but has an underlying air of misery about her, which we think does not encourage patronage.'

Winnie snorted. 'Let me see that!' and Mr Marshall handed over the paper. There, in uneven typing, was all that he had said, only some words were spelled wrong.

'*An underlying air of misery about her*'? It was so rude, it almost made her giggle. She wondered which of the people she had served recently had written it. A few possibilities stood out: a man in a bowler hat who claimed to be a salesman, the woman who came in wearing lipstick like a femme fatale, the two elderly men who said they were meeting an old friend but had suspiciously forgotten his name...

'Try cheering up.'

Easier said than done, thought Winnie.

Mr Marshall pointed at the photos of the silent film actresses that Trevor had once selected to adorn the wall behind the piano.

'Be like that?'

'I hardly think I can,' Winnie said. 'They're twenty years younger than me, for a start.'

'I'm just giving you advice.'

'Footfall – and look more like Clara Bow? And be silent too, I suppose?'

'Can't hurt,' he replied, downing his drink.

She had more chance of looking like Churchill, she thought. Good grief.

When Winnie thought of the day the telegram came – and she thought of it often – she felt sick. It had been a lunchtime, a Thursday. The telegram boy had tried the back, apparently, but no one heard. She only noticed him when he came through the bar, slowly, solemnly, like he was carrying the Crown Jewels.

What a job! Hermes the messenger delivering bad news. The boys got younger and younger for such a responsible task. Heavy on those skinny shoulders. This one looked like a Victorian boy. Fifty years ago, he would have been up chimneys.

Sid was still playing the piano back then and it was classical, which gave everything a slightly portentous air. The boy left her the telegram and disappeared in a flash. Bank robbers and telegram boys know about getaways. He probably would have preferred to be up a chimney.

The telegram said Trevor was dead.

Not even missing.

They weren't giving her a shred of hope.

Winnie had thumped the paper on the counter and pulled pints for Jim and Old Jim, who were staring open-mouthed.

'They've got the wrong one,' she said. 'How do they know it's my Trevor? Drink? On the house?'

Was it Toby or Jim who said, 'Mrs Eldridge, I think...'

'What?'

Cotton wool tones: 'You've had a shock.'

'You might have, I haven't!' she said. 'We all knew this would happen. Idiot man!'

She remembered them looking over her head, that way people do when they're thinking: *'we've got a right one here!'* Telling her to sit down. It was infuriating.

'Trevor is a popular name...' she protested, veering from one notion to the next. 'Every Tom, Dick or Harry is called Trevor.'

Nathan reread the telegram, as though unable to take her word for it.

'I'm sorry,' he said.

'No,' she told them. It was impossible he was dead. Was she still supposed to keep neutral?

'Have you a telephone number for Susan? I can give her a call,' Old Jim asked, wary-eyed. 'Or Mr Cuthbert? He's good in an emergency.'

'Don't you dare call Susan. Or Scott Cuthbert. This is my business.'

She had to call Susan. Had to go through a million different operators before she got to break the news to her that her father was gone.

She didn't know how Susan did it. She was back at the Castle by nine that evening – so grown-up, even then, at the worst of times. If Susan had got time off from her important work, then it must be true.

For someone so logical and reasonable, Susan was surprisingly superstitious. A rainbow stretching over the roofs of Kettering was Daddy saying hello. A feather floating on the breeze... Winnie wondered if Susan was saying it just to try to comfort her, or did she genuinely believe it?

Another time, a butterfly landed on the windowsill. 'Here's Daddy again.'

'He's a cabbage white now?'

Susan pretended not to hear the cynicism.

Winnie thought that if Trevor were sending messages from beyond the grave, then surely he'd choose something less ambiguous as a sign, or at least something he was interested in?

He was never interested in the weather, except if it was going to rain off football; and as for butterflies? It wasn't that he didn't like them, but he liked them no more than the average person in summer. But she didn't say that to Susan. Her girl had lost her father.

She thought about the dreams she and Trevor had shared: Trevor walking Susan down the aisle. The wedding party back at the Castle. Susan with a beautiful bump. Trevor saying, 'It doesn't matter what it is, as long as it's healthy,' and 'I can't wait to be a grandad...'

All dust. Left in some foreign field, thanks to a bunch of maniacs.

An underlying air of misery?! Less than a year after her husband had died? Just what the hell did they expect?

13

SPRING, 1941

Francine

Francine had been in Kettering for nearly four months, which was longer than she had been in Somerset. Sometimes, in school, especially in English or Latin or in any subject in which Francine found it hard to concentrate, she heard babies screaming in the corridor, but when she looked around, no one else seemed to have heard. Her fellow students were all heads down, smoothed hair, immersed in their tasks.

Sometimes, her sister Maisie would bounce right into the classroom, tug at Francine's pencil, or jog her elbow so that her writing slipped, and Maisie would laugh, then run off. And no one saw that either.

It wasn't even that the children never looked up from their books; once, planes roared off from the nearby airbase and they went wild, pushing back their chairs. Miss Lane tried to stop them, but then, realising resistance was futile, let them rush to the windows. She didn't have much control at the best of times.

'One, two, three, four – twelve.'

'Why are we counting them?' Francine asked but no one answered.

So they did look up from their books sometimes, but it had to be something substantial, not babies or little girls or weeping mummies.

They counted the planes back in a chorus of numbers. Nine.

Miss Lane said the other planes probably stopped over at the coast for refuelling. David shouted that the planes would have crashed, the pilots were probably dead and for a few minutes, Miss Lane couldn't speak, not even to tell them to pipe down.

Miss Lane had to teach them all the subjects, and it was easy to tell which she liked and which she didn't. She had a big smile when she was reading, didn't mind writing, yet bit her fingernails to the quick during arithmetic.

But Miss Lane was kind to Francine, kinder than the teachers at St Boniface, kinder even than the ones in London. Miss Lane was a good fairy. She even had a magical glow about her.

'You may have been taught different methods at different schools. We'll find a way around it.'

She made everything sound simple.

Francine understood the maths, but English was hard – Miss Lane was right, there were lots of things she hadn't learned before. There was a lot of comprehension, which Francine did not comprehend. They did a poem about the human race, and Francine thought it was about running. They did a poem about roads – Francine thought it was about roads but it was about choices.

'What did the writer intend?' Miss Lane enquired.

Francine racked her brain. If the writer intended it to be about choices, why did the writer not write that, she wondered? They could hardly use the excuse, like her, that they were not good at writing.

'It's like cracking codes,' Miss Lane said, which made the boys perk up.

But it wasn't. Codes, Francine liked. Poetry, she did not.

Most of the class used fountain pens, but Francine had never used a pen before. Miss Lane said Mr Williams, as a more senior teacher, would decide when she got the pen. She said that Francine wasn't the only child still using a pencil, but, when Francine searched for pencil-using peers, she could only see a sea of pens, scratching away, blue ink, inky fingers.

Miss Lane said Mr Williams thought she should wait.

What did the writer intend?, thought Francine.

At breaktime, Francine usually played skipping games with Pauline. Pauline wasn't as much fun as Lydia, but she didn't argue as much as Maisie. Francine enjoyed herself – but then Pauline announced that she and her mummy were moving to America, so Francine realised with a pang that there was no point getting attached.

In the evenings, Francine and Mr Cohen tucked into their jam sandwiches together, two pals, the wireless in the background playing the terrible tunes that Mr Cohen enjoyed.

He liked the Thursday evening comedy, *It's That Man Again*, and was forever repeating its gobbledygook phrases, like 'Lovely grub!' Francine didn't like the show, but she liked the effect it had on him. Other times, he could be morose. He claimed that the war was going worse than they reported.

And he had a theory that they held back the really terrible news, so people didn't panic. She thought that wasn't necessarily a bad idea: She had once overheard Mrs Froud and Mrs Hardman say her mummy was a panicker.

Francine mentioned that she still used a pencil.

'They won't let you have a pen?' he asked repeatedly, and she was concerned Miss Lane would get in trouble. She didn't want to hear that her kind teacher wasn't perfect.

'Just not yet.'

'It's not right,' Mr Cohen went on. The power of his indignation was spoiled somewhat by the jam on his cheek.

'Honestly, Mr Cohen,' she told him, wiping her face to encourage him to do the same. 'They'll give one to me soon.'

'But when?' He sounded in utter despair.

'When my handwriting is neater?'

'I don't like it,' he said, eyes narrowed. 'Not one bit.'

She distracted him by asking if they could sift through the photographs he kept in a shoebox. She liked the photos and the stories that accompanied them. Mr Cohen's family were from Russia but they had left in the 1880s. They planned to go to New York but, by accident, had ended up in England.

'The pogroms drove them out,' he said. 'You know what that is?'

Francine didn't.

'The Cossacks. Like Nazis.' He peered at her with his blurry eyes. 'It begins with something small. Like a pen.'

'It's only a pen,' she said defensively. 'It's not that serious.'

One photograph was of him and his children feeding pigeons in Trafalgar Square and another was of him astride a bicycle. He said his Ruthie had been planning to organise the photos one day and then he got sad again.

Francine wondered if someone had photos of Mummy, Maisie, Jacob and Joe. But she couldn't remember anyone actually taking photographs. Her mummy had always put it off, and now it was too late.

A few days later, Francine got home to find Mr Cohen had drawn criss-crosses on sheets of paper to create a series of grids.

'You get to practise your writing and I get to play my favourite game,' he said. He gave her a pen and all the ink that he had.

'Black, blue, whatever colour you want.'

The game was called Battleship, but that was perhaps the wrong name for it, because there weren't just battleships. Mr Cohen taught her: five spaces are a carrier, four spaces are a battleship, three spaces are a cruiser or a submarine, two are a destroyer.

'My boy, Dan, is on a carrier,' he said.

Without looking, they had to guess where they were on the other's grid, and shoot. If they were correct, they might guess where the rest of the ship was. The first one to identify – that is, to sink – all their opponent's ships was the winner. Maisie would have loved this. The babies too, if they had ever got the chance.

'You will get the pen, little Francine, if you persevere,' Mr Cohen said.

She kissed him on his papery cheek. She had got used to his smell and his false teeth.

Just before the Easter break, Mr Williams asked Francine to stay behind in class. Some children looked at each other fearfully. *He's just a willy-bum*, Francine told herself. He was all right with Barry and he liked Albert (although Albert hated him) but he had smacked Jack round the back of the head and once David wasn't allowed out at playtime for two weeks. But it was when he got the slipper out that the trouble started...

The children trooped out of the classroom, leaving just her, and her heart sank yet for once he was smiling at her.

'Where are you staying?' he asked, teeth glinting like a crocodile in a picture-book.

'I'm staying with Mr Cohen, sir.'

'The old man who lives on the King's Road?'

'Yes.'

'He's a Jew.'

She couldn't think what to say. Francine saw her mummy behind him, looking more concerned than ever. Jacob was on her hip, Joe clutching her leg.

'Is he?' she said finally.

'I can get you away from there.'

Francine didn't want to leave Mr Cohen and his jam sandwiches and Battleship.

'It's all right.'

'These people... You don't want to be involved with them.'

The dice said four. She had to say something.

'He's kind to me.'

His face darkened.

'I see,' he said, surveying her. 'Go before I change my mind.'

Francine fled.

. . .

A few days later, Francine spotted Mr Cuthbert doing his awkward stagger across the playground, dodging the footballs and the hopscotch. Francine thought a wheelchair would be easier, but she admired him for choosing the difficult way.

One by one, the evacuee children were pulled out of class and sent to the headteacher's office to tell Mr Cuthbert how they were doing.

First, he saw Albert, who came back to class laughing, then David, Barry and Jack. Then it was her turn.

'Francine Salt!' He seemed pleased to see her. 'How are you faring?'

Had anyone visited her and Lydia after they were sent to Bumble Cottage in Somerset? Francine didn't think they had. It made her feel protective of Mr Cohen for being under such scrutiny.

'Good.'

In a lower voice, he said, 'I am looking for somewhere permanent for you.'

She stared. He was suggesting more pass the parcel? What would be the point?

'I'm happy where I am.'

'Really?' He was more relieved than surprised. 'No problems? Anything at all?'

Francine shook her head.

'Excellent,' he said, and he seemed to mean it.

Her mummy was standing behind him, worried in her apron and curlers. She wished dancing, laughing, daytime Mummy came along to see her occasionally, but it was only ever anxious or unhappy Mummy now. She tried to shake her out of her head.

She wondered if she should say anything about Mr Williams, but there was nothing tangible, nothing she could put her finger on – and in a way, hadn't he also tried to help her? What persuaded her to say nothing was that she had only three months left at the junior school anyway: next September, she would be at Kettering High School and Albert said it was peachy there.

'I'm still chasing for news of your Southampton family,' Mr Cuthbert said, but even this couldn't put a smile on her mother's grim face. Francine had almost forgotten about her cousins.

'We'll do our best, but the address you gave us was...' He paused. 'Destroyed. Most of the street was.'

He blinked up at her. 'Was it definitely the army your father is in? I've been in contact with people, but...'

'Definitely,' she said, before pausing. 'The *Dutch* army,' she added. 'Papa is from the Netherlands.'

'Ah,' he said, pulling his tie looser, then closing his eyes. When he next opened them, he said, 'I didn't realise.' Then he turned over his notebook so she couldn't see what was written there.

14

Francine

A few days later, Albert came dashing over to Francine in the school playground, bouncing on his heels with excitement. He had heard that Francine might be getting her yearned-for pen.

'I heard them talking at breaktime,' he said. 'They didn't know I was there.'

Albert could be silent as an assassin sometimes.

'Willy-bum said you didn't deserve it. Miss Lane was arguing that you do.'

Please let me have the pen, Francine thought. She had worked hard and it would be recognition that she was not all bad. Things could go her way. She threw her dice. Three and above she'd get the pen. Below three, no pen.

She got a three.

. . .

It was in assembly that awards – and pens – were dished out, and, after the passages from the Bible and the sports reports, Francine squeezed her eyes shut, thinking, *Please, please.*

Who had prevailed? She had a sinking feeling that Mr Williams would have, but he wasn't there. (Was that a good sign?) It was Miss Lane who was at the front of the hall, her hands in a prayer.

'One child here has worked hard, not just this week, but all the weeks she's been here. Let that be an example. Come to the front…'

Francine may have stood up before she even heard her name. Someone tittered. It could have been a disaster, but fortunately 'Francine Salt' rang out only seconds after.

As Miss Lane handed the pen over, her voice was croaky. 'You deserve it.'

She went in for a hug, but Francine held out her hand, so she switched to a handshake.

'Your family would be so proud.'

Francine clutched the pen. This was her comfort, this was her safe place. This was her shelter. (But shelters didn't always work out.)

She returned to sit cross-legged next to Albert in the front row. Albert leaned over and said, 'I got mine years ago,' but he must have seen her face fall, because he quickly followed up with, 'Well done.'

Albert was living with farmers, the Martin family, four generations of them in the same house, and he was happy there. He had warm milk from the cows, collected eggs in an apron before school, and the farmer's wife tucked him in each night.

He invited Francine to a tea party that evening to celebrate and she was delighted to accept. Mr Cohen never minded if she went out, and Albert's stories of life on the farm made her nostalgic for things she'd never known.

In the street, the schoolchildren were gathering around the foreign soldiers. Francine pushed in too, and was handed some chewing gum. David shook one of their hands and Tommy said, 'Howdy, pardner,' and asked if they had guns. They didn't, but they had gobstoppers, which were just as good. They gave one to Albert, which he immediately gave to Francine.

It was her best day since her family had died.

15

Francine

Big band music was blaring out from the wireless when Francine got back. Mr Cohen would be loving those trumpets.

'I'm home!'

The party music matched her mood. Mr Cohen couldn't have chewing gum – his teeth! – and he probably wouldn't want the gobstopper, but she couldn't wait to show him the pen.

He was in his armchair as usual, but fast asleep with his hand over his heart. How delighted he'd be for her. She was glad that he would now understand that he was wrong and her teachers were good people (he had never been convinced).

While she waited for him to wake up, she thought she'd get on with chores before she left for Albert's house. Mr Cohen had left his cheese sandwich on the coffee table next to him, so she tidied that away – he'd taken only one bite and it had been sitting out a while – then she peeled some potatoes for his dinner. There wasn't much in the cupboards, so he'd have to have tinned fish.

She remembered the dinners at Mrs Howard's in Somerset, some of the best food in her life, but nothing tasted as good as her mother's home-made chicken soup. She'd make that again on Friday, if Mr Cohen could track down a bit of chicken.

By five o'clock, Francine was surprised Mr Cohen hadn't woken up yet, so she went to wake him before she went to the tea party at Albert's host family. But he didn't stir. He must have been really tired.

She put the potatoes in water to boil. She got out her school books and did her homework on the table near him. She liked being in the same room as him and she liked doing her homework, especially this evening, especially now, with her precious pen. She deserved it! Her family would have been so proud.

She twirled it between her fingers. She would have to be careful with it. The body of the pen looked strong but when you took the lid off, the nib was so fragile-looking, with its line down the middle.

Mr Cohen was going to be over the moon.

Maisie used to say she was a swot just because Francine could do maths and no one else did except her daddy. She felt for the dice. Should she wake Mr Cohen now?

One and six.

One and she would.

It was a one.

She should. Gently, she patted his shoulder. 'Mr Cohen?' But his head rolled forward.

· · ·

Francine pulled a blanket up to Mr Cohen's thin throat. It wasn't like he'd be cold, but she needed to do something. There was no telephone and nowhere to go. She didn't know how to contact Mr Cuthbert and there was no way she'd be able to find his building on her own, even if she asked someone where the recruitment office was.

She placed Mr Cohen's kippah back on his head and nudged him back into place. Should she take his teeth out? She much preferred them in his mouth than floating pinkly in his mug, but she wanted him to be comfortable.

She fed Tiger, but then the cat stalked away like she sensed trouble.

She thought about Mr Cohen's daughter, Ruthie Toothie, hiding in Paris, and his son, Daniel, on a carrier. She had no way of letting them know – and she doubted it was her place to.

She thought about Albert's tea party, but she couldn't leave Mr Cohen, she couldn't have fun and cake, warm milk and fresh eggs, while he was here.

It's That Man Again came on the wireless.

Francine got another blanket from her room, then settled down on the sofa. To soothe herself, she read *The Princess and the Pea*. The fact that the princess had a power she didn't know used to charm Francine. The power was a small thing, but it was absolutely the right power at the right time. Now Francine wondered – if she could have any power in the world, she'd definitely want something more substantial than to be able to feel a pea. Wouldn't it be more helpful not to feel a pea? Or to not feel anything at all?

She had just fallen asleep when her family came to her, she woke up and smelled burning. Acrid in her throat. Black smoke plumed in the kitchen. The potatoes had burned through the pan. She didn't know if the pan would ever be right again. She was so sorry, Mr Cohen, so sorry.

'Things will look better tomorrow,' her mummy said.

Francine woke up early and thought maybe she'd been mistaken yesterday, maybe Mr Cohen had just been heavily asleep, like she used to sleep in the shelter, maybe he'd taken himself off to bed in the night... But he was still there, in exactly the same position as before in the armchair, the blanket hanging around him like a cartoon of a wealthy man about to tuck into a huge dinner.

As she scrubbed the saucepan, she thought about taking the train to London. Mrs Hardman would look out for her – when she wasn't on the buses – but the idea of it was too hard. What would she say if Francine just turned up on the doorstep? Was there even a doorstep left in London? Perhaps the whole of London had disappeared in the bombings. Maybe she could go to Somerset? But Mrs Howard surely wouldn't welcome her, and she didn't even know where the nearest train station to Bumble Cottage was. She couldn't leave the cat on her own, either. Finally, she told Tiger she was going to school, and the cat agreed that was the best option. She left the saucepan to soak some more. Even so, she had spent too long dithering, which meant she was late, which meant not only was there no time to tell Miss Lane before the children came in but worse, she would have to stay in at lunchtime as a punishment.

Francine sat in the office with Mr Williams, who watched her with his cold expression and his glinting teeth. He said that he might have to give her the slipper. Outside, she could hear the other children skipping and singing songs she and Maisie used to sing in the shelter.

Oranges and Lemons say the Bells of St Clements.

Then Miss Lane came, needing him urgently, and he got up and told her she was a lucky girl. She didn't feel lucky. She felt even less lucky when she saw Albert, arms folded and expression sulky.

'You didn't come.'

'Albert, I'm sorry!'

'I told everyone you were coming.' Albert's hosts had a huge extended family. 'They were looking forward to meeting you.'

Francine couldn't think what to say, so she just ran away.

'It's like that, is it?' Albert called after her.

She tried thinking what Lydia or Valerie would do, but they wouldn't be in this predicament in the first place. Somehow, they always landed safely when they jumped. Not like her: bad things happened to her. Even when she thought good was happening – like the pen – it turned out to come with rotten conditions attached. She could have the pen, but her saviour would have to die. Her battleships got sunk every single time.

The golden roses were in bloom! They were at the foot of the pub walls and went all the way round to the door, and the door was wide open. From the pavement outside, Francine could see an enormous picture of Churchill, Union Jack bunting strung from the ceiling, and round tables and some hidey-booths. It was called the Castle, only the H was missing.

Francine would have walked past like she usually did, only the flowers were so inviting, and inside there was a man polishing glasses and singing along to the wireless and she recognised the song as one of her mother's favourites. It felt like it was calling to her.

'*We'll meet again, don't know where, don't know when...*'

Now, she could feel her mummy prodding her in the small of her back. *Go on then*, she said, through her down-turned mouth. *Tell them what happened.*

As she walked in, the man wiping the glass suddenly dropped it. There was a tinkling sound of breaking and a few men cheered. They were maybe the same age as Mr Cohen. Two of the old men at the counter were deep in conversation. A newspaper was stretched between them, and one man was doing a crossword and he asked the other man what was a person who was dishonest at gambling.

'As if I would know that!'

They both laughed.

Card-shark, thought Francine, a word her Daddy had called her as a joke. She knew she had to alert someone to what had happened to Mr Cohen, but she also felt terrible that she hadn't done so sooner. Would she get in trouble for leaving it this long? Mightn't it be better to pretend she hadn't found him and that she was as shocked as anyone? But then that would mean waiting for someone to come into the house – and no one ever came. Even Mr Cuthbert hadn't since that first day.

There was another reason she hadn't told anyone. She wanted that extra day to assimilate it into her, the time to adjust. When her family had died, there hadn't been a single moment, from the second she had woken in the cellar, bleary and itchy-faced, to all the commotion outside, to find the rescuers digging in the yard, to being dragged away, to being with Mrs Hardman, to being with teachers... she hadn't a moment to breathe. This way, she'd had one last night, and one last day, when it was still normal. The sweetest delusion. But now, it was time to face the music.

There was a round table in a corner with two cushioned stools. She took one, her feet didn't touch the ground. A different tune came on the wireless, and she recognised this too, but didn't know the title.

The waiter would come over soon and she would say that she wanted a milk tea, her mummy's favourite drink. Mr Cohen always made sure she had a shilling for emergencies. Was a milk tea an emergency? When nobody came, she realised she had to go to the bar. She had to stand on tiptoe to see over the counter. Her mummy was still with her, standing arms crossed. Her hair was pulled back tightly but the curly bits that Francine loved had broken free.

'Mama?'

'Why haven't you got your gas mask?'

She saw her baby brothers, Jacob and Joe. Baby Joe was swaddled, Jacob was holding a toy car. They screamed. She covered her ears.

'I said what do you want?'

Francine blinked at the barman. 'Milk tea, please.'

16

Winnie

Winnie was having a bath in the middle of the day. Yes, it was unusual, but Mac was downstairs ('hard-working and a friend to all', apparently!) and he was more than capable of quelling the thirst of a small party of elderly men.

Even now, a month after Mr Marshall 's visit, Winnie couldn't stop obsessing over it. How was she supposed to save the pub? *Should* she save the pub? That morning, she had woken up in the foulest temper. Nothing in particular had happened, it was just her despair was accumulating. Trevor would have told her to get on with it, but she felt so weary. That phrase, *an underlying air of misery*, had also punched her in the guts. It was true, that was why. Look at what she had become!

So that afternoon, she had taken herself upstairs to escape. She might have read a book too, only she had no concentration any more. She took jugs of hot water into the bath until she could be bothered no more. It was lukewarm when she got in. Still, she sank into the water so her face was covered.

She remembered Trevor would come in sometimes while she was in the bath, ignoring her protestations that she was in her birthday suit, telling her his latest gripes. It was a good life, but it wasn't the life she had imagined.

When she was young, she dreamed about going as far away as she could. The pyramids and the Empire State Building and the Taj Mahal. Her father said she could go and her mother said, 'That's what life is for, to do what you want to do,' and that surprised her, because her mother was a mouse whose life seemed made up of tea and plant cuttings. For the first time Winnie wondered if that was a deliberate choice, not accidental. She was doing exactly what she wanted and she wanted Winnie to do the same.

But now there was war, death and responsibilities that were hers alone to bear and sometimes, like today, they felt too much. Nevertheless, Winnie told herself to relax. There was something enjoyably illicit about an afternoon bath. She had the talcum powder lined up, and a towel she'd brought with her from her home over thirty years ago. Everyone deserved a treat – even this grumpy old bat.

Mac was banging on the bathroom door. 'Problem.'

'What now?'

'It's urgent,' he said and then coughed. 'It's not Susan.'

Clasping her house robe together, Winnie dashed downstairs, and when she saw the small girl, head bowed in concentration, for a brief dazed moment she thought it *was* a young Susan. The child had a drink in front of her that she appeared not to have started, and she was throwing dice, moving her lips into soundless words every time she scooped them up.

'Who is that, Mac?'

'That's it,' he said, his face revealing that he was as confused as she was. 'That's the problem.'

The girl looked up as Winnie walked over.

'I like the roses,' she said. There was no reason this should have thrown Winnie more than any other subject, but it did.

'Thank you,' Winnie said when she'd gathered herself. 'Are you with an adult?' she asked. But as she was speaking, she realised who it was, and quickly made her tone gentler. 'Otherwise you can't be here.'

'That's the thing,' said the child. 'My adult is dead.'

17

_____

Winnie

Winnie called the police first and as she did so she sent thanks to Trevor, for having had the prescience to get a telephone fitted. He had done it to bring people in – 'and while they're here, they'll have a drink!' – but she probably used it more than any customers. And then, after she had spoken to the local police station and they had promised to investigate, she had called Scott Cuthbert at his office.

'I'll be there right away.'

Only then did Winnie realise she was still in her house robe, and she hurried back upstairs to put some clothes on. A bath in the afternoon! What had she been thinking? She wanted to tell everyone that this was the first time she had done such a self-indulgent thing in all these years, but knew that protesting about it would make it sound worse.

She came back downstairs, dressed, made up and with a landlady smile pasted on her face – just as the man from the brewery had ordered (although it was unlikely he had anticipated anything like this scenario!). And then she got the girl another drink, this time a lemon cordial that had been in the back of the cupboard since the Vikings and – what did little girls like to eat? What did Susan like when she was that age? – a slice of bread with strawberry jam. She didn't expect her to be hungry, but she said, 'If it's no bother, Mrs,' and wolfed it down.

Winnie couldn't sit with her, other people needed serving, but she knew what the death of poor Mr Cohen signified and she didn't need a crystal ball to be able to predict what Scott Cuthbert was going to say.

It was what *she* was going to say that she wasn't sure of.

When Scott came in, flustered, he went straight over to the girl and took her hand. Winnie shouldn't have been surprised to see the rapport between them – Scott was a lovely man – but it still gave her a start.

'What a clever thing you were to come here,' he said, avoiding Winnie's eyes. Had he arranged this?, she wondered. But the girl said, 'I heard a song that Mummy liked, so I came in...'

'Which song was it?' Scott asked, like they had all the time in the world. But to Winnie's surprise the girl launched into, '*I know we'll meet again some sunny day*,' in a soft babyish voice, and Scott said, 'That one's lovely.'

Finally, he sidled over to Winnie. She expected him to beg her to take her in, so it threw her when he didn't. He mopped his brow with his handkerchief, and she caught sight of the monogram – S.J.C – that his wife, Ada, sewed on everything. 'In case I forget my own initials,' he always joked.

'This is a hindrance,' he said with a sigh.

She poured him his favourite drink. 'It's on the house,' she said as he rummaged in his jacket pockets.

'She'll have to go to a children's home... maybe London... There's nothing else for it.'

'Hmm,' said Winnie.

'You all right?' he asked, changing the subject – which was usually her job. 'Has the brewery given you your answer yet?'

'Not really. While half the men in the country are fighting overseas...' she paused – never wanting to make Scott feel guilty. 'They are just so concerned about footfall. They want me to magic up customers out of nowhere!'

She missed out the *underlying air of misery* – it might make Scott laugh, but she hadn't reached that stage yet, and anyway, there were more pressing issues than the brewery's opinion of her.

Mac came over self-importantly. 'Police are here.'

Winnie found some dominos for the girl, who was still on a stool, feet dangling. Winnie couldn't help noticing her tatty shoes.

'Do you know what these are?'

'I love dominos!' Francine's eyes lit up. Winnie thought she had a remarkable face – it showcased every emotion.

Mac agreed to keep an eye, so Winnie and Scott went to meet the police officer, Constable Michaels, round the back. It wasn't the most auspicious setting, next to a drainpipe, a gutter and the bins full of old bottles, but she didn't want Francine to see or hear the conversation, nor did she want to invite him upstairs. Whatever this was, she wanted it to be quick.

He was an old friend of Trevor's – everyone in Kettering was an old friend of Trevor's – and he'd been to the house to confirm that Mr Cohen had indeed... 'expired'.

Expired, Winnie thought, like a pint of milk. He said he tried to get an ambulance to take him away but of course there weren't any ambulances, they were all in Birmingham for the Blitz, so he'd put him in a vegetable van. Winnie wished he hadn't told her that.

'What's going to happen to the girl?' the constable asked, which struck her as odd. Wasn't he supposed to be the authority here?

'Children's home,' Scott answered. 'London probably.'

'There must be other foster families in the area,' Winnie said.

'There aren't,' Scott answered, looking not at her but at the constable. 'The system is overwhelmed with evacuees. It's a shame, especially since she's settled into the school here.'

'Can't Ada help?' Winnie knew she was clutching at straws.

'Ada is working all hours at the hospital. No, there's nothing else for it – I'll get her sent tonight.'

Even as he was saying it, Winnie knew she couldn't let this happen. Just like her father couldn't all those years ago. She might have a lot on her plate but sometimes, you had to decide which plate or which lot was more important. Or something like that.

The girl's family were dead. She had no one else.

'She can stay with me,' Winnie burst out.

Scott had the grace to look surprised.

'It's not too much?' he said, then before she could reply, he switched to, 'Would you do that?'

He was so disingenuous she could have punched him in the face. Wasn't this what he had planned for all along? Constable Michaels was slapping her on the back.

'Nicely done, Mrs Eldridge.' He cleared his throat.

'Trevor was a good man. One of the best. I'll leave the girl and the cat in your capable hands then.'

'What cat?' said Winnie. *For goodness' sake.*

Constable Michaels left not long after, and when it was just the two of them Scott put his hand on Winnie's shoulder.

'Look how well you brought up Susan,' he said. 'A more marvellous young woman I can't imagine!'

Winnie shook her head. Susan was an arranger, a sorter, a do-er. She used to take in presents for teachers and leave thank-you cards for the milkman. The number of times Winnie had fretted over forgetting some social nicety, only for Susan to tell her, 'Already done!' Susan had required such light parenting. When Winnie despaired about the war, which she often did, she consoled herself that the British had Susan. Whatever she was doing in the depths of the Buckinghamshire countryside, Winnie hoped that they were using her full potential (if anyone could).

'You had evacuees before,' Scott reminded her.

'That was when I was still a fully functioning member of society,' she said.

'You still are,' he said.

Winnie ignored that. Scott's view of her had always been overly-generous.

'Francine is all alone in the world.'

'Exactly – the other evacuees had homes to go back to. She doesn't.'

'Not many people understand what it's like,' he said. 'She mightn't be an orphan anyway. She's convinced there's a father out there somewhere.'

'How can I help someone when I feel so down all the time?'

Winnie had never told anyone about the tricks her brain played on her. That, even now, talking to Scott, looking perfectly sober and responsible (although still damp from the irresponsible bath), she had vivid images of the pub collapsing, a car somersaulting or an outbreak of typhoid.

An underlying air of misery? Hardly. Her misery was well and truly out in the open.

'Who better to help?' Scott said.

Winnie decided they should go to Mr Cohen's house straight away, before they told Francine the plan. Scott's expression suggested he disagreed but right now he would go along with anything Winnie wanted.

It was only a short walk, even at Scott's snail's pace. Winnie carried a cardboard wine box. Inside, it was homely and the windows were open. Scott was looking around him, surprised.

'I hardly recognise it.'

'How do you mean?'

'It's been cleaned up,' he exclaimed, putting a finger across the surfaces in a way Winnie had only seen women do before.

'You think the police did it?'

'Doubt it – I reckon Francine must have.'

'You said she was resilient.'

'And how...'

There was no sign of the cat at first. Apart from an empty bowl and the cat hairs.

'How are we going to do this?'

'Here, kitty, kitty...'

They both chuckled. It reminded Winnie of when they were kids, best friends, without a care in the world.

'There she goes!' yelled Scott suddenly. 'Get her!'

The cat was having none of it. Their laughter made it

worse; she skittled from one surface to the next, scowling at them, waving a paw, and what a meow!

'Get a treat to lure her in.'

'This is not funny!' she told Scott.

'It's desperate,' he said. 'That's why I'm laughing.'

She was laughing too. The situation was ludicrous.

'It would help if we knew her bloody name!' she said.

'Ah,' said Scott with a grin, 'about that – her name is Tiger.'

Winnie sighed. 'Of course it is!'

Somehow, they manoeuvred Tiger into the box.

'It's for your own good,' she scolded. She had to carry the cat, rattling against the sides and mewing angrily, along the street back to the Castle. She was heavier than she looked, and Scott was no help. At one point, Tiger made a jump for it.

'No, you don't,' Winnie told her.

Scott looked on approvingly. He'd got what he wanted. When they got back to the pub, he played dominos with the girl while Winnie slipped away to telephone Susan.

'I have acquired an evacuee and a cat,' she whispered, aware that walls have ears.

'Which is worse?' Susan asked.

Winnie felt choked suddenly. The poor old man, expiring, alone in his chair, and the poor little girl who had experienced more than any child should have to go through.

'Mum?' Susan asked. 'Are you all right?'

'Yes, darling,' she said in an unnaturally high voice, 'it's just this bloody war.'

'I know,' her wise daughter said.

18

Francine

The lady in the pub put a cardboard box on the table and, like a movie actress bursting out of a cake in one of Mummy's favourite films, Tiger appeared.

'You're here!' squealed Francine just as the lady declared she might live there too.

The lady looked weary, but didn't everybody nowadays? There was something gentle about her too. Her mummy would have liked her, Francine decided. But that wasn't good enough. Her daddy still wasn't back. But he might be soon, and, if he was, how would he find her here?

'I'd better go back to Mr Cohen's house, thank you.'

The lady paused, smoothing down her hair.

'You were close?' she asked.

Francine nodded.

'I can imagine,' the lady said. 'But I'm sorry, that's not possible. And if you live here you can stay at the juniors and

then start high school in September with all your friends.'
She took a deep breath. 'I hear you're doing well at school.'

'I got a pen,' Francine said. She, who never won things.
Despite everything, yesterday's achievement still astonished
her. The lady seemed taken aback by this.

'A pen?'

'A fountain pen. From school – because I write better
now.'

'Do you like writing?' asked the lady. She was pretty
when she smiled and that was like Mummy, too.

'No,' said Francine, scratching Tiger, who was purring
contentedly. 'But I like the pen.'

The lady showed her around the upstairs of the pub,
which made Francine think of her old house in Romberg
Road. Them on the top floor, the Frouds on the middle, the
Hardmans in the basement. She remembered that Mummy
used to worry that their flat would collapse.

She walked along the carpeted hallway. The woman was
talking all the time but, unlike with the blonde woman,
Francine found it – found *her* – reassuring.

'Call me Winnie,' she said.

'Winnie...' Francine played with the word in her mouth.
She'd never heard the name before. 'Like Churchill?' she
asked, and the woman laughed. 'I'll call you Aunty Winnie,'
Francine decided, because older people preferred it when
you did.

'This is the kitchen,' Aunty Winnie said as they carried
on touring, 'This is the door to my room,' and then, 'And this
room will be yours.'

The bedroom was a square room with sash windows, a
map of the world propped against the wall and a globe and
maths instruments on the desk. The bed had a pink eiderdown, a flat pillow and a raggy doll who was not half so nice

as Lydia's Margaret-Doll, but it was better than nothing. It wouldn't be a bad place to wait for her father's return, she supposed, although, oddly, she liked the big room downstairs too, where the people came and went and there was that smell of polish and hops and intrigue.

'It was my daughter, Susan's.'

Francine snapped to attention.

'Is she dead?'

The woman's face fell.

'No! She's away working for the war effort.'

Francine eyed Aunty Winnie closely. She was glad her daughter was not dead, but she could feel there was heartbreak here, and it was like she recognised it. Aunty Winnie, like her, was hurtling backwards on a train, while everyone around them was going forwards. They were in the same carriage.

She wanted to say something like this to her, but she couldn't find the words.

19

Winnie

Susan used to go off to bed early but would read with a torch under the blanket until midnight. Winnie would tell her to stop, but secretly she approved. But that first night, Winnie didn't know what to do with Francine – whether she too would take herself off to bed or whether she would need prompting...

At around eight, the girl stopped gawping at everyone in the bar and asked if it was all right if she went up. When Winnie checked on her ten minutes later, the child was fast asleep. Winnie supposed she might not have slept the previous night with the poor expired Mr Cohen in the house. She gazed at the sleeping figure in wonder. Winnie had felt alone after Trevor died – my goodness, this child had lost everyone!

. . .

The cat roamed around between pub and upstairs. That night, whenever Winnie let her out, she meowed to come back in. Winnie let her in and she meowed to go out. The girl might have been out like a light, but the cat was the opposite.

'Go downstairs, Tiger,' Winnie scolded, but the cat followed her. Two o'clock in the morning. Three.

Winnie went over all the things that she had to do the next day. Scott Cuthbert had said he'd still look for any other available foster carers and he'd absolutely look for the girl's family – but he had a billion other children to concern himself with and she was no longer an urgent concern. And she still had to face the threat of closure from the brewery, like a guillotine waiting to fall. She pictured Trevor's despairing expression if they closed the Castle down. Sometimes, she felt like she was a museum and she was in charge of the pub's legacy. Maybe, just maybe, the girl and the cat would help her bring it back to life.

Winnie must have eventually fallen asleep, because the next thing she knew she woke up, sensing a shadow over her. *At last, Trevor?*

It was a small white face, an almost pointed chin, long straggly hair. It was not Trevor. And Francine needed a haircut.

'What is it, darling?'

'I thought you also might be dead,' Francine explained.

'I'm not, as you can see,' Winnie said, pulling herself upright. She didn't do well on interrupted sleep. Trevor used to get up in the night to soothe baby Susan. And she was strangely embarrassed at her nightgown – so prim, so Victorian! She was not eighty. How odd she must appear to this sweet young thing.

And the damn cat was asleep at the end of the bed. How did she get there?

Francine tiptoed towards the door.

'I'm not...' What could she say? *I'm not going to die on you.* No one could promise that – well, they could, Trevor had promised exactly that. No one could *keep* that promise.

'Wait,' Winnie called. 'Do you want to sleep in here?' After all, Trevor's side of the bed was free. 'Just for a night or two?'

The girl nodded, pulled back the covers and crept in. Soon, once again, she and the cat were fast asleep and, once again, Winnie was not.

Winnie had rules yet within a week, she was breaking them. 'Do not let the children sleep in your bed'. That was gone by the wayside... 'Don't talk to Francine about her lost family. It will cause unnecessary upset.' In fact, Francine *liked* talking about her lost family. 'Avoid the subject of death.' Ditto. 'Don't let children in the pub' was another one that was proving impossible.

On her third morning there, Winnie realised Francine kept digging in her pocket and looking at something.

'What have you got?'

Francine's palms were trembling as she held out two tiny ivory dice, the way you might hold out a treat for a nippy dog. Winnie remembered seeing them before; now she realised they were special to the girl.

'Daddy gave me these.'

'What do you do with them?'

Francine threw them down.

'Two sixes. That means a good day.'

She threw again. A four and a three face up.

'Pretty good,' Francine corrected.

Winnie thought Francine was more similar to her than Susan was. Francine was small, as was Winnie, and delicate-looking – although, like Winnie, she did not have a delicate nature.

When Mr Marshall from the brewery next came in, he asked, 'Is this your daughter? She's the spit of you.'

'No,' Winnie said. 'She's a... an evacuee.' It seemed the simplest explanation.

His expression hardened. 'I'll have to inform the brewery, Mrs Eldridge,' he said.

'Of course,' she said. She didn't doubt it would be another black mark against her.

'I can help here,' Francine offered after she had been there about a week.

'I don't know if that would be right,' Winnie said.

Francine had a way of looking that said, *why?* without her having to actually say it.

'I don't want people thinking I got a child in to do my dirty work!'

'But I like keeping busy – it helps.' She pointed to her head.

Winnie nodded. This, she understood.

'I could do with the tables in the bar cleaning. Mac's cleared them, but...'

Francine's eyes lit up. 'I can also cook.'

'We don't serve food any more, what with the rationing.'

'I'll help you get more people in,' Francine continued.

Winnie smiled, but she was thinking she had to get Francine's change of address registered.

Then Francine asked where Mr Cohen was.

'Ah,' said Winnie, flustered. Surely she understood he was dead? 'He was buried.'

'Already?' Francine asked, her little face white. 'Did I miss the funeral?'

Winnie felt terrible. She hadn't even considered that Francine might have wanted to go.

'We can go to the cemetery,' she said, but Francine shrugged.

When Winnie told Scott that all her rules were being broken, he laughed.

'Is that such a bad thing?'

She told him in general it was going well and saw he was relieved. However, she felt he was altogether *too* relieved, so then she listed her worries: The girl hated to sleep alone. The girl thought her father was coming back – would he? The girl liked to work – could she? The girl—

'Winnie,' Scott interrupted, 'you know more about looking after people than anyone I know.'

'I only had Susan. And she virtually brought herself up.'

But not all children were like Susan. And Francine had been through the wringer – it was little surprise that she had a few issues around sleep, around school, around everything.

Now Scott was grinning.

'Just keep her safe, happy and fed.'

'It's more complicated than that.'

'Who does Susan take after, I wonder?'

'Ha.'

'Seriously, Winnie, you *are* capable,' he continued. 'You keep the customers under control...'

'They're grown adults.'

They were adults and yet they bickered and complained like children.

'Any news from the brewery?' Scott asked. 'Have you increased footfall?'

It was kind of him to remember when there was so much going on.

'Not yet,' she said. Sometimes, she thought Mr Marshall enjoyed dangling her on a string. Other times, she felt ashamed – good gracious, the country was on its knees and she was preoccupied with keeping a pub open. And yet, she told herself, wasn't the pub one of the freedoms people were fighting for?

Scott clinked his glass against hers.

'You'll find a way.'

'Maybe I'll end up at Susan's. Doing for the war effort.'

'You're already doing for the war effort here,' Scott reminded her. 'Don't you forget it.'

20

___

Francine

Francine liked upstairs. She liked the unremarkable lino floor in the kitchen, the simple lighting, the ducks across the wall that had been there since prehistory. She liked her bedroom and she liked Winnie's bedroom, where she spent half of some nights. The bathroom wasn't scary either. She liked the roses outside and the sparrows that came to settle on the windowsills. But Francine loved the downstairs of the pub most of all: the smell of the different drinks, the warm glow of the lights, the regulars with their memoirs and their crosswords. She loved the way peoples' personalities changed throughout the evening, like characters in novels. Some started off stiff and morose, and then a few pints later they were bleary-eyed, red-nosed, wet-lipped, declaring that they were glad to be alive. Winnie tried to steer her away, but Francine found it fascinating.

Miss Lane said Eskimos had many different words for snow: Francine would wager there were more different words for being drunk – well-oiled, three sheets to the wind, plastered... she had a whole new vocabulary!

If there was a downside about the Castle – other than missing lovely Mr Cohen, of course – it was Mac. He wasn't horrible, but he was irritating. Winnie said to ignore him, but sometimes he got under her skin. Tiger wasn't keen either. She always got under his feet or caused mischief when he was around.

Albert was still determined not to talk to her, but she saw more of Marjorie – Barry's big sister – because their paths crossed more often. (She and Barry were staying with a vicar who was forever dragging them to church.)

One time, she and Marjorie were asking some of the American serviceman for chewing gum when an older, earnest-looking man in a similar uniform came over and asked the men if they hadn't anything better to do. Then he turned to the girls.

'Were they bothering you?'

'No,' admitted Francine, 'we were hoping for a gobstopper!'

Maybe *he* had a gobstopper.

'Actually, *we* were probably bothering *them*,' agreed Marjorie, tossing her hair.

The man laughed. He didn't have a gobstopper, but he gave Francine and Marjorie some gum and Marjorie peeled away towards her house, pleased with her hoard.

'Your accent is funny,' Francine told him.

'So is yours,' he said.

Francine remembered Winnie's anguish about footfall. It meant she needed more customers.

'Why don't the Americans drink in our pub?'

He grinned. 'What?'

'Pardon. Mummy said you should say pardon,' Francine told him helpfully.

'Okay. For a start, I'm not American. I'm Canadian.'

Francine wrinkled up her nose. 'Same difference.'

He laughed. 'What pub did you mean? The King's Head?'

'Not the King's Head,' Francine said, aghast. 'The Castle, of course. Although it's missing its H.'

She thought he might laugh at her, like Mac usually did, but he nodded seriously.

'Is it your parents' pub?'

'No,' she said. 'It's Aunty Winnie's.'

He smiled at her. 'I don't know why we haven't been there.'

'You should!' Francine persisted.

'We might!'

She held out a crooked finger. 'Do you pinky promise?'

Winnie would be over the moon! He locked his finger with hers.

'Pinky promise. I'll bring in the boys soon as I can.'

21

Winnie

'Shall I get rid of him, Mrs Eldridge?' Mac muttered. Winnie looked up from her accounts. She hadn't even noticed the Canadian serviceman come in.

'Don't be daft,' she said, straightening up and wishing she had more bobby pins for her hair – everywhere was out of them. They were out of cold cream too, but Winnie felt the bobby pins were a greater loss.

'What can I get for you, sir?'

When Francine saw the man, she shot off her stool so fast it wobbled and nearly fell.

'You came!' she yelped.

'A promise is a promise.' He winked.

Winnie looked between them, bemused. 'What?'

'Pardon,' corrected Francine. 'He promised me!'

'Miss Francine here told me the Castle was the best pub.' He winked again. 'Far superior to the King's Head.'

Winnie blushed and made a *My Goodness* expression at Francine. 'Welcome.'

'Sergeant Ron Roscoe at your service, ma'am. You must be Aunty Winnie.'

Winnie realised she was sweating. She fanned herself. 'Pleased to meet you.'

Sergeant Roscoe was broad-shouldered and large-chested. His head was large but when she looked at his smiling face, she saw kindness there. There were other things too – exhaustion, curiosity, interest – but kindness was how he was looking at her now.

Right then, Winnie wished she were one of those people who could turn on like a light switch, like Trevor. Trevor could have been fixing the sink but as soon as someone came into the pub he was Mr Entertainment, while it always took her a minute or two to collect herself.

'What goes on here?' Sergeant Ron Roscoe asked, which struck Winnie as an unusual question. What did he expect went on?

'We will soon be putting on events,' Francine jumped in. 'From Battleship to bingo!'

Winnie looked at her. Where on earth had she got that from?

'Sounds fantastic,' Sergeant Roscoe said. 'I'll definitely get my men in.'

Perhaps she had underestimated the girl?

'You said you needed more feet falling,' Francine said proudly after Sergeant Roscoe had drunk up and left. 'So I thought I would see what I could do.'

The Canadians didn't come straight away, but then, when they did, they really did. They came in groups, fives and tens of them. Their accents made you pause a moment before you got the words. Winnie liked it. In a way, it was like travelling – only the travel was coming to her. A few foreign voices, a few foreign faces, and things looked less bland. Or perhaps it was like a fresh coat of paint! The stories these boys told! Fletcher had never left his village before the war. Peabody hadn't known what Nazis were. Foster's grandparents were English. Winnie could listen all day.

When she told Mac how interesting she found it, he grunted, 'You'll be welcoming Nazis next!'

'No, I wouldn't,' Winnie said. What a thing to say! 'I mean that it makes a change. We should be grateful.'

'I'm not!' Mac said bitterly. 'We can do without them.'

Winnie didn't think they could. The pub was buzzing again. Mac must have been able to see that. It was almost like the non-stop days before the war. The cash register was ringing. The drinks were disappearing. *If you could see me now, Trevor,* Winnie thought, as she struggled gloriously to keep up, *you would be so proud.*

Footfall was the word!

The Canadian boys seemed even younger than Susan, most of them. Smooth-cheeked, wide-eyed, and with such even teeth! They were polite, too.

'They've got better manners than our lot,' she said to Mac.

'They're guests in our country. Guests are always polite.'

But they were so much more than guests.

Regulars could get disgruntled when there was an influx of strangers – there had been a roving theatre group in town once, who stayed a month, and her regulars nearly rioted. But this time around, half of them didn't care, the other half were absolutely delighted.

'As Sandra, my granddaughter, always says, it's nice to see life in the old dog,' said Toby.

Winnie laughed. If she were to take offence at every badly phrased phrase, she'd be at the smelling salts all day long.

'Late is better than never,' said Nathan.

'I'll have proper help with my crossword now,' said Old Jim, although Winnie thought the soldiers were even less likely to get the clues than her. Which was saying something.

Sure as day follows night, young women found their way to the Castle too. They came one Saturday night and Winnie thought it might just be a lucky one-off, but then they came the next and the next.

The girls were looking at the soldiers and the boys were looking back, and Winnie thought, *Their parents are going to kill me!*

It must have been confusing for Mac – on one hand he wanted the girls there, but on the other, he resented the competition. The girls had always dressed up at the weekends, but this was off the scale. The clouds of perfume or hairspray caught in your throat. They were as colourful as wildflowers. How ingenious they were, making dresses out of curtains, improvising on tights, curlers and rouge. Like dominos falling, the local girls became smitten with Canadian servicemen.

Yet the man who had started it all off, Sergeant Ron, still hadn't come back. And Winnie couldn't help thinking about him, even when she didn't want to.

22

Winnie

The Blitz came to an end and the newspapers were trumpeting the stoicism and strength of the nation. It was May 1941, and Winnie, Mac and the regulars drank a toast to the king, to Churchill, to the country, and then Francine asked:

'Will I go back to London then?'

'Uh, no!' Who did the girl think she had to live with there? 'You're here in Kettering for the...' Francine's upturned face was expectant. 'Foreseeable...'

'I don't know what that means,' Francine said.

'It means for as far as I am able to see.'

'Like, for ever?'

Winnie swallowed.

'Exactly.'

Francine nodded before rolling her dice.

'Three,' she called.

'Is that good?'

'It means fine...' Francine raised her narrow shoulders. 'For the foreseeable.'

Francine had only been living at the Castle for six weeks, but she had settled in beautifully. Winnie found it easier to get up in the morning nowadays, knowing she would see that girl's face at the breakfast table – or on the pillow next to hers. She felt a whoosh of pleasure at seeing Francine's things around the flat – her shoes and her shoe polish – her mother had been fastidious about polishing shoes, apparently. Her hairbrush in the hall, her toothbrush at the sink gave Winnie a warm feeling.

She *had* been lonely since Trevor had gone, no point denying it. It was lovely not to be all by herself any more. Francine was sweet company. She understood when to talk and when not to. She liked jokes, both the telling and the listening to, and to make Francine laugh could make Winnie's day. She chatted to the birds: 'Are you having a good day, Sparrow Number Four? Lovely flying, Sparrow Number Five!'

The biggest issue she had – if you could call it that – was sleep. The girl did not like being alone at night. When she came into her bed, Winnie coaxed her back to her own, but she soon came back. A bedtime routine was effective but difficult, since Francine's bedtime was at the pub's busiest hour. Nevertheless, most nights, Mac permitting, Winnie slipped away, read a few pages of a story – she couldn't make stories up, however much Francine would have liked her to – and then Winnie tucked her in with a rhyme:

'Sleep tight, don't let the bedbugs bite.'

'Don't let the bombs give you a fright,' Francine would reply, which always caused a shiver to run through Winnie.

Francine didn't throw the dice so much as tip them.

Conversations at breakfast tended to be led by the dice. 'The pub is going to be really busy tonight, Aunty Winnie. The dice say.'

'I doubt that!' Winnie said. 'Now, do the dice say I need my umbrella today?'

The dice said she did.

Winnie became fond of if not Tiger herself, then of seeing Francine's pleasure at Tiger. No, she was fond of Tiger too. There was much to admire in her athleticism and her independence. Even the way she ignored you until dinnertime was charming.

Winnie had thought she would buckle under her new responsibilities, but strangely, they seemed to make her feel lighter and happier.

Trevor wasn't fading from memory, not at all, but he became incorporated into her routine in a way that wasn't as painful as it used to be. She would think, 'Trevor, you'd like this,' or, 'Trevor, you wouldn't like that,' but it no longer ached but instead was a rather sweet memory.

He would like the Canadians – or he would like their money. He would find Francine a pickle! He would find her dice-game intriguing. He would like the increased footfall and he would like the upbeat version of Winnie, rather than the one with the underlying air of misery. He'd probably make jokes about it: 'If you'd been this nice back then, I'd never have joined up!'

That gave her a lump in the throat.

Winnie got a summer cold. She hated being ill – such a waste of time – and this one floored her. For two days she couldn't get out of bed. Mac took charge of the pub and Francine brought her up hot lemon and honey drinks, or newspapers and buttered toast.

'Are you all right, Aunty Winnie?' the girl whimpered every time she coughed.

'I will be!' Winnie said, bursting with affection for her miniature nurse. 'I love you, Francine.'

23

Francine

When Mr Cuthbert came to the school to check up on Francine, she asked, 'Have you found my father yet?'

'If he is alive, we'll find him.'

If he is alive. If? Why had he suddenly introduced an if? Did he think her father was another one dead?

Tears came to her eyes. This was not what he'd said before.

It had been a terrible morning. Aunty Winnie's coughing had kept her awake all night. She wanted to get in bed with her, but Aunty Winnie didn't want her to catch it and sent her away. It reminded her of when she had chicken pox.

In the bar, there was a trail of feathers – which led to the body of Sparrow Number Two, her favourite rose-botherer, dead. Tenderly, she had wrapped the bird in yesterday's newspaper and disposed of it. She loved Tiger dearly, but she told her off. 'You don't kill my lovely birds,' she said. 'What would Winnie say?' But Tiger just slunk off, proud of herself.

'In the meantime,' Mr Cuthbert was going on at school in the classroom he commandeered for 'chats'. 'How are you doing at the Castle?'

Sparrow Number Two. Cassie. Jacob. Joe. Maisie. Mummy. Mr Cohen. Maybe Daddy now. Maybe Aunty Winnie next?

Francine couldn't speak for a moment – all she could think of was feathers. Was it a sign? The dice said it was. 'It's... it's good.'

'Do you like Mrs Eldridge?' Mr Cuthbert asked, his face half-hidden behind his notebook. This was why he had come to the school, she realised, rather than ask her in the pub.

Francine thought of the coughing. She preferred the coughing to the silence. Each time Winnie stopped coughing she thought, *That's it – another one down.*

'I like her,' she said cautiously. What did they all have in common?, she thought urgently. All these people, the dog, the bird?

One thing.

Her.

She loved them. They loved her. A two again.

Mr Cuthbert was nodding cheerfully. Francine waited. She knew what would come next. Sure as the chopper comes to chop off your head in the game of Oranges and Lemons.

'I hope you know Mrs Eldridge is fond of you too. Between you and me, I haven't seen her this happy in a long time.'

She said, 'I love you,' Francine remembered.

Suddenly the babies were screaming again and maybe it was a message or a warning. The list of the dead was growing. They knew.

Outside the classroom, Francine covered her ears with her fists and then quickly asked her dice once again what they thought. Five. No good. She had to protect Aunty Winnie. And Tiger. And even Mac. If Aunty Winnie loved her, it meant she had to leave.

Francine still had her key to Mr Cohen's house. The next day, instead of going to school, she went there. She hadn't said goodbye to him and while, logically, she understood he was not there, of course not, a part of her wondered if she might find him in his armchair, his sandwich on a plate to his side. Tea with the lemon left in the cup for extra flavour.

She knew where the scissors were in Mr Cohen's house because she was the one who had tidied them away. Second drawer down. The drawer with the knives, forks and spoons that didn't fit in the top drawer; also, spatulas, ladles, soup spoons – and not only that, odd bits, keys, padlocks, nail scissors. If she were a thing, no doubt she'd belong in the second drawer down too.

She would get in trouble if she rent – a new word for her, meaning ripped – her school uniform, so she cut her vest instead. It was one of Maisie's; it even had her name in the back. They'd always swapped because Maisie was big for her age while Francine was small. Somehow that it was Maisie's felt right.

It was usually only adults who covered their hair, but now she covered hers. It was like play-acting, but Francine was serious. She covered the larger mirror with the tablecloth, the smaller with a tea towel. She sat on the low stool that Mr Cohen had sometimes used as a footstool: she was not a relative, but she had loved that old man in the two months after he took her in and now she knew – it was probably because he had taken her in that he had died.

She found a prayer book and then the prayer called the

mourning prayer. It was in English and Hebrew and she wished she could read it in Hebrew and felt ashamed that she could not. Then Francine thought she would make herself a jam sandwich, but there was no food, not a crumb; someone had been in and removed it all. But they had left everything else exactly as it was. Even the burnt saucepan was in the sink. Francine thought it was mysterious, you could even say sinister, but perhaps it was ordinary – what did she know?

Francine went to Mr Cohen's house the next day and the next, instead of school, but she returned to Winnie and the pub in the evening. She knew what she had to do but she wasn't ready for it.

'How is your cough?'

'Getting better,' Winnie said cheerfully. She had colour back in her cheeks. 'Because you looked after me!'

Winnie moved to hug her. Francine backed away.

On the Friday, she didn't know how long she'd been in Mr Cohen's house before she heard a knocking, not at the front door, but at the kitchen window at the back. There she saw a familiar freckly face. She grabbed the key. Unlocking doors always made her feel important. Mummy had said she had to wait until she was thirteen before she had a key.

'I guessed you were here!' Albert said, delighted with himself. 'You missed country dancing and spelling! There's no F in teeth!'

Then he made his expression solemn. 'I only heard about the old man today,' he added. 'Sorry.'

'It's all right.'

'Is that why you didn't come to my house?'

Francine nodded.

'You really liked him, didn't you?'

'Mmm.'

'I wish you had told me.' Albert said.

She hated that the tears came again.

She didn't know if Albert would die if they were friends. Surely Albert didn't count? Surely she was allowed someone? She threw the dice, but they were inconclusive.

He came in and unlaced his boots. He had never visited her here and he relished taking in the ornaments, strange landscapes and still-life pictures, the prayer-books and the menorah.

'Did you see him dead?'

Of course Albert wanted the gory details. He was obsessed with death. All boys were. They were obsessed in London when she was at school there, they were in Somerset when she was at school there, and they were in Kettering – they played war all lunchtime. She remembered them once passing around a photograph of a dead soldier. Half of his head was caved in. She said he looked surprised, and one of the boys remarked, 'Wouldn't you be if half your head got blown off?' And then one of the boys had been caught by Miss Lane, who shouted and made him cry and then Miss Lane cried too.

She remembered them bringing out her mother, her sister and her baby brothers, white with dust. One of the rescuers was crying, heaving with emotion, and he shouted at her: 'Get out the way, child, this isn't the picture house!'

Francine smacked the side of her head as though to dislodge the thought. 'Albert, I really am sorry about the party,' she said.

His face softened.

'It was boring without you. So are you going back to London?'

'Not London.'

'Then where?'

Francine paused. She wasn't sure what she was going to do next. She liked Aunty Winnie, but she knew it was *because* she liked Winnie that she couldn't stay there.

'I've been in the Castle but I'm going to leave.'

'The Castle *pub*?!' This shocked Albert more than the second part of the sentence and Francine didn't know why.

'Yes...'

'Is it a real pub?'

This struck Francine as a strange question. Why would she stay at an imaginary pub?

'Yes,' she said.

'I'll have a Scotch, please!' he said in a funny grown-up voice, and they squealed. She was glad she didn't have to explain any more. His voices were great. Albert could always make her smile. He was like Lydia in that way. Francine was a respectful and obedient girl who avoided misbehaviour at all costs, but she adored anarchy in others.

Now, they pretended to drink alcohol. Glug, glug! He mimed pouring a bottle down his throat. He slumped back in the chair before curling up a fist and thumping the coffee table. 'Give me my beer!'

'You sound like the giant in *Jack and the Beanstalk*!' She giggled.

Now he staggered around, shouting, 'Just one more, you fucking idiot!'

'Albert!' He had turned into a monster.

'Who the hell are you to tell me what I can and can't drink?'

Francine had never seen this side of Albert before. He was always the sweetest thing – annoying maybe, but never aggressive. He was too good at pretending to be drunk. Now he slipped to the floor, rolling his eyes like a lunatic in a horror film.

'Albert! BERTIE!'

He sat up, laughing, snapping back into his normal self. It was a relief.

'You should be on the stage.'

He laughed. 'It's easy!'

'How do you know what being drunk is like?'

'I just do.'

He stuck out his lower lip, suddenly melancholy, as though the play-acting had taken something out of him.

'What do you want to do now?'

They put the wireless on and it was *BBC Dancing Club* so they did a dance, just holding hands and swinging in and out, and then, because Albert was worried it was too loud and they'd be discovered, she switched it off.

They lay on the living room floor side by side and he didn't complain too much about cat hair and she thought of Mr Cohen's feet, which were the only part of him she didn't love. Even then she'd have put up with the sight of them all day and night, if she got the chance to hear him say, 'my bubbalah' one more time.

Then she remembered: the shoebox of photographs and showed them to Albert. There was one photo of Mr Cohen and his wife at his wedding, hoisted around in chairs, lifted by the guests, and Albert wanted to re-enact it. The kitchen chairs would be the most suitable. He couldn't lift her, but she could, just about, lift him.

'You're light as a feather!' she mocked.

There was the photo of Mr Cohen's son flexing his muscles on the beach. Albert took his shirt and vest off and did that too, like he did in football. He had a plum instead of a bicep, but that didn't stop him being proud.

There was the beautiful one of the just-married couple. She and Albert held each other, copying the pose. They were both the same size, peas in a pod.

'Albert,' she whispered. 'You smell of something bad!'

She suddenly felt guilty. The babies were screaming again. She covered her ears and then realised Albert was staring at her, concerned.

'What?' he asked. 'What's happening to you?'

She rubbed her face and was about to tell him about Mummy and the ghosts, but thought it would sound stupid. Instead, she corrected his 'what' to 'pardon'. He had moved on anyway. He had found the Battleship grids and wanted to know what they were. She promised she'd teach him to play.

'It's how I got my pen,' she said, waving the papers. 'Thanks to this.'

Just after four, Albert said he had better head home or else his people would be worried. 'And Francine?'

'Yup?'

'Where are you going to go?'

Francine didn't know, but she found herself saying, 'This is still my home...'

If she became too friendly with Winnie, then Winnie would probably die too. Everyone did. Maybe that was why Lydia and Valerie stayed away. They knew she was a bad-luck token, like a mascot but the opposite. If you took her to a match, your team lost. If you took her to a house, you died.

At this her mummy scowled, shaking her head vigorously, but Francine knew better than her. After all, which one of them was still alive?

At the door, Albert hovered. 'I can ask my people, the Martins, if you can stay with us?' he suggested.

'It's all right...'

She did not want to kill Albert!

He said he'd come back tomorrow. He wanted to play pubs again – could he be landlord next time? She agreed. He said he'd be strict and he would kick out the drunks into a heap outside the window, but she couldn't imagine it. Albert was too nice.

This time, instead of going back to the Castle, Francine decided to stay. Distancing herself from there had to be done and quickly. She had just been drawing out the pain. It was strange to be alone now, but she wasn't alone for long. She could hear Maisie and her Mummy bickering and the babies screeching. She took herself up to bed, but they followed her up there.

'It's all right, Mama,' she told her. 'I can look after myself.'

But her mother screwed up her nose like she smelled old herrings.

It was dark and the moon was a sliver, a half-hearted peeking thing. This was the moon the Nazis liked best. It was a night like this when they'd bombed her life upside down.

24

Winnie

'Francine wasn't here today,' the woman in the school office said, flicking through a register. Most of the names had ticks against them. A few had red crosses. Winnie glowered at the woman, trying to contain her surprise, then tried to look for Francine's name upside down among the others.

It was four o'clock. Mac and the pub this afternoon were driving Winnie mad. And there was a constant buzzing in her head: 'King's Arms are doing this – what are the Castle doing? How are you going to save the pub?' All the unanswerable questions.

Thank goodness she had stopped feeling poorly. Her throat was no longer sandpaper dry, head no longer fuzzy, so she had thought to surprise Francine by meeting her at the school gates. Now she was the one surprised.

Francine had left the house that morning the same time as usual, her satchel criss-crossed over her chest, socks pulled up to her knees and plaits still tidy. She had thrown her dice and announced: 'Today is going to be a better day.'

'Is there a problem?' the woman with the register asked.

'No,' lied Winnie, filling up with shame. 'My mistake.' She turned away.

'Mrs Eldridge,' the woman called, her finger pressed a line on a register. 'Francine hasn't been in school all week.'

Winnie felt sick. How could this have happened?

When it came to the pub, Winnie had an antenna for trouble. Usually those drunken rows or alcohol-induced infringements withered on the vine, but occasionally they turned into something more menacing.

When she got back to the Castle from the school that afternoon, fraught with worry about Francine, it was obvious straight away that something was amiss. The Canadians were unhappy. A young soldier was leant over the bar, demanding attention.

Winnie wasn't stupid. Trevor wouldn't have asked what the problem was – his philosophy was, 'Let them come to you' – but Winnie would always try to nip whatever it was in the bud. (That was one of the many differences between Winnie and Trevor.)

'What's going on here?' she asked.

The soldier spun around. He was holding up his pint glass and glaring at it.

'This!' he spat out. 'It's watered down.'

'Sorry?'

'I said' – the Canadian's voice was loud, as though she were deaf as well as stupid – 'It's WATERED DOWN.'

'What?' snapped Winnie. This was no time for 'pardon'! Trevor would have gone out of his mind if he'd heard the pub's integrity challenged in this way. There could be no greater insult. Her regulars looked over anxiously.

'Taste it,' the young man said, offering the glass around. The other men shook their head.

'I know my beer,' Winnie said. Her back was up. Trevor was dead. Susan had left. Mac was useless. And Francine? Francine was off, God knows where.

She thought – who *are* you? I have opened this pub every day – even the day my husband died we stayed open. I have cleaned it, supplied it, serviced it, done everything – and you are telling me that I am doing it wrong?

'It's not watered down. We would never do that. NEVER.'

The King's Head had done that once and it was a shameful escapade. For all the pub landlords. Trevor's fury had been righteous: 'A pub's existence is based on trust. They don't just let themselves down – they let us all down.'

'It *bloody* is.'

The serviceman roared with laughter, and the other Canadians joined in. He was putting on an English accent and taking the mickey out of her. The cheek of it! Especially since she had been so positive about them being there in the first place.

'How dare you walk in here and accuse me like that?'

He sneered in response.

To her horror, she realised Sergeant Ron Roscoe had arrived. He clocked the situation immediately and was putting out his hands as though urging restraint.

'The question is: how dare you serve us this muck?'

'Now then,' Ron Roscoe spoke reasonably. 'Let's not jump to—'

'It's not muck!' Winnie yelped. 'And no one else is

complaining.' She gestured to her regulars, who seemed to have shrunk not only in size but in number.

'So you save it for the foreigners then?'

'No,' said Winnie. 'Don't be ridiculous.'

I am at the end of my tether, she told herself. This is what tether's end looks like. Francine was missing, she was fighting to keep the pub going – and now she was being accused of the basest, worst thing a landlady could do.

Ron Roscoe was telling them all to calm down. There was more banter. Calm down? She would not calm down.

'Are you trying to poison us?' the young man asked, and again the soldiers laughed.

She was so outraged, so shocked by these arrogant young men, she could have smashed all the glasses, flung over the tables, run out of the door screeching. She was one second away from that, one millisecond.

'How dare you accuse me?'

Ron had one hand on her shoulder, the other in front of the soldier's chest, but it was too late. Winnie had had it up to here!

'Get out. All of you.'

'Come on,' she heard Ron Roscoe say. 'This is unnecessary—'

'You too – out!'

The young man was arguing. 'I want a refund.'

She didn't need Mac. She grabbed the mop that she'd done the floor with earlier and charged. Mop underarm, like a toddler having a tantrum, she ran at them. 'Out! Do you hear me? OUT!'

After the Canadians had been chased out, and that included Ron Roscoe, the Castle fell silent as a graveyard. Then Old Jim suggested that Winnie went upstairs to 'powder your nose, or whatever it is you ladies do...', and Jim said he'd look after the bar. Two old fellas came in, talking about cricket, unaware that there'd been a scene.

'Who are you to tell me what to do?' Winnie was disturbed at how hysterical she sounded.

'I am your friend,' Old Jim spoke firmly, 'and Trevor's friend too. No one wants to see you distressed like this.'

Winnie nodded. She might be at tether's end, but she couldn't stay there, she had to find a route back. At that moment, the thing she most wanted to do was get blind drunk.

'I'm all right,' she said, putting the mop away, ignoring her shaking hands. 'Stuff and nonsense about our beer being watered down. How dare they? Can you imagine what Trevor would have said...'

She felt like sobbing suddenly. She was trying to keep it to his high standards, but she would never be as good as him.

'Good riddance to bad rubbish,' she called. 'Cheers.'

Her regulars chinked their glasses, and, if some of them still looked perturbed, Winnie ignored it. She tried not to think about the surprise on the Canadian's kindly face. The way he held up his arms as if in surrender. The way he had tried to keep the peace.

Her temper would be old news soon. Hopefully. Then she remembered Francine again. Francine who should have been back by now. Francine who had missed every day of school this week. Francine who, contrary to what she had thought, had *not* settled in beautifully.

'I'm leaving,' she said abruptly.

'What?' Mac was not happy.

'I have to go out. Keep an eye, please.'

Winnie didn't see any disgruntled Canadians on the way to Scott's office, she wasn't sure how she would react if she did. She climbed up to the third floor, each echoey step amplifying her self-loathing.

'She's usually back at four? It's only five now.' As usual, Scott's first reaction was to pour oil on troubled waters. 'You know kids! She's probably out, climbing trees.'

Winnie told him what the secretary at school had said – that she hadn't attended all week.

'It's not unusual to have setbacks—' He stopped. 'I saw her just the other day. She seemed fine.'

Scott was trying to calm her, but Winnie knew him well enough to see that he was concerned.

'We just have to think. Where could she have gone?'

'I have no idea,' admitted Winnie.

Could this day get any worse?

25

Francine

When she heard the knock on Mr Cohen's front door, Francine guessed who it was. She did consider hiding – she knew the best places to disappear into – but she also felt a weariness that kept her glued to where she was; her old bed. The sheets hadn't been changed and the familiar scent and the familiar view from the window were enough to make her feel this was where she should be.

Mostly, she wanted to be back in the shelter where once everything had felt safe: to be entangled in her sister's arms, the sound of the babies murmuring, her mummy snoring, their simple, underground mole-like lives. She couldn't be bothered with the present, when her heart was stuck in the past.

Somehow Mr Cuthbert and Aunty Winnie let themselves in, she heard their low voices. Her heart was thumping. Aunty Winnie probably wouldn't throw her out for running away, but it would sour everything, the way the death of Cassie the dog had soured everything for her in Somerset. Yet the thing was, the contradictory thing perhaps but what also made perfect sense, was – she *wanted* Aunty Winnie to throw her out. Aunty Winnie had to throw her out, because she was bad news.

Everyone she loved died. Aunty Winnie had said she loved her.

They called out her name a few times and then Mr Cuthbert added, 'Francine, the cat is missing you,' and her heart sank at the thought of poor Tiger looking for her. It was unfair of Mr Cuthbert to use that.

A dice fell from her pocket and rumbled from the mattress onto the stone floor. Four. Aunty Winnie raced up the stairs. Francine knew it was her because Mr Cuthbert was always so slow. She burst into the room, white as a sheet, but she didn't tell Francine off, she just said, 'Here you are,' in an unsurprised voice, and 'Let's take you back.'

'To where?'

'To the pub.' Aunty Winnie paused. 'Home.'

Wasn't Aunty Winnie aware that people around Francine died? *Always* died.

No, she didn't seem to be.

Downstairs, Mr Cuthbert mumbled, 'You gave us a fright,' but he didn't sound angry, more sad.

She wanted to tell them that she was bad news, but she couldn't find the words, she couldn't. She asked Winnie how was her cough, and she said, 'Fine, thank you for asking,' in a surprised tone.

Out on the road, they walked on either side of her and each took hold of a hand. This was what her mummy and daddy used to do, and, like her mummy and daddy, they both looked over her head and smiled at each other.

'Are you two married?' she asked. Suddenly, everything

made sense: Mr Cuthbert and Aunty Winnie were a family. Francine was used to the idea that men and women didn't live together, since the war.

But they jumped apart.

'No, Francine!' Aunty Winnie said while at the same time, Mr Cuthbert said, 'We're old friends, that's all!'

'Like me and Albert?'

'Exactly.'

'Good,' said Francine, because actually she thought the kind Canadian with the accent and the extra-large head would be perfect for looking after Aunty Winnie when she was gone... And she would go.

26

Winnie

That day when they'd fetched her from Mr Cohen's house, Winnie's heart had bled for Francine all over again. When she had found her, huddled on the bed, she seemed like a wild creature caught in a trap.

Winnie had been complacent. Happy-ever-afters weren't likely for any of them, she realised now. The most she could hope for was a happy-for-a-bit. She felt foolish and also, although it was unfair, betrayed. She had thought they were getting on.

When they got back to the Castle, Winnie said, 'You mustn't do that again.'

'I am here for the foreseeable future,' Francine repeated automatically.

'Is that all right?'

Francine shrugged.

'Do you have any questions?'

'Yes,' she said.

Winnie braced herself.

'Where are the Canadians? They always come on Fridays.'

'There was an incident,' Winnie admitted. 'They'll be back.'

'What incident?' asked Francine.

'Adult business. Nothing for you to worry about, Francine.'

'She threw them out!' Mac called from behind the till.

Winnie grimaced at him. He was supposed to be on her side. Hard-working and *loyal*? 'It wasn't as bad as all that...'

'It was,' Mac insisted.

Francine's eyes were wider than ever.

A few evenings later, Francine sat on one of the bar stools and scribbled in her notebook like she was pretending to be a businessperson. It was a sweet game. Other children played doctors and nurses, or cowboys but Winnie wasn't going to complain about Francine playing offices. But then Francine came over to her, with a determined look.

'I have ideas for increasing footfall...'

As he poured a drink, Mac snorted.

'Go on,' said Winnie, more to pull up Mac than because she thought Francine might be on to something.

'First, you must get the Canadians back,' she said. It was funny, thought Winnie. Francine's voice shook much of the time, but it never shook when she was talking about the pub. 'They're VITAL.'

Winnie shrugged. 'They'll come back in their own sweet time.'

'Na-ah,' echoed Mac. 'We can manage without their pity.'

Francine folded her arms. 'You're making this more difficult for yourself,' she scolded.

Winnie realised suddenly that Francine didn't see this as
a game at all.

Next Friday night, two pretty girls came into the bar. Winnie
gave an effusive landlady's welcome, while Mac lit up like
the sky on Bonfire Night. You see! People still came. The
Castle would always be popular. These were much better
than argumentative Canadians. Francine didn't realise this.

Winnie recognised the smaller one from Susan's school.
She had taken over her father's hardware shop in town. She
was putting on lipstick without a mirror.

'Where are the foreign boys then?' the taller one asked.

'Are there seriously none here?' the smaller one who
knew Susan said.

Winnie realised she might have got this wrong too.

'They'll come in later!' Winnie suggested. 'Probably...'

The girls downed their drinks in ten seconds and then
left before Mac had even rung up the till.

Winnie was about to go and wish Francine goodnight
when Mr Marshall from the brewery arrived. He had impec-
cable timing – he always turned up when she least wanted
him to. Last week, the Castle had been packed like sardines
and he hadn't come. Now he was here it was a graveyard.

She couldn't leave him with Mac, either. Well-inten-
tioned as he was, Mac couldn't help peddling rumours.

Mr Marshall was already unhappy about Francine.

'It suggests you're not one hundred per cent committed
to the Castle,' he scolded her.

'What rot!' Winnie burst out. She was losing her temper
a lot these days. That's what war did to you. 'I'm more

committed than ever because I need to support and house this young girl. And' – she was into her stride now – 'I used to have a family here, remember – Trevor and Susan – and so does the landlord of the King's Head *and* the White Horse...'

Mr Marshall ignored this and instead counted the drinkers, his finger working across the room. 'Just seven? On a Friday evening?'

'It's been a difficult week,' Winnie insisted.

'But then, you've got the Canadians... I expect they are on manoeuvres or something.'

'Absolutely,' said Winnie, her heart sinking. She couldn't really have scared them all away *permanently*, could she? One little mistake? 'On manoeuvres, yes...'

'What time do they usually come?'

Winnie threw up her hands. 'Who knows. Double, is it?'

'Please.'

After more questions, which Winnie did her best to answer, she asked for five minutes and galloped upstairs to put Francine to bed. Mac would have to hold the fort. Sometimes she had conversations in her head with Trevor about Mac. In her head, Trevor was rather scathing about him – in her head, Winnie would always end up defending him.

'Sorry, sorry...'

Francine looked up from her *Princess and the Pea*.

'I thought you had died,' she mumbled.

'What?'

'You took so long, I thought something bad had happened.'

Winnie sat down on the side of the bed. This wasn't normal.

'I was just downstairs.' She paused, and then she had a strong intuition. 'Is this what it was about? Your running away?'

Francine looked at her and for once Winnie couldn't read her expression. For a while, Francine just leafed through the pages, and then she slammed the book shut.

'Everyone I love dies,' she said finally.

Winnie's first reaction was to argue that this was nonsense but she waited a moment to absorb what Francine had said. And then she felt she understood.

'I felt like that after my husband died.'

Francine blinked at her. Sometimes she reminded Winnie of the small bird that the chemist's shop used to keep in a bamboo cage at the window. One day, the latch hadn't been put on right or something and the bird had got out and flown away. Winnie had thought how wonderful, but the chemist said it would never survive in the wild.

'I felt that I must have done something to be singled out in this way. That it was about me.' Winnie explained. 'But it wasn't that. It wasn't me.'

'It might be.' Francine said slowly. Her fingers clenched on her dice.

'It isn't.'

'I loved Mummy and Maisie and my brothers.'

'Yes...'

'And Cassie the dog.'

Winnie didn't know who that was, but she said, 'Go on...'

'And I loved Mr Cohen.'

'Yes...'

'Now they are all dead.'

Winnie wanted to say, *but other people aren't!* but she didn't. She couldn't. Instead, she waited. Francine sniffed.

'So I mustn't love you, you see. Otherwise you will die, too.' She shrugged like she'd reached an undeniable or well-evidenced conclusion.

Now Winnie took her hand. Her bony fingers were so fragile, so breakable, she thought.

'That's not how it works, Francine.'

'If I love you, you will die. Like Sparrow Number Two.'

Winnie put her other hand on Francine's so the girl's hand was sandwiched in her own. Oh, how she loved this girl. And this surprised her. It had happened so quickly and she didn't think she was capable! But it was love, she knew it.

'If I die – and I'm not planning to...' She smiled, but Francine did not smile back. '*If* I die – it will be because my time was up. It will have nothing whatsoever to do with you, I promise.'

'How do you know?' Francine whispered. She wiped her eyes and blew her nose on the square handkerchief she kept under the pillow.

'Because you're not that powerful, darling. That's not how life works.' She took a wild guess. 'Did Tiger kill a bird?'

Francine nodded, her face full of woe.

'She's a naughty cat,' said Winnie. 'But that's what they do, sweetheart, it was not your fault.'

Finally, Francine gave Winnie a watery smile.

'We really should play bingo in the pub.'

That was another thing about Francine: she had the attention span of a flea. Nevertheless, a flea with more business acumen in her little finger than in Winnie's entire being.

By the time Winnie got back downstairs, Mr Marshall had left.

'Was he in a good mood?' she asked Mac.

'Not really,' he said, 'I told him about you and the Canadians.'

Ye gads, thought Winnie.

. . .

The next afternoon, Winnie related the conversation she'd had with Francine about dying to Scott Cuthbert.

'Survivor's guilt...' he said gloomily. 'It's natural under the circumstances.'

'What can we do about it?' Winnie asked, her heart falling. She was glad that Francine had told her, and she found it encouraging that what Francine was feeling was something that was recognised, had a label even, yet she also found it heart-breaking that this feeling was so widespread that it did have a label.

'I don't know,' he said.

About one week after Mr Marshall 's visit, Mac followed Winnie down to the cellar, calling her name, his footsteps echoing off the walls. She hated him coming after her and even the way he said her name annoyed her.

Goodness, she *was* a grumpy old bat.

'May I have a word?'

He was going to, whether she liked it or not.

His eyes were frantic and his hands were shaking. Even his breath smelled anxious. Winnie felt an unusual sympathy for him.

'What is it?'

'You're going to be angry with me.' Mac said this often. He was usually right.

'I'm sure I won't,' Winnie said.

Perhaps he was going to hand in his notice, she thought. It would be impossible to replace him. Strong men like him were not lining up in the streets of Kettering looking for work like they used to. When they came, with their hopeful eyes, Trevor used to try to find them jobs. (Winnie didn't go in for eulogising the dead, but Trevor was such a generous man. In nearly every memory she had of him, he was trying to help.)

'I can't do anything right,' Mac said.

Winnie wiped the sweat off her forehead. She had a bar full of elderly men complaining about the war and what they would do if they were in charge: naturally, everything would be much better; Hitler and his cronies would be mincemeat by now. She didn't have time for Mac's existential angst.

'What is it?'

Did he kill the bird? she wondered wildly. Perhaps Tiger was the innocent party here!

'I watered down the Canadians' beer.'

'Wha—? Why?'

'Because how are we going to make any money otherwise? I thought it would help...'

'Why didn't you tell me?'

Before you bloody did it!

'You've been so busy with the girl! I didn't want to add to the—'

'So instead you humiliated me?'

As soon as the words were out, she regretted them. He hadn't humiliated her. She had humiliated herself. He seemed to shrink in front of her. This was worse than she'd expected. She recalled her rage. Had she really charged at the Canadians with an actual mop?

'Are you firing me?' Mac asked.

The ridiculous thing was that part of her determination to keep the pub open was to keep poor Mac in work – and his poor mother sane.

She took a deep breath, to keep her anger in. Right now, the only reason she wouldn't fire him was because she was desperate.

'I'm not, but it was a terrible thing to do.'

He hung his head in shame.

The next day, Mac came in with an apple crumble. 'Mummy says there are more of these.'

He must have told his mother and now she was trying to make it up to her.

Naturally, Francine wanted to know what was going on. Trevor might have said, 'Children should be seen and not heard,' but Francine was not just any old child. She cared about the pub.

'The Canadians will come back,' Winnie explained defiantly, 'and when they do, I'll apologise for watering the beer down. All right?'

Mac nodded eagerly now that the blame had shifted, but Francine blinked at her.

'They won't.'

Winnie laughed. 'Not everyone is as stubborn as you, Francine.' She winked.

Francine giggled but then she turned serious, 'I saw Sergeant Roscoe the other day. He told me they definitely won't be back. Not until they get an apology.'

Winnie gulped. She was going to have to do something drastic.

The airbase was closer than she thought to the Castle – twenty minutes, fifteen if she hadn't dawdled to chat with Jim's wife. Mac had offered to come with her – after all, he said, he was responsible for this – but she told him to stay and man the bar. She was still furious with him and trying to keep her distance until she cooled down. It wouldn't do to chuck an apple crumble at his head!

Over the years, Winnie had grown to feel affection for the Castle, its customers and the life it had given her, but Francine had fallen in love with the pub straight away. She seemed to glow in the bar, she basked in the community and she loved making plans to increase footfall. Francine had unexpectedly become yet another reason she had to keep fighting to keep them open. (Like she needed more incentives!)

Winnie had written a card that was apologetic and heartfelt. She wrote how mortified she was, 'especially mortified because you are our brave allies'! Francine had checked it over solemnly. Winnie thought she might say it was too much, but she didn't.

'It would be better to talk to him yourself,' she concluded, but Winnie thought that was unnecessary. She didn't say she found the whole episode was excruciating. Francine hadn't seen how out of control she was. Fingers crossed though, all would be well. The Castle was nearer than the Kings Head to the base so it had that in its favour.

There were barbed wire, sandbags and 'keep out' signs all over the airbase. Once, she would have found all the military paraphernalia intimidating. It is amazing how quickly you get used to terrible things, Winnie thought. They should do studies on it.

Past the honeycombed fence of the perimeter, Winnie found the entrance. Trucks were coming out as she approached the security guard.

'Could you give this to Sergeant Ron Roscoe,' Winnie said, showing the guard the envelope.

How did Canadians have such impossibly white teeth?

'I'll get him for you.'

'No-no, it's just—' Winnie said quickly, but the man held up a hand.

'He'll be here in two minutes.'

'I don't want to be a bother,' Winnie added, growing alarmed.

'No problem.'

If smiles won wars, victory would be theirs right now. Or at least his.

'I'd rather not,' she said weakly.

Goodness me, she thought, what had she started?

'Here he comes,' the man said, pointing at a silhouetted figure hurrying out of a nearby building towards them.

When Ron Roscoe had last seen her, she was raging at him and his men. Winnie felt so red and hot she would like to have dunked her head in cold water. She wished she had made more of an effort. She was wearing a brown winter coat and a brown hat that she had thought matched but on second thoughts probably didn't. She didn't like looking in the mirror any more because it was like looking at a bad-tempered version of her own mother and her mother had been no Clara Bow.

He was smiling as he approached, or was he smirking? It was hard to tell.

'Good to see you again.'

Winnie bowed her head, momentarily stunned by his bright blue eyes.

'I wrote a card...' she began but couldn't remember the rest of the sentence.

'Yes?' he prompted.

'To apologise. It's all there.'

It was definitely a smile. 'While you're here, why not have a look around?' he suggested and he took her arm.

· · ·

There was work going on everywhere. It was a hive of activity. *It took me nine months to secure the brewery's permission to put up hanging baskets*, she thought. How fast things moved when it came to war.

'We're still fixing things up,' Ron Roscoe said as they walked. He pointed things out. 'Living quarters, offices, the mess... we had a projector the other night and watched Charlie Chaplin movies.'

'Ha,' she said. Being on the back foot made her nervous. And he made her nervous. Put the two together and she could hardly speak.

He took her to a canteen, where they had coffee. He said hello to some passing soldiers and one of them nearly walked into a table, he was so busy craning his neck to see who Ron was talking to.

Then Ron read the note while she watched him nervously: her handbag on her knees like a shield.

She said that she was mortified.

'You already said that,' he said, pointing at the note, 'twice.'

'I truly am!' Winnie continued, fanning herself.

'I do appreciate your apology,' Ron said.

'Wonderful!'

'But I'm afraid it's too late. The boys have found somewhere else that is keen for custom,' he said.

'Not the King's Head?'

'I don't want to say, but...'

Winnie hung her head. Trevor would say she was an idiot. She *was* an idiot. 'Never turn down good money,' he used to say. She should write all his advice down before she forgot it.

'We're keen for your custom too.' She blushed on her blushes. 'Francine has all sorts of bright ideas.'

'She's a clever thing.'

'We'll be running bingo nights, card games soon. All the things she said.'

He hmm'd, smiling at her, his expression was so kind, it made her tearful. 'I'll see what I can do,' he said. And Winnie found herself thinking that, even if he couldn't get all the others to come back, she would be happy just to see him again.

27

Winnie

The Canadians didn't come back to the Castle right away. But then, just as Winnie had given up hope, some came, in twos and threes at first, and then, some days later, in larger groups. There was room for them all and – Francine's idea – Winnie opened the back room. Back in the day, she and Trevor had served both sides of the pub: the lively crowd congregated at the front of the house while the more elderly, or the ones who just wanted peace and quiet, tended to prefer the back room. It was lovely to see it busy again.

Sometimes they didn't have enough spirits, but they certainly didn't water them down but answered straight. Some drinkers left and went looking elsewhere. Others didn't look the slightest put out but said, 'How about an alternative?'

But Sergeant Ron Roscoe didn't come back. Winnie most certainly wasn't looking out for him, absolutely not, but she would have liked to have served him a drink on the house and to apologise once more. It was the least she could do.

Things felt different nowadays. Winnie could feel that she was recovering and ridiculously, pathetically, that made her sad, because part of her didn't want to recover. She wanted Trevor back, not to be 'over' his loss. Every time she felt better, it made her ashamed, it felt as though more distance was coming between them. But life goes on. The country was pulling together. Churchill's speeches couldn't help but fill you with pride and courage – his painting behind the bar couldn't help but remind you: We can do this. We are doing this. Purpose and passion.

The brewery still hadn't made a decision as to which pub would get to stay open. Mr Marshall often came to inspect, and he must have noted how crowded it was.

'Don't hurry us,' Mr Marshall said, which had not been Winnie's intention. 'You want us to make the right decision, don't you?'

After he visited, it always felt like the guillotine that was poised over her slipped down a notch.

But Winnie had Francine – her secret weapon. Slamming the door on her way out to school, chewing a pencil at the bar, giggling with the customers. It was absurd and she would never admit it to Mac or Scott Cuthbert, but in some ways it was like having a very enthusiastic business partner. They began playing poker in the back room on Friday. Sundays became Bridge night. For a child who hated English, Francine was good at thinking up adverts: 'Special Deal for OAPs on Wednesdays!' She was terrible at crossword clues, but she had a go, and she attentively listened to Toby's memoir.

'It's a real book!' she cried at the end of chapter six.

Toby said there was no greater accolade.

Winnie's 'underlying air of misery' seemed to have dissipated. There was pride and even contentment. Her first thoughts in the morning were of Francine. Sometimes, she wondered idly if she would have felt this – this tenderness – towards any eleven-year-old girl. No, no matter how wholesome and loving any other eleven-year-old might have been, Francine simply *was* the most special of them all.

One Sunday evening she put the wireless on to clean up to, and it was the Vera Lynn song that had brought Francine into the pub: 'We'll Meet Again'.

'My mummy liked this one,' Francine said.

Winnie smiled at her, wistfully.

'So did my Trevor.'

To her surprise, Francine got up and, with a low bow, asked Winnie to dance.

Winnie laughed. She was going to say that she couldn't, she had the floor to sweep, then mop, the accounts to go through, but then she changed her mind. Francine deserved attention. Francine deserved so much more – she was a diamond.

She took the young girl's hand.

They came closer. Cheek to cheek. They moved around the room in time to the music, Winnie careful not to tread on her toes, dreaming of Trevor, Francine probably dreaming of her mother. This was making the best of it, Winnie thought, and this she could do. Sometimes it was all you could do.

28

Winnie

Mrs Hardman, Francine's neighbour from London, visited, and she brought her chocolate ration for Francine. Before the visit, Winnie feared this Mrs Hardman – who she had heard alarmingly little about – might want to adopt Francine, or at least take her back to live with her in the house in Romberg Road, especially now that the Blitz was over. Winnie did not feel up to a fight, but she would be devastated if Francine left now. She would not be back to square one, as Scott had once suggested, she would be way, way back, in the minus numbers.

Once she met Mrs Hardman – Jean – though, Winnie realised, with relief, that such speculation was unlikely. This modest woman, who wouldn't say boo to a goose, had no designs on Francine. Winnie couldn't help wondering if the war had made her this meek, or if she had always been this way. The first thing she said was that she was exhausted, hadn't had a day off in goodness knows how long. She was wearing a strange starchy uniform and an odd, peaked hat, which she explained was what she wore as a bus conductor, and looked out of place here in Kettering.

Winnie didn't like to ask why Mrs Hardman wore her uniform on her day off, but she launched into an explanation of it herself: 'I feel braver when I wear it – silly really...'

'Not silly,' Winnie said, since it made sense. She put on her uniform as armour, while Winnie lived in a Castle. They were both a kind of self-defence.

'I would never have imagined I'd have a job on the buses!'

Winnie understood this too, because she could never have imagined ending up in a pub. It was grief and then it was Trevor. You get pulled into things.

She'd fancied being one of those new airline stewardesses, but she was too short to reach the lockers where they put the luggage; and as for working on a boat, she'd get seasick. She enrolled in an evening class to learn Spanish instead, but the teacher, dashing Miguel, only went off to join the civil war and no one else took over.

Winnie remembered in her first few weeks at the Castle, Trevor's happiness was overwhelming. Winnie was happy too, but not like he was. Newly married and hoping to get pregnant. But at the same time, a little voice, *her* little voice, was protesting: *I thought you were going to leave Kettering?*

Once, one of her old teachers came in. After she'd stopped teaching, this teacher had been force-fed in prison for demanding the vote, and everyone talked about her like she'd gone crazy, but Winnie had always liked her.

'Is that Miss Winnifred?'

Why had Scott also had to be there that evening, sipping his shandy at the bar, eavesdropping on everything?

'Yes, it's me,' Winnie said slowly.

'Here's the girl I thought was going to travel round the

world. I thought you were like those Victorian women climbers. With nothing but a parasol and a girdle.'

'I think they had more than—'

'I was certain you'd be in Timbuktu by now.'

'Here I am instead,' Winnie said. It hurt to be talked about like this.

'What made you change your mind? You were born five minutes from here.'

This was excruciating, especially with her audience.

'Love has a way of doing that to you,' she said.

Scott had clinked his glass towards her. 'So say all of us.'

It was one of the moments in your life that feels pretty embarrassing at the time, but when you look back on it, it's even worse.

Now Winnie shook herself from her reverie and tried to pay attention to the yawning woman in the uniform in front of her.

'What about your husband, Mrs Hardman?' Winnie asked, pouring the tea.

The woman paused as though selecting an answer. 'He's dead,' she replied eventually in a strange flat tone. So they had that in common as well.

After the tea, Francine wasn't due back for another hour, they went downstairs and had a tipple together for good luck. The occasion seemed to call for it.

'How is your daughter – Valerie, is it?'

'She's in Somerset. Evacuated. Do you have any children of your own, Mrs Eldridge?'

'My Susan is in Buckinghamshire.'

'What's she doing there then?'

Winnie laughed. 'To be honest, I have no idea!'

But Mrs Hardman took that the wrong way; she mistakenly jumped to the idea that Susan was estranged from her mother.

'It's not like that,' Winnie clarified 'Susan is not allowed to say. It's all hush-hush.'

'Of course...' the other woman said quickly. 'That's what I thought...'

Mrs Hardman also filled in some of the gaps about Francine's life in London before her family were lost. Their endless nights in the shelter, the chicken pox. The smell. The burning. The loud noises.

'Is she all right with loud noises now?' Mrs Hardman asked.

'She is,' Winnie said.

'Good,' Mrs Hardman said. Every time she lowered her heavy eyelids, Winnie thought she was going to fall asleep.

'She worries about people – loved ones – dying...'

'I can imagine.'

Her tone was light, but she dabbed at her eyes, which Winnie noticed were wet. Everyone had to be so brave nowadays, Winnie thought suddenly; why couldn't they just have a big old howl or a roll on the floor, legs kicking – the situation merited it! This war was brutal. But Mrs Hardman was as stoical as you had to be. She put her handkerchief back in her handbag and cleared her throat.

'I'm pleased you're looking after her.'

Then Francine arrived back from school and Winnie saw the affection between them. Francine was hungry for news of Valerie and Lydia, but Mrs Hardman was surprisingly vague about them. Mrs Hardman cupped Francine's face in her hands and, thank goodness, she didn't mention the chicken pox scars. Instead, she said, 'Your mother would be proud.' And then she did cry.

. . .

Later, Winnie walked weary Mrs Hardman back to the station, while Francine stayed back to check on the sparrows or to plot new schemes or whatever she did.

'May I ask—' Winnie said, grasping the opportunity. 'About Francine's father? What was he like?'

'He's very foreign,' Mrs Hardman said, which caused Winnie to raise an eyebrow. Very? As opposed to *quite* foreign? 'But he's a nice man.'

What Winnie meant to ask was: If he is alive, will he come? She might as well enquire directly.

'Will he try to find Francine, do you think?'

Mrs Hardman looked puzzled.

'Of course! She's his daughter!' she exclaimed.

He probably wasn't alive then, deduced Winnie. It was unbearably sad, but at least she'd get to keep her girl.

29

SPRING, 1942

Winnie

It was Francine who brought the knitting circle to the Castle. She was twelve now and indomitable. She'd found the knitters on a park bench in the rain and persuaded them to come up to the Castle, lured them in with promises of cut-price gin and a warm fire.

One of the knitters, Mrs Wyatt, a widower of indeterminate age (but upwards of eighty-five), lived in a house only four doors down from the Castle but had never actually stepped foot inside.

'I've not been in a public house. My husband didn't like ladies at them – I thought they were places of ill repute.'

Winnie smiled. Things were changing, but men with views like Mr Wyatt stayed the same.

'The war had got me out the house,' Mrs Wyatt said and then whispered, 'Is that a terrible thing to say?'

'It's what a lot of people think,' Winnie said.

Another of the knitters grabbed her arm.

'That girl is just extraordinary,' she said.

'Who? Francine. Yes, she is pretty special,' Winnie responded proudly.

'She told me all about her life – how she is waiting for her father to come back.'

'Did she?'

Winnie felt that prickling sensation she always got when Francine's father was mentioned. Please, please let him come back – but not quite yet. She didn't want to say goodbye to Francine. It wasn't just the Castle that the girl had brought back to life.

'And she loves you,' the woman said. 'Clear as a bell.'

One of the knitters was a lovely young woman with a toothy smile and a big pretty birthmark down the side of her face. She was Mrs Phelps. She was a widow with a baby, Lester, who never shrieked, even though she was soft as toffee with him.

Mac said he'd serve so Winnie could join the group. She resisted at first – it had been a long time since she'd made anything more creative than a Bloody Mary – but then the pull of the wool took her over. Mrs Wyatt helped her cast off. They were making jumpers for 'our boys in the navy'. Francine was also pleased that Winnie joined in.

Winnie had to concentrate on her knitting needles, so she didn't notice that Mac was smiling at Mrs Phelps like all his Christmases had come at once.

There were stories of battles and pictures of devastation all over Europe. Winnie read the newspapers early and then hid them from Francine. She wasn't sure why. No doubt the girl would catch up with all these things – and worse – at school, but Winnie wanted to protect her as much as she could. Francine didn't need to know the details. Francine didn't need to hear that the Nazis might yet win. Winnie knew she was probably protecting herself, too. These were conversations she didn't want to have.

Winnie was also thinking of other ways to increase footfall. When she wasn't in the pub she was queuing: the war shortages bit long and hard. Having a community helped. The family that Albert stayed with, the Martins, had kept a pig back from the officials, and before too long, the whole town had extra pork.

One thing that surprised her – the number of engagements and marriages there were. It wasn't just that war wasn't stopping them, it seemed that it was positively encouraging them. *Marry in haste, repent at leisure*, thought Winnie sourly, hating herself for her bitterness. Young Jim got engaged between tours in Italy and Nathan's daughter married a new fella after her first husband died. 'He's not even cold yet,' people muttered slyly.

Then there were the Canadians – not shy at coming forward. The boy who had accused them of watering down drinks – yes, rightfully – was engaged to the butcher's daughter. The daughter from the King's Head had already left the country.

'Just got to ask my boss, and then we're all go,' one Canadian told Winnie as Maggie Hartle beamed out from under his arm.

'You can't put your life on hold just because of the stupid old war,' Maggie said.

'Wonderful,' said Winnie.

Oh, to be twenty and your whole life stretching out ahead of you!

Maybe, if Francine had family of her own, it would be possible to dream about an alternative future for herself, but

Winnie took her task of looking after the girl very seriously indeed. Francine had long overtaken the Castle as a priority in her life – which was interesting, because the Castle had a momentum of its own now.

The pub's oak-panelled booths were rarely empty. It had become known as a place where both individuals and groups could take refuge. It wasn't just the Canadians, the poker-and bridge-players or knitters, there were the men who were working in the allotments. The ladies from the hospital. Servicemen back on leave, drinking to chase the demons away.

Trevor would have loved it.

The 'stupid old war' was everywhere and involved every-one. A woman Winnie had gone to school with was killed while nursing in Malta. Another customer got a telegram – when he was in the pub – that his brother had perished in Egypt. Winnie looked after them all.

There was talk of a Castle rugby team starting up. In the end they didn't have the numbers, but a group of former players did come for drinks. One of them played 'Chopsticks' on the piano, badly. Nevertheless, the mood was such that customers clapped. To Winnie's surprise, Sid rose from his quiet corner.

'Sid?' she questioned, before she had time to think.

He shrugged at her, then gestured at the rugby player to move off the piano stool.

'I can't listen to that!' He winked at her. 'Who's it hurt-ing, eh?'

Winnie gave him a smile. This was a change and a half. She hadn't thought she'd ever see Sid back at the piano.

'Need me to turn your pages?'

'It's all here,' Sid said, pointing to his head. 'But if you would sit by me, I'd be much obliged,' he smiled awkwardly before adding, 'It helps with the nerves.'

He played wonderfully. Some classical tunes and some dancehall numbers. And then he rubbed his hands, said he had to stop for today – he was out of practice.

'Bravo,' the customers cried.

'Thank you,' said Winnie.

He patted her hand on his shoulder. 'Thank *you*, Mrs Eldridge. You have to go on, don't you?'

He was talking not only about his son, but about her Trevor too, and for a moment she couldn't speak.

From then on, the piano was played a lot. Jazz or classical, swing or church songs, something for everyone. Mrs Phelps from the knitting circle proved to be a pianist too and when she and Sid duetted, they brought the house down.

Although the pub was thriving, the brewery still hadn't come to a decision and there was one other thing on Winnie's mind – there was no sign of Sergeant Ron Roscoe. The fact that he didn't actually fly planes was small consolation. She longed to see him again, but knew that if she did, it would only bring confusion or guilt – one way or another. Maybe it was for the best if they never saw each other again. Nevertheless, she couldn't resist asking one of the men she recognised as one of his squadron had he been transferred?

'Nope,' the lad said cheerily, 'Old Roscoe's still around. Want me to give him a message?'

'Absolutely not,' Winnie said, to his surprise.

Sometimes she was sure that when she looked up, Churchill was winking down at her.

She realised what it was – Sergeant Roscoe was probably married. He was – at a guess – forty-five? Just slightly older than her. They called him *Old* Roscoe! His wife was probably a capable woman who swam thirty lengths of a pool and wore an Alice band. Her name might be Arabella or perhaps Jacqueline, and she would come from a good family.

Or perhaps he didn't have a wife, perhaps he just didn't like Winnie. If so, Winnie told herself, that was understandable because what man in his right mind would want to get involved with a grieving pub landlady?

Winnie's favourite time was early evening – there was something sustaining about the streaks of gold in the sky and Francine and Albert doing their homework with some of the regulars trying to interfere. But it wasn't all cosy knitted jumper, sing-songs and engagements; one night, the Castle descended into chaos. It was men from a nearby town – not her regulars. Winnie didn't know what started it: it was about communism, Cripps or Chamberlain.

One minute, Sid was playing a rousing rendition of 'Roll Out the Barrel', the next, there were punches being thrown. One of the men was even trying to puncture another man's shoulder with a dart!

Francine and Albert had been playing Battleship at the counter but now Winnie shooed them out of the bar so fast that Albert nearly lost his boot.

'Why were they like that?' Francine asked later. 'We're all on the same side, aren't we?'

Winnie didn't know the answer, but she could guess. 'They had too much to drink.'

'But why?'

'They drink to forget.'

Winnie kissed Francine's cheek, grateful that for herself the temptation to drink to oblivion had gone.

30

Winnie

Almost a year after she'd last seen him, Ron Roscoe came back to the Castle. He looked exhausted. His blue eyes were so narrow, she wondered how he could see out of them. His skin was sallow, while everyone around him was golden and seemed to be toasting themselves in the English sunshine.

Her heart went out to him.

As an aircraft engineer, the most senior there, he was responsible for every single plane.

'We had a few losses,' he said, head bowed. 'Lots to deal with.'

Winnie kept as still as she could. She couldn't think of anything comforting to say. It was just so terrible.

The next time he came in, a few weeks later, they talked intently. He told her about where he was from, Burlington, Ontario, and how he spoke French 'almost as well as English'. (Later, Winnie found Burlington on the map in Francine's room – always good to picture a place – and it looked spectacular.)

He asked about her: Had she always lived in Kettering? Yes. Did she speak any other languages? Sadly no, although Old Jim had taught her some Welsh and Nathan some Gaelic.

It was amazing how familiar Ron seemed to her. All the feelings he'd evoked in her from the first moment she'd met him were still there – no, even more than before; which was, she reminded herself, ludicrous. Had she lost her mind? It wasn't as though she had room for him – what with Francine, Tiger, Susan, the pub she certainly didn't have time for anyone else. And absolutely, definitely not with a someone from the other side of the world. Plus, of course, she barely knew him.

'How's your wife coping with you being away?' she couldn't resist asking. She pictured Arabella perfecting her front-crawl.

Ron looked puzzled. Quietly he said, 'I'm not married. Never have been.'

Winnie could feel something rise inside her: hope? pleasure? 'I just assumed you would have a lady waiting for you back home.'

'No lady,' he said. 'Apart from my mother.' He was smiling now. 'She's counting the days.'

'That's good.'

'Is it?'

He looked her directly in the eyes, but then they were disturbed by Nathan.

'You wouldn't happen to know the capital of Canada? Six across.'

. . .

The next time Ron came to the Castle, he brought daffodils.

'You needn't have!'

She put the daffodils in a vase on the kitchen windowsill. A splash of colour, an assertion of life. But what did it mean? Trevor never got her flowers. What would he have thought? At first she could hardly bear to look at them, at the muddle of confused feelings they evoked, but then she found herself smiling.

Mac had a headache and since there were only a few stragglers in the bar she let him off early. Old Jim and Jim pushed off homeward too, and so did Nathan. Then, just as Ron was saying his goodbyes, Francine dashed in demanding to play cards and, far from minding, Ron was happy to oblige.

The pair played a game Winnie didn't know, called Pig. And then a second game called Cheat. Francine found them both hilarious, but she also liked to come out on top.

'Play with us, Aunty Winnie!'

'Help me,' Ron laughed.

While they were playing, she found out more about him. His dad was a farmer, he had a younger brother who had been brain-damaged in a farm accident, and his mother was the best mother in the world. He had an engineering business that he had to get back to. His father was looking after it now, but...

Francine had won again.

'Aunty Winnie, you're useless!' she crowed. And then, 'You'll never guess – Sergeant Roscoe has never had Bovril before!'

'We'll have to fix that!' Winnie chuckled.

She couldn't stop smiling as she went upstairs and made it. As she brought it to him, she thought, *what am I doing?* But another voice said, *am I not entitled to have fun?*

Ron took a sip, then a second and a third, before he

announced it was quite the most disgusting thing he'd ever encountered, next to jellied eels and kidneys, and were English people out of their minds?

At this, Francine laughed so much that she hiccupped.

He taught her how to shuffle. She kept dropping the cards at first and then looking up like she expected to be told off, but she soon got it. Then it was her bedtime. Winnie expected Ron would leave, but he said, 'I'll wait, if you like.'

Unprompted, Francine gave him a kiss on the cheek goodnight and she never did that!

The bedtime routine went smoothly. Francine said, 'You can go if you like!' with a broad grin, and Winnie was back downstairs within ten minutes. She found Ron reading a newspaper.

'I'm still mortified about barring you that time. I'm sorry, again.'

She thought of how she had raged at them.

'Don't apologise,' he said. 'Well, you can apologise for trying to kill me with Bovril. Dreadful stuff.'

She blushed.

'It's life, isn't it?' he went on. 'Throws some curveballs – especially during a war.'

Winnie loved his accent. He could read aloud a shopping list and it would sound like poetry.

'Thank you for making Francine laugh,' she said.

'She's a sweetheart.'

He paused and she guessed what he might be about to say before he said it.

'How long will she be staying with you?'

'I don't know.'

Was it evacuation? Was it fostering? It was in a blurry grey area, and blurry grey areas were her least favourite. Scott was determined that Francine wouldn't go into a children's home. Beyond that, he said, it was 'playing it by ear'. Whenever he said that, she heard 'playing with fire'.

'It must be hard looking after a pub and taking on a grieving child.'

'And a ruddy cat,' she added.

'And a ruddy cat,' he agreed.

What was it about his face that made it so lovely to confide in?

'It would have been harder not to take her on.'

The next time Ron came to the Castle was about a month later, and he had something tucked under his arm.

'You shouldn't have.' Winnie blushed. 'The daffodils were more than enough!'

She had kept them for longer than she should, feeling reluctant to throw them away even when they were brown and withered.

Ron went scarlet. 'It's for the pub... it's a dartboard.'

She went scarlet too. They were like a couple of red socks.

'Francine thought it would be a good idea.'

Of course she did.

Winnie had got rid of her dartboard after Trevor died; the arrows whizzing around willy-nilly reminded her of bullets and drove her mad, so, when it fell off the wall, she had packed it away in the cupboard under the stairs.

'I see you used to have one.' He pointed to the circle on the wall where the flocked wallpaper was lighter than elsewhere.

'It's a distraction,' he said. 'From all the' – he gestured around him – 'bad news.'

Winnie hesitated. Part of her thought it was intrusive.

Another part thought it sweet that he was looking out for his men.

'I'm sorry,' he said. 'I can take it back.'

'Not at all,' she managed. 'Let's play!'

Her first throw didn't hit the board, but the wall behind. The second flopped on the floor. The third hit the board but not within the point zone. She was so bad that she thought, forget the rainbows and red admirals – *this* was a message from Trevor, although she didn't know what the message was.

'I can teach you,' Ron was saying.

'To be honest,' Winnie said. 'I don't care for it.'

He grinned, his white teeth all in a pretty row.

'Don't blame you.' He plucked the darts off the board. 'What *do* you care for, Mrs Eldridge?'

Funny how a question like that can make you emotional.

'I don't know,' she admitted.

'You don't have any hobbies?'

'Not particularly.' She was almost afraid to say it. 'I always dreamed of travel...'

'Me too,' he said. 'Maybe it's something to look forward to, after the war.'

She didn't know if he meant she or he or they, and she blushed again.

31

AUTUMN,1942

Francine

The next time Francine saw Mr Cuthbert, he explained he was still looking for her Southampton family. 'Don't give up hope,' he said.

'How about my dad?'

'Him too,' he added quickly, but she didn't believe him.

'Do you love Aunty Winnie?'

He stared at her. 'What makes you ask that?'

'My dice,' she said and he laughed.

'Well?' she added since he had still said nothing.

'The truth is: I did once,' he admitted. 'But after I was injured, I married Ada, she married Mr Eldridge and it all ended happily ever after.'

'But Mr Eldridge is dead,' Francine explained to him as if he were an idiot.

'I know. But maybe she'll meet someone else.'

'Maybe she already has,' Francine said lightly.

A few weeks earlier, she had bumped into Sergeant

Roscoe in the street while she was feeding birds. She had asked him why he hadn't come back to the Castle.

'It's complicated,' he had said.

'It's not!' she insisted. 'Aunty Winnie misses you.'

He laughed. 'Is that so?'

Something about him made her bold.

'Someone needs to take care of her. Anyway, got any gobstoppers?'

Now she smiled at poor Mr Cuthbert. He really had no idea.

Francine loved her Aunty Winnie and felt protective towards her. And she loved the pub and, if she did her homework in time, Winnie let her help and even paid her! Getting a wage was a thrill. She didn't know many nearly-thirteen-year-olds who did.

They had done a raffle and collection tins and raised £200 towards a Spitfire. It had been Francine's idea. Not only was there cards, but they had regular darts tournaments now – proceeds to the war effort – and these were also Francine's ideas.

Francine's favourite thing was bingo. She had made the bingo set herself and she called out the numbers from a shopping basket which Winnie had jazzed up with flowers. Everyone had a card – some people played two or three at once – and they had to get a line and then a house and no diagonals were allowed. Francine was surprised how many people did not know the rules.

People donated prizes – although Winnie and Francine had to check for suitability. The things people gave away! Winter coats to Zippo lighters, a silver-plated necklace to two old crayons and a pack of tissues. Winnie said they went from the sublime to the ridiculous.

Winnie still insisted Francine went up to bed before closing time, but that was all right. And Francine always managed to get up for school in the morning.

Now at high school, Francine was good at maths, still hated poetry, and revelled in the fact that there was no more Latin. She didn't see Well-Developed Marjorie much any more (Marjorie was now sixteen and in the Land Army, dating all the young farmers she could find), but she and Albert were inseparable. He was the only other child Winnie allowed in the pub and in the bingo he had won a pair of candlesticks and an old copy of *The Wind in the Willows*, which he was surprisingly pleased about.

Francine went over to see Albert at the Martins' farm sometimes and they played football on the scrubby land there. His host family were always pleasant, if distracted.

Occasionally, Francine thought back to her time at Bumble Cottage in Somerset at the start of the war. The noisiest thing might be the cows mooing in the fields or the chickens crowing in the morning. She hadn't liked that strange peace; she preferred a rowdy environment. She liked it best when Paul Howard, the host mother's son, came home from boarding school and told funny stories or gave her piggy-backs.

'Lydia is too girly-girly for me,' Paul once said. She remembered it because he was the only person in Somerset – possibly the only person ever, apart from her family – who preferred her to Lydia. Everyone else adored Lydia and saw Francine as her shadow.

Lydia and Valerie must have heard by now what had happened to her family. Francine imagined Valerie writing a letter, with all the correct words, and wondered if she would ever listen to one of Valerie's stories again. She pictured a pink envelope flying towards her filled with Lydia's stories of Bumble Cottage, Rex and Mrs H. She would still like that, no matter how unlikely it was.

As for her mum and her baby brothers and dear sister, it was hard to miss them since they were still with her. Always. Sometimes, she'd be mopping the floor and she'd hear the babies howling, or her mother shushing them, and she'd look around and they would be staring at her. Her mother's sorrowful face made it hard to remember when she used to be happy...

'You missed some,' Maisie might interrupt gleefully, crossing her arms, 'I could do it better than you.'

She was healing, but she wasn't sure she would ever be *healed*.

32

Winnie

Keeping the pub open was Winnie's way of commemorating Trevor and providing a home for Francine. Francine seemed to be born for it. Winnie let Francine collect glasses. She let her organise groups and events; she let her do raffles and games. But would all these initiatives, all these changes, be enough to convince the brewery?

Winnie couldn't imagine how Francine would react if they lost the pub. They'd have to move, and she didn't know where. It would be too much, and although Winnie wished she hadn't put Francine in a position that was so precarious, she didn't know what she could do about it. Increasingly, it felt like the pub was Francine's baby. And Francine was not only healing the pub, she was healing Winnie, too... even if Winnie did live in fear that maybe one day Francine wouldn't be hers any more.

Mr Marshall came in, even more officious than usual, and asked her customers what they liked about the Castle.

Winnie squirmed. Please don't let them be silly, she thought, her livelihood depended on it!

The regulars talked about community, sociability, getting out of the house. They weren't silly at all: it made her quite tearful. A serviceman on leave said that when he was on tour, he had thought of nothing else but his beer here. His friend said the Castle was one of the few places where he felt he could be himself. Where nothing was demanded of him.

Mr Marshall scribbled in his notepad. Then he turned to the Canadian servicemen who were filling up the back room.

'I like the grandfathers here,' one said. 'They remind me of mine at home, sitting on the porch drinking whiskey.'

'I like the alcohol,' said another with a nose as red as a rose. 'A few gin and tonics and I don't care about anything any more.'

'I like darts,' said a man who threw a sixty every single time he played. He had, naturally, been nicknamed Cupid.

'It's cosy,' one man – boy, really – told them. 'It's good to be somewhere that isn't all about the war.'

'I like the music,' said Captain Franklin, who loved to sit alongside Sid as he played.

'Are we only allowed to name one thing?' a deep voice asked.

Winnie looked up. Ron Roscoe was beaming at her. When had he arrived? She loved her chats with him. No one seemed to get her as much as he did. *And* he smelled divine.

'No.' She laughed. 'You can say as many as you—'

'Only one!' interrupted Mr Marshall, scowling at Winnie.

'That's difficult...' Ron pondered. 'Okay, it's the landlady,' he said with that shy smile of his.

He must be joking, though, she told herself. This homely face? This long-lost figure? Her cheeks burned.

'The landlady?' repeated Mr Marshall, with raised eyebrows. 'Do you mean Mrs Eldridge?'

'I do,' he said. 'She is what I like most about the Castle.'

'Oh, you!' Winnie said. Gathering herself, she waved a dishcloth at him. 'It's nonsense, Mr Marshall!'

But Mr Marshall was scribbling in his book.

'I meant it,' Ron whispered once Mr Marshall had left. 'You know I did.'

When the letter arrived in the post two weeks later, Winnie knew exactly what it was. She hurried into the bar, holding it aloft, glad Francine was still at school so she could prepare herself.

'I've got the decision,' Winnie called at no one in particular. 'From the brewery.'

She sank down on a bar stool. So here it was. This letter would tell her the shape of her future. She had been so worried about this that she was even tempted to visit the travelling medium who read palms, but she'd resisted. Trevor would have laughed. One of the magazines had a 'how to read your own palm' section too, but when she did it herself all she found was that her life line had so many breaks you could hardly call it a line, it was more a series of dashes and dots, a cry for help in Morse code.

If the brewery said no, she'd go, and she'd go with dignity. It wasn't like she was going because she was no good, it was just circumstance. It was the times they lived in. She'd look for war work somewhere with accommodation attached.

Before they opened the envelope, Mac said they should definitely contest it – so it was clear what he assumed it said.

'What'll happen to the regulars?' he whispered.

The thought of her old boys – Nathan, Sid, Toby, Jim,

Old Jim, all with their individual heartaches – trudging around to find alternative public houses made her heart twist.

'We can't keep going just for them,' she said and he pulled a face. 'Read it for me, Mac.'

Mac couldn't. He passed it to Toby. Toby stood up as if he'd been waiting all his life to make this announcement.

'We regret to inform you that...'

Winnie nearly fell to the floor. She'd feared it, but she hadn't believed it. That was her scuppered. What the hell would she do now? Jobless, homeless... Francine might yet end up in a children's home after all.

'Bastards,' she hissed.

'No, wait. We regret to inform you that the White Horse and the King's Head will be closed for the duration of the war' – he looked around wonderingly – 'while we continue to support the Castle.'

He jumped off his chair.

'They believe the Castle is still viable. You're staying open!'

Now Winnie stood, shocked that her jelly legs could support her.

'We're still in business?'

Mac was already pouring drinks and lining them up.

And she still had a home?

'That calls for a drink,' Mac said.

'A celebration!' Winnie said. 'What do you think swung it for us?'

'They say what swung it for us,' Toby said, brandishing the letter – and for a moment she thought of Chamberlain's White Paper and what a mess that had turned out to be, and then she told herself to stop being so silly. The pub had been saved – wasn't that exactly what she wanted?

'Footfall!' Toby said. 'The Canadians are saving us. In more ways than one.'

'I guess you could say that,' she said, thinking of Ron. '*She is what I like most about the Castle.*'

When Scott Cuthbert came by, he insisted he'd never doubted it. It was lovely to hear, but also made her feel flat. It *had* been in doubt – it was only through ingenuity and hard work that they had made it. Without Francine, she knew it wouldn't have. She couldn't wait to tell her.

33

SPRING, 1943

Winnie

One evening an old school friend of Trevor's arrived, full of bonhomie and looking for his old pal.

'Smoking behind the bike sheds, is he?' the man joked.

'Not quite,' Winnie stuttered. 'He joined up and...'

The man put both hands on his head.

'What? No! I thought he was past it!'

Well, he is now, Winnie said to herself.

The conversation didn't break her heart as it would have done before. She was healing from the devastation of Trevor's death. She was getting over the shock, if not the loss.

She hadn't had dark thoughts for a while now either. There were reasons enough to have them – the war news was horrendous – but these days Winnie could open up the pub without thinking the door was going to flatten her. She could walk down the street without expecting a plane to crash on her. Perhaps the Nazis would invade. Perhaps the pub would be taken over by men in jackboots. But Winnie was coping; she could deal with anything.

Francine was no trouble – no, that was the wrong phrase, she was much more than 'no trouble'. When she had heard the pub was saved, she didn't believe it at first, then danced around the pub, elated. She was happy at school and happy in the holidays. How contented Winnie felt wishing the girl 'Goodnight!' or listening to her singing along to some song on the wireless. Sometimes they'd look at the globe – Francine always spun it too vigorously, like it was a conker or tennis ball – while Winnie would moon over the exotic names.

Francine would say, 'You should go!'

'Not on my own,' Winnie said playfully. 'You'll have to come with me.'

'I'm not going anywhere!' Francine shrieked.

These were fantastic moments and Winnie was aware she had gone from thinking she was the unluckiest woman in the world to thinking she was one of the luckiest. Perhaps she was just too busy to have such black fantasies any more. There was a pub to run, regulars and non-regulars to look after, a child to bring up, a brilliant daughter to worry about, darts competitions to organise, a memoir to help write, crossword clues to answer...

Scott was right: Francine had helped her recover. It was annoying, but true. And helping her recover had helped the whole pub recover. This was also true.

Ron Roscoe didn't come back for another while, and that was all right. It was good she wasn't in a position to escalate this, whatever 'this' was. It was enough to know that he was there, not far away, doing his thing. But after several weeks had gone by, he returned to the Castle. Came in with those twinkly eyes, the accent that was so exotic to her, and had he got even more handsome? When he smiled at her, she thought, he has, he really has.

There was a frisson about him that evening, a nervous energy that Winnie felt was directed towards her. *He's going to ask me for a date*, she thought. She felt like a young girl around him and the prospect made her feel flattered and excited. Why shouldn't she? Things might be busy, but she felt stronger than she had for a long time. She could do with a night out, dancing on the airbase; she had heard they had a wild time there. The young women who went couldn't speak highly enough of it. Not that that was why she wanted to go out with Ron...

But Ron pulled a face, and she realised why he had come: it wasn't for a date, it was almost the opposite.

'You're leaving?'

'Fraid so.'

'I thought...' she began. She hadn't thought enough. 'You were going to be here for the duration of the war.'

For the foreseeable, she thought – like Francine.

He swallowed. 'I'm not going back to Canada.'

'Oh?'

'I'm being sent somewhere else. While we're at war, we have no control over our lives.'

It seemed impossible that he wouldn't have control over everything. He wasn't a spotty-faced new recruit, he was a seasoned professional. She was surprised how distressed this news was making her feel.

'I thought you were in the kind of role where you stayed in one place.'

He grimaced. 'So did I.'

She always enjoyed his company. His calm authority, his kindness. His humour. The gifts. They had never, though, declared themselves to each other, and now she saw that it was too late. Like the daffodils, they had less time than she had imagined.

'The regulars are going to miss you.'

He had been helping Toby with the memoir, Nathan with the crossword clues, Sid with his confidence.

'I'll miss them too.'

'And Francine,' she added, thinking, poor child, who still believed everyone she liked went away in the end.

'And Francine,' he echoed. 'You've gone above and beyond for her.'

'Thank you.' She couldn't think straight. 'I guess it's goodbye then, Ron.'

He walked towards the door. Churchill was glaring at her back, wondering why she wasn't saying what was on her mind.

'Wait!' she called and he returned to the bar. 'I mean, when you come back it will be good to go out with you.'

'If I get back...'

'Don't say that!' Winnie was horrified. 'Of course you will.'

'Anyway, there's nothing I'd love more,' he said, smiling broadly now. 'It will give me something to look forward to.'

'It's difficult to predict the future,' she said earnestly. 'But after the war, Francine might have her father back. Or perhaps her cousins, and things will look very different.'

'I thought you were just asking me to go dancing?'

Once again, Winnie was mortified. Why had she leapt ahead like this? She knew why – because it was what she had been thinking! But now she had said it out loud, he must think she was a crazy lady. She couldn't speak.

'Whatever you meant, good,' he said hastily, his eyes locked on hers.

'Good,' she repeated. Dear God, what was the matter with her?

Then, in an unexpected move, Ron Roscoe leaned across the expanse of the counter, the sticky, beer-marked counter, and somehow, without thinking about it, she had leaned towards him too, and he pressed his lips on hers.

And it was wonderful.

34

Francine

On the wireless, they said, 'Love is in the air,' although Well-Developed Marjorie had just broken up with her latest boyfriend so it wasn't true for everybody.

It was after school and the boys were playing football on some scrub wasteland. Francine and Marjorie were half-watching. Marjorie had a very rare afternoon off. It was London kids versus Kettering kids, it always was. A Canadian soldier had agreed to referee, but he hadn't turned up. Maybe he'd found out how feisty the game got.

Francine was now thirteen, and among her peers she was known as a grown-up thirteen. She liked it when Marjorie confided in her, although she would have liked to join in with the football too. She did like football; Mr Cohen used to say, 'Why not play, bubbulah?' but when she tried, the boys didn't pass to her – even her own team, even Albert didn't – and when she did kick the ball, however accurate it was, they pretended it was rubbish. Even the nicer ones said things like, 'Better luck next time,' and she didn't want to think about what the nastier ones said.

'What do you think?' Marjorie asked, chewing a blade of grass.

'It's a good game.'

Albert went down, grabbing his ankle and calling for a free kick. However, when he realised no one was paying any attention, he jumped up and whacked the ball in the opponents' goal.

'No, about me breaking up with Nigel?' Marjorie clarified. She produced a pear from her bag and peeled it deftly with her penknife. She handed Francine a slice and Francine regretted nicknaming her 'Well-Developed Marjorie'; it was unkind, even if it was only in her head and she'd never dream of saying the phrase aloud, even to Albert.

'You don't *need* a boyfriend, do you?' Francine said, which was what Mrs Froud always used to say to Lydia, who was obsessed with love and marriage and had designed her wedding gown and cake several times over.

Marjorie agreed and then, after she ate her pear slice, she said she was in love with one of the young farmers. She didn't know his name yet but he was 'like Rhett Butler'. Francine didn't say it but the thought made her sad. She'd liked the idea of Marjorie being a friend and not anyone's girlfriend. She would have liked to lean her head on Marjorie's shoulder. She smelled so sweet. Sitting in the sunshine, eating pear slices, watching a game of football, her dice safe in her pocket, Francine was happy.

'What about you and Bertie?' Marjorie asked, eyelashes lowered.

'Huh?' Francine laughed. Albert was running around, his arms outstretched, as the Kettering boys booed him. 'Albert and I are friends.'

'That's how it begins...' Marjorie claimed.

Albert was now doing victory somersaults on the pitch. He turned to look at them, flexed a tiny bicep and waved. Francine waved back.

'He's sweet on you,' Marjorie was giggling, but it felt to Francine like a dark cloud came over them. She decided she would ignore it for as long as she could.

35

Winnie

Winnie got used to Ron Roscoe not being there. She was in the same position as so many in the country – missing someone. Not knowing where someone was. Trying to keep faith that her someone would return. And Winnie was luckier than many in that she had so much to occupy her.

Since there was a glass shortage, she asked regulars to bring in their own – another of Francine's ideas. Winnie had thought they would be annoyed, but Jim said, 'Apparently, that's how they're doing it in London,' which was the greatest vote of confidence there ever was.

The brewery had eventually sent a full report on their decision and Francine was pleased that so many of her ideas had been noted.

'Special commendation to the groups...' read Winnie delightedly. 'We hope to encourage other public houses to do the same...' That's all down to you, Francine.'

Francine paid attention to the minutest details of how the Castle was run. She had noticed that the brewery controlled everything.

'Wouldn't it be better if you did?' she interrogated Winnie, pen in hand.

'But that's impossible.' Winnie remembered having similar conversations with Trevor. 'They're good – compared to some.'

'But they could be better?' Francine asked.

'I guess.'

Francine's acumen was remarkable, but sometimes it was too much.

Winnie liked to be involved in Francine's life, from her schoolwork to her sparrows, to her hairstyles and her nutrition. Had she eaten? Why wasn't she wearing her coat? Susan had become fiercely private when she hit thirteen, but Francine was always happy to hear Winnie's opinions – she invited them, even. Their relationship made Winnie happy. On her occasional flying visits, Susan always remarked on the positive change in Winnie. Winnie could tell Susan was relieved about this.

Scott came in one lunchtime and Winnie's defences went up – what was amiss? – but he was grinning from ear to ear.

'I bring good tidings.'

'Francine's father?!' Winnie's heart raced.

'Ah, no. Sorry.' Scott looked embarrassed. 'It's her Southampton family.'

Winnie clutched her chest. Scott drank his beer and wiped the bottom of the glass. 'Turns out they're not actually in Southampton any more but they're desperate to see her.'

'Gosh!' said Winnie.

'You weren't expecting this?' Scott asked, biting his lip.

'I have been hoping for it,' Winnie lied. *Please let them be nice*, she prayed, but at the same time another prayer slipped through: *please don't let them take her away, not just yet.*

36

Francine

Aunty Winnie didn't like the idea of Francine getting the train to Brighton – which was where the Southampton family now lived – all by herself.

'I'll be fine!' Francine reassured her. 'What's the worst that could happen?'

This phrase was a mistake; Winnie turned puce.

Francine laughed. 'Don't worry, the train is safe as houses.'

Winnie didn't find that persuasive.

Winnie had lent her a carpet bag. She proposed popping a bottle of cider in it, 'for your relatives?', but Francine squealed she wasn't taking that across country, and Winnie hurriedly agreed. 'What was I thinking? Forgive me, Francine, I'm all over the place!'

It had been arranged that Francine would go for one week. Francine thought a week was too long, but she didn't like to say. She got the idea, from their excited exchanges on the telephone, that her cousins expected her to go and live there 'for the foreseeable'.

Winnie went puce about that too.

As the train puffed away from Kettering station, Francine could feel her mother's nervous anticipation and the babies yelled at the noise and Maisie screwed up her nose. 'Why do you get to go everywhere and I don't?' Francine looked around her to see if anyone else had heard them, but, as usual, nobody else had.

She had to change trains in London. It was there that she saw the devastation in the streets: rubble and masonry, bricks and wood. No matter how many times she'd heard about this on the wireless, it was still hard to take in. There were lots of men in uniform, but they didn't offer her chewing gum like the lovely Canadians. Two women in WAF uniform were laughing about a party. An old man without a hat asked for directions, but she couldn't help.

On the railway platform in Brighton, Marcie Rosen hugged Francine like she was saving her from drowning. She was her mother's cousin and she looked like her mother in some ways, but in others she didn't resemble her at all. Her hair was dyed red, but the roots were grey, and she had her mother's high cheekbones. Daddy used to say, 'You could slice bread with those!'

Marcie and her daughters Annie and Rachel worked all day in a factory and then the girls went out socialising most evenings. Marcie's son, Raymond, was in the air force. Marcie's husband, Larry, had also joined up.

Francine wasn't going to ask what happened in Southampton, but Marcie had no qualms about telling her. They had been bombed out, she had been sent to the local hospital and then the hospital was bombed.

'It collapsed like playing cards – all of us were packed in

the cellar. One woman gave birth in there! You think you're in the safest place. Can you imagine?' Marcie bit her lip. 'Sorry. I'm sure you don't need to imagine.'

They were staying in three rooms in a large terraced house. There were families all over the place, and the cousins were having an ongoing dispute with the landlord about the shared bathroom, though Francine couldn't work out exactly what.

The decor was strange – there was the head of a reindeer or a moose stuck on the wall, and an empty fish bowl – but it was habitable, and Marcie wasn't as aggravated about the decor as she was about the bathroom.

She kept asking, 'Are your people good to you?'

Francine said Winnie was, but Marcie was sceptical. 'Why didn't she bring you here then?'

'She's busy with the pub.'

Marcie didn't agree with pubs. Not in wartime.

'What's not to agree with?' Francine asked, but Marcie just shrugged.

That evening though, she said, 'Your grandfather was a drinker and a gambler.' She explained that had always put her off.

Francine explained it wasn't all about alcohol. She thought of the Brewery report, which had commended them for 'community spirit and the variety of groups who met there'. She mentioned they had raised funds for a Spitfire. She said Winnie was a great landlady and Marcie softened and said she supposed so.

Francine wished Winnie had come along. Everyone who met Winnie liked her, impossible not to.

'Any news about your father?'

'Not yet.'

If Daddy is still alive, you'll throw a 1 or 6. If he's dead, you'll throw a 2 or a 5. Don't know is 3 or 4.

Marcie's fingers knitted together. 'Do *you* think he's still alive?'

'I do.'

'Then he probably is,' Marcie said illogically. 'People have a feeling about these things. I knew the instant my father died.'

Marcie had work too. The flat was exceptionally tidy and needed nothing doing. After two days of sitting in the cold and waiting for her to come back, Francine decided she had had enough.

'I have school. And friends. And Tiger, my cat.'

'Are you sure? There are schools here, of course.'

'I'm sure.'

Marcie didn't say any more, but Francine thought she looked a tiny bit relieved.

Even though the cousins were a long way from Kettering, it felt nice knowing they were there. And even though Marcie Rosen couldn't possibly know if Francine's father was alive, the conversation about him had left Francine with a good feeling. She decided not to tell Winnie that her cousins had invited her to live with them – maybe Winnie expected her never to come back? Maybe Winnie *wanted* her never to come back? But when she returned to the pub, Winnie stopped serving Old Jim and rushed over to her.

'What's wrong? Didn't it go well?'

'It went well,' Francine said. 'But I prefer it here.'

'Oh?'

'I told them I had to come back early. For the Castle.'

Winnie smiled at her, misty-eyed.

'*Just* for the Castle?' she teased.

Francine shrugged, equally playful. 'Maybe I like being with my Aunty Winnie too.'

Winnie was beaming.

'Like? But not love?'

'Never.' Francine giggled and stuck out her tongue.

37

SPRING, 1944

Winnie

The country was still at war, yet Winnie felt almost at peace. The pub was safe for now and it was popular with regulars, community groups and Canadian servicemen. Francine was thriving. Sometimes, for a joke, Winnie would ask her to throw the dice and then they would debate the answer. Sometimes they would just see who got the highest or the lowest.

One time, Francine said something that made Winnie pause.

'Why don't you talk about my family?'

Winnie took a breath. 'I don't want to upset you when you're happy or make you sadder when you're already sad.'

Francine shrugged. 'They're with me all the time.'

'How do you mean?'

'The babies are always crying and Maisie is usually cheating and Mummy is frightened.'

'I'm sorry.'

'It's okay, I'm used to them now.' Francine's face was full of fortitude. Winnie loved her more than ever then and wished only that she could wave a magic wand and make it better. Only later did it occur to her that she had not once had a single vision, sign, or whatever you might call it, from Trevor. She had the opposite problem to Francine. Searching for reasons, she came up with ridiculous hypotheses: he died in France, he didn't love her, she wasn't receptive enough... Whatever it was, it made her heart ache.

'We thought it would be over by Christmas.' Toby was up to chapter twelve of his memoir. 'We were wrong. We thought it would be over by next year. We were wrong.'

'Nice use of repetition,' said Winnie.

Sometimes, Toby hit the doldrums. 'Is it worth bothering with?' he'd ask, a glum expression on his usually cheerful countenance. 'Does anyone care?'

'It's important,' she'd say to encourage him, 'lest we forget.'

'No one cares though, do they?'

'I care,' she said.

'And so do I,' Francine joined in and Winnie gave her a quick squeeze that she hoped conveyed, 'Good girl'.

'Thank you,' Toby said, stoically.

The pub was so busy, Winnie thought about getting someone in to help in addition to her and Mac, but then Francine persuaded her that she could do it, so Winnie let her do four hours after school and most of Saturday. She might only be fourteen but Winnie even let her take over the accounts – she couldn't do much worse than Winnie, could she?

She was with her for the foreseeable future, after all.

The D-Day landings were all over the news. The liberation of France was slower than everyone had hoped, and more terrible and more bloody, but it was happening. Finally, the tide was turning. And they were no longer drowning in the tide either, not in the same numbers anyway. They just might be winning the war.

Winnie thought about Ron Roscoe a lot. Where was he? Was he fatally wounded on some French beach? She was fairly certain she would hear if anything happened to him. No message had come, not yet. Sometimes, it felt like they had such a connection. She couldn't explain it – it was like they knew each other intimately, or had a deep understanding of each other.

Or maybe she was mistaken. Maybe he was like that with everyone.

Maybe he had met a younger, more suitable woman, a go-getting nurse with curly hair and sharp eyebrows and no flock of people dependent on her. Or perhaps a glamorous ENSA performer with dyed hair, tight clothing and the voice of an angel who could follow him all over the world. Why on earth would a man like him settle for a woman like her? Why would Ron Roscoe be interested in someone with so many complications when he could have anyone? It didn't seem plausible. The war must have turned him mad, that must be it. If he was still alive, that is...

38

Francine

Francine didn't like using the lavatories at the school with the strange gaps between floor and door, so usually the first thing she did when she got back to the Castle was to rush to the loo upstairs. It was one afternoon while she was doing exactly that when she first saw him.

She tried to go straight through the bar, like a dart to her target, without anyone noticing her, but Winnie called her over, her voice high-pitched.

'Francine, FRANCINE! Remember Mr Williams from your junior school?'

Francine smiled non-committally. Mr Williams eyed her up. His hair fruitlessly reached from one side of his head to the other and his skin had a waxy quality to it she hadn't noticed before, a candle about to melt.

'We meet again, Miss Salt!' he said.

He was in a group including some of the teachers from

Francine's high school. Three women, two older men, all smiles.

'Mr Williams was just telling me that he's going to become headteacher at your school! Isn't that exciting? And he's going to bring all the teachers here on Fridays as an...' She searched for the word. Mr Williams helpfully broke in, 'appreciation for all the work they do and all the hard work you do.'

'That's it!'

Winnie's peals of laughter made Francine feel even more uneasy.

Despite the go-ahead from the brewery, the Canadians and the community groups, Winnie was still desperate for customers. It was as though her fear had become ingrained and, even though the threat of closure had been removed, its spectre remained. Her daily refrain was, 'We've got to work hard to stay open.' Or more simply, 'Footfall!'

'Did you ever get your handwriting pen?' he asked.

Francine nodded. Didn't he remember? Didn't he remember his animosity towards her?

'Well deserved,' he said warmly.

Perhaps he wasn't as bad as she recalled. Perhaps he wouldn't be as bad as last time. People change, she reminded herself; Aunty Winnie always said so. Plus, it had been over three years now. Perhaps some people get nicer?

The next morning, Winnie was relishing the previous evening's bar takings.

'Such a relief. That was' – she counted on her fingers – 'seven teachers! And some of them can put the drink back! If they become regulars...'

Francine helped Winnie dry up the dishes. She usually liked this, standing side by side with her evacuation mother in the kitchen. Today, Winnie, in her apron and curlers, was in a brighter mood than usual. She clutched Francine with soapy hands. 'Trevor used to say, "One door closes, another opens."'

Surely the relevant point was: what were those doors opening on to?

Albert and Francine met most mornings at the oak tree to walk to school. The next day, he was nose down in a comic, which he dramatically shut when he saw her.

'I heard,' he began. 'He used to be so horrible.'

'Perhaps he won't be now. New school, new role...'

'Doubt it.' Albert was really down in the dumps. 'What do they say about leopards and spots?'

'That they'll eat your face off, given the chance?' Francine joked, but he didn't laugh.

As they walked, Albert kicked stones with his big boots and they went flying all over the place. He had power but no accuracy. He was tall now – how did that happen? He was a foot higher than her and it was as though he didn't realise it. He was always knocking into things, or her. 'He isn't used to his frame,' Winnie said kindly when Francine complained. He still had the same kind, freckly face though.

That morning he ran off out of sight for a moment, then came back with a daisy.

'To cheer you up,' he said shyly, handing it to her.

She looked at the yellow centre with its white petals. Daisies never failed to put Lydia in her mind. There was something about the freshness, the prettiness that was her to a T. She pulled at the petals the way Lydia would have done.

'He's still horrible. He's not horrible any more...'

She grinned at Albert.

'He's still horrible. He's not horrible any more...'

At last, he laughed.

She ended with a daisy stripped of its petals on: 'he's not horrible any more'.

'That's a good sign,' she said, holding up the stem.

'I don't know if that would stand up in court.'

Albert's voice was different now too. For a few weeks last year, it had swung up and down and you didn't know where it would land. Now its tone was so deep, sometimes she couldn't catch what he was saying; it would get lost in the wind in the leaves or in the rumble of the milk float.

Marjorie wasn't the only one who said Albert was in love with her. Others said it too. This fascination with putting people in twos: 'The animals go in two by two' also reminded her of Lydia. It felt like they were spoiling or smearing something that was precious to her. It felt like they were plucking the petals off her friendship.

They walked alongside the brook. Albert knew the names of all the wildlife. He loved the farm where he lived. He had perfectly slotted into the country way of life. It was hard to believe that he'd spent the first nine years of his life in a tenement block in the East End of London.

'Don't worry about Willy-Bum. I'll look after you, Francine,' he said.

She threw grass at him, laughing. 'I don't need looking after.'

39

Winnie

Winnie was opening up the pub at midday when a man she didn't recognise came barrelling in towards her.

'Be with you in a minute,' she called.

He wasn't one of her old regulars, nor one of her new locals. Not one of Mr Williams' teachers; and he definitely wasn't one of the Canadians. He was unshaven, in demob clothes. His breath smelled and his beard was grey and matted. Even Tiger didn't look impressed. Winnie wondered if he was one of those who had been fighting in Normandy. Poor fellas. She knew what Trevor would do. A pint on the house and a currant bun from upstairs to soak it up and then send him on his merry way.

'Mrs,' he called. He might have collapsed if the bar hadn't saved him. She detected a foreign accent.

'Take a seat,' she instructed. 'Let me hang up your coat. I'll get you a drink.'

He looked surprised.

'I need to know... Is there a Francine Salt here?'

That was when she realised who it was.

Winnie led Francine's father through the pub and up into the flat upstairs. She ran him a bath and he didn't resist. Some of the poor souls came back from fighting with all sorts: maggots and fleas weren't the worst of it. He waited as she carried pans of hot water through, leaning against the wall with his eyes closed, like a small child expecting a punishment.

When Mac came in she didn't tell him about the new arrival, she wanted Francine to be the first to know, but she asked him to try and acquire a razor from the village shop – Mac made a half-joke, half-enquiry about why she suddenly needed a razor, but she didn't explain.

Francine's father stayed in the bath for so long, and was so quiet, she wondered if he'd drowned.

Just before Francine was due back, she knocked on the bathroom door, told him it was time to come out and gave him an old shirt of Trevor's to wear. It was too big for him – he, like Francine, was slightly built – but it would do for now. Winnie was filled with nervous excitement. What was this going to mean for Francine, and for the family they'd built? She wanted to ask him questions – Was he planning to take the girl away? – but it was not her place to speak. One thing she knew – Francine had been waiting for this day for most of her young life.

40

Francine

Cycling home from school, Francine was dreaming of numbers and card games. There was a shady nook in the playground that was perfect for poker and that was where she was most lunchtimes, making shillings off older students.

Far from being the expressive one, nowadays Francine was famed for her poker face. The older students said she didn't give anything away, which she felt was funny because she felt stuffed full of raw emotions and it seemed incredible that they weren't visible to the rest of the world.

She was pleased that she had only seen Mr Williams once at school recently, and actually, he wasn't too bad. He'd simply said, 'How's the Salt child?'

Why he talked like that she didn't know.

'Fine, thank you, sir,' she had managed to respond, so maybe the daisy was right and he wasn't horrible any more. Certainly, he liked being in the pub and Winnie liked him and his friends being there too.

The bicycle was new. A Canadian soldier had given it to her before he left. Albert was sad because there were fewer of their dawdling walks to school, but some days she would wheel the bike next to him, and other times he had other things to do anyway.

Francine propped the cycle against the pub wall. As usual, her mind was on the lav. Hurrying across the bar, she called out 'Good afternoon!' to the regulars, and 'Fine, thank you!' when they asked after her day, but then, unusually, Aunty Winnie came out from behind the counter to greet her. Before she could protest, Winnie had her hand on her shoulder and was guiding her to the armchairs by the fire.

'What's go—'

Francine couldn't believe it at first. She scrubbed her eyes and blinked, as if the image in front of her might disappear. But no, it was still there. Like the sight of the collapsed shelter, this image would be there for the rest of her life. But this was a beautiful sight. She threw herself at him, and he held her so close she wasn't sure if she was dreaming. It was him, it was. And she was so happy, and at the same time, shocked, confused, guilt-ridden.

'My girl,' he said, over and over again, weeping. He smelled of Aunty Winnie's soap.

'I'm sorry, Daddy.'

They should all have been here – Mummy, Maisie, Jacob and Joe. They should all have greeted him home. She was the eldest child, she should have been able to save them. She had been sent out because of chicken pox and everything about that was wrong.

'I couldn't help it,' she hiccupped into his chest, her daddy's chest, poker face gone. 'I couldn't help them.'

She should have died, she thought. She was ashamed that she hadn't.

'You are here,' he said. He clutched her like he would rather die than be parted again. 'You made it.'

41

Winnie

Francine's father looked like a hermit with his yellow beard and his yellow teeth. He also seemed to have a permanent cold; he snorted into his handkerchief constantly. It gave Winnie bad memories of the Spanish flu. (Please God they wouldn't have another epidemic.)

Francine wanted him to stay on the sofa in the living room.

'What about the bed and breakfast you stayed in when you first came to Kettering, Francine?' Winnie said. 'It's not far.'

Francine blinked slowly in surprise and Winnie saw that she was hurt.

'Your father might be more comfortable there,' Winnie added. 'I'll pay, of course.'

Francine nodded, distrustfully. 'Can I go with him?'

Winnie was about to say no when she thought: What was the matter with her? Trevor would have knocked himself out for this serviceman and father. She needed to put her own anxieties behind her – or at least address what these anxieties were really about.

Winnie hadn't really believed Francine's father was still out there. There were so many dead or missing now, stacked up like used pint glasses, she had presumed that, even if Mr Salt had survived, unlikely, it would be impossible for him to be found or for him to find them. Scott Cuthbert had said after six months of shouting at people to look for him in the wrong place, it was virtually impossible.

And if Winnie had ever dared to dream that Francine's father would make it back, she hadn't pictured a traumatised stick figure who looked like he'd blow away in the first gust of wind.

Francine was turning the dice in her hand. She was exuberant and she couldn't understand why Winnie wasn't. Winnie realised she had to be careful that this didn't come between them. They had become so close over the last three years, it would be a shame to lose all that over the return of her father. This was the fulfilment of Francine's wishes.

'Of course he'll stay here!' she managed. 'I'll put bedding out in the living room, and you can both sleep there until Daddy works out what to do next...'

Francine squealed, 'You're the best!' and skipped off to tell him.

Winnie gulped. It was going to be a long few days.

Once he had shaved, cut his hair above his collar and put on clean clothes that actually fitted – Sid brought in a bagful of his son's – Mr Salt didn't look so out of place. He was only thirty-three or thirty-four, Winnie realised, and although there wasn't much he could do about the teeth, or the nose-blowing, within a few days he looked completely different from when he'd first arrived.

He helped out upstairs – he wasn't averse to dusting or washing up – and he also helped downstairs in the bar. He lugged barrels up from the cellar and delightedly answered the telephone in his foreign accent: '7893 – Ze Castle in Kettering. May I ask who speaks?'

He was definitely growing on her.

He broke up arguments in the bar – one about someone who was using the black market and another between two doctors at loggerheads over the Beveridge Report on welfare – he sat at the piano with Sid, he listened to Toby read extracts of his memoir and made helpful suggestions. Admittedly, he was less adept when it came to answering crossword clues.

He made Winnie strange-tasting tea and brought home dried fruits. He liked the windows open, but didn't mind when she went around shutting them, and he changed the light bulbs she'd been meaning to get round to. He was better at odd jobs than Mac, but he didn't rub it in his face and was instead polite and deferential to the other man. Probably politer than Winnie was.

'Why are you wearing that silly scarf?!' Winnie had enquired of Mac, who was wrapped up even though temperatures were rising.

'It's a nice scarf,' Mr Salt commented mildly. He was a born peacemaker, a mediator by disposition.

He quickly found a room in town in return for help with jobs around the house. Winnie suspected Scott Cuthbert had had a hand in that. He was also looking for work.

'What about here?' suggested Francine. 'Aunty Winnie always needs staff. She hasn't had a holiday in donkey's years.'

Winnie held her breath. Mr Salt laughed, a rasping sound.

'Mrs Winnie has had too much of me, I think.'

Winnie muttered something about not being able to afford to take anyone on – which was true.

'What kind of work are you looking for?' she asked.

'Anything,' he said.

'That's the spirit!' Winnie said, brightly. She liked him, she was adjusting to his being around, but she also looked forward to things getting back to normal – whatever that was.

42

Francine

Francine's father had been fighting with the Prinses Irene Brigade. He was in the Med, he was at the Nile, he was all over the map in her room. Francine marked the locations off with her pen, but he did not want to tell her much.

'Can't we talk about something else?' he muttered as she cuddled up to him, his braces leaving sweet indentations in her cheek.

That first night, Aunty Winnie had brought them in tea, apologising for the lack of biscuits, yet she mostly kept to herself in the pub, and Francine appreciated the space. Her father had headaches and sores, stomach pains and blisters. He got tired quickly – he reminded her of a travelling man Winnie once had to throw out of the pub. Beneath all that though, he was still Papa.

'You've been here all this time?'

'Not quite,' said Francine, wondering how to explain her experiences. 'I've been to other places too.'

He ran his fingers through her long hair. He called her Rapunzel.

'Don't be silly, Daddy,' she said.

'Why? She lived in a castle like you.'

Instinctively, she understood that in her father's mind she was still eight years old. She understood this because in her mind her father was still dashing and debonair, adoring husband to her mother and play-monster to his children.

They both had a lot to catch up on.

Sometimes she indulged him, but sometimes that didn't work. She brought out *The Princess and the Pea* and he wept. She introduced him to Tiger, and he adored her, but he didn't much like the sparrows. He asked if she still did cat's cradle (no), jacks (no); but when she showed him the dice he'd given her and told him she kept them with her at all times, he roared with laughter. She couldn't predict how he would react to anything.

He mightn't want to talk about his experiences in the war, but he did want to know about the night of the bombing.

'Do you remember?' he asked. His soapy smell had gone, replaced by cigarettes and whisky.

She remembered that, a few evenings before it happened, she and Maisie had had a rotten row. It always upset Mummy when they argued, but the urge to bicker was stronger than concern for her. It was over a game of dominos. Maisie was cheating but refusing to admit it. She remembered nappies hanging on the line and the babies had less milk than usual and Mummy was fretting because the supply ships were getting bombed.

The babies had cried and she remembered Mummy clapping her hands over her ears, moaning, 'Just let me sleep.'

She remembered the last morning when she woke up in

the shelter: the all-clear had gone and the kettle was whistling, but Mummy was louder.

'What's that on your face?'

Francine didn't know anything – but she did feel an itch on her belly and, as she moved in to scratch it, Mummy yanked up her nightie.

'Mu-um!'

They both looked down and saw a dot-to-dot on her tummy, like the ones she used to do at school. She was repelled by them yet, at the same time, enchanted.

'I can't have you ill now,' Mummy implored, as though Francine had deliberately connived to have spots in order to make Mummy's life more difficult.

Francine had stood patiently as she examined her.

'No school for you. Go in the house and go to bed. Stay away from the others.'

'But, Mummy—'

'Run back to the house. I'll sort you out in a minute.'

Mummy didn't come back in for another hour. While she waited, Francine wrote a letter to Lydia complaining about how bored she was. When her mother came in, she was no longer so tense, she was resolute. She'd come up with a plan.

'You'll stay at Mrs Hardman's. She's already had it. Go now.'

'But what about the bombs?'

'It's just for a little while, darling. If the sirens go, run to the cellar.'

Her mother kissed her on the forehead absent-mindedly, and Francine trooped off.

Mrs Hardman was out all day and in the evening, too. When the sirens went, Francine made her way to the cellar. She didn't hear Mrs Hardman return. When she woke up the next morning, she was thinking of porridge and toast, and hoping that Maisie would get spots and join her, because, she had just realised, Maisie wasn't so hateful after all.

Where was the all-clear? Why hadn't there been an all-clear?

Then there it was – a flash of white light and the most terrible noise, a roar, a rushing like the sea, and then nothing and everything vanished and then people poured into the yard. The whole shelter was gone. Disappeared. So obliterated, they didn't even know where to start the digging. It had all become nothing. 'Vanished into thin air', as Mrs Howard had once told her, a phrase invented by Shakespeare.

How could she tell her father this?

'Nothing at all,' Francine lied.

Daddy's eyes were squeezed shut. 'That's for the best.'

43

Francine

Francine saw Mr Williams in the pub on Friday evening, and he was nice as pie. Winnie fluttered around him and the other teachers and introduced them to Francine's father. Mr Williams thanked him for his service, clasping his hand between both of his and calling him a 'charming man'. But then when Francine next saw him at school, a few days later, he went narrow-eyed and cold. It was in the school hall and he called out her name. At first, she mostly felt embarrassment; the fear came later.

'What have you got in your hand?'

She'd been caught with her dice – when she was usually so careful to keep them hidden. She slipped them in her mouth.

'I haven't got anything,' she said, palm-up, look! Could he spy the dice in her cheek like a squirrel's hoard of nuts?

'See me after school, Francine Salt.'

Whenever anyone used her full name, it meant bad news.

She remembered Well-Developed Marjorie saying that it was only certain Londoners who piqued Mr Williams' interest. It seemed she was one of them.

His office was about three times the size of Mr Cuthbert's and nothing like it.

'So you *are* a Jew-girl,' he said in a resigned way. 'I did wonder...'

She held on to her dice and imagined her father punching him on the nose although that didn't seem likely. She wondered if she should deny it. How did he even know?

Mr Williams continued to glare.

'What have you got to say for yourself?'

'Nothing, sir.'

'You didn't tell me.' He kept pointing his finger close to her face.

She didn't know what to say.

'You tried to cover it up. Hide it from us.'

'I didn't, sir. It just didn't—'

'I don't like being lied to,' he snapped, and Francine stared at the inkwell and wished she could drop down into it. Swim away in a river of ink, back to Aunty Winnie or Papa. She wasn't sure what Mr Williams was more angry about: the dice? Being Jewish? Both? But he was very angry and she couldn't ask.

'Write it out. "I do not lie to my headteacher".'

'How many times, sir?'

'Two hundred times. Or I will beat you to Satan's Synagogue and everyone will thank me.'

Francine often heard the babies screeching but not this time; they were gazing in open-mouthed horror. Mummy and Maisie looked petrified.

'Take that shocked look off your face. You people make me sick.'

'I'll tell my host father.' Albert's mouth was a grimace. Hands in pockets, he kicked a stone until it disappeared under a hedgerow.

Francine shook her head wildly. 'It'll make things worse.'

She had been kept in the office for two hours. Mostly Mr Williams scowled at her, his teeth glinting. She had a strange yearning to cut off his hair, or at least tip it the other way.

'He'll probably forget about me,' she said, with more hope than she felt. 'Or move on to someone else.'

Mr Williams was in the pub that Friday. He drank with the other teachers, and got squiffy. He even called her his best student, to Winnie's delight. But then, maybe a month later, when she thought the threat had passed, she was walking alone in the corridor and he burst out of his room.

'You were running,' he said.

'But I wasn't,' she told him, bewildered that he could think so.

'My office, after school.'

It was raining, that bouncing rain that couldn't last long, and she and Albert usually loved a rainy walk home. She imagined Albert waiting patiently for her at the school gate, hands in pockets.

'Two hundred lines: "I can't be trusted".' He scowled to himself. 'There will be a reckoning soon.'

Next morning, Francine didn't want to go to school. She feigned a stomach ache, but Aunty Winnie wasn't having any of it and shooed her out at the usual time. Francine didn't go to school; instead, she walked to Mr Cohen's house – her last refuge. She went round to the back and tried the door, but it was locked. She put in the key, wiggled it, but it didn't fit any longer.

Someone was coming.

Francine darted back round to the front of the house. There was a mother with a baby on her hip looking out of the window, worried. Guiltily, Francine raised a hand and waved. She didn't want to frighten her.

On the way back to school, she dropped the keys into a bin, and they clattered like skeletons.

She didn't always see Mr Williams. Some weeks went by without her hearing his particular tread or seeing that comb-over. But every now and then she did, and his teeth would twinkle like rogue stars.

'To my office, Francine.'

She never knew what she was there for. She asked one time and he chortled. 'That says it all, doesn't it?!'

Even thinking of Lydia or Valerie didn't help. They'd never get in such a mess.

'Does Mrs Eldridge know you're a Jew?' he asked one time.

Francine shrank from him. 'I don't know…'

'Louder.'

'I don't know.'

He laughed, horribly. 'You people.'

She hadn't thought about it before. It had never been mentioned, which she supposed meant that Aunty Winnie didn't. She remembered overheard conversations. The man from the brewery talking about the landlord of the King's Head – 'tight as a Jew.' One of the Canadians saying, 'Hitler might be a bastard, but he was right about the yids,' and Mac laughing like a drain. And Winnie never said anything. 'No politics in the Castle,' was her motto. Or 'We need to be neutral.'

He pushed a paper across the desk.

'One hundred lines.' He'd decided two hundred took too long. '"I will not be sly".'

And then there Mr Williams was, at the Castle on a Friday night again. In her castle, her home, her sanctuary, pretending nothing was amiss.

'Come and sit with us,' he said, patting a stool.

'I'm going upsta—'

'Have a chat first,' Winnie insisted, smiling. Winnie thought a headteacher who was interested in his pupils was a marvellous thing. 'Get him on side,' she whispered. 'He's influential.'

'Has Mr Salt found work yet?' Mr Williams asked.

'Not yet,' mumbled Francine.

'A shame,' he said. 'I wish I could help.'

Another teacher, the white-haired lady, who had a faint moustache and taught history, said, 'Run along, sweetie, you don't want to be stuck with us old folk!' But Winnie came over, drinks lined up on a wobbly tray and her Cheshire-cat smile.

'Another round, please, dear Mrs Eldridge.'

'Coming right up.'

Francine knew what she was thinking: footfall. The Canadians would be going home soon, and local customers were worth their weight in gold.

That night, Francine was supposed to do the bingo. She dealt out the cards to each of the tables and could feel him watching her again. She walked to the front, but nerves made her clumsy and she dropped the basket of balls.

'Francine?' Winnie was watching her, with tilted head. 'We're waiting!'

Aunty Winnie, who she loved.

Francine ran upstairs. She leapt into her bed. He was spoiling everything. The babies were screeching again. She covered her ears.

Winnie was calling after her, her kind face wreathed with concern – just like her mother's.

Tell her? Tell her not?

'What happened, darling?' and when Francine said nothing, 'Do you want me to get your daddy?'

'Just let me sleep,' Francine said, rolling away from her.

44

Winnie

Winnie observed Francine and her father closely. Sometimes, they went out for walks, played cards or listened to the wireless. Sometimes, Francine's father cancelled because he was too poorly. He didn't seem to be making plans for the future and Winnie didn't know where she stood. After a few weeks had elapsed, she asked him outright.

'Will you be taking Francine away?'

He raised a trembling hand and said, 'I thought she liked it here.'

'You're her father,' Winnie replied, trying to hide her incredulity. Was he a man or a mouse? 'You decide.'

This seemed to tie him in knots. Had he not thought that that was the reasonable thing to happen?

'I don't have a home or a job yet,' he mumbled.

'I know,' said Winnie. She didn't know what she felt. Disapproval? Pleasure? Both? 'Francine can stay for as long as she likes. Obviously.'

She didn't know why she said obviously. There was nothing obvious about it. She was disappointed for Francine that she was saddled with a weak father, but for herself she was pleased: it wasn't the worst possible outcome after all.

Winnie had the sewing alliance doing an event in the back room. They were a fantastic group of ladies, and had been thrilled to find a home – they'd seen one of Francine's notices. There was a crossover with the knitting circle and also with the book group on Tuesday mornings that had opened with *I, Claudius*.

It was early evening and already busy. Winnie was stacking the chairs in the back room – the sewing alliance left a terrific mess – when she heard a commotion in the front bar, and hurried in. She was not in the mood for a drunken brawl. She saw someone was being hugged. Someone was being welcomed. Then she heard that distinctive deep voice, that lovely accent that rumbled straight to the core of her.

'Hello, Mrs Eldridge. Long time, no see...'

'Look who's here!' Jim and Toby shouted as one.

'The man of the hour!'

'The wanderer returns!'

Ron shook everyone's hand – why was he taking so long?! – before he got around to her, and then he gazed right into her eyes: relief, happiness, fear, it was all there. It had been over a year since they'd seen each other. She'd had no idea if he was even alive.

'Good to see you, Ron,' she said, as she had imagined saying ever since he'd left. She delivered her lines perfectly, then held out her hand to shake, but he pulled her into a wonderful bear hug instead.

Be careful what you wish for, she thought. It's been so

long. He's bound to have met someone more suitable, someone young and free. Or he might have forgotten their tentative overtures... the kiss – only one kiss, but what a kiss! Yet as his eyes locked on hers she knew, she just knew, he hadn't forgotten.

'You're a sight for sore eyes,' he said and blushed.

Winnie gulped. She was beset with awkwardness and self-consciousness. Enough with the emotions. She told him business was surprisingly booming. Francine was a great assistance. He chuckled. 'I can see that.' When she got to: 'Francine's father is back', his eyes lit up, there was no mistaking that.

'Wonderful! And he's well?'

'Pretty well,' she said. They could get into that another time. She was sure Ron would know more about the frayed nerves of soldiers coming back from war than she did.

He nodded thoughtfully. 'And you?'

'Surviving.'

'You can't say fairer than that.' He smiled. 'And Tiger?'

'Still a raving lunatic,' she said. Oh, it was good to hear his laugh.

Jubilant, Sid got on the piano, and some of the regulars sang along. She couldn't stop marvelling at his return and he occasionally glanced back at her and, when he did, he gave her an I'm-glad-I'm-here smile.

Winnie called Francine down to see Ron, and she did so without dissent, but before too long, she trooped back upstairs. Winnie realised suddenly that she was hardly ever downstairs these days.

'Isn't she growing up?' she said, although Francine hadn't been growing, particularly. She looked much younger than her fifteen years.

'That's what happens.' He grinned. She thought he

would say more, but then his friends called him over and apologetically, he said, 'Looks like we're doing a pub crawl tonight.'

'Good luck with that,' she said.

'I'll come back some time when it's less busy.'

'Do that! Absolutely!' she said too loudly and too keenly, but he smiled, thank goodness, and said, 'I can't wait.'

Over the next few weeks, Ron was busy with work and the pub was always crowded, so there was little danger of them speaking alone. Winnie and Ron exchanged small talk and a joke or two. Sometimes she could feel him gazing at her, and maybe he knew she was watching him, but that was about the extent of it until one evening he asked if he could help clear up afterwards. He said it would be nice to catch up.

My goodness, thought Winnie. What did 'catching up' entail? She couldn't concentrate for the rest of the shift and could only think how his kiss had made her swoon. She felt like a woman possessed. When it came to closing time, she sent Mac away early and she and Ron cleared up together. He didn't speak much while he was helping, just, 'Like this?' and 'Shall I put these over here?' kind of thing, but when Winnie said he'd done enough, he should get himself a drink, he did.

He leaned towards her and in a softer voice he said, 'Is Francine all right?'

'How do you mean?'

'I don't know,' he said. 'She seems different.'

'How so?'

'It's like a light has been dimmed.'

Winnie felt insulted. Of all the things to say, this was

probably the most hurtful. Was he suggesting she was negligent?

'In what way?' she asked icily.

'No, you've done a terrific job.' He realised she was hurt and was now trying to backtrack. 'It's probably just growing up.'

Winnie wiped down the already-wiped counter. Sometimes, she wished she could be more like Churchill and come up with something both cutting and funny. 'A light has been dimmed?' The phrase wouldn't leave her. It was like one of those propaganda ones. Keep Calm. Dig for Victory. She had, of course, noticed Francine was quieter than usual, but she had told herself it was age-related, boy-related, grief-related, nothing to worry about. Ron voicing this meant she couldn't dismiss it any more.

'Winnie,' he said, 'I didn't come here tonight to upset you... I came here to say I missed you.'

'I missed you too, Ron,' she whispered.

'Tell me if there's hope.'

Winnie's heart was fluttering wildly.

'How do you mean?' she asked, stalling for time.

'For us. I don't want to start up anything if there's not a possibility... I'm not that type of man. It's all or nothing with me.' He paused. 'And I think you're the same.'

Winnie swallowed. She didn't know what was the right thing to say, or what she wanted to say, and if they were the same thing or not.

'I don't know,' she admitted finally. 'I'm still a bit lost.'

'I see that,' he said. 'But I'm not lost. I know exactly what I want.'

And then Mac came crashing back in. Somehow, the mad cat had got in his bag and stolen his ration book, his mum would kill him if he didn't find it, and the catching up was over.

45

SPRING, 1945

Winnie

The end of the war was coming. Susan had been saying it since last year, Scott Cuthbert had been saying it since Christmas. The wireless had been saying it since February or March. Despite all the warnings, the Castle was running out of drink. After six years of keeping the place open through thick or thin! Trevor would have been apoplectic.

Winnie really did have to water down everything – with the customers' knowledge, that was. She begged the brewery for more deliveries and they said they'd do their best, but it was the same all over the country. The nation's drinkers had started celebrating already.

'What if it's a false alarm?' Francine asked cautiously. Winnie's pessimism had rubbed off on her.

'It's not,' Winnie told her. 'Oh, Francine! Can you imagine not being at war any more?'

Even at this momentous news, Francine hardly raised a smile. Ron wasn't wrong, she was different. No matter how

Winnie cajoled her, to 'lighten up!' Or 'give us a smile' (the
same lines her customers used on her), Francine was melancholy. She also kept losing things: her coat, her plimsolls, her
key. It was like her head wasn't screwed on properly.

Winnie realised she probably should have arranged a
victory party at the Castle – one final push – but not only
was the pub depleted, Winnie felt that way too. So when
Ron asked her to join the celebrations with the Canadians on
the airbase instead of opening the pub, she made the decision
to go. She had been stalwart for a long time, why not do what
she wanted for once?

Over the telephone, an exuberant Susan had agreed.
'Time to put yourself first, Mum!' she said. When Winnie
asked what Susan was planning to do, she said she had been
offered work in New York for a new international organisa-
tion. It was tremendously exciting.

Winnie gulped. 'I meant tonight?'

Susan laughed. 'Tonight is for letting our hair down.'

She also said: 'Mum, thank you for never holding me
back,' which made Winnie glow with pride.

The war was over! And Ron Roscoe, wanted to spend
this special night with her. Being with him was like being
wrapped in a warm blanket. She felt cocooned in his attention – was that the right word? She felt comfortable yet ready
to emerge.

Naturally, Winnie worried about Francine, especially on
such a big occasion, but Francine said not to worry, she had
plans with Albert anyway. Mac was also happy not to work.
He'd pulled his apron over his head, getting tangled in that
daft scarf: 'I'm off...'

'Five across,' said Old Jim, 'ENJOY – that's for you,
Winnie!'

Sid played a jazzy number before thumping down the

piano lid. They'd asked him to play the organ at the church. Toby said he had been visited by the muse, so he was going home to get chapter thirty written. Nathan was rereading Anthony Trollope. Jim had family to see. And some of the demobbed servicemen were having an early night – or as one of them put it, trying to get their wives in 'the family way'.

So Winnie closed up and got ready for the party with Ron.

'It's all or nothing with me,' he'd said.

All, she thought, *definitely all, tonight.*

46

Francine

Albert was delighted to be asked to the Castle and Francine felt nervous that he was delighted for reasons she didn't want to contemplate, but she stuffed away these reservations. She and Albert were old friends, friends like she, Lydia and Valerie used to be, that was all.

'You didn't want to go to the street party?' he asked from under his cap. He was acting shifty, though, shiftier than usual.

Several neighbours were putting out tables in the streets and bands were readying to play. Winnie had been loaning out tablecloths and spoons all week.

'Not really, you?' Francine replied.

'I'd always rather be with you.' His voice shook. Francine glared.

'Where's Mrs Eldridge anyway?' he asked.

'Dancing on the airbase with Canadians.'

'Dancing?' Albert laughed at the prospect. 'Isn't she too old for dancing?'

'You're never too old,' Francine scolded him.

'Be good, kids,' Mac said. He'd come in for some beer he'd stashed away. He put his fingers over his lips. 'Don't worry, it's all paid for.'

Albert grinned. 'We weren't.'

'Don't do anything I wouldn't do,' Mac finished before racing off, full of excitement.

Francine wondered what he wouldn't do. Nothing, she supposed. The man was a liability.

'You seen your dad lately?' Albert asked.

'I'll probably see him tomorrow.'

Her father had got a job in a barber's shop. 'You cut hair?' Francine had squealed.

'I have many talents you don't know about,' he told her, mysteriously.

Francine and her father had settled into a routine. He came in the pub on Friday evenings and they spent Saturdays or Sundays together. Sometimes in the pub, sometimes walking or at his shop.

From the moment Albert met him, he had been fascinated by Francine's father. His story, his experiences, everything about him intrigued him.

'Does he like me, do you think?'

Francine shrugged. Her father talked about many things, but he had not once mentioned Albert.

'I don't know. Aunty Winnie certainly does though. She loves you.'

Francine teased Winnie that she would have preferred to have taken in a boy. Winnie always chuckled and said, 'They'd be less of a bother than you!'

Albert grinned, content with that. 'I like her too.'

. . .

Francine couldn't tell her daddy about what was happening to her at school. Daddy was jumpy these days. Loud noises made him sweat. He bit, not just his nails like her, but the skin around them until it bled.

He kept saying, 'If your mum were here, everything would be all right.'

Well, she's not, Francine wanted to say. *Get used to it, I had to.* But her mummy shook her head, looking sadder than ever.

If, a few years ago, she had imagined herself and her daddy walking off into the sunset, now she had different impulses. She didn't want to go anywhere. The thought of leaving Kettering filled her with dread, even if it was with him. She feared this would seem disloyal, but fortunately, her father didn't seem to be making moves to take her away either. He accepted that the Castle was Francine's home. It was hard to describe – she felt linked to it, in a way she hadn't to anywhere before. Maybe not even the flat at Romberg Road. But she understood her position at the Castle was also precarious in a way that it hadn't been at Romberg Road.

Albert had never been in the bar when no one was there before. The lighting was low and their voices echoed off the walls. He rolled his hands across the mahogany surfaces, he spun round on one of the stools, then he asked about the pictures.

'They're silent screen actresses,' Francine explained. 'That's Clara Bow – I don't know the others.'

Francine knew that when she ran the pub – *if* she ran the pub – she would put these pictures in the back room and get some new ones in here. She often thought about giving the place a freshen-up.

'How was Willy-Bum this week?' Albert was the only one who still called him that.

'Didn't see him, thankfully,' said Francine, and he gave her such a sympathetic look tears came to her eyes.

'Want to play?' she asked.

Albert never said no to that. 'Always,' he said.

'Let's get drunk!'

The last time (and first time) they'd played this game was at Mr Cohen's house that time. Albert must have remembered it because he immediately started staggering around the bar and drooling.

'Fwancine!' he called, miming a drunk. 'More!' and then he fell into the coal scuttle. He picked himself up, laughing, and brushed himself down.

'This time we'll do it properly!' Francine said, grabbing a bottle of Scotch. 'Look what I got!'

Albert stood up straight, no longer acting.

'I'm not doing it *really*!' he said. 'Just pretending.'

'It'll be fun...'

Albert's mouth fell open and he stared at her, as though he didn't know her as well as he'd thought. Francine's skin prickled.

'No,' he said, horrified. 'Absolutely not.'

'Why not?'

'Because...'

'Because you're scared?' she teased him, but she was hurt. Albert was supposed to be her friend. Lydia would have drunk with her. Lydia would have done everything, the naughtier the better.

'It'll be fine! It's what all the adults are doing.'

'I said no,' he snapped.

Albert pretended to be adoring, but he wouldn't do this one thing for her? He walked round the bar and grabbed his coat from the hook. There was a finality about his actions that surprised her. She hadn't realised how strongly he felt.

'Bertie?'

He buttoned up his coat, pulled the sleeves over his wrists. Then he looked at her, with a pained expression.

'My parents drank a lot. It's not nice.'

'It's not the same.'

'It *is* the same.'

The main door was locked and bolted in a million ways.

'You'll have to go out the back way,' she told him. Now he wouldn't even look at her. He scuttled off, not embarrassed, more hurt.

She thought he would come back, change his mind, join her, like he always did. She imagined him returning contrite. She would hold out before forgiving him, but then forgive him she would.

He did not come back. She was on her own. Again. She was always on her own.

She unscrewed the cap of the bottle and poured herself a drink. That sound, that soothing sound of liquid on glass. That smell, like something unleashed. What was it Winnie said about the troublemakers who came to the Castle? 'They drink to forget.'

Francine had lots of things to forget, an entire mountain of rubble, so maybe a drink would be as good a place as any to start.

She remembered something else about the night of the bombing. She hadn't been able to sleep. The cellar was horrible. It was agony for her to be alone. She'd never liked it, not in London, not in Somerset. And it wasn't just that; the chicken pox was keeping her awake too. As soon as one spot's itchiness faded, another clamoured for attention.

The garden was in blackness, and you weren't allowed

torches or candles since the Nazis could see everything. She crept out though, grass and weeds scratchy against her itchy legs. Stubbing her toe on something. The darkest night. She remembered rat-a-tat-tatting on the shelter door and then, when no one opened it, forcing it open it herself.

'Out!' Mummy had yelped, startled, half asleep.

'Please let me stay here.'

'I can't, darling,' Mummy said. 'I'm already going out of my mind.' She gave Francine a blanket. 'Everything will look better in the morning.'

Those were the last words she ever heard her mother say.

47

Winnie

The sun went down and then the most impossibly beautiful streaks of colour and possibility lit up the sky. How nice to watch the sky and not think in terms of whether it was a good night for bombing.

'I still can't believe it's over,' Winnie said, as Ron signed her in at the gate. She had been saying that a lot.

'In Europe,' he said. His voice was so deep, it rumbled right through her. 'We've got Japan to beat yet.'

'Sorry,' she said, and he smiled.

'There's plenty to celebrate.'

The relief was exquisite. The Nazis were defeated, the Japanese would be soon. And Canadians knew how to hold a party.

The air-force band was already playing when they reached the hall, and Ron pulled her onto the dancefloor. She was one of the oldest women there, but she was used to that. Ron wasn't so young himself. Plus, she could keep up with the best of them. How happy she was in Ron's arms, one hand on the small of her back, the other encasing her own; how easy it all felt, how natural. Occasionally someone would yelp, 'Victory!' or, 'We stuffed those Nazis,' or, 'Never again!' and everyone would clap, whistle or dance harder.

It went on for hours, wonderful hours, dancing, kissing, whooping. Winnie had celebrated the end of the Great War but she had never known a night like this. Even as she danced, it felt historical, it felt significant. She couldn't stop smiling; sometimes, she even let out a laugh. Many people would be mourning tonight for all those lost, but for Winnie tonight was about the living.

Ron had never looked so handsome. He twirled her around, nuzzled her collarbone. She felt so at ease with him. Sometimes, they broke off for drinks or to talk to some of his people, but mostly he was attentive just to her.

Then, and it felt way too soon, the bandsman was apologising: 'Time for bed. Some of us have work tomorrow!'

And there was more clapping and cheering.

When Ron asked Winnie if she wanted to see where he was billeted, she had already decided, had known from the start of the evening, what her answer would be.

All.

Ron had shared with a man who'd, fortuitously, gone back to Canada last week, so now he had the hut all to himself. There wasn't much to see: two wooden chairs, two beds, two desks, one trunk, one man.

He sat down on one of the beds.

Winnie felt like she could hardly breathe. She should leave now, she thought, she couldn't face his loveliness or her own desire for him. It was overwhelming. It demanded too much of her. And what about her dear Trevor?

'Come over here,' Ron said gently.

It had been a long time since she had felt like this. She sat on one of the chairs and he shook his head, slowly, deliciously.

'Not there,' he said in such a low voice it was a wonder she could hear. He patted his legs.

'I don't know if I can...' she whispered.

'Come on,' he said. 'There's plenty of room.'

Of course, whether there was enough room wasn't what she was worried about. But she got up and, if it's possible to die from self-consciousness, she thought she might. She went over to him, her face aflame.

She lowered herself onto his lap and managed not to sigh. He brought his lovely arms round her. This plain old hut was the most wonderful place in the world. His head was over her shoulder, and she stayed still as she could. He gently moved her head so that he could kiss her.

She looked him directly in the eyes and she could resist no longer.

'Oh, Ron...'

Winnie wanted to stay here, in Ron's arms, where she belonged, for ever. They were in bed together, under the sheets. The war was over – and she had just made love, twice! with a man who had been patient and accepting and loyal. And more than that, Winnie thought to herself, as she went to the bathroom and tidied herself up. She couldn't resist a satisfied giggle, remembering the last few hours. So much more.

He told her he was attracted to her from the moment they first met but the moment he *really* fell for her was when she came to the base and kept saying she was mortified.

'It was the way you said it,' he elaborated. 'That and your red cheeks.'

Winnie laughed and said mortified again and again until he kissed her to stop and moved on top of her.

As for the love-making, she had thought she might have forgotten what to do! Ron had certainly helped her remember. But difficult as it was, she had to go back – actually, she *wanted* to go back too. She wanted to check up on Francine and the Castle. She still had duties and responsibilities. She was not a flibbertigibbet – even when she was young she hadn't been.

Ron wanted to walk with her, so they set off, and there was something soft in their bodies and relaxed in their mood, after all the noise and exuberance of the night. It was a quiet, reflective journey – until they banged into Mac and one of the young women from the knitting circle.

'Just taking Mrs Phelps home from the street party,' Mac said quickly.

Mrs Phelps looked the worse for wear, and the street party had finished hours ago, but Winnie was hardly in a position to judge.

She and Ron kissed at the pub door. She didn't want him coming in when Francine was there. Especially not recently, with Francine's unpredictable moods. Who knew what would push her over the edge? But Ron understood anyway; he was the perfect gentleman. Yet tonight – maybe it was the drink or the excitement or the possibilities in the air – he still wanted everything clear and above board.

'They will be sending me back any day now, Winnie,' he said. 'But I don't want to say goodbye.' He paused. 'Do you understand what I'm saying?'

'I'm not quite sure,' Winnie said, suddenly shivering.

It was one thing to have a man who wanted to be with her on this most special of nights. It was quite another to have a man who wanted to spend all his tomorrows with her. To make plans, to invest, to give himself. That was something else, that was something she hadn't dared to think about.

'I want you to come home with me, to Canada.'

48

Winnie

Winnie thought she might burst with joy. Ron Roscoe
wanted to be with her. He wanted her. And she wanted him.

Twenty-five years after she had first dreamed of getting
away from Kettering, of a life of exploration and travel, she
was being offered the chance. Away from here, away from
the pub, away from the dreary English weather. Off to somewhere new. Different. A change. Even if she didn't like
Canada, at least it would be new and exciting but Winnie
knew she would love it. She was made for Burlington. Her
heart was singing – not just for Ron but for this brave new
world, this bright new life that was waiting for her.

It was what she had always wanted, before she'd lost
track of what she wanted.

But then doubts followed joy. Confusion took her over,
just as soon as Ron had disappeared from sight.

There was Trevor, the Castle and all his dreams, and all
her memories, and all that she knew. Even if she could work

her way around that, there was a far bigger obstacle –
Francine. Francine, her traumatic past and her fear of being
left. Francine who seemed to be getting quieter by the day.
However, as Winnie undid all the locks, she had a revolu-
tionary idea. Not fully formed yet, but a blurry suggestion, a
potential plan.

Francine could come to Canada too! When they used to
look at the atlas, it had mostly been Winnie speaking,
Francine giggling, but it had, she hoped, at least stirred a
curiosity in the girl. Winnie imagined them embracing this
new world together, hand in hand: 'This is my other daughter.' Why not? The cousins no longer in Southampton
wouldn't object, and her father was so docile, how could he
object to anything? It occurred to her, crudely, that it was a
blessing in disguise that Francine's father was so placid.
While he frustrated her, she should be grateful. A stronger
man might have whipped Francine away from her and
broken her heart.

Ron would agree – of course he would – you could say
that he and Francine were friends first! It was Francine who
had brought him into her eyeline. It was Francine who had
supported their relationship all the way.

She would say yes to Ron. They both would say yes.

That was when she realised there was someone in the
bar. She could smell it, sense it: she was not alone.

Trevor had told her what to do if there were burglars. Get a
weapon, and attack first, don't give them a moment, they
won't expect it. Then run. Winnie strode behind the bar and
reached for a bottle. She would smash whoever it was over
the head. She was surprised at her cold efficiency. She could

handle an intruder. She hadn't got through the war just to be robbed at the end of it.

'Who's there?'

There was no reply.

Winnie edged around in the darkness, ready to strike, and then saw something. A body on the floor. Oh God.

Then she saw it was Francine curled up like a baby. Winnie put the bottle down and flew to her side.

'Francine, FRANCINE!'

The girl was out cold. Winnie's eyes slowly adjusted to the dark as she looked around for the criminal.

'Who did this to you?' she demanded. How dare they? She would make them pay...

She grabbed Francine's outstretched wrist, feeling for her pulse. She was alive, but not of this world. The wrist was too thin, too fragile, she thought; and – Winnie was noticing everything all at once, noticing and panicking – there was vomit too. It was caked in her hair and under her chin. It was now on Winnie's knees. Francine's school skirt was dark and damp.

Winnie took this all in, in one second, two. It hadn't been done to Francine, Francine had done this to herself. Winnie crouched low beside her. She didn't know what to do. She felt utterly out of her depth. Ron would be nearly back at the base by now. Mac was out. Susan was miles away. Trevor... Trevor was dead.

She got up and switched on the light and it felt blinding. On the floor, Francine moaned. Did she need the hospital? It was a hard decision. Winnie prevaricated. So many decisions she had to make on her own. If she'd been sick already, maybe not. Winnie slumped down onto the floor with her feet out in front of her.

She couldn't move her. She wasn't strong enough. It

would cause more damage; Francine might hit her head on the counter or the floor – maybe she already had. She ran upstairs and got pillows, blankets for both of them. Settled in for a long night.

She held the girl's hand, but her fingers were limp

'Francine, it's all right, I'm here.'

'Ly... dia...'

Lydia? The girl who didn't write?

'Do you know where you are?'

For one second, Francine's eyelids flicked open, although the eyeballs barely focused. 'Home.'

Despite her fears and her fury, that simple four-letter word nearly made Winnie smile.

'Yes, darling, you're home. You're safe.'

The sun broke in, stealthily, through the pub windows around five, bringing the colours of the stained-glass door to life. Winnie had been watching the rise and fall of Francine's chest for hours. What a relief to see it though. What a horror it had been to find her this way. She thought briefly of Ron – last night felt like an eternity ago. She would have to give him an answer sooner or later, and she no longer knew what it would be.

Francine woke up, looking wretched. She was like a broken sparrow. Her eyes were back to how they were when Winnie had first met her – haunted, horrified.

Whatever she had done, she had stolen Winnie's heart. Nothing would change that.

Unsteady but resolute, Francine staggered to her feet. She clutched the pillow and blanket and went up to bed.

49

Winnie

Francine didn't want to talk about what happened. When she was squeezed to say something, her answers were terse and Winnie wasn't sure whether she believed them or not.

'Was it your first time doing that? Francine, put the newspaper down and answer me!'

Francine looked aggrieved. She said of course it was.

'But why? Why would you do that?'

Francine wouldn't say. Or rather she said she 'didn't know'.

Then who does know, Francine?

Winnie had left that door between the flat and the pub open for years – she'd have to lock it now. But she also knew that would be solving the symptoms, not the problem.

Francine had been through disaster and loss, but that was years ago. She had been managing, Winnie had been sure of it. Out of the flames, she had risen. She had friendships, she had fun, she had manners, she had ambitions. At least, Winnie had thought so. How had she got this so wrong?

Winnie tried to bring it up again, in different, less obvious ways. She mustn't let herself be put off by the weariness on Francine's face whenever she broached the subject.

'The other night, you mentioned Lydia.'

'Did I?' Francine looked puzzled.

'Perhaps you should get in touch with her?'

Francine wrinkled up her nose.

'I'll help!'

'No...'

'I just meant, I could get you some ink for your special pen.'

'Don't bother.'

Winnie was flustered. She felt as though she was watching her dreams being conveyed away from her, like on the escalators you see in fancy department stores.

'Francine,' she said lightly, 'what would you say if I said we were invited to Canada – you and me?'

Francine looked up and brushed her hair from her eyes.

'What would I say?'

'Yes?'

'I would say no.'

'I don't mean *now*,' said Winnie desperately, 'in a year or so.'

'Never,' said Francine. 'This is our home.' She scowled. 'Our Castle...'

'Darling,' Winnie said, trying to keep her cool. 'What happened? Why are you so sad?'

But Francine wouldn't even meet her eyes now.

There was only one explanation that Winnie could think of.

· · ·

Francine's father was cutting a man's hair when Winnie came into the barber's. He greeted her with his extravagant smile.

'I'm not good at women's styles,' he said apologetically. 'Although I'm always happy to have a go...'

'It's not about my hair,' Winnie said self-consciously, cupping it: did it look atrocious? Before the war, she used to go to the salon every couple of weeks. Now she was lucky to go every six months. She had done it herself for the party at the Canadian airbase, and Ron said it was like a film star's, but that was honey talk. With no products to keep it in place, it went unruly.

She pulled her coat around her so that he would know she wasn't staying.

'Could we have a chat?'

'I'll come to the Castle later.'

'That won't be necessary.'

'Oh?'

One thing about Francine's father was that he was awfully familiar. He seemed to think they were old friends. She liked him and, of course, with Francine they had a huge interest in common, but that didn't mean they were family. She found herself talking like the man from the brewery with him, as if to draw a line between them.

He had wanted her to call him Mossy – strange name – but she had insisted on Mr Salt and eventually he got the message and Mrs Eldridged her back. Now, she was glad she had stuck to her guns.

As she waited, Winnie tried to avoid the sight of herself in all the mirrors. There was never anything good to see there. Ron liked her, she reminded herself, but thinking about Ron and what she had to decide made her queasy.

Mr Salt finished polishing the old man's shiny bald head

with a puff brush. The man was surprisingly pleased with his work, preening like a small girl.

'Anything for the weekend, sir?' said Winnie's father as the man paid.

'Please.' The man smirked at Winnie. Refusing to indulge him, Winnie gazed at the stone floor, where his tiny curls were scattered like seeds for chickens.

Eventually the doorbell jingled and the customer went on his way, his pockets stuffed, and she had Mr Salt to herself.

'I haven't got another customer until four,' Mr Salt said brightly. 'What can I do you for, Wi – Mrs Eldridge?'

He kept moving as he talked. He swept around the chair like she did at the pub. It felt different when you were the one on the chair. She would have preferred him to sit down. He cleaned the equipment. He sprayed the mirrors. He put his brushes and razors in order. Was he being deliberately thorough on purpose?

'Francine is having a few problems at the moment.'

'Oh,' he said. 'I didn't know.'

'Yes, it's... yes.'

'Right.'

He washed his hands, dried them, then sat opposite her, still at last.

'I have a solution, but I'm not sure you will like it.'

'What is it?' he asked.

'Since Francine seems agitated by your return...'

His shoulders flopped back in the chair like she had shot him.

'...I suggest you see her less.'

Winnie could see this was shocking to Francine's father, so she backed down. 'Just until her doldrums go away.'

He didn't understand what she was saying initially. 'You think I am the cause of her... doldrums?'

'I don't kn–'

'You think me going away will help?'

'I...' Doubt rippled through her. But Francine's – what could you call it, malaise? – had started around the time he had reappeared. It was too much of a coincidence to think otherwise.

'It's not that you're a bad influence,' she lied. 'It's just that it brings it all back – what happened with her family, the trauma of it.'

As she said it, she realised, *it happened to his family too*, and he would have been within his rights to protest, to fight for his daughter, even. But Francine's father was docile and he agreed. She couldn't help thinking he was too docile, and perhaps *this* was the problem. She didn't get him at all. Why was he so placid? It didn't feel like a blessing in disguise any more.

'I'll do anything for my girl,' he said. And she thought, *why do you have to make these grandiose statements? Why can't you be practical for once?*

'I'll stay with the cousins, if you think that would help?'

'I do.'

'One month or two?' he pressed.

'Maybe longer, maybe less – until we see a substantive difference in her attitude and well-being?'

'A substantive difference...' he repeated. Maybe he didn't understand the English. Whatever. He had aged before her eyes. Somehow, once again, he looked like he had that first day she'd met him.

As Winnie walked away from the salon, she felt Mr Salt's reproachful eyes upon her and she was uncomfortable. It was like throwing people out of the pub and she always felt regretful about that too, but, as Trevor would have said, rather throw them out *before* they do anything than give them the time and have them smash everything up.

And she knew – Mr Salt would smash everything up.

There was still excitement in the pub about the end of the war, and Winnie tried to join in. Everyone was making plans and clinking glasses. 'War's over!' There was still shouting in the streets. There were still celebrations. It was the news they had waited for, for so long. The news they didn't dare imagine.

Winnie set a smile on her face and deliberated about what she was going to say when she next saw Ron.

On Friday the teachers poured in as usual and, although she hadn't planned to, Winnie called over Mr Williams. He looked impressive in his hat and pale mackintosh. As he approached, his expression changed; he seemed wary, defiant even, and she was glad to put his mind at rest. She would not like a confrontation with this man!

'Don't look so worried.' She gave him her best landlady smile. Ron had told her that her smile was what he noticed about her first. 'It's not about you!'

He chuckled performatively. 'What is it?'

'It's my Francine – have you noticed she seems...' Winnie couldn't find the right word. To Mr Salt she had used 'doldrums', but this seemed to understate it. What about 'malaise' or 'gloomy'? Since Mr Williams was a headteacher, and no doubt well acquainted with a dictionary, she decided on, 'discombobulated'.

'The whole world is discombobulated,' he said. He still seemed like he was readying for a fight.

And now she too gave a fake chuckle. 'You can say that

again. I wonder whether it ever was combobulated,' she said, laughing at her own joke, hoping he would join in.

He waited a moment before saying, 'I barely see Francine in the school day. It's a large establishment, over three hundred children, and I hadn't noticed Francine was troubled.'

'Oh, she's not *troubled*.'

Winnie wished she hadn't started this. For one, Francine would kill her if she knew. She liked to keep her life at home and in the pub separate from her school life. And for another, you didn't want to get a reputation for 'troubled' – that sort of thing could accompany you your whole life. 'Just—'

Mr Williams interrupted, 'I'll take extra care of her, if you like.'

'That would be...' Winnie felt a rush of relief. 'Wonderful.'

Trevor would have told her not to suck up to those in power, but wasn't it marvellous when you could? That feeling of Francine being in safe hands was priceless. Combobulating even.

'I thought Daddy was coming,' said Francine in the sullen tone Winnie had come to expect nowadays. They'd made an arrangement for card games and darts.

'He is not,' Winnie said, then, regretting her abruptness, she added, 'I saw him today. He apologised, but something cropped up.'

'Oh?'

'Now the war is over, everyone is all over the place.'

'Hmm,' Francine said, but she didn't seem bothered, which Winnie took as further proof that Mr Salt was the cause and not the cure. She was more agitated about the sandwich Winnie was making.

'Please, no more spam! I can't face it.'

'There's nothing else and you must be hungry.'

'I thought things would improve once the war ended.'

'They will do, just not right away, Francine.'

Winnie had queued at several shops, yet it was a waste of time. She too surveyed the grey loaf despondently. Everything looked drab, smelled drab, tasted drab – It was the hope that killed. They were saying rationing was going to last some time yet.

'Oh, there is a slice of celebration cake Mr Williams got from the school governors,' Winnie had remembered suddenly. Francine loved cake. But, surprisingly, she didn't want any of that either. She must have been very low.

Francine's dad did not turn up the next week either. Winnie knew she should say something to Francine, but she couldn't figure out what.

'Perhaps he's poorly...' Francine wondered aloud. 'I'll go to the barber's.'

Winnie didn't feel like she could stop her.

Once she'd gone, Winnie felt terrible. Had she done the right thing getting him to leave? She hadn't *insisted*. She had hardly run him out of town. If he'd put up a fight for his daughter, he'd still be here. Nevertheless, she accepted she was largely responsible and so she remained on edge. She hadn't seen Francine flourish since last week, but it was early days. At least Mr Williams was aware and was looking out for her.

On her return, Francine said flatly, 'They said he's gone to stay with the cousins.'

'That's probably for the best,' Winnie said.

'Why? And why didn't he tell me himself?'

'I don't know. He probably...' *What did he probably?* 'Needed to see people he used to know – there's comfort in that.'

Francine refused to call out for the bingo that evening, which meant Mac had to step in. He was pretty useless, but they got through. Francine did sit by Sid when he played 'Für Elise' though, so it wasn't all bad. *She's going to get better*, Winnie thought. It mightn't look like it, but that was the way with things – one step forward, two steps back. This was progress.

The next day, Winnie braced herself for the return of Ron Roscoe. She had decided a holding pattern was the best answer – and probably the truest answer; she really didn't know what was for the best.

'Ron said to apologise, but he's been called urgently to London,' one of the men explained. 'He's helping organise the journey home...' He winked. 'All the visas for the wives and girlfriends.'

'Good-o,' said Winnie, light-headed. That could be her – could have been her. 'Important work...'

50

SUMMER, 1945

Francine

Francine had a head cold and unusually, Aunty Winnie let her stay in bed. (Usually, Aunty Winnie was a great believer in if you were ill, the best way to get better was by pretending you were not.)

Albert called in a couple of times. Francine told Winnie to tell Albert that she was asleep. Winnie didn't like lying to Albert, but Francine didn't feel guilty. Albert was with David and Barry a lot these days. They boxed together and talked endlessly about their left – or was it their right? – hooks and 'how to be more powerful'.

Winnie kept suggesting Francine write to her old friends. Francine said she might, but this was more lying. *Open herself up for more abandonment?* Hadn't there been enough of that already?

Francine was enjoying not going to school. She was enjoying being free from Mr Williams, although if she thought she heard his pompous voice downstairs, she snuck under the covers and when she did that, Maisie called her 'stupid girl' and the babies howled with rage. Mr Williams never said things about Jews in public – he saved them all up for her: Evil, lazy, devious, Christ-killers. If she told anyone he would 'make life very difficult'. Not just for her but for Aunty Winnie, and 'that filthy father of yours too'.

He made her feel dirty. Ashamed. Disgusting. A burden. She didn't know what to do with these feelings; they were hers and hers alone.

After several days, Aunty Winnie insisted on taking her to the doctor's. The surgery was about halfway between home and school, a nice-looking house that had been converted into a surgery with a flat above. There were framed postal stamps on the walls, and Winnie, being Winnie, gazed at them like they were the most interesting things in the world.

'This one is from the Belgian Congo!' she called. 'This one is from Burma! When I was a girl, I wanted to go to all the places on the stamps.'

'You've told me that,' said Francine.

Winnie loved everywhere except here, she thought. She hadn't mentioned going to Canada again, but Francine hadn't forgotten. Why would she go anywhere else, she pondered? Why would Winnie want to? You were still you whether you were floating in a canoe down the Amazon or in a teahouse in Kyoto. There was no escaping you and she was not going to try.

There were lots of people waiting in the waiting room. Twenty minutes passed, then another twenty. Finally, the doctor emerged from a side door and announced that he needed a break. Only after that should the next patient knock. Winnie was growing more agitated. She had to open the pub. They were – if Francine counted correctly – sixth in line. Winnie kept glaring at the clock until finally she whispered, 'Throw the dice, Francine, let's see if we should stay.'

Francine threw a three. 'It thinks we should go home,' she decided, so they crept away.

On Saturday, Winnie was in the kitchen, making soup between shifts. The cabbage and carrot floating around aimlessly in the vat of hot water made Francine, who had just got up, feel worse.

'Daddy is another one who has left me,' she said. 'What did I do to deserve this?'

'Your daddy loves you, it's just...'

Francine gave a hard laugh. 'What is it?'

'Circumstances,' Winnie said, putting the lid on the pot.

Rather than face the soup, Francine decided to go to the cinema although Winnie was so delighted and over-the-top about her going out, 'at last!' that she almost changed her mind.

Before the film there was a newsreel: Richard Dimbleby's report from the Liberation of Belsen, one of the Nazi concentration camps.

There had been rumours about this, even in the playground, but she had never, never, never imagined what was really happening to the Jewish people in mainland Europe. The hairs on her arm stood on end.

The other people in the cinema were munching on their humbugs or fiddling with their binoculars. One man said, 'They'd better hurry up with the main feature.' And the woman he was with said, 'Depressing, ain't it? I don't want to hear about it, now the war is over.'

They didn't seem changed. Not in the way she was.

She thought about Mr Cohen's attempts to convey something to her about human nature. A dot-to-dot. A line. A name-change. A pen. An office. About where it started and where it could end. And although she tried never, ever to let herself think about him, because once he was in her mind she could not shake him out, she thought about Mr Williams.

Was this what he wanted? Was this his plan? Would nobody stop him? Why did nobody stop *them*?

She left before the main feature and, by the time she got home, she really did feel sick.

51

Winnie

The thought of life going on here but without Ron felt desolate. It felt old and ugly and timid. The queuing. The drab. The rain. The empty shops. Mac. Mr Marshall's visits from the brewery. It all got to her.

Trevor had been happy as a pig rolling in muck – but she wasn't. How long would it take her to learn that you can't put on someone else's dreams? Sooner or later, they will feel too tight or too heavy. You have to wear your own. Life is short – there is no point not being true to yourself.

Did she owe the country? Did she owe the people who had fought for the country? Yes, and yes. But was the answer to stay here? This was a question she couldn't resolve.

They had fought for freedom – shouldn't she therefore be free to leave?

She remembered Peter and Paul's father with his motor-bike and side-car saying, 'This country is finished.' She didn't believe that, never had, never would, but she wondered if *her* place had finished. Winnie had been here in 1919. She had helped rebuild the country once before. People didn't like to talk about it these days, but it was a dark and dismal time, worse even than now. Starvation was widespread. Unemployment was high. People were grief-stricken. Winnie knew people who looked back with nostalgia, but it was their youth they were nostalgic about, not the time itself. That time had nothing to be nostalgic about.

She should leave, she told herself. Winnie knew she shouldn't live her life according to how a dead man wanted her to. Not only that, but how did she know exactly what Trevor would want? He'd wanted the Castle to thrive and she had accomplished that. Surely it was enough that she had kept it open every day through the war? It was an achievement. It was too soon to be proud of it, but Winnie knew that she might be one day.

Trevor would understand. He would. He wouldn't want her giving up her life for a ghost.

There was only one remaining piece of the puzzle: the piece called Francine. Her darling girl was troubled. And when it came to it, this was the only piece that ever really mattered. She should go, but no, she couldn't go. Not without Francine.

Ron Roscoe was trying not to show his frustration, but it was clear the more she put him off, the more he was struggling. Ships were leaving for Canada all the time. You saw them in the newsreels. The people waving their goodbyes haunted her.

She suspected Ron would have gone already if it wasn't

for her. He was holding on for her. He wanted honesty, not excuses. And, after that precious night they had shared together, he had a right to know.

One evening, he asked if he could stay behind after closing again. It was decision time. Or rather, it was time to tell him the decision she had come to.

'Have you given my proposal any thought?' he asked, his beautiful eyes on her.

He didn't know she had thought of little else?

'I am,' she said.

His head shot up, delighted.

'You are? Coming with me?'

'I mean I am thinking about it all the time,' she explained quickly.

She had to make him understand.

'Thing is, I thought when Francine was reunited with her family it would be happy ever after. But it has been difficult.'

Ron took her hand. 'I can imagine,' he said gently.

She could have sunk into his voice and he was saying what she wanted to hear. But it wasn't as simple as that.

'She's distressed. She fears abandonment. She has' – she remembered Scott's useful phrase – 'survivor's guilt.' What was it Francine had said? *What did I do to deserve this?* That surely was as plaintive a cry for help as there ever was.

'What does she say?' Ron asked, taking her hand and caressing her fingers.

'I asked if she wanted to come.'

He looked surprised but then nodded eagerly.

'And?'

'She said no. I haven't been able to ask her how she would feel if I left.'

Winnie was certain it would be the end of her world.

He sighed, removing his hand. 'Maybe you should.'

Winnie shook her head. He was missing the point. He hadn't seen Francine coming back from the cinema feverish. She had thought the girl was pretending but this time her temperature really was high, and she was trembling.

'Then there's Susan.'

At this, he smiled ruefully. 'Susan will be working in New York, won't she?'

Winnie half-wished she hadn't told him.

'Even if she weren't, she doesn't need you to take care of her,' Ron continued.

'I know,' admitted Winnie. Susan never had, not really. It was a strange thing to have brought someone so – island-like – into the world, but there it was. Susan was born to fly. For the first time, Winnie wondered if maybe she was more similar to Susan than she had previously realised.

'It's just so far,' she sighed.

'We have boats. We even have airplanes.' Ron forced a smile. 'We have mass movement of people.'

'For war, yes.'

He didn't answer for a while. Then he said, 'People move for war. You won't move for me?'

She opened and shut her mouth. Then she looked up at Churchill, who looked as though he too was waiting for her response. Sometimes she thought the painting was one a child could paint, other times that it was one that would take years to understand – the meanings, the layers.

'I don't know what to do.'

'You keep moving the goalposts,' Ron said, leaning away from her.

'I don't know what that means.'

He was red at the tops of his cheeks. 'You change the rules of the game.'

'I have to react to what's in front of me.'

'What's in front of you is Francine's father is here, her cousins aren't far, she has friends. I don't know Francine like you do, obviously, but what I do know is that she wouldn't want you to give up your life for her.'

Winnie looked around cautiously, then whispered, 'I'm not sure about her father.'

'He loves her, Winnie!' For the first time, Ron snapped.

'Something has gone wrong though,' Winnie persisted. 'You said it yourself. You said "her light has dimmed". It's true.' She said it out loud now. 'I can't leave her like this.'

She thought of the sick matted in Francine's hair. The way she lay in bed nowadays and had given up on everything. School missed. All those unsent letters in her room to Lydia and to Valerie, telling half a story.

She couldn't abandon her. She had to persuade Ron of this, but he was frowning now. He probably thought she'd turned the goalposts the other way – made it so that it was impossible to score.

'I get it.'

'You don't.' She had to make him understand. 'I do want to be with you, Ron.'

He nodded. 'I know how much you love Francine.'

'I really do.' She was crying now. It was all too much.

'And it makes me love you even more to see how you are with her.'

Winnie sniffed. 'Thank you.'

'You gave her a great and safe and loving home during the war,' he paused. 'And now the war is over. I thought that was the deal.'

'That wasn't the deal.' Winnie blew her nose, tried to pull herself together. She would not be self-indulgent; such a horrible trait.

'That's what evacuation was, wasn't it?'

'It was much more than that. For us.'

'Okay,' he said with a finality this time. 'I didn't realise. I guess that's that, then.'

He stood up, walked off, and she knew this might be the biggest mistake of her life.

52

Francine

Francine went back to school. Sometimes, Mr Williams was nice to her. 'This hurts me more than it hurts you,' was one of his favourite lines. Or, 'I don't *want* to do this...' Mostly, he was not. Even when she didn't see him for a few weeks, the fear that she was just about to hung over her like a forecast of hail. Winnie remained oblivious – it shocked Francine how oblivious she was.

'Bless him!' Winnie might coo, or, worse, 'I don't know where I'd be without my teachers... now the Canadians are going back, everything hinges on them.'

Francine's family didn't help – how could they? They were dead. Ghosts. They just stood there, looking on, horrified. Even Maisie.

'Mummy,' Francine whimpered once when he was shouting at her, but that encouraged him further and he laughed, teeth glinting. 'She can't hear you, girl. The only good Jew is a dead Jew. You all need rounding up.'

· · ·

She hadn't seen him at school for about a month, which was worse as it meant she was going to see him soon, and it was always worse after a break. He pulled her into the office.

'What did you tell her?'

'Who?'

'Mrs Eldridge.'

'Nothing,' said Francine, backing away from him.

'Good.'

He made her write 'I will not tell tales' one hundred times, and he sat there, shaking his head so that the ugly hair-wave flip-flopped.

'You people think you're so special...' He was working himself up. 'Chosen ones, my arse!' he suddenly yelped. She didn't know what that meant. 'We shouldn't have stood in Hitler's way,' he went on. She kept her eyes fixed on the paper and tried to block out every sound other than that of the pen scratching.

At the pub one Friday, Mr Williams took over the bingo. *Her* bingo. Her game. Her favourite thing. When she complained, Winnie said, 'But you said didn't want to do it any more!'

'I know, but...'

'He's better at calling out the numbers than Mac.' Winnie tried to stroke Francine's back, but Francine wriggled free. 'No offence to Mac, but he reads like there's a gun at his head.'

'Number four, knock on the door!' Mr Williams called out. 'Two fat ladies, eighty-eight!'

How the regulars laughed!

'Thirteen – unlucky for some.' He met Francine's eyes. 'Devil's favourite number.'

Francine got up.

'Where do you think you're going?' Winnie called.

'Upstairs.'

Winnie was chasing after her, pulling at her arm. Her face was beetroot. Understanding-Winnie had gone, replaced by Winnie-in-a-temper.

'What *is* going on with you recently?'

'Nothing.'

'Then why are you so...'

'So what?'

'I am doing my best, I am giving up the world for you!'

'I didn't ask you to do anything!'

Francine felt like pushing Winnie then.

But Winnie had covered her face with her hands. 'Forget it – it's nothing, darling.'

Francine didn't push her, but she had wanted to.

Mr Williams was right, Francine was evil.

'No room at the inn,' Daddy sighed when he came back from the cousins; but just as Francine thought, that's good, he'll stay here, he said he would only be able to see her once a month from now on.

'What? Why?'

At first, he talked about the demands of the barber's: so many people needed haircuts since the war ended. It was a hairdressing emergency! She didn't know if he was being serious or not, but then he added softly, 'Maybe I'm too much for you, doll?'

'I don't know what you mean.'

He stroked the bristles of his chin. He was like a daisy without petals, she thought.

'I don't know,' he said. 'I don't know anything any more.'

She hated to see her daddy so feeble. And he wouldn't let her help. It was like she made him feel that way.

Then Mr Cuthbert visited her at school, all walking sticks and papers. He put his hat on the desk between them and said, 'I hear you've been despondent, Francine.'

It didn't make her angry with Aunty Winnie, just sad.

'I'm fine,' she told him in a sing-song voice.

'If ever you need to talk...'

'I know.'

Seeing him made her feel worse too. That strange man getting on with life despite his broken legs while here she was, struggling to get out of bed. She was the most pathetic being who ever lived.

53

Winnie

It was put-on-a-brave-face time again. The Canadian boys wanted farewell fusses and the girls wanted big goodbyes.

The girls were complaining – 'They won't let us on the ships yet...'

'It's servicemen first,' Winnie snapped. 'You'll get your turn.'

She knew the reason she was impatient with them was just because she was jealous. They could simply get up and go. Didn't they realise how fortunate they were not to be manacled to this life?

Ron didn't come back to the Castle, and she was glad because it would be awkward, yet she was also upset because the thought of him disappearing was breaking her heart.

Francine kept asking where Ron was and what was going on, and that didn't help.

'Nothing. And I don't know.'

She sounded more like a teenager than Francine did sometimes.

Winnie wanted to see Ron on the airbase – they needed privacy – but if she went there, he might assume she had changed her mind and she couldn't bear to see the disappointment on his face a second – or would it be a third? – time round.

She remembered working in the old people's home all those years ago, before the pub. Sometimes she had had to tell people with poor memories bad news. She would tell them once, then a second time, and a third time, and there came a point where she just had to stop.

So she didn't go to the base; she was too busy watching Francine with an eagle eye anyway, and managing the Castle, of course. She pulled pints and sat by Sid and helped Old Jim with answers for his *Telegraph* crossword. She listened to the men come from war with their terrible stories of exploding mines and booby-traps and things too horrible to tell. And she listened to Toby's memoir.

'If someone had understood just a little of what we'd gone through it would have been easier, but no one did. This was loneliness. To have given my all for a war in a foreign land and no one appreciated it. A soft word, a kind smile would have made the difference.'

'Oh, Toby,' she said, goosepimples on her arms. Every time she heard his story, it felt like history was repeating itself, again and again.

And then Ron came back.

'I'm off tomorrow.'

'Let me get you a drink on the house,' she said automatically. From the corner of her eye, she took in how handsome he was. Maybe not to everyone, but definitely to her. She loved everything about him: the greying temples, the tanned skin, the rough chin that would grow the thickest of beards if he left it. Under that shirt was the chest that shivered if you touched it, and when he made love his eyes were half open, half shut in a way that was both dreamy and thrilling. Did he think about that night – at least, did he think about it as longingly, as fondly, as she did? It was impossible that he was going. She couldn't bear the thought that she'd never see him again.

She was collecting glasses and he was about to throw his first dart when he said, almost casually, 'You haven't reconsidered, Mrs Eldridge?'

Winnie took a deep breath. 'If the situation changes, I will. Absolutely.'

'Is the situation here likely to change?'

The definition of madness is doing the same thing over and over again and expecting a different result. But if at first you don't succeed, aren't you meant to try, try again?

'It might, Ron, one day...'

Ron threw three darts in a row – 20, 18, 3 – then ripped them from the board. Winnie felt like her pull to him was irresistible. She had never felt so torn in her life. It was like she was in an invisible tug-of-war.

'Francine *deserves* for me to stay,' she said. Perhaps she should have let it go but she felt this need, not only to explain but to get him to agree with her.

'What about you? What do *you* deserve?'

Winnie couldn't trust herself to speak.

'Most evacuated children have gone home now,' he said.

'It's complicated,' she admitted.

He threw the darts again, as though to distract himself, or maybe thinking, *here's something simple.*

She watched the feathers whizz through the air like something easy, like everything should be as easy as that. They made a swishing noise and then a smacking sound as they landed. This time a 60, 18 again and another 60.

'Bravo,' she said.

His mind wasn't on the game. She intercepted him on his return from the board.

'Ron,' she whispered, 'why don't you stick around tonight after I've closed?'

She had pushed Trevor's hand away the night before he left. Never again.

'Won't it make things worse?'

'Probably,' she admitted. She was already tearful, but she was more certain than she had been that she couldn't leave things like this.

The next morning, Ron crept out of Winnie's room with Winnie right behind him. On the landing he bumped into Francine, who said, 'Oh hello!' as if him being there was perfectly normal behaviour, hugged him goodbye, promised to write and then went back into her room.

Why had Winnie ever worried about what Francine would think on this score?

Tiger was doing her heartiest meowing in the kitchen, even though Francine had just fed her.

'Ignore her,' Winnie said crossly, 'she's just trying it on.'

Ron laughed but he had tears in his eyes.

By the back door, he held Winnie.

'No regrets.'

She couldn't tell if it was a question or not, but she did have an answer.

'No regrets.'

'I'll write – and you'll let me know if...'

'Straight away.'

It had been the most beautiful and heartbreaking night of her life. And then, with Tiger chasing after him, he was gone.

54

WINTER, 1945

Francine

Everyone had said how good life would be once the war was over. Not for Francine. She used to love school – not any more. She used to love the Castle at the weekends – not any more. Most of the Canadians had left, taking their chewing gum, Hershey bars and gobstoppers with them. Winnie's mouth was turned down all the time. The only person whose mood had improved was Mac, and he drove her mad.

One morning, Francine didn't go to school. Instead, she took a bus across town to where she had heard the Jewish cemetery was. She had no idea where Mr Cohen's grave might be, but after about an hour of searching she found it in a far corner, close to some trees with low-hanging branches, in what looked like a newer section.

The headstone was smooth and white and inscribed in a language she didn't understand, except for the dates and the name Abraham Cohen. And next to it, almost exactly the same, was the grave of his dear Bertha.

Flowers didn't seem to be the thing – the graves were decorated only with pebbles – but Mr Cohen had always been fond of flowers, so Francine put down the yellow roses she had brought with her from the pub. She didn't think he would be annoyed. He never was constrained by convention. She imagined him chuckling away to his wireless shows.

'What shall I do?' she asked him. Mr Cohen hadn't only laughed. He had been good to talk to about serious things, even if she hadn't always understood what he meant.

She had to do something about Mr Williams, but what? Sometimes it felt like she couldn't think straight and if she could just use logic or sense maybe, she would be able to work out a way.

Mr Williams had inveigled his way into the Castle with astonishing speed. He was now a 'regular', beloved by Jim and Old Jim since he was good at crosswords, loved by Toby since he was a fan of memoirs, loved by Nathan because he enjoyed discussing Trollope and loved fiercely by Winnie because he had brought in all the teachers and therefore all the teachers' wallets.

'It begins with something small. Like a pen,' she remembered Mr Cohen saying. She used to think he was being over-dramatic.

All the gravestones nearby were very plain, the most ornate one with a musical note on it and another with a carving of a wave. If she had organised Mr Cohen's grave-stone, and if she had free rein, she wondered what she might have put: a jam sandwich maybe, or one of those funny quotes, like 'Lovely Grub'.

She had never been to her family's graves, but she supposed they too might be somewhere like this. She didn't feel any compulsion to go, maybe because she didn't feel as if they were there.

Looking back towards the low building, she saw that her mother was striding towards her, perhaps to tell her off – she wouldn't like her here, children in adult spaces were a bugbear of hers – but as she approached, she saw the woman wasn't angry or distraught, and that, in fact, it wasn't her mummy.

'Can I help you?' the woman asked. Francine was no expert, but she thought the lady was wearing a wig under her hat: she had an exceedingly straight fringe that was an unnatural brown. She had a way about her like a teacher, firm but kind. Francine told her no, thank you.

'Are you a member of the synagogue?'

'No, I was just...'

'Visiting a friend?' The woman smiled at her, and it was a smile that expected nothing. 'I'll just give you our address in case you ever need it.'

She pressed a note into Francine's hand. 'You're always welcome.'

In the middle of assembly the next day, Mr Williams called out in front of everyone.

'You cheated in your test, Miss Salt.'

Francine stared at the floor. She did not dare even roll the dice. He usually left her alone for three weeks or so, but she'd only been to his office a few days earlier.

'I would expect nothing else from you.'

The hall was silent although she could feel Albert squirming next to her. Everyone's heads were down.

'I did not cheat,' Francine said quietly.

'I don't think she did,' Albert spoke up, and so did Barry from London.

'No break, boys,' Mr Williams said, and Barry let out a groan. 'And you, Francine Salt. See me after school.'

'Shh,' she said to Albert, who was itching for a fight. 'It's all right.'

Her mummy was there. 'Things will look better in the morning,' she whispered.

Francine was about fifty lines in – *I repent for the sins of my people* – when he snatched her pen and snapped it in two. Her precious pen.

'I will not have your defiance any more,' he said.

He moved over to the desk where he kept the slipper and opened the drawer.

55

SPRING, 1946

Winnie

Winnie missed Ron, but there was no doubt that she would have missed him even more if she hadn't been so worried about Francine. The girl occupied her every waking thought. Sometimes it felt like they were right back to where they started, that afternoon when Francine first appeared at the pub: 'My adult is dead.' Francine either stayed out or didn't go out at all. Her school attendance was patchy. She had stopped taking an interest in the pub.

'I'm never going to leave you, Francine,' Winnie said. She said it often, but Francine shrugged like she couldn't care less.

Had she gone to Canada, everything would be different – yet Winnie didn't see how she could have gone. Francine had no one. Her father was at best incapable, at worst feckless. The cousins hadn't stepped up – maybe they would if asked, but they showed no inclination to ask themselves. No, Francine was her duty and hers alone. And of course, she wasn't just a duty – Winnie adored her – but goodness, right now she was blooming hard work.

She remembered Francine worrying about losing those she loved – had that fear returned? Winnie asked her, but Francine was blank-faced, adamant there was nothing wrong.

'I swear,' she said, 'on my life.'

'You're my girl,' Winnie pleaded. 'And I love you no matter what.'

'Thank you,' Francine said, crossing her arms. 'May I go?'

Winnie accepted this until, a few days later, she overheard Francine talking about her 'life' with Albert. How she was looking forward to being reunited with her brothers and sister. How she couldn't wait to be in her dead mother's arms again.

The licensing laws changed – the hours the pub could be open were shorter, since the government wanted people to return to abstinence. The comfort of a beer, so important in wartime, was no longer encouraged. And restaurants and cafés were opening up instead of public houses. Winnie would have to be nimble if the Castle was going to survive the next decade of changes. The White Horse had started serving breakfast and, while she wondered who on earth would go out for breakfast, she had heard that it was packed with construction workers. She should have thought of that. Another place was serving a dish called 'spaghetti Bolognese'.

'It's long and thin like snakes,' Nathan explained with authority. 'Impossible to eat without getting sauce down your collar.'

'That won't catch on!' Winnie chortled. Goodness, Trevor would have said they were stark raving mad!

'Scissors,' Toby advised. 'My granddaughter, Sandra, says that's the way.'

'It tasted like meat loaf,' Jim said.

'There's nothing new in the world,' Old Jim said, and everyone agreed.

Winnie had worried that, once the Canadians left, the Castle would go quiet again but people were coming back to live in Kettering all the time – soldiers in their demob suits and young women who'd been in the Land Army, or in factories or nursing overseas. And even if they didn't stick around, there was Mr Williams and the teachers too – thank goodness for them! She really was indebted to him.

Not long after Ron left, Scott Cuthbert came into the Castle. He hadn't been in for a while. He was working on a Parliamentary report on the care of children.

'You're not going to Canada then?' he asked.

She felt suddenly bitter. Trapped, she supposed. If it hadn't been for him pushing her to take in a little girl, she might have been free.

'I thought you wanted me to look after Francine?'

'I do,' he said with his characteristic honesty. 'But I also want you to be happy.'

'I'm happy when Francine's happy.' She wasn't happy now.

Scott didn't say anything and Winnie felt disgusted with herself again. It wasn't his fault, this time or last.

During quiet moments, Winnie would go over what she'd say to Lydia or Valerie if she ever met them.

'You abandoned Francine in her hour of need,' she might

scold. Or 'She loved you both, but you never wrote, you never visited!'

She probably wouldn't do it – even if she got the chance – but she wanted to hurt them the way they'd hurt her girl. But then Winnie's rational self would tell her they were just silly children who made mistakes. And anyway, maybe she should stop wanting to be a knight in shining armour. Maybe she wanted to say something to them because she had been so tempted to let Francine down – she had seriously thought about leaving the country, crossing the ocean, hadn't she? Perhaps her preoccupation with them was to deflect attention away from her own (massive) shortcomings?

Winnie jumped at a knock on the pub door. It was Albert. Albert was different. Albert had always been there, through thick and thin. Winnie dreaded to think what life would have been like for Francine without him. What a pal!

'She's not back yet but you can wait for her here... Would you like some squash?'

Winnie had been watching the way Albert looked at Francine for the last year or so. How he pedalled over to see her, and waited, smiling. He was a lovely chap.

Then she wondered if this was what he'd come for. To declare himself? Perhaps Francine had been lovesick all this time. Maybe she wouldn't let herself fall in love with Albert, for the same reason that she hadn't let herself love Winnie all those years ago. She was scared whoever she loved would die. It made sense.

Albert wouldn't come in, but hovered on the step, twisting his cap in his hands.

'What is it, dear?'

'Things are difficult for Francine,' he said.

'I had noticed,' she said. *I have done everything I can*, she thought. And she had a sinking realisation that asking

Francine's father to leave had made no difference. In fact, it had probably made things worse. 'Can you think why, Albert?'

Although he was staring at the ground, Albert gave a nod, so tiny that Winnie wasn't sure at first that she hadn't imagined it. *Did* he *really* know why?

'Can you tell me – is it... me?' she asked fearfully.

This time Albert shook his head. He had regressed to being a lost boy.

'Is it her father?'

It was, wasn't it?

Sternly, Albert shook his head.

It wasn't him?

'Then what?'

'School,' he mumbled.

But Francine had always liked school. She had friends, she liked the lessons, she liked her pens. Winnie couldn't understand.

'It's the children at school?' she asked, her voice high as she grew increasingly flustered.

'No.'

Albert didn't want to say it, whatever it was. He looked at her with a wretched expression.

'It's the...' Winnie racked her brains. 'Teachers?'

Again, he shook his head, eyes pleading.

'Then what?'

'It's the head teacher,' he whispered.

Mr Williams? Mr Williams was the problem? Winnie grabbed her coat and her hat – she didn't know why, force of habit maybe – and then shouted at Mac to keep an eye.

'I won't be long,' she yelled, although who knew how long this would take. She would go to school now. Have it out with him. Find out what this was.

Albert was protesting – 'Don't tell her I said,' but she ignored him.

She dashed along the road towards Kettering County High, dimly aware Albert was hurrying after her. At the school, she marched down the corridor, not knowing where to go but knowing she had to find her girl.

She heard voices – no, not voices, *his* voice.

That was the room. That was the place. There was a square glass window in the door. She peered through it. There they were.

'You are a devious people, a filthy Jew-girl,' she heard.

Winnie froze. Francine's head was bowed. Winnie could see the white snake of the parting of her hair. Her messy writing on the desk, dozens and dozens of lines. Hours and hours of punishments. Francine's hand was stretched in front of her.

He was holding something, his arm up in the air and then with force, he smacked it down onto her palm.

Francine jolted.

The door didn't open immediately, so she pushed against it and then it did.

'Mrs Eldridge!' he called out in surprise.

Something whipped past her, a shadow figure, and then Albert had punched Mr Williams in the face, and he stumbled, fell against the desk and then to the floor. He was like something soft, made of hot air.

56

Francine

'I just don't understand – why didn't you tell me?' Winnie kept asking.

'I don't know,' Francine muttered.

Because. Because a hundred reasons because. Because it was too ugly to put into words. Because it was terrifying. Because it was probably her fault. Same as her family's deaths were probably her fault. Because it was nothing more than she deserved. Because he would make things bad for her father. Because he would make things bad for Aunty Winnie. Because Aunty Winnie liked him and needed him and said things like, 'We're so lucky Mr Williams and the teachers come to us!' or 'He's so polite and helpful!' And whenever he was in the Castle, her laugh went on and on.

And then Winnie gave up asking and instead kept saying, 'I'm just so sorry, my darling. I let you down.'

'It's not your fault,' Francine sniffed.

Despite the coal shortage, Winnie lit the fire in the pub.

She wrapped Francine in a blanket as though she were an invalid. It wasn't even very cold. She wouldn't let anyone put on the wireless because, she said, it might make Francine more miserable.

'It won't!'

But Winnie couldn't take that chance.

Albert had disappeared, and Francine felt sick and scared – was he going to get in trouble because of her? Winnie insisted he wouldn't, everything would sort itself out, then she looked as though she were about to start on the 'why didn't you tell me?' line again, but managed to contain herself.

'It's going to be all right, Francine,' she said and that was lovely, it felt like being gently let down – like falling with a fine silk parachute made from elderly ladies' night-gowns rather than plummeting smack bang wallop into the earth.

Albert did come back later, with six eggs, only one cracked, from the farm. He had on his most solemn expression. Only after Winnie kept slapping him on the back, cuddling him, calling him a hero and pouring him ginger ales did he let himself smile.

Once Albert had left, Winnie knelt down by Francine's armchair and Francine braced herself for more questions.

But instead Winnie said, 'There's something else...'

'Yes?'

'I owe your dad an apology.'

'What? Why?'

Winnie took a deep breath.

'I got it wrong.'

Although Albert had been the one to punch Mr Willliams in

the face – left hook, naturally – Mr Cuthbert was the one to pick up all the formalities.

'He'll never work in a school again,' Mr Cuthbert had said furiously. 'I can't believe this was going on right under our noses.'

Mr Williams disappeared from Kettering County High the very next day, 'due to health reasons', and no one cared enough to ask what they were or if he'd be back. Francine couldn't believe it.

Aunty Winnie still flapped around her too much and Albert worried, but on the whole Francine felt like when she'd sunk all Mr Cohen's battleships. She'd won.

'Is there anything else you want to tell me?' Winnie asked one day.

Francine thought about her secret designs on the pub. Sometimes, these dreams had been the only thing to keep her going. She knew Winnie didn't love the Castle like she did; the Castle was work for her, whereas for Francine it was a passion. One day, Francine wanted 'Miss Salt – Landlady' on the wall. The first thing she would do would be to fix the H in the outside sign. First impressions are important! But Winnie had looked so worried and uncertain all over again that Francine had just said, 'There's nothing.'

A few evenings later Albert, Francine's dad and Mr Cuthbert were together in one of the Castle booths. Francine brought them over drinks and then let her daddy hold her hand. Winnie had gone to see him the day after the showdown, and when she next saw him he had told Francine that it wasn't Winnie's fault, she was just trying to do her best and, 'no hard feelings'.

Now they called Winnie over from the bar.

'You need to help us with an argument, Winnie,' Mr Cuthbert was saying.

She came over, smiling.

'Francine and Albert here claim that your real name is Winston.'

'It is, isn't it?' Albert's face was shining.

'It definitely is,' Francine said.

'Winnie is always short for Winston,' Albert added.

They both looked to Francine's father for support, but he raised his hands. 'Damned if I know! Names were my wife's department.'

'Good grief!' Winnie said. 'You're both wrong. Winston? Really? In my case, Winnie is short for Winnifred.'

Francine and Albert were shocked, Mr Cuthbert was victorious – 'You owe me a shilling!' – and Francine's dad made a face like they were, each one of them, clowns.

Francine thought it was another thing that just went to show that you can know someone for a long time and not really know them at all.

Not long after it had all come out about Mr Williams, Albert invited Francine to go with him to the cinema one Friday evening.

'I don't know if I fancy it,' she said.

'You should go.' Aunty Winnie was giving her the look.

'Why?'

'Because Albert was kind to you. Remember?'

Albert *had* been kind to her, but Francine had already thanked him repeatedly. She didn't see why the rest of her days should be spent doing things out of gratitude. Nevertheless, for Aunty Winnie's sake, she said yes.

As they queued up for tickets, Albert seemed in a funny

mood. He smelled different to usual and was fumbling around in his pockets. Then he offered Francine a cigarette.

'Since when do you smoke?'

Francine had never seen Albert with cigarettes before. She'd assumed he associated them with his parents. He lit one and shrugged. Then coughed. He wasn't good at smoking and neither did it suit him. Then, more strangeness: Albert insisted on paying her admission.

She did argue – the money she earned from weekends and evenings in the pub wasn't bad, while Albert worked on his host father's farm and didn't make much – but he wouldn't let her.

'There's going to be more wars. Against the Soviet Union next, I think,' he said, running his hands through his hair.

Maybe that was why he wasn't himself today, she thought wildly. Maybe he was worried about the conscription. Or the threat of a nuclear war.

'I thought we were allies with the Soviet Union.'

'Not for long,' he said.

Albert was never going back to London. His parents were alcoholics.

'They can't help it,' he always said, but Francine knew everything about it hurt him deeply.

In the cinema, Albert wouldn't stop jiggling his knees, which made the whole row of seats judder. It reminded her of being on the train to Somerset, in the bench seat long ago, when Lydia had slapped her thigh – 'Stop it, Francine, you're making me nervous!'

'What's the matter with you today?' Francine whispered. Sometimes, she thought she sounded like Lydia when she spoke to Albert too. The same impatience bleeding into her voice.

'Nothing.'

The unfamiliar smell was cologne, like Ron's. It was nice, but overpowering in the confines of the cinema. The film wasn't an interesting one and a few rows in front, a man was snoring loudly. Francine nudged Albert to point him out, but Albert leaned towards her.

'Francine...'

'Uh-huh.'

His face was right in hers, alarmingly close. She blinked, pulled her head back, whispered, 'What are you doing?'

'I thought you liked me!' he returned, flustered.

'I do!' she said. She didn't just like Albert – she adored him. He was the most loyal friend. There had been countless occasions when he had supported her, not just in standing up for her against Mr Williams but with everything. More than that, he was fun. He was nearly as brilliant at cards as she was. He loved bingo as much as she did. His smiley, freckly face was the backdrop to so much of her life in Kettering.

'I thought you *really* liked me.'

'I do!' she repeated, confused. She suddenly remembered that long-ago day in Mr Cohen's house when she had been able to lift him, yet he couldn't lift her. Things had certainly changed since then. He had matured, and all the boxing he did with Barry and David had filled him out even more. She thought to herself, *He even looks like a box!*, but decided not to say that. Whatever his size, Albert could be thin-skinned, and he was so odd today.

'Then...' He inclined his head towards her. This time his lips were puckered, and this time they found their way; they landed on hers, and she thought of a plane finding its runway, the way the wheels come out from nowhere.

He murmured her name and it was plaintive and sweet and unbearable.

Pulling away, Francine felt bewildered. She didn't understand what he wanted from her? 'What about the film?'

'You said you'd seen it before.'

'Yes, but...'

It had never occurred to her not to watch! The couple on the screen were arguing. They both were furious – oh no, *he* wasn't furious. He grabbed her for a big kiss, she shrieked, resisting – How dared he? But then, to Francine's horror, she succumbed. And kept succumbing.

Albert was trying to mirror what he saw on the screen. Francine pulled back again, shaking her head.

'No, Albert.' She said it firmly, like she did to Tiger when she was whining after she had already been fed.

'What do I have to do?'

'What do you mean?'

She didn't really want to ask.

'To get you to kiss me.'

Francine thought of the old aunts and uncles who used to gather in her house for Friday night dinner or at Saturday lunchtimes, her mother insisting she kiss each one, and having to do a circuit of the room. To get her through, she used to imagine she was a dinosaur deciding which one she would eat later. (Aunty Lily was the fleshiest.)

Nevertheless, Albert had a point – he was her best friend. And he did have the most beautiful, smooth skin. She should be able to kiss him. She puckered up and gave him a noisy kiss on his freckly nose.

'You don't know what I mean?' he asked, staring at his boots.

Maybe it surprised them both that he would know something before her. Apart from English, where he knew everything before her.

His voice was croaky. 'I want to kiss you like a boyfriend kisses a girlfriend.'

'Uh, that's... No.'

Out of nowhere, an image of Well-Developed Marjorie flickered into her mind, Marjorie kissing her various boyfriends.

'We are allies, that's what!'

As soon as she said it, she knew it was the wrong word. Hadn't he just told her how allies switch?

For a moment, she thought maybe she should just lie back and think of England. Maybe this was what was expected of her – maybe this was how every girl felt when a boy made a pass at them. You got used to it, perhaps.

'What can I do to make you love me?' he said in a low voice. It was perhaps the saddest question she had ever heard.

'I do love you,' she whispered. She would not get used to it. 'Just not like that.'

He peeled away from her.

'You can't *leave*, Bertie!' she said.

'I hate it when you call me that!'

'Then I won't – Albert...'

As he got up, his jacket caught on the arm of the chair. He shook it free. The people seated nearby had had enough.

'Quiet,' one man behind snapped. 'We've paid for this.'

Albert hesitated, but pulled on his cap and started off along the row. It reminded her of the night she'd got drunk. Now people all over the cinema were glaring at them. On second thoughts, they seemed to have decided this beat the film they'd paid for.

Once Albert got to the aisle, he walked quickly. She considered chasing after him, but felt herself frozen to the spot. She could only stare at the screen, where the hero and his girlfriend were getting married.

The pub was closed by the time the film ended, and Francine was glad she wouldn't have to go through the regulars. They were lovely but they always had so many questions. Winnie, who never stopped, was in the kitchen making potato cakes. There was flour on the surfaces and a dusting on Winnie's sweet face.

Francine greeted her, then went to her own room, but Winnie followed, untying the strings of her apron.

'Did something happen?'

She could read Francine like a book.

'Everything's fine.'

This was where Lydia and Valerie would have been so useful. Francine imagined they'd give excellent advice. No doubt Lydia would have kissed lots of boys by now and Valerie would have researched it.

Winnie hesitated. 'Film no good?'

'It was fine.'

'Albert all right?'

'Albert's fine, too.'

Francine paused, contemplating whether she could tell Winnie. But she couldn't. She told herself it was because she didn't yet know what she thought, but mostly, it was because looking at Winnie's hopeful expression made her realise again just how strongly Winnie felt about her and Albert.

57

Winnie

During the war Winnie had told herself, *once the war is over, you can be happy*, yet here she was, miserable again. Actually, Winnie woke up most mornings quite happy, but then within seconds, the shame about Mr Williams kicked in, and it was like a sack of bricks, weighing her down. She had taken in Francine and let her down! It was the most *mortifying* thing she had ever done (in a crowded field!).

Yet Francine had got over it with astonishing speed.

'You have to forgive yourself,' she told Winnie. 'How could you have known?'

Once, Francine asked if she might cook chicken soup on Friday for her and her father, and although the broth was thin and watery, it was also lovely. And Francine's father put a small round piece of material on his head and said prayers, and that was lovely too. He had got over it too, he said, it was what it was, and he would have done the same, etc, etc, but she couldn't forgive herself. She just couldn't. What a failure she was.

On Saturdays, Winnie served the knitting circle and the Castle darts team while Mac dished up a stew, the ends of his daft scarf dangling in the pan. They were serving more food in the pub these days and it was popular. Then, because everything appeared to be under control, Winnie went upstairs; she'd had a letter burning a hole in her apron all morning and she couldn't wait any longer to open it.

Ron, bless him, still wrote. *Why is he still writing to me?* Winnie wondered. *It's not like it's going to work out... He must realise that by now.* It was not all: it had turned out to be nothing. Still, his persistence, single-mindedness and being an obstinate old git were qualities she admired almost as much as his being a soldier with kind eyes and a heavy handsome head.

As she read, she couldn't stop smiling at Ron's anecdotes of life in Burlington – the descriptions of the people and the work he did. Even more than that, she liked the miss-yous at the end of every letter and the kisses, which she counted each time to check she was not out of favour. They were as consistent as the rest of him.

It felt like he was one of the few who ever saw the real her. Even to Trevor, dear Trevor, she had always been a means to an end – a means to the pub. The brewery had wanted a married couple and, ding-dong, Trevor had proposed. With Ron, it was not a case of killing two birds with one stone – in fact, this stone was not doing much at all, which was a good thing really, thought Winnie, poor birds.

And sometimes, not very often, Winnie let herself remember that wonderful V.E. Night (before the subsequent disastrous events at home) and also their very last time together. They did have something special, they really did.

She still might get to be with Ron one day. Just as soon as Francine was married, no matter how long that took. She might be young but anyone who saw Albert and Francine grinning together would know they were a match made in heaven.

That was her mission now.

She began her reply. *Dear Ron. It is always so wonderful to hear from you.*

58

SUMMER, 1947

Francine

Francine had left school with just a few qualifications under her belt. She was now seventeen years old and people no longer said she was wise for her years. Nor did they say she was still growing, since it was glaringly obvious she was not.

One time, Albert came into the pub, all dressed up like he was going to a funeral. He'd passed his exams and was now working full-time at the farm. They hardly spent any time together, not since the cinema incident last year.

'Have a drink with me, Francine,' he said, patting the stool next to him.

'I'm working.'

But it was early and hardly anyone was in. Jim was taking Old Jim to an appointment. Toby had indigestion, Nathan was visiting his brother, Sid and his wife were on a coach tour to Cheddar, and they had no groups in until the Scrabble players at four.

Francine went over to Albert's table. She hoped they

could be friends again. She missed him awfully, but she had been avoiding him so he wouldn't get the wrong idea.

As soon as she sat down, she realised – he still had the wrong idea.

'You think you don't deserve love,' he launched in, trying to take her hands. Francine thought he had picked up these lines from someone else. They were, like cigarettes, very un-Albert-like.

'You think you're alone, but you're not. I love you, I've always loved you, from the first day we met.'

Francine couldn't think of anything to say. Would 'thank you' cut it? Or, 'That's sweet but no...'

He squeezed her fingers gently, not the way Mr Williams used to when she tried to get away.

'You don't want to be like Winnie.'

This jarred. 'How do you mean?'

'Her and Mr Cuthbert. Everyone knows they were in love as kids but when he came back from the war injured, he didn't want to burden her – so he set her free.'

Francine had not known this.

'It affected their whole lives,' he went on, 'when they could have been so happy together.'

'Albert,' she said, careful not to call him Bertie, 'I don't think we are like them at all. And anyway, they've been hap—'

'It's not about them!' he said impatiently as though he hadn't been the one to bring them up. 'I'll wait for you,' he added. 'But I won't wait for ever.'

He got up, even though he'd hardly touched his drink and he was usually scathing about other people who left theirs. He stalked over to the door, his expression tight as his braces. This time she did follow him.

'Don't wait,' she told his retreating back. 'I am not going to change my mind.'

She couldn't be clearer than that, could she?

He let the door swing shut behind him.

Mrs Hardman visited that week, which Francine was pleased about, not least because it was a brilliant distraction from the Albert situation.

Mrs Hardman was excited about Valerie's latest wireless show. It felt pretty incredible to Francine too. The last day she had seen her, Valerie was listless in a hardware shop. She was now doing a job that involved half the country!

'It's called *The Woman on the Clapham Omnibus*,' Mrs Hardman said, then added nervously, 'It's about buses!'

'Wow, I bet you were a great resource,' Francine said, but Mrs Hardman's expression had turned stiff. 'Did she not ask you?'

'Not directly. I suppose she remembered stories I told her...'

Francine could only guess how much that must have hurt Mrs Hardman. Valerie and her mother's relationship had always been strained and Francine could never understand it. The sympathy she had once had for Valerie had evaporated since she'd lost her own mother. Gosh, if Mrs Hardman were her mother Francine would hug her all day long, never mind give her a teensy boost by asking her about her war work.

'Are you courting, Francine?' Mrs Hardman asked. Since Francine had left school, everyone had been asking her that like it was contagious.

Francine hadn't planned to tell but found herself baring her soul to her old neighbour.

'There is someone who wants to court me, but I don't feel the same.'

How she wished she felt the same. How she wished she and Albert could be happy together – it would be perfect, it would make everyone so happy – but in her heart, it didn't feel right, and because she loved Albert, although not in the way he wanted, it wouldn't be fair.

'I wish my mother were here to tell me what to do.'

Mrs Hardman's response surprised her.

'Obviously I'm not your mother, but I imagine she would say to follow your heart, Francine. I remember her saying, "there are many nice men in the world, but that doesn't mean you have to marry them all."'

Francine wasn't sure if she was joking or not, but then she realised that Mrs Hardman was deadly serious.

'It's all right to wait for the right person,' she continued timidly, 'or even not to marry at all.'

Francine felt suddenly tearful.

'How did you decide you loved Mr Hardman enough to marry him?'

Mrs Hardman pressed her hand over her heart, and she made a huffing sound. 'That's a good question,' she said, but she didn't say, and this time, Francine didn't feel she could push her for an answer.

59

Francine

'My granddaughter is coming,' Toby announced at the counter. 'My granddaughter, my greatest critic!'

Francine got him his usual.

'Has she read your book?' she asked.

'Read it? She hates it!' He laughed. She presumed he was joking. His memoir was a page-turner.

'Will you bring her in?'

'I can't *bring* her anywhere. Sandra does exactly as she pleases.'

'Sounds like my cat.'

Sid had recently told Winnie and Francine that Tiger stayed overnight at his house, oh, at least three times a week. Tiger had a favourite spot under the shelves in the larder. Winnie and Francine bent double laughing at Tiger's antics. So that's where the sneaky one went when she wasn't at home!

Toby grinned at her, his drinks' foam making a comical moustache. 'I imagine you two will get on.'

Not far from the pub, there was a hall. For as long as Francine had been living there, it had never been in use. She had had her eye on it for a while – and now there was a sign up in the garden that said FOR SALE. Francine got off her bike. She could feel her mummy was with her again, prodding her anxiously in the shoulder blades. She shoved at the door and to her surprise it opened into an airy, large room, a light place with big windows.

Francine was now working full-time at the pub, and one of the things she enjoyed most was hosting the many groups who met there. Nowadays, the back room was constantly occupied. There were over fifteen groups, including the knitting circle, the sewing alliance, bingo club, cards, darts club, Friends of Canadians, memoir-writing, and chess and other board games.

Being in the heart of the community was something Francine had never expected, nor even wanted, but it was an excellent place to be. Now, she wanted to expand the business. Take it out of brewery control, bring it up to date... Maybe even find a place to turn into a bingo hall? Francine didn't have the money yet – but one day she would. She had big dreams.

A few days later, a young woman appeared in the Castle. She had corn-coloured hair and wide-set eyes and her skin was golden. Her teeth were so white and straight that Francine thought she looked more Canadian than British. She was wearing a beautiful dogtooth-checked coat – another thing you didn't see around here – and Francine watched as she hung it on the stand, and then because she didn't want to be caught watching, Francine dealt the beermats out onto the counter. Underneath the coat, the young woman was equally stylish – or adventurous maybe; she was wearing mannish trousers with a pretty white blouse and it was a curious mix.

'You must be the famous Sandra?'

'No,' the young woman said. She had heavy lids and pale eyelashes. There was something about her – not just the clothes – that attracted attention.

Francine licked her lips, feeling stupid.

'Oh, sorry!'

'I'm Sandy. S.a.n.d.y.'

Sandy was a good name for her; not only was she golden but she was gritty too.

'I'm Francine,' Francine said. 'F.r.a.n.c.i.n.e.'

'Good to know.'

Sandy played darts with her grandad. Francine watched from behind the counter, pretending not to. Sandy had straight posture and strong-looking arms and her darts all hit the board, but she didn't get the 20 she was looking for, and grew frustrated. When they'd finished she came back to the bar, smiling.

'That's my dream of a career in darts dashed...'

'How long are you here for?' Francine asked. The girl could drink too. She was on her third pint.

'I've got time off work, but what's there to do here in Kettering?'

Bizarrely, Francine couldn't name a single thing. 'Uh, there's loads.'

'Like what?' Sandra said, sipping at her drink.

'Um... bingo, cards, piano, views, cycling...'

Sandy laughed.

'You'll show me around?'

'Sure,' Francine said, although the idea made her feel nervous.

You couldn't tell how tall Sandy was when they were on bikes, but when they stood side by side there was a real difference. Francine was barely five feet; yet it wasn't just her height – or lack of it – that sometimes made her feel stunted. She felt like she hadn't been able to grow to her full potential. By contrast, Sandy was the vision of health.

Francine tried to see the village through Sandy's eyes. Some shopkeepers and business owners – like Winnie with her rose-pruning – went to enormous efforts to make their establishments look inviting. Others did much less. Some had exquisitely dressed mannequins in their windows, others looked like they had given up trying long before the war.

The airbase had a deserted look about it. There were still a few trucks and people in uniforms, but it was a big change from in its heyday – if that was the right word for an airbase.

As they cycled past, Francine told Sandy what Aunty Winnie had told her, which was that a production company was interested in buying up the place and turning it into film studios to make war films. Winnie had confessed to having reservations about this development, but Francine had told her that it would invigorate the town and bring in lots of people – possibly to the Castle as well.

'Oh yes!' Winnie had agreed. 'I hadn't thought of that.'

Recently, Winnie was less interested in the pub than ever. Yes, she was there physically, but it felt like her mind – or her spirit – was far away. Sometimes, Francine approached her with plans and she would say, 'Ooh, how interesting! I'll think about that!' and maybe she did, but she never did anything about it.

Sandy was also uninterested in the transformation of the airbase, and more preoccupied with what had happened when the Canadians were there.

'Did you go out with the Canadian boys?' She had a way of posing questions that felt like being poked with a sharpened pencil. It made Francine realise that other people – Winnie, Mr Cuthbert, even Albert – trod lightly around her.

'No.'

'I bet they queued up to take you dancing.'

'Never.' Francine dabbed her forehead with her handkerchief. 'Although they did give me sweets.'

After they'd ridden through town, they left their bicycles and began the steep ascent up the hill on foot. It wasn't a proper path but one that had been worn in by walkers. There were stones and rocks that were easy to trip up on and a couple of times Francine had to grab hold of Sandy to stop herself from falling. Sandy was steady as a mule.

Sandy had brought liquorice and Francine had a flask of sugary tea. They'd walk through lunch, which was all right since she didn't have much of an appetite. Francine wondered if Sandy would ask about her family. She didn't know what she'd tell her if she did. She only told people once she knew them well, but she didn't want to tell Sandy the usual pat or rehearsed version of the story; there was something about this woman – she had the charm of Lydia and the intellect of Valerie – that made Francine feel like she wanted any conversation she had with her to be from the heart.

Sandy worked in insurance.

'The only people I talk to are dull types in bowler hats and it's all about risk and disaster,' she said. 'I'd rather work in a pub.'

Inevitably, the conversation turned to where they were in the war. Sandy, who was from Liverpool, had been evacuated to the Cotswolds.

'It was fine,' she said, chewing liquorice. 'A family took in my older brother and me. Then Mum was evacuated and we went to stay with her. We all keep in touch.'

'Nice.'

'How about you?'

Francine lay back, shielding her eyes from the sun.

'There's nothing much to tell, not really.'

'People don't like talking about the war, do they?'

'Not really.'

'Do you ever say anything other than not really?'

'Not really.'

They smiled at each other.

'My grandfather is writing his memoir because he feels it's important. Personally, I think it's self-indulgent tosh.'

'Oh?' said Francine. 'Have you read it?'

'I read the prologue,' Sandy said, 'I prefer fiction.' Although Francine found reading more difficult than many, she had been alongside Toby for every chapter and had shed many tears as he relayed his experiences. She was surprised that Sandy, who mentioned several times how much she loved books, hadn't.

Francine tried to explain. 'Your grandad feels people should know about what he went through... Maybe if people understood the horror, then it could have averted another world war?'

'I don't think his memoir will change minds, will it?' Sandy grinned. 'Would it have changed Hitler's mind, do you think?'

'I don't suppose so, but he'll have done his best. That's important too.'

'He's wasting his time.'

Did she mean to be so rude, Francine wondered? Out of nowhere, she remembered Mrs Howard quoting: 'The quality of mercy is not strained...' She had liked that.

Now she looked at Sandy.

'Sometimes there is a tyranny or an ideology that is so bad that you have to stand up to it, to fight it, in whatever way you can. I don't think a memoir will stop wars or anything, but it's all drops of compassion, isn't it?'

'I'm a pacifist,' Sandy announced suddenly. 'And I don't think it would have been that bad if we'd just surrendered, that is, not actually declared war back in 1939. Better to be friends than enemies. You don't have to fight all the time, especially not on behalf of foreign countries like Holland or Poland.'

As Sandy said those names, her face was contorted as though they were a food she disliked.

Francine, who rarely got annoyed, now felt a spike of fury. Sandy was talking like an idiot – and about Francine's father's country – and Francine just hadn't expected it. She had been so drawn to this woman, thinking her a kindred spirit, yet now she felt alien. It just showed, Francine thought sadly, that you shouldn't judge a book by its cover. Still, she continued trying to express herself.

'Good people don't want war, but sometimes we have no alternative.'

'There's always a choice!' Sandy chuckled to herself. She seemed to think Francine was the stupid one. Francine shook her head. What an insufferable know-it-all. 'People could just choose peace. And then it would be fine.'

Francine could take it no longer. Something about this reminded her of being trapped with Mr Williams. Never again. She felt for her dice, then got up, relishing Sandy's evident surprise, and strode off. Sandy could find her own way home. It was only ten minutes or so and, besides, she thought bitterly, Sandy had peace on her side.

At the base of the hill, Francine was still annoyed as she pulled her bicycle from where it had been tangled up with Sandy's, like lovers entwined. She was still annoyed as she parted them, and still annoyed as she cycled away. She heard Sandy yelling her name, twice, three times maybe, but then she must have given up.

By that evening, Francine was so angry with Sandy she could hardly contain herself. At the same time, she was asking herself, *why are you so angry?* People in the pub said ridiculous things to her all the time. Winnie always insisted part of their job was to keep up with the issues of the day yet to nod along serenely, no matter what nonsense the customers came out with. She was there to make them feel safe, relaxed, comfortable. She was not there to challenge opinions or to put forward her views (however right she was!). And Sandy was not like Mr Williams, she really was not.

So why had the girl got under her skin?

France rolled her dice yet wasn't satisfied with the answers.

That night and the next few nights, Francine struggled to sleep. It wasn't only her family keeping her awake any more, it wasn't the miserableness of her mother or the frustration of her sister or the howls of the babies: sometimes it was Sandy yelling her name, once, twice, three times, and then falling silent.

60

Winnie

Winnie was always delighted when Albert came into the Castle. Such a pleasant young man! Perhaps she would have liked a son, as Francine liked to tease her. Perhaps he was just a lovely young lad who had this effect on everyone. Or perhaps she was just waiting for the day when Albert would lay his hat on the counter, cards on the table, and announce, 'I'm going to ask Francine to marry me.'

Albert and Francine had so much in common. They were like the two dice Francine kept in her pocket – they added up to so much more when they were together. They brought something special out in each other. Like Francine, Albert hadn't gone back to London, although, unlike Francine, he did still have family there. Winnie knew he wasn't keen on them and that they had never visited him here.

Winnie had of course noticed that Albert had been in the pub less than he used to be, but there could be many explanations – it was lambing season and all sorts. Farmers were no slouches. She was so hopeful of a match between Albert and Francine that she had even had set aside a ring. Her wedding ring would go to Susan, but the gold band that Trevor gave her for their tenth anniversary would be Francine's. She'd discussed it with Susan, who didn't mind, but said, 'isn't it a bit premature?'

Not really. Winnie had a plan for the wedding – everyone back to the Castle, naturally! She also had an idea for Francine's trousseau. Francine didn't often dress up but that was partly because of rationing. She'd have no excuse when she was the bride.

Winnie would never forgive herself for the Mr Williams debacle, never, ever. It was the biggest failure of her life. But if Francine and Albert married, it would be a good way to get some redemption. So yes, her goalposts might have moved, *thank you for that, Ron*, but actually they had moved with the times. Adaptation was key.

Now, as Albert reached the bar, Winnie chased over to get to him before Mac.

'Usual, is it?' She fetched a ginger ale.

Albert winked. 'Thanks, Aunty Winnie.'

He was adorable!

And then Winnie realised something else: close behind Albert was a young woman with curly blonde hair, peachy cheeks and big eyes behind round glasses – she couldn't have looked less like Francine, although there was something similar to Francine in the way she carried herself. Did Albert have a sister? Or was this perhaps one of the Martin farm girls?

Albert ordered her a blackcurrant and paid for them both. Now, Winnie saw he looked worried, proud and shy all at the same time, and she would have asked what was going on, or even made a joke, but thank goodness she didn't because then she saw they were holding hands.

Albert had a girlfriend. This was his girlfriend. Not Francine. Her heart plummeted.

'This is May,' he said. 'May, this is Mrs Eldridge.'

'May?' Winnie pulled herself together. She mustn't forget she was a landlady, a hostess, here to serve. 'That's a lovely name.'

'I wasn't born in May,' the girl informed her. 'But my parents didn't like April.'

'Quite right,' agreed Winnie. She didn't know what she was saying. This wasn't the plan. Didn't Albert know the plan?

'May and I are engaged,' he said and the two of them chinked their glasses together.

Evidently not.

61

Francine

In the bar, May was talking about the wedding plans. They'd booked the church. They weren't in a hurry, but there was no point waiting, was there? May's parents were arranging everything. They were very traditional. Albert would have the family he wanted, the family that Francine could never have given him.

'They love him already,' May said. 'Dad hopes he'll join the family business, but Albert is determined to stay on the farm.'

Albert blushed behind his freckles.

This could have been me, thought Francine. And there was a tiny part of her that wished it was. The part that knew that Albert would be magnificent: Husband. Son-in-law. Father. Provider. It was all he had dreamed of being.

It was a fork in the road and she had – almost inadvertently – gone one way while he had gone the other. It was correct, but that didn't mean it didn't prickle her. Sometimes, she wished she were a straightforward person who it could have worked out with. Right now, she also wished Aunty Winnie wouldn't keep looking at her with eyes full of sympathy.

'I'll do the bingo tonight,' Francine said cheerfully. She had to prove to Winnie that even if Winnie's heart had broken over this, her own heart remained intact.

Francine took over from Mac, who was making a dog's dinner of calling, and pulled the balls from the basket.

'Red number four.'

'White twenty-two...'

'Quack, quack,' everyone replied with varying degrees of enthusiasm.

May was the first to get a line. She let out a high-pitched shriek, then leaned over and kissed Albert, who had never looked so proud.

Francine didn't falter: *We are not Winnie and Scott*, she reminded herself. *It's all going to work out.*

And her thoughts drifted, as recently they inevitably did, to the bicycle ride and the argument on the hill with Sandy.

It wasn't until one Saturday afternoon, after another couple of months had passed, that Sandy next came into the Castle. Francine didn't recognise her straight away – her lovely hair was concealed under a patterned headscarf and she was wearing sunglasses even inside. Francine was writing special offers on the new blackboard. They were doing spam sandwiches at the weekends now, which were proving a surprise hit.

Sandy came up to the bar but not straight away, after a few minutes. Even then it wasn't direct; she zigzagged over.

'Sorry I upset you,' Sandy said.

'It's all right.' Francine shrugged as though she hadn't given it a single thought. 'What are you having?'

'Oh...' Sandy seemed surprised that her apology hadn't prompted a conversation. 'G and T?'

When she had her drink, she waited as though to say more, but Francine went away, so eventually Sandy backed off. She chose the smallest corner table.

As she served the other customers, Francine couldn't help wondering what Sandy was doing here. Then she wondered why the young woman provoked something in her that she didn't understand. It wasn't irritation exactly, but it was close to that. Or it *was* irritation, but it was the kind where she wanted to be with her more rather than less. It was like a spot she needed to scratch.

'When are you next free?' Sandy asked Francine when she next came to the bar.

'Not until midnight. Today's our busiest day.'

The customers gathered around the wireless on a Saturday afternoon to listen to the football results. They'd be a big cheer if Birmingham City or Coventry Town won. Silence if they lost. Wins were better for pub takings, of course. Who could resist a celebratory beer? A lose wasn't bad – a beer to cheer yourself up? A draw was the worst, in terms of profit.

Sandy examined her nails. 'Have you got a light on your bike?'

Francine eyed her cautiously.

'Why?'

'Fancy a ride out in the dark?'

'Tonight?'

'Sure...'

After that Sandy sat reading a magazine. She got up only once, to use the ladies. One of the darts players, Fred-the-feather, asked Sandy if she wanted to play. As she waited, Francine found she was holding her breath. Sandy must have refused, since he went over to his pals, saying, 'No luck.' Then another of the men went over, and she must have said something similar to him because the others slapped him on the back in commiseration.

They shut the pub promptly that night as everyone was tired. Sandy asked if she could help with the clearing up. Francine was going to say no, but changed her mind and got her to wash the glasses so they were able to leave sooner.

'I can see why you don't like talking about the war... It's personal, isn't it?' Sandy said.

'It's personal to everyone, isn't it?'

'It's more personal to you than most.'

Francine sniffed.

'Grandad told me he heard you are Jewish.'

'So?'

This made Francine feel uncomfortable. She knew she couldn't control the dissemination of information, but out of all the things Toby could have told his granddaughter, why had he chosen that? Why did people care so much when she didn't? Why did they want to put her in that box when she didn't know much about that box herself? She could remember her mother kept kosher before the war – which meant she followed religious dietary rules – but very little other than that. She didn't want to be secretive, but at the same time she was prickly about people knowing – no, it wasn't knowing, it was *expecting* certain things because of it. The Mr Williamses were everywhere. Just because he'd gone didn't mean another one wouldn't pop up in his place.

'If you had been on the Continent you might have been murdered too, or at least gone into hiding. And if the

Germans had managed to invade, you'd have been one of the first against the wall. So it IS more personal to you.'

Francine frowned. 'It's impossible to measure but most people appreciate the necessity of fighting against Hitler, whether they're Jewish or not.'

She thought about Mr Cohen's daughter, his Ruthie, hidden somewhere in Paris. She'd never find out where she was now, she supposed.

'Mm,' said Sandy. 'You're probably right…'

At the top of the hill Sandy wanted to look at the sky. Francine sank down awkwardly next to her, grass prickling her calves and arms. The night did look beautiful. The white lights flickering in the black seemed to be pulsing with life, little heartbeats.

'I arranged the stars especially for you.'

'Ha.'

Sandy put serious things in a joke and jokes in serious things. It was hard to keep up.

She had brought sausage rolls and blackberries. Francine tucked in hungrily. 'Have you heard of the Famous Five or Mallory Towers?'

'Nope,' said Francine. 'Are they films?'

'So' – Sandy sat upright, animated again – 'They're series of books, for children really, and they couldn't be further from how I grew up, but I loved them. A real escape.'

'I see.'

'In the books, the children are always racing around, eating picnics and having' – Sandy put on a funny posh accent – 'Lashings of ginger beer.'

Francine laughed. 'We sell that in the pub.'

Smiling, Sandy continued, 'So I thought, why not have a midnight feast – with you?'

Why not indeed? thought Francine. She thought again of

what Albert had said: 'You think you don't deserve love.' It *wasn't* true.

Sandy peered at Francine. 'You have...'

'What?'

Leaning in, she touched Francine's cheek. 'Something. A crumb or a...'

Francine touched her wrist. 'It's my scars.'

'I'm sorry, I didn't—'

'I had chicken pox when I was little. I kept picking and picking and... *voilà!* I'm covered in marks.'

Tiny reminders, she thought of them as. Of the worst time.

Sandy shook her head. Francine could see she was embarrassed. 'Did no one tell you not to?'

Francine smiled ruefully.

'They tried. At the time, it wasn't something I cared about.'

'You have a beautiful face,' Sandy said.

Francine didn't know how to respond. Sandy was the joker in the pack. Still, it was much more fun being with her when they weren't disagreeing.

'So you and your family always lived here?' Sandy asked.

'No, I was evacuated from London.'

Via Somerset, Francine thought, *via Mr Cohen*.

Sandy put down her sausage roll, mouth open in surprise. 'I thought you were here long before the war.'

'I came in January 1941 – in the middle of the Blitz.'

'With Winnie?'

'No... I moved in with her later, in the spring.'

'Oh, wait, I thought Winnie was your mum?'

'No, she's not,' said Francine, surprised Toby hadn't imparted that to her. People were strange in what information they thought was pertinent and what was not. 'It's a long story.'

Sandy leaned on her elbow and looked at her. Her eyes were as green as meadows. 'I'd love to hear it.'

'Another time.'

'There will be another time, then?'

Her skirt had slipped over her knee and Francine could see the place where her stockings ended and her suspenders began. She had this wild urge to put her hand there. Just rest her fingers on the edge where the material met the pale skin of her thigh.

Francine felt her dice. Tell this girl about the destruction of her family. Don't tell her. Tell her something else.

She got a 3 – don't tell. She decided to ignore it.

62

Winnie

It had been a long, long day. The kind of day after which she and Trevor would have taken turns at resting their aching feet in a bowl of hot water.

Somehow the community groups had been double-booked. Fortunately, the newly formed women's liberation army – Winnie did raise her eyebrows at that – had got on with the knitting circle like a house on fire and they both overran by half an hour. There had been a fractious darts tournament and a queue of regulars wanting to tell their stories. The ex-servicemen often had very sad tales and, while Winnie encouraged them to share with their families, their doctors, their bosses, most of them preferred to talk only to her over several pints of beer.

Francine was making tea upstairs in the kitchen. After Albert's engagement, Winnie had looked for signs of distress in Francine. She hadn't see them yet but who knew what Francine felt? She was an expert in covering things up.

'Can we have a talk?' Francine asked and Winnie said of course they could. She sat on the kitchen stool, and waited for bad news. When did people ever want 'a talk' for good news?

'Aunty Winnie,' Francine said in the clear voice she used when she was calling out the bingo numbers, 'why didn't you go to Canada to be with Ron?'

This wasn't what Winnie had expected. She didn't like to be the focus of the talk.

'I didn't want to,' she said lightly. 'Now about Albert... It's not over until—'

Francine snorted. 'That's not true. I know you and Ron love each other.'

Winnie grimaced.

'And I know you wanted to go.'

'I wanted to, but I didn't,' Winnie admitted. 'And I had made a promise to myself.' And to Ron, she remembered. 'That I wouldn't until...'

'Until what?'

'Until you are settled,' Winnie said. 'It's the least I can do.'

Perhaps she should have discussed it with Francine before? She dismissed this idea. Francine was still a child, her responsibility. Any parent would feel the same.

She pushed on. 'Now I know this May girl might feel like an obstacle...'

Francine snorted.

'But you shouldn't give up hope. Albert loves you more than her.'

Francine poured the tea then handed Winnie the mug.

'Aunty Winnie, I'm not going to marry Albert.'

'It doesn't have to be Albert,' Winnie said generously – although she would have preferred it was Albert. Albert was the quintessential good husband and son-in-law. This May girl was lucky but that didn't mean it was set in stone. Goodness knew, Winnie was more aware than most that feelings can change on the spin of a sixpence – or a stint in the trenches.

Francine was shaking her head slowly, another thing Winnie didn't like.

'Albert *is* nice,' she said, 'but I've no interest in marrying him.'

'As I said, it doesn't have to be him.' Winnie knew it sounded even worse second time round than it had the first, but she was convinced she was right.

This girl was a victim of the Blitz, of the fostering system, of a gross bully and of her, a dozy Doris who didn't see what was going on in front of her nose. She had taken her eyes off Francine only once in all her time at the Castle and look at the damage that had ensued! That maniac Williams! She had trusted him and he had fooled her. She didn't know who to trust now – all she knew was no one was going to hurt Francine again, not on her watch.

'I'm not going to marry anyone.'

'You say that now,' said Winnie, sipping her tea. Francine must have been hurt by this May girl to come out with such proclamations. It was like that for her after Scott had chosen Ada. She probably said dreadful things and thought even worse. But then she met Trevor and they had had a tremendous run of it. She wouldn't have missed that for the world. 'You'll meet someone else some day, Francine.'

Francine sighed. 'So what excuse can you use now?'

'What?'

'What's your excuse for not going to be with Ron?'

Winnie spluttered.

'It's not an excuse. I want you to be settled down before I

leave. You've gone through so much, Francine – losing your family and then Mr Cohen and then...' And then the disastrous bit *she* was responsible for. *How would she ever get over that?* 'Anyway, it's not about me.'

'It is,' Francine said sternly. 'I'm not going to ever settle down the way you want me to.'

'I said it doesn't have to be Albert!' *Third time lucky.* 'There are plenty of young men...'

'I don't want to be married, ever, so if that's what you're waiting for, please just go.'

'What?' Winnie said, half-expecting Francine to correct her with a 'pardon'?

'Go to Canada and be with Ron!'

Winnie felt like sobbing suddenly. She felt as if she didn't have any skin, she was all ugly flesh and shameful desire – and as if Francine knew. Francine knew she was torn and half of her wanted to be with Ron. She had tried to hide it from the girl, but she hadn't succeeded.

'You love him. And you always wanted to explore the world. You never wanted the pub to consume your whole life.'

'It's not like that,' Winnie tried to explain. 'I didn't want to be married when I was your age either, but then I changed my mind.'

'That's not going to happen to me,' Francine said firmly.

'All right,' said Winnie, holding her hands up in surrender. 'Time for bed.'

'No, wait. I have something to show you.'

It turned out Francine had done something completely underhand. Winnie would never have imagined the girl who seemed oblivious to romance, obsessed only with business, to have done this. Indeed, if it had been anyone else, Winnie might have blown a gasket. The outrage, the interference, the poking her nose in!

Francine had written to Ron! Not only had Francine written to Ron, Ron had written back immediately. Ron had written back in his big Canadian CAPITAL letters – Winnie didn't know if his writing was a Ron-thing or a Canadian thing, but whatever it was, it was lovely. Each letter stood like a great oak tree, like Ron commanding you to lean on him. And he didn't put too many words on a line or too many lines on a page; there was a nice amount of clean space around them that made Winnie feel ridiculously that he would give her plenty of space, too.

Tell Winne, yes I am still in love with her and I would love her to come here.

Francine stood, hands on hips.

'Now do you believe me?'

'What is this?' Winnie felt ganged up on. They'd been communicating without her, about her?

'He *wants* you in Canada. How much clearer do you want it to be?'

'It's complicated.'

'But you love him, don't you? I know you do.'

'I do, but it's not just about love, is it?'

'What is it about then?'

Winnie had tried but she couldn't shake the absolute horror of the classroom that day from her mind. She could never forgive herself for her role in it. Stupid bystander. No, worse. She pictured herself telling Francine, 'Get him on side, he's influential!' or worse, asking Mr Williams, 'Have you noticed she seems discombobulated'?

It was an albatross round her neck – and she felt she was

doomed to carry that big bird around with her until the end of time.

'You're my girl,' she whispered.

Francine was shaking her head at her so tenderly.

'And you're my Aunty Winnie. Nothing will ever change that.'

'I failed in my duty to you.'

'You didn't. Not at all. And you can go – you must.'

'I don't know.' Winnie couldn't resist returning to the letter. 'When did he send this?'

'Just last week. Listen, Aunty Winnie, I've got my dad now. I've got' – she hesitated – 'friends here. I've got my cousins. Bertie and I are still pals and I love running the pub.'

Winnie felt exhausted again. Not tired for bed – not anything putting her feet in hot water would cure – but bone-tired. Like she had been running in the wrong direction this whole time, and now needed to get back and start again.

'You want to take over the Castle?'

'I would love nothing more,' Francine answered immediately. 'I love it here. And I want to expand... I'm' – She reddened – 'bursting with ideas, actually.'

Winnie swallowed. What would Trevor have said to this?

'You'd still be the proper boss,' Francine continued. 'But I'd be the manager on the ground, as it were.'

Again, Winnie felt like she was being pulled in all different directions. How was it she couldn't decide? To have freedom and not know what to do with it struck her as being as difficult as having no freedom at all.

She was being ridiculous. Trevor would be happy. And even if he wasn't, was what Trevor thought the only salient point here? What did *she* want?

'I think of you as my other daughter.'

'I will always be yours,' Francine said. 'Wherever you are.'

'So you've no place here for little old me?' Winnie whispered.

'No place for you at all,' Francine joked.

If they were the hugging sort, Winnie knew they would have hugged then. Winnie knew her answer – she *knew*.

'You have been such a light in my life.'

'And you,' Francine returned gruffly. 'You saved mine.'

Francine offered to help draft a reply to Ron, but Winnie said she'd be fine doing it herself.

'I'll do it tomorrow.'

'Write it now,' insisted Francine. 'You've wasted enough time as it is.'

Winnie hesitated. Never had a paper looked so blank.

'Do you want to borrow my special pen?'

Winnie, Scott Cuthbert, Francine's dad and Albert had clubbed together to buy Francine a replacement for her first special pen after they found out what had been happening at school.

Winnie looked up at the earnest face of her evacuee or her foster child? Neither label fitted, she was just her Francine.

'Go on then.'

Dear Ron

I'm hoping to have an extended holiday in Canada – with a view to a permanent stay – and I was wondering: what are your thoughts?

Yours, mortified,

Winnie

'Much better than a dumb old wedding,' Francine said, and Winnie laughed, although secretly she thought it would have been nice to have a dumb old wedding and then go.

But nothing turns out exactly as you hope it will – what turns out is always different, and sometimes what turns out is even better.

63

WINTER, 1948

Winnie

It wasn't easy telling the people she'd known all her life that she was leaving, but it was easier than it might have been because of Francine. The pub was in safe hands. Safer than it had been since Trevor left. Francine was the Castle's true heir, Winnie thought. The natural successor. It felt like it was written in the stars.

'Francine virtually runs it all now anyway,' she told people – even when they didn't ask, especially when they didn't. 'Better than I ever did.'

It was true; the pub was in Winnie's name, but Francine had taken over everything. She did the books. She did the deliveries. She had, thank goodness, taken over all communication with the brewery. Francine lit the fire on the cooler days, washed the windows, double-checked the glasses – since the war had ended, there was more lipstick on the glasses because there was more lipstick. She had even got the H in TH CASTLE re-installed, something that Trevor, in twenty years, and Winnie, in thirty, had never got round to doing.

'It was nothing,' Francine said – she always insisted what she did was nothing. 'Jim knew someone who knew someone, who did it at a fair price.'

She was trying to raise money to buy them out and free them from brewery control. Winnie had mixed feelings about this – it felt like a rebuke. Should she have done it sooner? It also felt like a whole lot of bother – this *wasn't* nothing. But it was up to Francine now.

And Francine wanted to buy another pub or four. She was also keen to open a bingo hall. She had been predicting that bingo would be the next big thing for a while.

'I don't see how that would work.'

Francine shrugged in her Francine way.

'We'll see... if I can get the finance.'

Winnie was pretty certain she wouldn't. She was an eighteen-year-old girl, for goodness' sake; the only way she would ever get the finance was if she had a wealthy husband, or even a working husband (like Albert!), but there was no telling Francine that.

There was nothing in the plans to alarm a Castle regular. But people will always surprise you. Some of the customers, ones Winnie thought would be distressed at her departure, were chipper and full of 'Good luck!' Or 'About time too!' Others, ones she thought hadn't noticed her, who had never said more than two words to her beyond, 'Pint, please,' were woebegone.

Some people didn't like change. She used to be one of them, so she sympathised.

Miss Lane was worried about bears in Canada. She'd done a project about them with the children. With the myriad things Winnie was worried about – and there were enough to keep her up at night, with Francine, Susan, the journey, Ron, Ron's family (would they like her?), Ron's friends (ditto) – bears hardly figured. In fact, she'd prefer to worry about bears, she decided. Counting bears might help her fall asleep.

A few people didn't know the difference between Canada and America – to be fair, Winnie was vague on the subject too.

'Don't they speak French there?' Nathan asked.

'Oui,' Winnie said. 'In some parts.' She had taken out a French textbook from the library and when the pub was quiet, she would practise at the bar. It wasn't necessary but she wanted to surprise Ron. She knew all the members of a family in French. Interestingly, it was one of the first things you had to learn.

There were no words to describe the relationships she had with someone like Francine, Old Jim or Scott, of course.

'What?' Old Jim asked suspiciously when she practised on him. Jim said he had never heard an accent like hers.

'Ma tante a un parapluie!' said Winnie.

'She should see a doctor about that,' Jim quipped.

Mrs Wyatt from the knitting circle said she was going to hide away in Winnie's trunk.

'I've always had a thing for the Mounties,' she explained. 'A picture book I saw when I was a child, stayed with me all this time. How handsome they looked in their red jackets! I envy you!'

'Ron isn't in the mounted police...'

'But still,' insisted Mrs Wyatt. 'He's as close as I'm ever going to get.'

Would she write to the children? This was bear-botherer Miss Lane again. 'Or find pen pals for them?'

'Or perhaps' – Miss Lane's face lit up – 'we could twin schools? Don't laugh, Mrs Eldridge, everyone's doing it!'

Mrs Phelps who didn't say boo to a goose said that she had heard over 60,000 women had married Canadians during and since the war. It was hard to tell if she approved of that or not.

'I'm not sure Ron and I are,' Winnie said, blushing. 'It's an exploration, for now.'

Mrs Phelps ignored this. 'You have to have a medical to show that you've not got TB.'

'How do you know so much about it? Are you planning on going?' Mac asked in a strangled voice.

'Not me,' she said, looking up at him with her startling blue eyes. 'I'm never leaving Kettering.'

Scott Cuthbert was the one Winnie was dreading telling the most. She was waiting until he came into the pub, but he was away on work business, or away with his wife, no one was sure.

Then one day she was walking in town when she noticed the recruitment office was all cleared out. Winnie wanted to know who was moving in and why, and how much the rent was. She had just read the sign stuck on the window when she noticed the lights were on in the offices upstairs and, spontaneously, she decided she would find Scott and tell him her news face to face. There was nothing to be scared of. Now, nearly thirty years later than planned, she would actually be leaving town.

Scott was scrabbling around on the floor among dozens of paper files. Looking for families, looking for children. Winnie wondered what a file on her would say: *Unexceptional middle-aged woman with a homely face and ideas above her station.*

He wasn't surprised to see her.

'I have something to tell you,' she said, wringing her hands.

'Help me up then.'

He held out his hand and, as she grabbed at it, she nearly toppled over. Finding a balance was something they never found easy. They both laughed and then he struggled into his chair. Was he finding it harder than usual? Probably. The indignities of getting older adding to his injury. She remembered reading about life expectancy falling with injuries such as his.

He lit a cigarette and offered her one. She usually wouldn't but she thought, what the hell? It was that kind of day. Plus, cigarettes help you live longer, the advertisements said. And these days she was in the business of living for as long as she could.

'I already heard,' he said. 'The whole town is talking about it. You're going to Canada, aren't you?'

'I am.'

'Lucky Ron,' he said wryly.

'Lucky me,' she said.

He blew out smoke. The small office grew misty, but she was glad of the drop in visibility; he wouldn't see that she was teary.

'What about Francine?'

'She has given me permission, yes.'

'Is that so?'

'Don't make it harder than it already is, Scott.'

A part of Winnie had always wondered if Scott had installed Francine with her not only to keep her going when she was so close to giving up on life, but also to keep her back. If perhaps having her foster Francine was his way of keeping her in Kettering, keeping her close to him. If so, she did not hate him for this, quite the opposite.

'I don't mean to,' he said. 'It's just I'm going to miss you more than you know.'

'I do know,' she said. She stubbed out the cigarette, admitting defeat. Smoking wasn't for her. 'Because I'll miss you too.'

She wondered – if he hadn't been terribly injured, hadn't met Ada, hadn't thought she wanted to leave, might things have been different between them? No matter. Things had turned out all right. She had met Trevor and they had been happy – and so had Scott and Ada. And now... now she had something else and someone else to look forward to.

Scott probably thought he knew what was right for her, but he didn't understand that people can change.

They looked at each other. His face no longer boyish or round, the hair no longer wild. She knew his pain and suffering and he knew what she'd allowed him to see of hers. She felt emotional. Old friends' faces will do that to you. Like double vision. You see the faces of back then at the same time as you see the faces of now. You see the dreams and the punishments of the past. The laughing child and the hurt adult. The journey they'd gone on from then to be the person you see now. It was all there. It was never just now. It was never just a face. He had the same face; how could she think it had changed?

'My best friend,' she whispered. Of course, that's what they would say in the English-French book. *Mon meilleur ami.*

He shook his head. She could hear the tears in his voice. 'My sister.'

64

Francine

Daddy was going to London to test drive a car. Everyone was having babies or getting cars. Albert had got a second-hand Buick and young Jim had acquired a Ford Anglia. There was still rationing on fuel, but car-owners were optimistic that it would end soon.

'It might be boring,' Daddy warned. 'But I'd love you to come.'

They decided to make a day of it, so Francine packed lunch: her father's favourite – herrings – which stank and made the passengers in the train carriage scowl; plain old jam sandwiches for her.

Daddy was in a nostalgic mood. He told her how he met her mother at a language school in Euston where he was studying English. Such a pretty girl! She was the receptionist and he used to bring her flowers and try to practise verbs with her.

'I was sure you met at a dance!' Francine said, confused.

'Second date was dance,' he said. 'Third date I asked her to marry me.'

It was perhaps the first time he'd mentioned her mother without crying.

They went back to 67 Romberg Road. The street had plenty of bombsites, like a mouth full of rotten teeth. The last time Francine had been there was nearly eight years ago, January 1941.

A neighbour came over as they stood wondering who still lived there and pointed with her thumb, said, 'She's always at work. She's probably at the BBC today.'

'Hoity-toity,' mocked Francine's dad.

'Da-ad,' warned Francine. 'Mrs Hardman isn't hoity-toity...'

They rang the doorbell on the off-chance and for once they were in luck.

'Rare day off,' Mrs Hardman said, delighted to see them. When Francine's dad said how impressive it was that she was at the BBC, she laughed. 'I'm a lowly dinner lady.'

'So?' he said.

'What about the Frouds?' asked Francine, meaning, what about Lydia? Her heart beat faster when she talked about her. Mrs Hardman said that her parents had left the flat after the war and Lydia had chosen to stay on in Somerset. She didn't like the city, apparently.

That was the Lydia she knew. While everyone else ran around in circles, trying to keep other people happy, Lydia always knew what she wanted, and she wouldn't deviate from that.

Mrs Hardman said, 'I'm glad you came. I've got some photographs for you.'

She handed them an album. She must have put it

together herself because Francine couldn't remember anything like this. Black pages, sticky tape holding the photos in place.

Francine held her breath. There was Joe and there was Jacob. Joe holding his bottle. Jacob playing the recorder. She had forgotten that damn instrument. It was hers, then Maisie's, and Mummy had said her grandfather was a great musician so what the hell happened to them that they were all tone-deaf?

Oranges and Lemons, say the bells of St Clements.

Now Daddy cried and said Dutch words that she didn't understand but could imagine. He wasn't long on his grieving journey, she appreciated, while she was years further down the line. He had found out other things too, since the war ended: He had found out about some cousins in Amsterdam who hid in a basement for three years of the Nazi occupation. He had found out about some cousins who did not.

Afterwards, they wandered around the car showrooms with their expensive-tyre smell, and it was a good change of scene. Her father in his baggy blazer, faded trousers and heavy bags under his eyes didn't look like he had enough money, and at first the smart young men treated Mr Salt if not with disdain then certainly with disinterest. Francine couldn't bear to see it.

At one showroom Francine's father asked for a test drive in the Morris 8 E Series, and the young man stubbed out his cigarette and pulled a 'ho-kay!' face.

Francine's father was excited by the four doors. Francine didn't say it but somehow four doors made her sad, made her think of her siblings, the tiny hands that wouldn't open the doors, small bodies that would never get to bounce on these leather seats. As they drove out to the road, her father talked about the mechanics and the wipers and how responsive the brakes were. Then, once they were on a roll, Daddy started asking her questions.

'What will you do once Winnie is gone?'

'I'm going to run the pub.'

'You are?' A mixture of incredulity and admiration in his voice.

'I virtually do anyway,' she said. She felt disloyal saying that, but Aunty Winnie spent most of her time mooning over Ron Roscoe's letters and phone calls – and why not? Good for her.

She told him her plans to regenerate the Castle and to open other pubs. 'I just need to raise some money.'

'How much?' he said – straight to the point.

'Four thousand pounds,' she said.

'I don't have that much,' he said sadly. 'Would it help if I don't get the car and gave you the money instead?'

'No, get the car.' She laughed. 'You need it. That won't make the difference.'

She would go to the bank with a business plan, she explained. She had made some appointments already.

'You don't want to marry, have children?' her father asked.

Francine took a deep breath.

'Not sure...'

A few days earlier, she and Sandy had gone for another picnic on bikes, this time in the day. It was horribly hot and every time they found some shade the sun moved again as if determined to follow them.

'Are you staying in Kettering?' she'd asked.

'Grandad wants me to,' Sandy had said. 'He needs me to, as well.'

'Is that the only reason?'

Francine thought she knew most of Sandy's expressions

by now. The face she made when her bicycle tyre got a puncture and the satisfied face when she had fixed it. How she had looked when Francine told her about her family. Francine knew her face when she was talking about the war or her Enid Blyton books. How she looked when Tiger jumped on her lap. This expression, however, was unfamiliar.

'It isn't the only reason, no.'

She had leaned over and suddenly a shadow fell over Francine as Sandy's face loomed at hers, her lips coming towards her, landing on hers.

'Woah!'

Francine pulled back and Sandy did too, immediately, running a hand through her hair, shaking her head.

'Have I got this wrong?'

'Got what wrong?'

Francine was muddled. Sandy had kissed her?

'I thought... oh, it doesn't matter.'

Sandy stood up, pulled at her trouser legs and gave Francine a look that Francine couldn't decipher.

'I'm heading back. Coming?'

Since then, Francine couldn't stop thinking about Sandy. Everything was about Sandy. Her unblemished skin, not a spot or scar on it. Her hair when she tied it up in a ribbon or with too many bobby pins. Her hair when she let it down. Her pretty pale neck. The in-out shape of her in her blouse and trousers. How she got moody when she talked about cruelty to animals or was elated when she talked about the National Health Service or soft when she talked about her grandad.

Now, Francine looked at her father. He had come back in the end. Made it through the war when so many others hadn't. Lost all his loves – except for her. She didn't want to disappoint him ever. He had had four children and now he had only one. Whatever she did, she could not make herself four or make up for the loss of three. She could only be herself.

'Why don't you want to marry?'

At least his eyes were back on the road. A truck went by, and then some shouting boys on bicycles who made her think of Albert. And then a dog that made her think of Lydia. If Lydia were here, life would be so different.

Francine wondered what it was about her that meant that she lived with one foot in the present and one in the past. Were Valerie and Lydia like that or was it just her? Did everyone live with this exhausting prod of memories? She doubted it. Most people avoided straddling present and past. She wished she could.

'I don't know if marriage is for me, Daddy.'

When he next changed gear, he patted her on the knee.

'Whatever you think. You lead your life, Francine, I won't interfere.'

She thought again of Sandy and all the possibilities that lay there. Possibilities she would have to be bold to explore. She didn't know if she had the courage. There were so many different types of bravery and, although she knew she was brave in some ways, she wasn't sure she was brave in this particular way. Perhaps it was time to find out?

'Smooth, isn't she?' he continued. For a moment, she thought he meant Sandy, and she nearly let out a laugh when she realised he meant the car.

'What do you think?'

'I think you and she will be happy together!'

. . .

Francine sat outside on the kerb while the negotiations went on in the car showroom. She would have liked to have been involved. Negotiations were her bread and butter nowadays and she enjoyed them – especially when she was being underestimated, which was most of the time. She was fascinated by the car business too, but her father had made it clear he'd rather do this alone.

The discussions looked heated, but then, just as they looked most like breaking down, the men were suddenly hand-shaking and back-slapping each other.

I'm out with my dad, she thought to herself, *my father is buying a car*. And it was unremarkable yet remarkable too.

She remembered when he joined up, as a reservist at first. It must have been about three months or so before war broke out properly, early summer 1939, when it was an ominous rumble heeded only by some. Maisie and Mummy were thrilled, but Francine was so perturbed by the sight of her father in uniform, all spick, span and unfamiliar that she wanted to hide. He had laughed and then held her. 'I'm still me!' he'd tried to reassure her.

On the way back to Kettering, they stopped off to get provisions for the farewell party she was planning for Winnie. Her daddy was in love with the car and didn't stop talking about it. She marvelled at the human capacity for pleasure. At the joy of acquiring things. Some people look down on those who covet material goods, but they're usually the lucky ones, the ones who've got everything they want, nice and safe.

You will get the pen, little Francine, if you persevere.

This car was her daddy's pen.

Her father drove her back to the Castle and then he was off, to show his new purchase to 'a lady-friend...'

'You don't mind?' he asked.

It helped that Aunty Winnie – who knew everyone and everyone's business in Kettering – had warned her this was on the cards.

'How could I mind?' Francine replied.

He grabbed her hand, kissed it. 'My girl,' he said.

65

Winnie

Winnie spent most of the day packing and repacking her trunk. Half the clothes that she was contemplating taking she hadn't worn for years, but she might be a completely new person in Canada, mightn't she? She might want to wear a two-piece navy pencil suit with a pearl necklace that made her look like a sleuth in a movie. She might want to wear a floral dress with a lace collar that she had last worn at Susan's christening. It still fitted – almost. It was difficult deciding which to take and which to leave, but it was a happy task. Winnie was humming to herself to the tune of 'Pack up Your Troubles in Your Old Kit Bag'.

Would Francine like this beige skirt with the attached slip that Trevor had been given by an old aunt and that Winnie had never worn? Probably not. Would Susan perhaps like this wide-brimmed hat that Winnie had only worn once (to Old Jim's wedding)? Doubtful.

These weren't troubles and nor was it an old kitbag she was packing, but she liked the sentiment.

Ron had been as reassuring on the other end of the telephone as a man could be, but he was no good at advising what to bring beyond, 'Honey, you can get anything you need here!'

All week she had been going around in a sort of dream state, telling herself: 'This is my last time at the butcher's' or 'This is my last time taking in a delivery.' That way of thinking didn't calm her nerves.

The only way she could deal with the move was by telling herself it wasn't actually final. That she could 'always change her mind'. That phrase gave her room to breathe. It enabled her to act.

At night, she thought, *It's so far, it's too far, I can't!*, but in the morning, she told herself, *Pull yourself together, woman*, and that helped too.

Francine peeped round the bedroom door, winced at the piles of clothes, then said, 'Don't come down until I say so!' so Winnie did have an inkling that something was going on downstairs, but she had no idea what.

When she walked into the pub the tables, booths and bar were all full and there were groups of people standing in between, and everyone cheered. There were sheets hung over the walls and written on them was FAREWELL and BON VOYAGE and WATCH OUT CANADA, HERE COMES WINNIE!

'What have you done?' Winnie scolded Francine. 'You pest!'

Francine laughed. 'Me?'

'I told you not to make a fuss!'

'We couldn't let you go without a party.'

The regulars were all there. Sid was at his usual place at the piano. He must have been warned not to play anything melancholy because he launched into 'Daisy Bell'. Sid's wife was there, hand resting on his shoulder and muttering that he was more than half-crazy.

Winnie thought, *I will have someone to sit by me and someone to sit by for!* She couldn't wait.

Francine wouldn't let her go behind the bar. 'Not tonight. You've got to circulate.'

'If I must.'

She greeted Old Jim and his crossword.

'Country in the North American continent,' he said, 'Six across.'

'CANADA?'

'Is lucky to have you,' he finished, winking at her. 'If only I were twenty years younger!'

'Twenty? Forty more like!'

Nathan was gloomy. 'Who will I talk books with once you've gone?'

'You can always talk books with me,' called Francine across the counter.

'Do you like Lawrence?'

Francine looked doubtful. 'Uh. Lawrence of Arabia?'

'D.H. Lawrence.'

'I can try!' Francine offered cheerfully.

Winnie grinned, thinking of Francine's struggles with English at school and her throwing books across the floor. 'Who cares about the writer's intention, Aunty Winnie!'

Toby whispered into Winnie's ear: 'I have news too... The memoir is finished. I'm sending it off.'

'Amazing!'

'If it weren't for you, I'd never have done it!'

That wasn't true, she thought. Nevertheless, she appreciated the sentiment.

'You'll have to come on a book tour to Canada.'

'I will.' His whiskers tickled as he kissed her cheek. 'I'll
even bring the girls.'

Girls? Winnie wondered. Who did he mean? Behind the
counter, Francine had turned red. She was blushing a lot
lately, but then it did get hot over there.

The Castle darts team – the Archers – asked Winnie to join
them for a game. She would have liked to go out with a bang,
but her performance was more of a whimper – three darts
and she got a 19, an 8 and one miss. Nevertheless, they made
such a fuss of her, you'd think she'd got a bullseye.

Some ex-servicemen thanked her for listening to them.

'It's been a privilege,' she told them. It had been.

The knitters had come along too, still knitting. No occasion was big or small enough to stop them. Winnie admired
the way they could knit, drink and set the world to rights, all
at once.

Mac was especially attentive to them.

'Before you go,' he said, 'there's something I want to tell
you.'

'You've taken up knitting?' she joked.

He ignored that and said, 'Mrs Phelps and me are
engaged!'

Although overjoyed, Winnie was also irked with herself
that her usual romance early-warning system had failed her
so dismally. She must have been too caught up with Ron and
Francine to have noticed love blossoming right in front of her
nose.

'When – how?'

'She knitted me this,' he said, gesturing to the scarf he had been wearing whatever the weather. Crikey, thought Winnie, how on earth could she have missed this?

'From that moment, I wanted her to be mine. It's taken a few years, but I managed to persuade her.'

Winnie gulped. My goodness, she had never imagined Mac would find his love – how short-sighted of her. 'You must tell everyone.'

'No. This is your party.'

'Rot!' Winnie pulled the young lovers to the centre of the room.

'Love is in the air!' she said, eyes filling with tears. 'You just have to let it in!'

Sid's wife pulled at his shoulder as he played a jazzy version of the Wedding March. 'Don't you be getting any ideas!'

Winnie had already said her goodbyes to Susan, on a trip to London two days earlier. Susan had refused all offers of clothes, eau de cologne, the painting of Winston Churchill, or Winnie's three monkey ornaments.

'Do I look like I want them?!'

Winnie knew better than to be offended.

'It's not goodbye,' Susan had also said unconvincingly over the thick black coffee she insisted on drinking in the basement bar she frequented near Westminster. Susan rented in London, but she never invited Winnie to her rooms. 'They're too small,' she'd say, or, 'The landlord doesn't like visitors.' Winnie accepted this as another of Susan's quirks. 'It's see you soon,' she went on.

Winnie wished there were windows here. Wasn't this like being trapped in an underground air-raid shelter? Hadn't people had enough of blinking around beneath the surface like moles? Susan hadn't, apparently.

'Coffee houses like these are everywhere in the cities in Canada.'

'Are they?' Winnie was thinking they'd never catch on and even if they did, she wouldn't voluntarily go. She smiled to herself. But she'd go for love.

'Public houses are finished, Mum,' Susan continued. 'You got out just in time.' Winnie nodded vaguely. Susan would be in New York next year. She was formulating a plan to meet up with her there.

'I'm proud of you, Mum,' Susan said suddenly. 'It's hard to rebuild your life at your age.'

Winnie ignored the 'at your age'. What did Susan think she was? Some grand old dame of ninety? She wasn't yet fifty!

'I haven't done anything yet.'

'No backing out now,' Susan said briskly. 'You're the best, Mum. You inspire me.'

Winnie remembered a time long ago when she, Trevor and Susan had taken a precious day off from the pub to go to London Zoo. Susan was on a mission to see penguins. Winnie and Trevor had watched her indulgently, squeezed against the railings, desperate to communicate with the birds. The penguins waddled, swam and ignored her, but, whatever they did or didn't do, Susan was spellbound. Trevor had turned to Winnie.

'She turned out all right, didn't she, our girl?'

At the time, Winnie had seen that as tempting fate, so she had shushed him: 'Don't speak too soon.'

Now she thought, *yes, Trevor, you were right.*

. . .

At the farewell party, Winnie danced with Francine's dad, who was a surprisingly nifty mover, Jim, Old Jim and even Mac. Then Francine tapped a spoon against a glass and said that she had been told to give a speech, so here goes.

'The Castle was built in 1868 and they called it the Castle because there once was a Roman castle nearby. It has always been a place of community and sociability. It saved many people from that most horrible of afflictions – loneliness.'

There was a shout of 'Hear, hear!' And 'God bless Trevor and Winnie!'

'I came to Kettering in 1941, during the Blitz, and this town, but especially this pub, was a place of...' For a moment, Francine was too choked to continue. 'Sanctuary or refuge for me. We will miss Winnie, but the spirit of the Castle will endure.'

The regulars and the not-so-regulars all cheered.

'We'll look after her for you, Winnie,' Old Jim shouted, and Winnie wasn't sure if he meant the Castle or Francine – nor was he particularly capable of looking after anyone these days. But still, what a beautiful thought.

After everyone had left, Winnie and Francine cleared up. As they moved chairs and wiped tables, Winnie said you should never go to sleep on a row – although she'd done that enough times – and you should never go to sleep on a messy pub either. Then she said, 'I do think you should get in touch with Valerie and Lydia.' It was her last chance to give Francine advice.

Winnie remembered the half-written letters she used to find on Francine's desk. The girls' importance in Francine's life was something she had underestimated. Francine was as well-rounded an adult as anyone could hope to be, but still there were ragged edges and difficult memories that perhaps could only be smoothed out by old friends.

'Aunty Win,' Francine warned, 'stop it. I'm fine.' And then, in an awkward change of subject, she said, 'I'm surprised Mr Cuthbert didn't drop in.'

'I said goodbye yesterday,' Winnie said.

Francine searched Winnie's face. 'Hmm. One day, I hope you'll tell me the whole story about you and him.'

'There's nothing to tell,' replied Winnie, wide-eyed.

She was leaving at five in the morning. Francine's dad was driving her to Southampton. She'd offered him money but he'd refused gruffly: 'Least I can do.'

Francine snorted, said Winnie should take advantage of the offer. 'Any excuse to take the car for a long drive,' she'd said, which made Winnie feel less guilty.

'Don't get up,' Winnie told Francine now. 'You need your sleep now you're the landlady.'

Winnie was glad to leave the Castle in safe hands, but she felt wobbly too. Trevor had loved his pub. She remembered his smile after a busy night, when the conversations were animated, when they ran out of glasses, when the piano was being played.

'This is the life,' he would say, happy as a pig rolling in muck, and it was probably because of this happiness that when the war came along he felt obliged to do his thing, because hadn't he been fortunate? And wasn't it fair to share the load?

It was his life. And she was glad she'd been there, so glad they'd enjoyed it together. But he was the Castle. She was not.

'So, Churchill, what do you think of all this?'

The other Winnie grinned, his cigar at the ready. 'You took your time,' he might have said.

Would Francine take down the portrait once she was left to her own devices? Winnie didn't know and she didn't mind. The policy of neutrality had never really worked for her. Anyway, Francine would be a much better caretaker of the Castle than she had ever been.

Winnie didn't think she would sleep, not with the gin swirling in her belly and the nerves rattling in her head, but she counted Canadian bears and before too long her alarm clock was ringing.

Just as she was leaving – for the last time – she thought Trevor was there.

Ninety-five per cent of her knew it was just her conjuring him up, but five per cent wanted to believe it was him.

No rainbows. No butterflies. No thunderbolts. Nothing like that, just a whisper of something as she locked the door for that one last time. Scent of yellow roses.

'It's all right, Win, you get on with it, darling.'

And as she walked away from her home of thirty-five years, she looked up and saw a figure at the window – and that felt like Trevor too.

It was only much later that she realised that it was Francine, her second daughter, waving her off.

66

Francine

The day after Winnie left, Francine went to an address that had been scrawled on a beermat. The letters and numbers all leaned to the right, which gave it a sense of urgency – an urgency that Francine hadn't responded to. It was over three weeks since she and Sandy had last seen each other.

Francine knew the road but not the house. When she arrived, she saw a pretty, terraced building that looked as though it were looked after. She noted the floral-patterned curtains –still drawn at ten in the morning – and the bright red front door. She pushed open a gate that squeaked and noticed the empty glass bottles that had been left on the step for the milkman. There was lavender at the foot of the front wall, like purple socks on white legs, and a bee that seemed to have its eye on her. The bee would be the only other witness to her bravery, stupidity or whatever it was.

Sandy opened the door, yawning and her hair askew. She was in men's pyjamas that Francine had never seen a grown woman wear before, but Sandy had a way of making whatever she did seem normal.

Sandy scowled at the sight of her.

'Grandad's not in.'

'It was you I came to see.'

'What is it?'

Francine had hoped her attitude would be less confrontational.

'You didn't come to see Winnie off.'

Sandy huffed, then said, 'I didn't know if I was welcome.'

Gosh, she was making this difficult.

'You are always welcome, Sandy.'

Sandy pulled another face. She didn't move; she wasn't planning on inviting Francine in.

'I've come to say sorry for the other day,' Francine said. 'I didn't mean to react like that.'

'It's all right. I took a risk and it didn't come off. It's a...' She was groping for the right word as the bee moved closer. 'Gamble.'

Francine understood a gamble.

'But maybe it did come off,' she said slowly.

'How do you mean?'

Sandy wasn't going to forgive her that easily. Francine was going to have to spell it out. 'I... like... you... too,' she said slowly.

Francine had always liked the enigmatic, complicated people. Maybe it was a personality flaw in her? How might the more erudite Mrs Howard phrase it? Maybe she would say that Francine's tragic flaw was her eagerness to fly close to the sun?

Sandy shrugged. Francine edged closer to her. Very close. She was so bright and irresistible. Sandy was about six inches taller than her, and she smelled of sleep, and she was... wonderful.

'What are you trying to say?'

'I'm saying – if you tried to kiss me again, I might not be so taken aback this time.'

Sandy stepped back, wordlessly inviting her in. Francine followed, and then Sandy kicked the door shut behind them and the bee did not get to witness anything.

67

Winnie

You could fit maybe forty Castles into the Cunard ocean liner. It was enormous. It had its own English pub, the Crown, too. Winnie had decided to steer clear. She was supposed to be changing her life! She also steered clear of the tennis courts – not for her, not with these knees, the funny coloured swimming pool and the dark-panelled coffee shop. Susan was right – coffee shops were taking over the world!

Winnie liked being in her cabin best, or mooching around the top deck, or admiring the views from the deckchairs. It was only five days. She could do this.

Before she'd got on board, she'd told herself not to speak to anyone – this wasn't a busman's holiday, she wasn't the landlady now. Yet, surprise, surprise, within hours she had cracked and was talking to everyone and having a lovely time. She couldn't walk five minutes without having a chat about the view from the bridge or the macaroons or whether they sold plasters anywhere. There was the woman with a lisp who was going to marry her Canadian fiancé, who she had never actually met.

'We are pen pals!' she said cheerfully. 'But I know' – she laid her hand on her heart – 'he's the one.'

Winnie thought upturning your life was hard enough when you were in love with a person you already knew. She couldn't imagine doing it for someone who only existed on the page.

She met a family of seven who were going on a holiday round the world.

'Grandma left us some money in her will – something to remember her by!'

The mother whispered to Winnie, 'She was a tyrant!' Then she raised her glass and said loudly, 'God bless Grandma!'

She met a nervy soldier in a wheelchair who was going to meet a girl who had moved away to be with her married sister. 'I let her go once,' he said. 'Hope I'm not too late...'

And she met a mother in a hat, whose daughter had been evacuated to Canada. She hadn't been able to save up the money to get out there sooner. Finally, she had sold her long hair to a wig-maker. She removed her hat, revealing a cropped head.

'It's been so long,' she moaned. 'What if she doesn't love me any more?'

Winnie thought of Francine and her unwavering love for the late Mrs Salt, and she patted the woman's hand, 'She's going to love you all over again,' and the woman leaned back in her chair and closed her eyes with relief.

She still had self-doubt. The first night on board, she thought she should go back, turn round, take up a quiet life. But there was no way back. There was no land in front, there was no land behind. Security was an illusion; life was like this – endless sea, waves and tides and ocean, and the propulsion of the boat.

What if she and Ron were just a holiday romance? But they hadn't been on holiday – the opposite, in fact. It wasn't like they only saw each other relaxed and tanned. They had never seen each other like that. The last few years had been stress upon stress. Maybe they wouldn't know what to do with each other when they didn't have problems? Winnie scolded herself – she was second-guessing everything.

The self-doubt was a small, temporary thing that in the morning flew off to find itself a better, more permanent host. It was lost as she watched the flat line of the horizon, the birds swooping low across the sea.

Francine had managed to build a new life in the worst of circumstances. Winnie would manage too. She was getting closer to being the person Scott Cuthbert had always thought she was.

Days later, the ship sounded its horn, a momentous noise, and passengers crowded to the sides of the deck to watch their arrival. Land ahoy! Only Winnie didn't. She stayed in her tiny cabin, squinting in the bathroom mirror. Her face was drained of colour and her eyes minuscule. What if Ron had changed his mind and fallen in love with a woman who played tennis or a heroic curly-haired nurse? What if he didn't want her any more?

Out on the deck, she saw so many people. She thought Canada was supposed to be underpopulated! Everyone seemed to be at the port that afternoon, waving to the ship. And everyone on the ship was waving – could it tilt over?

It was overwhelming. The woman with the lisp ran past her, shouting, 'Good luck!' The family went skipping off with their maps and umbrellas ('God bless Grandma!'). The woman with the hat raced off to reunite with her long-lost daughter. The soldier in the wheelchair wheeled down the ramp, refusing offers of help. Winnie was going to be one of the last off at this rate.

And then she thought she saw Trevor again. Leaning in the doorway of the ship, only it was the pub door. He had a backpack and was carrying a sack, wearing his new uniform. And he was smiling, blowing her a kiss.

Almost before Winnie could think she was going mad, he had gone. And then she saw Ron waving at her from land-side. The closer she got, the more she could see how worried his expression was. Her heart went out to him – he was afraid too! 'I'm mortified,' she mouthed and he might have laughed. Her fear lifted, and as she drew nearer, smiling, fit to burst, there was only joy in her heart, and as she walked down the gangway and into his arms she knew she'd made the right decision.

'New York. Toronto. And then home to Burlington.'

'Sounds good for a start.'

She grinned, and he leaned down to meet her lips with his own.

68

SPRING, 1949

Francine

The banks wouldn't lend Francine any money. Four thousand pounds? And a lone female? What was she thinking?

'No, we don't do that.'

'How old are you again?' More sucking of teeth. 'Nineteen?'

'It's impossible!'

'Is there a husband?' one asked as if she were hiding one under the desk.

Maybe Francine could have asked her father to help, but she didn't think that would work either. Anyway, Sandy said they'd find a way. They'd have to. Francine was determined to build an empire.

Sandy had never liked her job in insurance and Francine liked to joke, 'What's the point of doing something you can't stand in an office when you could be doing something you can't stand with me?!' so Sandy worked at the pub now. Actually, she liked it. She was a breath of fresh air. She was better at small talk, for one thing. Francine always felt her personality was closed; by contrast, Sandy was the classic open book. And she had more energy than Mac and Francine put together. She would think nothing of mopping the floor at midnight or fixing a leaky barrel at 2 a.m.

Sandy had also moved in. Officially, she was in Winnie's old room. If Mac suspected anything untoward, he didn't say: he was too busy organising his forthcoming wedding to Mrs Phelps and looking after his young stepson.

Sandy loved reading aloud and Francine found she loved being read to, so once the pub closed for the night, they went through Sandy's Famous Five books. George was their favourite character; they both claimed to be like her.

'Who would Lydia be?' asked Sandy, who by now had heard all about Francine's 'London friends'.

'Anne,' Francine had said, sniggering. They found the Anne character tiresome.

'And Valerie?'

This was less easy. Francine considered. 'Julian maybe. Or Uncle Quentin!'

Laughing about them with Sandy helped Francine get over the hurt. Eight years now and they still hadn't been in touch.

As much as she loved living with Sandy, Francine found it nerve-wracking: they couldn't say they were sisters, and they were hardly 'old' friends. Francine knew it wasn't against the law – for women – but it certainly felt like it was. Sandy said to stop being a worry-wart but Francine couldn't help it. So when a policeman arrived in the pub asking for her, Francine's heart crashed to her boots: she immediately thought it was bad news. Fight or flee, she thought. Or hide in the cellar and wait for the explosion.

'Dan Cohen,' he said. 'You were living with my dad when he died.'

He had been in the area and wanted a chat. The relief! Then came curiosity and delight.

Maybe Dan looked like his father had as a young man, but he was nothing like the elderly man Francine had known and loved. Dan was tall and broad-shouldered, with dark hair sprouting up like broccoli and a handshake so firm that Francine wondered if her wrist would ever recover. Sandy was looking over, full of curiosity, and Francine was able to mouth back, 'It's fine!'

She served Dan a soda – 'No alcohol, thank you,' he'd said – and they sat together in the armchairs by the fire. Francine was suddenly embarrassed at how shabby the place looked, but he looked around approvingly and said, 'It's cosy!' Occasionally, there was a thud of a log on the fire like a punctuation in time. In the back room, the Castle Archers were in the middle of a heated match, while some poker players were due in shortly.

'How did he seem to you?'

'Lovely. We ate jam sandwiches and played Battleship.'

'I bet he enjoyed that,' he said, his voice croaky.

'What happened to your sister?'

She remembered the old man's eyes when he talked about his Ruthie Toothie. How afraid he was of the Nazis.

'I don't know,' Dan said. 'She was in hiding in Paris and it seems she was betrayed. I have no further information.'

Francine thought of the newsreel she had seen from Belsen that had shaken her to the core. She had probably been too young to watch such frightful images – although what would be the right age? Belsen wasn't the only place like that by any means, either. These execution camps were all over Europe; and while some people had looked away, some had joined in. How right Mr Cohen was to be afraid. She found it unbearable and in her mind it would forever be inextricably linked to Mr Williams' bullying. No longer did she tell people she was Jewish. It would be asking for trouble. She also told Sandy not to tell anyone. It was something that seemed only to isolate or separate her from everyone else and she couldn't face it. She needed camaraderie and solidarity, not to be told she should go away, or that her people did this or that. It was one of the ways she was less brave – despised herself that she was less brave – but she didn't see how she could fix it.

She thought often of Mr Cohen's desperation and the way he swung from believing that all would be well to fearing that everything was doomed.

'I'm sorry,' she said in the space after Dan finished speaking.

He downed his drink and then wiped his lips with the back of his hand. She searched again for any resemblance between him and his gentle father, but she still couldn't see it, although she thought she glimpsed a Star of David round his neck, barely visible under his collar.

'I just wanted to check you were all right.'

'I am,' she said, "I will always be grateful to your father. He opened his home to me when I was most in need.'

He stood up. 'Also... to give you this.' Digging into a trouser pocket, he handed over a folded yellowy envelope with her name on the front. 'From Dad.'

She shook it for clues. 'What is it? Photographs?'

'Open it when I'm gone,' he said.

They shook hands again – more of that terrible grip. Just as he was about to leave, Tiger barged into his legs and he yelped in surprise. For once Tiger didn't do her loud meowing but just purred and purred, contented.

Softer now, Dan stroked Tiger and promised he'd be back to see her, then left. Francine went back to sit by the fire and to see what she had been given.

Inside the envelope was exactly four thousand pounds.

69

SPRING, 1954

Francine

There was something Francine had been longing for, and the urge became stronger as time went on, and that was for the three of them – three little girls from Romberg Road, herself, Lydia and Valerie – to be reunited.

When she talked it over with Sandy, Sandy always said, 'Do it!' but something always got in the way: another argument with the brewery. Another place to convert into a pub. Another building to transform. More bar staff to employ. Francine and Sandy still lived upstairs at the Castle, but Francine now ran three pubs and one bingo hall. The more there were, the busier she was, the safer she felt. She was not the parcel in pass the parcel any more, she controlled the game.

'I'll look them up if you like,' Sandy offered.

You couldn't tell Sandy a single thing or she would spring into action. Deeds not words was her motto.

'I was just say—'

'No such thing as just saying,' Sandy said. She twisted her hair behind her ear, then went to lug another barrel up from the cellar.

A few days later, Sandy was leafing through the telephone directory. 'There are Frouds in Frognall Lane, West Hampstead!'

'That won't be her. Anyway, Lydia will have married and changed her name by now.'

'*You* haven't,' said Sandy with a grin. Francine gave her 'the look', which Sandy always said made her look like Winnie.

'But Lydia really wanted to – it was her main ambition.'

Probably her only ambition.

'There are no other Frouds,' said Sandy, sounding disappointed.

Francine's father now ran the new barber's shop that had started up in the old recruitment office below Mr Cuthbert's. He had remarried, too, and his new wife, Angela, helped in the shop. Francine thought Angela put up with a lot. She never complained, only hinted at problems. Daddy had terrible nightmares, sweats, guilt, headaches and stomach aches. 'I'm not a well man' became his catchphrase, although it didn't stop him driving like a lunatic. Angela cut Francine's hair for a discount price and would insist on tweezing her eyebrows too. She offered to fix Francine up with one of her friends' sons, but Francine always said she was too busy with work.

Francine's mother, her sister, Maisie and the babies were still with her, but she had devised ways to help her cope. She no longer covered her ears or eyes when the boys were screaming or Maisie was accusing or her mother was melancholy. She tried to remain calm and let them be. She tried to let them glide over her.

Sandy asked her what was up – was it her 'ghosts'? Francine didn't know if Sandy believed in them or not.

Her mother wouldn't have remarried, Francine thought, she was certain of that. But it was important not to be resentful.

Francine had to face it if a get-together with Lydia and/or Valerie were to happen, she would have to be the one to arrange it. She understood that it was difficult. She and Winnie used to talk about it. People crossed to the other side of the road rather than console even family members. People didn't have the vocabulary to speak to someone who'd experienced trauma.

Francine still threw her dice, out of force of habit really. Once, they told her to get in touch with Valerie at the BBC and she did it as soon as the dice told her so, knowing that otherwise she would find a reason not to.

'It's so GOOD to hear from you,' Valerie squealed. She was still working in the wireless department. She was also married.

Francine yelped at this news.

'To Paul Howard?'

She was sure it was him.

The line went silent.

'Valerie?!'

'Uh, no. I met Godfrey at work, he works in wireless too.'

For a moment, Francine was too stunned to speak.

'You're happy to meet up?' she asked eventually.

'Very!' returned Valerie.

'Super. Do you have a way I could contact Lydia?'

Either the phone line was dead or Valerie was taking another exceedingly long breath.

'Why not try Bumble Cottage?' she finally asked.

'She won't still be there, will she?'

Another deep breath before Valerie said, 'She might...'

'They didn't have a telephone when I was there.'

'Everyone's got one now.'

Francine got Sandy to try for her. It was silly that she felt so nervous. The number rang and Sandy covered the mouth-piece with her hand.

'There's a dialling tone. Sounds like they've got a phone!'

She passed the receiver over to Francine and a house-keeper answered and said, 'I can get Mrs Howard.'

Francine couldn't help it; she was still nervous of this woman. Brace yourself, she thought. It was just a means to an end. Mrs Howard would surely know where Lydia had disappeared to. And then a voice came down the line. A voice that was younger, fresher, less posh than the one she had been expecting.

'Mrs Howard speaking.'

'Lydia?'

'Ye-es?'

Lydia was Mrs Howard? Who? What?

It turned out Lydia had married Paul Howard. Francine knew she didn't remember those three months she'd spent in Somerset as clearly as she might have, but what she did remember pretty emphatically was that Paul never had any interest in Lydia – or vice versa – and Lydia's letters, when she did bother to write, were mostly complaints about how close Paul and Valerie were. What on earth had happened?

70

Francine

Lydia had turned so glamorous, it was hard to believe it was her, yet at the same time it seemed impossible that she could have turned out any other way.

There were few people who Francine still knew from before her life imploded, but after her father Lydia was perhaps the most important one. And her father wouldn't talk about her early life any more. 'Angela doesn't like me going over it,' he said, but Francine knew he was the one who didn't.

Lydia and Paul Howard arrived in a slick black car that must have been double the size of her father's (and his wasn't small). She and then Paul hugged her, and they were happy to see her, they couldn't have been acting. They had also brought enough luggage to stay for weeks.

She led them into the Castle. Both of them said 'Wow!' a lot. Lydia's fingers fluttered on the counter and then on the chairs and Francine was glad that, thanks to Mr Cohen's legacy, the armchairs were one of the first things she had been able to replace.

'I love that you live in a castle, Francine!'

'It's not a castle...'

'I always knew you'd become a princess,' Lydia continued obliviously. 'Like *The Princess and the Pea...* although I had never heard of Kettering before. What's so good about Kettering?'

Francine thought to herself, there's a community here who I look after and who look after me and a woman I'm madly in love with. And I'm building modern-day castles of public houses and bingo halls. People come and go – *boy, did they come and go!* – but her pubs, her businesses were forever.

But she just said, 'I was here during the war.'

'I can see that would make you attached to a place,' Lydia replied. 'I'm the same as you.'

We're not the same, thought Francine and she wondered why she had been so keen for this reunion. Lydia was not a god, she was not all-knowing, she was just a normal, fallible human being.

While they waited for Valerie and Godfrey to turn up, Lydia told Francine all about the beauty pageants she'd been in – she seemed to imagine Francine would find this impressive. Maybe other people did. Francine nodded along, mystified, wondering how their worlds could have been so far apart. Lydia listed the names of the English seaside resorts that held pageants and then explained what she used to do.

'We walked around the pool and then we answered questions and then—'

'And then you won?' Francine said playfully.

'I was usually placed third or fourth.' Lydia paused. 'They were fixed, you see.'

'Really?'

'I believe so.'

Francine looked at Paul, who was studiously avoiding her eye. It didn't surprise her that Lydia had taken to pageants like a duck to water, for weren't these contests exactly like their experience of evacuation? Even at nine years old, that day in that hall, Lydia instinctively knew what was required of her. She had sat there fluttering her lashes, while Francine and even Valerie hadn't the faintest clue about what was going on.

'How is your mother?' Francine managed to ask Paul. 'Mrs Howard senior?'

'She's been unwell,' he said, 'but we have people to look after her, take her to the theatre, or read to her... It's not as bad as it could be.'

Lydia was still talking. Apart from the beauty pageants – and despite having two children – Rex, her dog, was her other favourite subject.

'How old is Rex?'

'Twelve.' Her lovely features looked pained. 'In human years, he's older than my dad! Sometimes when he drinks, his ears go in the water, I just think, what if my ears did?'

Francine and Paul grinned at each other, then both burst out laughing.

'What?' Lydia snapped. 'What's so funny?'

Francine was taken right back to how it used to be. 'You are! What about your children?'

'Oh, them.' Lydia shrugged. 'They're sweet. I just thought you mightn't want to talk about children.'

'Why ever not?'

'Well...' The babies in Francine's head roared. 'It's all right that I don't have any.' She saved Lydia magnanimously. 'Actually, I do have a cat.'

'I *love* cats!' Lydia squealed. 'Paul says no, but I'm determined to get one.'

Paul rolled his eyes and Francine knew and he probably knew too that there would be three or four cats in his home this time next year. That was Lydia!

Francine thought Valerie, unlike Lydia, had hardly changed at all. Her face was as bright and appealing as ever, her hair clipped back in the same tortoiseshell clips she used to wear. The main difference was the jam-jar glasses and flat mannish shoes.

Francine instantly liked Godfrey. Generous, quiet, kind. She could understand why Valerie had married him. They seemed a good match.

It made sense that Valerie was working in wireless too, because she had always helped Francine find her voice. She'd always wanted to tell stories or write reports or imagine comeuppances of her own. And she'd always had a backbone when Francine hadn't.

Francine watched as Paul and Valerie greeted each other. And she thought they might have agreed beforehand, 'We're all grown-ups here' or 'We can do this – we have to do this!' because nothing seemed amiss, there was only a sense that everyone was on their best behaviour.

Valerie grabbed Francine's hand. 'Tell us – how have you been since we last saw you?'

Francine smiled, uncertain where to begin. There were so many no-go areas: Mr Williams, Sandy (for very different reasons obviously). They didn't even know the first thing about her dear Winnie. Or the return of her father.

'I didn't expect this,' Valerie was saying, gesturing around her.

'What did you expect I'd be doing?' Francine asked.

Valerie looked embarrassed. 'I don't know, just... not this!'

Did it make sense that she ran a pub? Did it have an inevitability about it, in the way Valerie and her wirelesses and Lydia and her pageants did? Since her family had died, she had found family in strangers. And where better than in a public house? The clue was in the title! But in other ways, the businesses, her skill in making them run was something that even to her seemed left-field especially when she thought of how timid she used to be.

And then being with Sandy made perfect sense to her but probably, their love affair would never make sense to the rest of the world.

Paul gestured to her glass. 'Do you drink alcohol, Francine?'

'Never,' she said.

He thought she was joking.

'Oh, not quite never,' she added, smiling, for being back with them made her happy. 'But once was enough for me! We also do darts, cards and bingo here...' She paused. 'And in my other pubs...'

They didn't pick up on the *other* pubs – and that was fine.

'You always loved playing games,' Valerie said.

'That's right, I did.'

Valerie was wandering around now. Francine hoped she was impressed. It wasn't just a pub, it was her everything.

But her ghosts were back too. Her mother had her head in her hands and Maisie was stomping her feet. As Francine was trying to block them out, Paul leaned over to her. 'You've done amazingly...' he said. He was such a well-brought-up boy.

. . .

Mac was delighted that she shut the pub early. His wife was expecting and his other son – he didn't call him stepson – was playing up. They'd had a busy few days as another film was being made at the air base-turned-studios. Whereas once planes or battles dominated conversations, now the customers were more likely to talk about lighting or sound.

Jim, Old Jim, Toby and Nathan left, grumbling, but Albert winked at her. He had started coming in again, now May was expecting her third, and neither of them ever mentioned what had happened or what didn't happen between them. Scott Cuthbert said, 'Move along, gentlemen, give them some space.' He winked at her. 'Enjoy yourself, Francine. If anyone deserves to, you do.'

Sandy served them and, because she was serving them, she was invisible. Lydia clicked her fingers, which was ghastly, but when Sandy came over Lydia was polite and said to her, 'I'm sorry, are we keeping you up?'

'It's fine,' Sandy said, winking at Francine, who prayed no one saw.

Valerie raised her eyebrows at Godfrey, who shook his head, smiling, and said, 'No, you are not going to make a radio show about pub landladies, Val. And Francine doesn't want to be in it.'

'Ooh, I might!' Francine laughed.

And they talked about their families and their mothers. Lydia's was in London, running nurseries for children of working mothers – she *was* the Mrs Froud Sandy had found in the telephone directory. Her younger brother Matthew – did they remember? A roly-poly, smiley soul – was now a strapping young man who did something in shipping.

Valerie's mother had remarried. She worked in the same

building as Valerie at the BBC. Valerie coughed, admitting she found that 'quite challenging!'

They all drank a lot, they drank like it was wartime, and Francine was worried that lowered inhibitions might lead to an argument – but it stayed good-tempered, enjoyable even. Paul looked over at Valerie sometimes as if he was about to say something, or at least take her in some more, but if she was aware of him she didn't show it. Godfrey had his arm round her. Lydia leaned into Paul.

They were still drinking as it grew late. 'Did the bar-lady go home?' Lydia asked.

Why was she so interested?

'She lives here,' said Francine. She should have left it at that, but found she couldn't: 'There's plenty of room upstairs.'

Maybe Paul would work it out. He lived in the art world after all, where the bohemians were. And he made his living by observing the things others mightn't notice. But Lydia or Valerie? Unlikely. The idea that she and Sandy were lovers seemed preposterous even to Francine sometimes, so no doubt it would to them too.

'What does the woman who took you in do now?' Valerie, ever the enquirer, asked.

'She went to Canada a few years ago and married a soldier she met in the war – she fosters children there.'

Winnie took children out into the wilderness, or on boats or sometimes to explore Montreal. She sent photographs of her and Ron. Usually they were windswept, outdoors, waving self-consciously at the camera, with gaggles of children pulling funny faces. It was a world away from the Castle, but it was exactly what Winnie had always wanted.

'Nice,' said Lydia. 'What's the plan for tomorrow?'

Lydia was never content just to enjoy a moment.

When Paul said he needed air, Lydia didn't offer to go outside with him, so Francine did. He was leaning against the wall by the yellow roses, smoking. Francine didn't know much about men – her expertise was limited to Albert and the elderly customers at the pub – but she knew Paul wasn't as happy as he used to be. Yet, she asked herself, who was? They had all seen too much or heard too much... no one had got away unscathed. He grinned at her though as she came towards him. One of his skills had always been making you feel like you were the only person in the world.

'Did Lydia tell you about Cassie, our old dog?' he asked.

Francine hadn't expected this. She shook her head.

'It was Lydia's fault she died. She left out the cake with raisins,' Paul paused. 'But she let my mum think it was you,' he said, exhaling sorrowfully.

Francine nodded. Somehow, it made sense. If she hadn't done that, maybe Francine would have gone back to Somerset after her own family had been killed. Life might have been easier, she thought, but maybe it was for the best it turned out this way.

'I thought you should know,' Paul continued. 'I hated that you would think that you'd done it. All this time.'

'It was a long time ago,' Francine said. 'And it was an accident, really.'

Paul rubbed his face, he seemed relieved. It must have been weighing on him.

'What are the children like, then?' Francine asked.

'The oldest, Margaret...' he began.

Margaret-Doll, thought Francine, Lydia's favourite.

'...is absolutely nothing like me. In looks, in tastes, anything. It's hard to believe she's mine.'

Even if she hadn't seen Lydia for over ten years, even if Lydia had betrayed her in a way, Francine was a loyal friend, and now she stared blankly at Winnie's roses. What was Paul suggesting, she wondered? Well, she knew what he was suggesting, but why?

He dragged on the cigarette, his handsome cheeks becoming narrower as he did so.

'And the youngest?' she asked.

He exhaled. 'Dennis is creative. He loves to get his hands dirty – drives Lydia mad.'

Francine could imagine. 'Another artist in the family?'

'Hope not,' he said wryly. 'I hope he does something impactful.'

She wondered if maybe she'd got it wrong, if the cause of his discontent wasn't Lydia but something else – his work, perhaps? She knew there were ludicrous articles about him, critics who labelled him a traitor for moving on from painting the fish that had launched his career. People were furious Paul Howard didn't give them what they wanted. Worse, he had started painting dogs, which they considered 'sliding into sentimentality'.

'And you and Lydia?' she asked vaguely. She hoped he wouldn't ask what she really meant. She meant – *how does that work?*

He smiled at her. The smile of a boy who chased around pretend-shooting, who would throw a bucket of water at you if you stood still but who would cart you across the lawn, saving you, if you'd seen a scary insect.

'She's a handful.'

Francine put her arm through his. 'You are, too.'

He grinned. 'That's definitely one thing we have in common.'

Back inside, Lydia was still impatient for plans for the following day. Valerie and Godfrey looked at one another like a point was being proved. There was something mature about them; you'd think they were ten years older than her and Lydia, not two.

'I've borrowed bikes,' Francine said. 'We'll go up my favourite hill.'

The hill where she and Sandy, in their haphazard way, became more than friends.

'Cycling?' asked Lydia, not able to hide her disgruntlement.

'We'll have a picnic...'

'It sounds wonderful,' said Valerie and Paul in the same sincere tones and at the same time.

'Did we ever cycle in London?' Lydia asked. Francine couldn't help thinking Lydia had a memory like a sieve.

'Only in Somerset.'

'You hardly did there, if I remember rightly.'

'I was afraid,' Francine admitted.

'You were afraid of everything,' Lydia said. Then she peered at Francine. 'You've changed.'

In a flurry of goodbyes, Paul and Lydia left for the Good Bed and Breakfast. Valerie and Godfrey were taking 'Sandy's' room.

'So kind,' Valerie said, concerned. 'I hope we're not inconveniencing you.'

'No!' said Francine. 'Not at all!'

Sandy was waiting for her in bed when Francine snuck in.

'How's it going?'

'Weirdly,' admitted Francine. 'I don't know what I expected, but...'

It wasn't this. They couldn't remember things that Francine knew word for word, or they remembered things clearly when Francine had no idea what they were talking about.

'That's the way it is,' Sandy said sleepily. 'People get lumped together – people made friends in the war, but the war was the only thing they had in common.'

'It wasn't like that with us,' Francine said. 'We were closer than that – before the war – our whole lives were intertwined.'

'Did you ask them why they didn't write?' Sandy asked.

Francine realised she might well be able to make Lydia and Valerie feel guilty about their treatment of her in the past, yet she didn't want that. It was just another ache that had faded with time.

'I'm not going to bring it up.'

'Right,' Sandy said from the pillow. She searched for Francine's hand under the sheets and gave it a squeeze.

71

Francine

The telephone in the bar was ringing and Francine raced down, hoping to get it before it woke anyone else. It was just gone six o'clock. After she had replaced the receiver she stood, for just a moment, before she could bring herself to go back upstairs.

'Valerie, I need to talk to you.'

Valerie came out the bathroom, drying her hair with a towel. Her glasses were steamed up; maybe that was good – she wouldn't be able to see the horror on Francine's face.

'What is it?'

Francine swallowed. A few minutes ago, she had felt important because she had been entrusted to deliver this news. Now she wished she hadn't been.

'Your mum has had a heart attack. I'm afraid it's—'

Valerie gripped her hands.

'Severe. She's in hospital. They don't know...' Francine

licked her lips. *How to phrase this?* 'They don't know what's going to happen.'

Valerie had turned so white, her skin looked translucent.

In the bar, Francine offered Valerie a whisky. She thought she wouldn't accept, but Valerie chugged it back, without ice or water, then wiped her mouth with her sleeve.

'I'll go to the hospital. She and Mr Carrington haven't been married for long. Poor him.'

Poor *you*, thought Francine, realising that her friend maybe didn't understand yet that her mother's life hung in the balance, or that the outcome might not be the one she was hoping for. Again, it reinforced for Francine what an awful lot she had lost at such a young age – but this was about Mrs Hardman and Valerie now, and she was thankful that her experience meant she could be of service to her old friend.

Valerie paced, gulped back more whisky and wavered between catatonic shock and appearing completely normal.

Just after seven, Lydia and Paul came from the Good Bed and Breakfast. Paul was bright-eyed, bushy-tailed, Lydia was full of complaints

'Boiled egg and soldiers? At that price!'

'It wasn't—' Paul began.

'I didn't bring any walking shoes.'

Grinning, Paul had his arm around her waist. 'I did tell you.'

'Why am I such an idiot?'

'I'm not saying anything...'

Finally, Paul, then Lydia, noticed Francine and Valerie's devastated expressions and their smiles dropped.

'What *is* going on?'

.   .   .

Godfrey was packing. Francine was impressed that he was capable, but then thought, *of course he was*. Efficient Valerie wouldn't waste her time with a chap who couldn't place a few shirts in a suitcase.

Sandy was standing by the kettle in the kitchen, so bleary it looked like her eyes were still shut.

'I'll go to London for a few days. It'll leave us short-handed, but...'

'Do what you have to do. I'll call Mac.'

This was another thing wonderful about Sandy. She was accommodating to the nth degree.

'I'll be here when you get back,' Sandy said.

'Don't forget to feed Tiger.'

'As if I would!'

Francine loved her then, especially since she wasn't great in the mornings. She clasped her and kissed her. On the mouth. Just as Paul walked in.

'Ah, sorry to interrupt,' he said, reddening. At heart, he was still the sweet boy with the tennis racquet, chasing a ball that kept running away from him.

'Paul will drive us back to London,' said Lydia, taking command. 'I insist.'

'No,' said Valerie equally firmly. 'Paul, you drive Godfrey back. I'll go with the girls on the train.'

'Whatever you say,' Paul said. He saluted her, then quickly took his hand down.

'We didn't ever do the journey back to London together, did we?' Lydia said as they waited on the platform. 'Just the outgoing one.'

How the events of the war years weren't engraved on her heart, Francine would never understand.

'I know,' Valerie said. 'I just wanted us to be together on a train again – like coming full circle.'

'Absolutely,' said Lydia. She had been bending over backwards for Valerie all morning.

Francine remembered the journey out so clearly – but then she had never stopped replaying it. The night before they left London the first time, she and baby Joe, Jacob, Maisie and Mummy all slept in the same bed, the musty smell of grown-up sleep, the tangle of the bedclothes.

'Why must I go, Mummy?'

'It's so you're safe.'

The morning, dressing with care, the name tag round her neck, Mummy staring at her with dismay.

'You will remember us, darling...'

'Of course! The teachers say I have a good memory.'

On the train, she had played the peacemaker. Lydia and Valerie had never quite got on, but both would act like friends for her sake. Dice in her pocket, while Lydia held on to Margaret-Doll and would only let you hold her if she was busy with something else, and Valerie so good at her stories – they were two strong personalities, whereas she was weak, piggy-in-the-middle.

Some generations had it worse than others. Francine knew: they had it worse. You can't say they didn't – there were sixty-five million dead because of the war. Would she change it all if she could? Yes. But no one ever gets that chance. You have no choice, you just had to submit to the great waves of time.

Valerie was talking about work (again). Lydia asked if her boss was married (Lydia always asked who was married!) and

Valerie said she thought he might be homosexual. Francine blushed.

'I didn't know they actually held down jobs!' Lydia said in wonderment. 'I've never met a homosexual in my life!'

Francine didn't dare meet Valerie's eye. She had thought it was widely known that Mr Froud, Lydia's father, had a love affair with a man during the war: apparently not. Lydia still thought her parents' marriage was like Humphrey Bogart and Ingrid Bergman in *Casablanca*.

'Funny how it all turned out,' Francine said, to change the subject.

'We were just three silly kids from London,' Valerie said.

'What are we now?' Francine enquired.

Lydia grinned. 'Paul says we are muse, producer and mogul.'

They burst out laughing.

'Paul always had a way with words!' Valerie snorted.

'I'm so sorry,' Lydia said. And Francine knew that the sorry contained multitudes, but also that, if she was asked specifically what she was sorry for, Lydia would deny it or deflect or shrug.

'Godfrey is a gentleman, isn't he?' she said to Valerie.

Francine watched them both carefully, still not convinced that they weren't going to start bickering.

'He's a darling,' agreed Valerie. And she didn't say, 'But you still stole Paul from me,' or anything like that, she just gazed out of the window at the expanse of sky.

'Your mum is going to be fine,' Lydia said, but Francine thought, how could she know? Only someone who had never lost a loved one could make such bold predictions.

'I hope so.'

'You'll get through this either way,' Francine couldn't

resist saying. She knew it made her sound depressing, but it still felt truer than what Lydia was saying.

Valerie nodded. 'I'll end up making a wireless show about it,' she said tearfully but smiling. 'It transpires that's how I deal with everything.'

'We all need something.'

'It's better than...' Valerie looked around as though searching for something to make a comparison. 'Having a nervous breakdown,' she settled on awkwardly.

'Exactly. Try to avoid that,' Lydia said dryly.

'There's another thing,' Valerie said slowly. 'I think I'm pregnant.'

They both congratulated her and Valerie went red and said, 'I didn't do much!', which made them cackle, then Lydia launched into a speech about the wonders of pregnancy and childbirth, before adding finally that Valerie would be brilliant at it.

'You're the first people I've told. I haven't even told Godfrey.' Valerie paused, her eyes filling with tears. 'I hadn't told Mum yet.'

'You'll be able to tell her in a couple of hours,' insisted Lydia.

Francine held the dice in her hand: two. It told her not to say anything, but she did.

'Mrs Hardman will be so pleased, Valerie.' She didn't add, 'if she survives.'

They leaned their heads on each other's shoulders, Francine in the middle, as the train took them back to where they had started.

72

Francine

At the hospital, they were met by a tall freckle-faced man whom Valerie introduced as Mr Carrington – her mother's husband. He ran his hand through his dishevelled red hair and told Valerie that it was only one visitor at a time, and he would dash home to fetch some things.

'And is she awake now?' Valerie asked brightly, although Francine thought it was obvious from his expression that she was not.

He told her no, then added it was early days yet, and then he hurried away without looking back: he was crying, but he clearly didn't want them to see that he was. Valerie's hopeful expression faded.

Francine squeezed her friend's hand and said 'Go on,' but Valerie hesitated. 'What if she doesn't wa—'

'Just go,' said Lydia.

. . .

Lydia and Francine waited for news in the long narrow hospital corridor with criss-cross wooden floors and walls without pictures. Again, Lydia leaned her head on Francine's shoulder.

'I didn't expect our long-awaited reunion would end up like this.'

'No,' said Francine, because she couldn't think what else to say.

'The first few hours are the important ones,' explained Lydia.

'How do you know?' Francine asked, suddenly impatient with know-it-all Lydia.

'From working with dogs,' Lydia said.

Francine sighed and shut her eyes, thinking of her own mother. She remembered Mrs Hardman had initially told her that her mother and siblings were sleeping, and how confused she had been. Mrs Hardman who explained rain was good since it put fires out quicker. That jittery woman with, as Aunty Winnie always said, a heart of gold. A heart of gold with a fault-line in it, apparently.

'I need to say something,' Lydia said.

Francine straightened up. The corridor smelled of disinfectant and somewhere there was the clanging of a mop in a bucket. Lydia was biting her lower lip.

'I'm sorry I didn't write,' she said in a rush. 'I didn't know what to say, I've never been great with words – and as time went on, it grew harder and... I should have...' She trailed off.

Francine gulped. She had always wanted an explanation or an apology, but now she had it, it didn't seem to matter.

'I just thought you didn't like me,' she said.

'Oh no!' Lydia cried out so loudly that a nearby porter pushing a trolley looked over in alarm. 'I hate that you would think that. It was me not you. You have always been my favourite person in the world – apart from Rex, that is.'

There were a million things to say to that – what about Paul, her children, her parents? But Francine knew Lydia.

'You do know Rex isn't a person?' she said, laughing.

'Isn't he?' Lydia pretended to be shocked. 'All right, you are my favourite person in the world. Full stop.'

Francine was still laughing when Valerie came down the corridor. Everything about her was different from before; she was sparkling, her steps buoyant.

'Mum woke up,' and it was as though the words bounced off the walls in celebration. 'She made it!'

Mrs Hardman had asked to see Francine, apparently. Francine shook her head – it wasn't her place, she thought – but Valerie insisted.

There were four beds in the ward, and Mrs Hardman was in the one nearest the door, which, Francine the landlady evaluated, was the best for a quick getaway.

Mrs Hardman looked so fragile; sleeping, just a tiny face peeping out from a stiff blanket.

As Francine sat down in the chair Valerie had just vacated, Mrs Hardman opened her eyes.

'Francine!' she whispered, smiling weakly. 'I never told you how strong you were, did I?'

'It's all right,' Francine said softly. 'Please rest, Mrs Hardman.'

'I miss your mother so much,' she said. 'She was my best friend. We all were so close in that house. Did you know that?'

'Kind of,' Francine said.

'Before the war, Mrs Salt was so full of love and light and promise. You probably can't remember her like that.'

Francine couldn't speak.

'I just wanted to tell you, remind you, how much she loved you. She always wondered whether she did the right thing staying in London and then bringing you back, but she just couldn't do without you. You don't blame her for that, do you?'

'I don't.' Francine said, 'I never did.'

She had always been grateful for that extra time she had with her mummy and with her brothers and sisters.

Mrs Hardman smiled and closed her eyes again.

When Francine went back out to the corridor, Paul and Godfrey had arrived, and Lydia and Paul were getting ready to go and collect their children. Lydia was pulling on her coat and flapping over bags. Godfrey had his arm round Valerie as if to keep her from running away.

'We'd like to contribute to any costs,' Lydia said earnestly, and Paul nodded.

'That's the joy of the National Health Service,' Godfrey said, pushing his glasses up his nose. 'It's free at the point of delivery.'

'Anything over and above,' Paul said. 'Carers, medicines or whatever you need. Just let us know. It's the least we can do.'

It looked like Godfrey was about to argue again, but Valerie interjected. 'Will do,' she said. 'Thank you so much, both of you.'

'I can't wait to give my mum and dad a big hug,' Lydia said unexpectedly, and then she burst into tears.

Francine helped Valerie through the next few days. While Valerie visited the hospital and Godfrey was at work, she went food shopping and made wholesome dinners and packed lunches: food to keep your strength up. 'Especially in your condition.' Valerie had now told Godfrey, who was, predictably, over the moon.

On Friday evening, Francine made a simple chicken broth and lit candles. Valerie, who looked exhausted and was feeling sick most of the time, said this 'would go down a treat'.

'Your mum was good to me,' Francine told her.

She remembered Mrs Hardman gently applying calamine lotion to her spots. A simple kindness when her world had collapsed.

'She always had a weak heart,' Valerie said, eyes down-turned. 'I should have been prepared.'

'How could you be prepared?' Francine asked. 'You can't treat someone as though they're going to drop dead any second. It's no way to live.'

Valerie shrugged, unconvinced. Then she put her hands over her still-flat stomach.

'Mum and I have been talking about names.'

This was exciting. Valerie – who was still only eleven in Francine's mind – was having a baby! And she was going to be part of it.

'Little Godfrey, is it?' Francine suggested, making Big Godfrey, who was tucking into the soup, splutter.

'I wouldn't wish that on anyone!' he said.

Valerie took the hand that wasn't holding the spoon. She was smiling nervously.

'If it's a boy, we're thinking Joseph Jacob, and if it's a girl, Maisie... You don't mind?'

Francine's eyes were watering. 'I don't mind one bit.' She went over to hug her friend.

. . .

After a few days in London, Francine too felt shattered. She realised her reminiscing, her *craving* for Lydia and Valerie, wasn't only about Lydia and Valerie. It was about what they represented. She associated them with the young version of herself, the free her, the loved her. They represented those years of her childhood when, thanks to her mother, her world was safe and predictable.

Her yearning to see them again was a yearning to go back, to return to pre-loss Francine. That's never going to happen, she had now realised. You can't go back. Lydia and Valerie were mere ciphers, stand-ins, for all the nostalgia and remembrance of things lost. They were not the cure. And yet since she'd been with them, a lightness had come over her. These people were the rare few who knew and remembered the pre-loss Francine. She wasn't entirely a reinvention. She was not all 'after' – she had a 'before' as well. She was known. In a way – this was so strange – it was like they'd never been apart.

The last train back to Kettering was quiet, and then the town was peaceful too. It had rained and the pavements were shiny and full of puddles just as when Francine first came here, and she enjoyed the walk from the station to the Castle. The fresh air helped her think. Both pub and upstairs were in darkness. It was not like the days when Winnie would be behind the counter fussing: 'Have you eaten?' 'Why aren't you wearing a coat?'

Sandy was asleep and Francine didn't like to wake her. Sandy needed a lot of sleep, which was something Francine had learned the hard way.

There were official-looking letters about the purchase of another pub, the Duchess, from the brewery. The word mogul was a ridiculous one, but Francine was making a success of herself – and she knew it. Her father said she'd always been a small girl with big plans. She felt in her pocket, where she kept two things for reassurance: her enduring dice and the address, on a torn piece of paper, of the Kettering synagogue. One day, that might be an avenue she would go down – but not now.

In the middle of the pile was a postcard from Winnie. Francine got one – or a letter – at least once a week. This had a picture of a distinguished-looking man in a red uniform on the front. On the other side was a mystifying message: 'It took me ages to find this! Please show it to Mrs Wyatt from the knitting circle'.

Francine laughed. Aunty Winnie was finally living her life exactly as she had dreamed. She was proof that it was never too late – and Francine couldn't help but feel proud, and inspired too, by that.

'Miss you, my darling. Love to you and Sandy.'

Did Winnie know? Francine wondered. She liked to think this might be Winnie giving her acceptance but more likely it was just Winnie being her thoughtful self.

Their lives together in the Castle hadn't just been healing for her, they had also been healing for Winnie. Francine had been a broken child, but Winnie had been a broken woman too. And together, through some strange alchemy of patience, community, love and defiance, they had somehow managed to rebuild themselves. Francine would never stop loving her wartime mother.

In the bedroom, as Sandy snored lightly, Francine pushed open the sash window and breathed steadily in the night air. Her mind kept taking her back to all that was stolen from her in the war. As she stared into the darkest blue sky, it seemed to her there were more stars here than in London. Of course, though, you could just see them better from here – she could see everything so much better here.

Here they are – her family in the shelter that turned out not to be a shelter.

Her mother was no longer looking anxious, angry or bitter. She looked different now, so calm and accepting. Just how she used to be before the war. There was no fear left in her now that Francine was happy. She stared right into Francine's face, and Francine felt seen – beautifully seen, as clearly as she could see the stars.

Her mother was talking to her:

'Let go of my hands, darling.'

'I don't want to,' Francine whispered.

'It's okay, I promise.'

Francine turned to see her sister. Maisie was not cheating, whining or blaming anyone any more, she too was serene and charming. 'I'm not arguing with you,' Maisie declared primly as she put the dominos back in order. 'And I'm not arguing with you!' Francine responded, but she saw that Maisie didn't hear her.

The babies, who had been screaming for so long and had torn her apart each time now... now they were two little boys who were just peacefully asleep. Eyelashes soft on their cheeks. Things would look better in the morning.

Finally, Francine pulled down the sash window and rested.

A LETTER FROM LIZZIE

Dear reader,

Thank you so much for reading *The Wartime Mother* – the third book in the Wartime Evacuees series. I hope – I can't assume – that you read the other two before getting here, although if not, don't worry, they can be read out of order!

If you want to be kept up to date with all my latest releases, just sign up at the following link. Your email address will never be shared and you can unsubscribe at any time.

www.bookouture.com/lizzie-page

It has been lovely immersing myself in the lives of Valerie, Jean, Lydia, Emmeline, Francine and Winnie. I feel like I have been living and breathing Hardmans, Frouds, Salts and Eldridges for the last two years!

In each book in the series, we have entered a different milieu of 1940s and 1950s Britain, from bus stations to beauty pageants to public houses... Why pubs? I'm probably more of a Winnie than a Francine when it comes to them – which was something I wanted to explore. My great-aunt had several London pubs and my grandmother worked in them. I have mixed memories of my visits there. Writing this book has been a journey into my own past in some ways 😊

This is the second book in which I have touched upon British anti-Semitism (the first was *When I Was Yours*). I was surprised that some people did not think it was a thing. It IS a thing and it's sadly becoming more of a thing, which is why I wanted to explore it here. Mr Williams is a made-up character, but nothing that Francine heard or experienced is made up.

This is the first time I've written about the brave men from Canada who came to Britain to help the war effort, particularly those in the air force. By the time the war ended, more than 18,000 members of the RCAF had given their lives in service for peace.

What next? I hope to be bringing you more historical fiction books with my wonderful publisher, Bookouture, and I hope you will continue to enjoy them.

And if you'd like to reach me via social media, I can sporadically be found at the links below.

Thank you again and much love,

Lizzie

- facebook.com/LizziePage
- x.com/LizziePagewrite
- instagram.com/lizziepagewriter
- amazon.com/stores/Lizzie-Page/author/B079KSR8PZ

ACKNOWLEDGEMENTS

I wouldn't be writing this if you weren't reading this, so thank you, thank you, thank you for reading the Wartime Evacuees series.

I can't tell you how grateful I am.

Huge thanks once again to the brilliant team at Bookouture. *The Wartime Mother* is book 13 – unlucky for some, but hopefully not for this one! I feel enormously privileged that I get to work with such great people to bring you my books.

That includes my wonderful editor, Lucy Frederick, who inherited me at the end of Book 1 in this series, but has stepped up to the page admirably. Thank you, Lucy. I'm sorry about my messy/sprawling timelines! Forgive me!

Massive thanks also to copy-editor Jacqui Lewis – she's a marvel. And thanks also to superb proofreader, Jane Donovan. Without you two dastardly nitpickers, I don't know where I'd be 😊 They never fail to improve my work.

Thank you also to all the tremendous people working behind the scenes at Bookouture. Keep on keeping on, you brilliant people!

Massive thanks also to my wonderful agent, Thérèse Coen at Susanna Lea Agency, and the (ever-expanding) team there. Many years ago now, Thérèse match-made me with Bookouture and, from my point of view anyway, it's been a match made in heaven.

Thanks also to my family: Steve who's been distracting

me since meeting in the fateful spring of 2006 and the kids who've been distracting me brilliantly all their lives yet somehow especially this year. I feel pretty confident that you won't ever read this, but if you do, I love you, guys, even if sometimes you drive me up the wall.

PUBLISHING TEAM

Turning a manuscript into a book requires the efforts of many people. The publishing team at Bookouture would like to acknowledge everyone who contributed to this publication.

Audio
Alba Proko
Melissa Tran
Sinead O'Connor

Commercial
Lauren Morrissette
Hannah Richmond
Imogen Allport

Contracts
Peta Nightingale

Cover design
Eileen Carey

Data and analysis
Mark Alder
Mohamed Bussuri

Printed in Great Britain
by Amazon

59320277R00231